# FORTUNE'S RISING

Text copyright © 2014 Sara King
Originally published by Sara King 2012

Published by 47North, Seattle

www.apub.com

Amazon, the Amazon logo, and 47North are trademarks of Amazon.com, Inc., or its affiliates.

ISBN-13: 9781477823996
ISBN-10: 1477823999

Cover design by Gene Mollica Studio

Library of Congress Control Number: 2014904251

Printed in the United States of America

*To my personal heroes, the storytelling geniuses who got me hooked on writing character-driven fiction: Stephen King, Joss Whedon, Orson Scott Card, Anne McCaffrey, George Lucas, and George R.R. Martin. If I ever get to meet any of them in person, I can guarantee you that my inner fangirl will pee herself like an overexcited Chihuahua puppy (minus the leg-humping).*

# DISCLAIMER

**(a.k.a. If You Don't Realize This Is a Work of Fiction, Please Go Find Something Else to Do)**

So you're about to read about cyborgs and aliens and laser pistols and life on other planets. In case you're still confused, yes, this book is a complete work of fiction. Nobody contained within these pages actually exists. If there are any similarities between the people or places of *Outer Bounds* and the people or places of Good Ol' Planet Earth, you've just gotta trust me. It's not real, people. Really.

# TABLE OF CONTENTS

# Fortune's Rising

# CHAPTER 1

# Anna's War

THE SCREAM OF THE SHIFT WHISTLE TORE THROUGH THE MILI-
tary razor wire and punctured the flimsy metal walls of the hut,
startling Magali out of a dead sleep. She braced herself on the cot, heart
pounding even though she'd had twelve days to grow used to the gut-
wrenching shriek.

Immediately following the shift whistle came the tinny thunder of
soldiers walking down the rows of huts, pounding on the doors with
their rifles in case the ear-shattering screech hadn't been enough for the
eggers to drag their exhausted bodies out of their cots.

A soldier found their door and made a brief aluminum rumble
before shouting, "Two minutes, folks. Be out here. Dressed and pissed."
Then she moved on, assaulting another egger's hut with her badge of
office.

Magali hated them.

Aching from not enough sleep, she climbed out of her cot and
pulled on yesterday's work clothes, still grungy and stiff with Shrieker
slime from the day before. Once dressed, she squatted quickly at the

bucket in the corner. Like most Yolk facilities, Yolk Factory 14 was still too new to have flushing toilets. They were lucky to have running water at all, considering the camp was little more than a bunch of metal huts haphazardly slapped together over the top of a Shrieker mound, then surrounded by razor wire. Magali's sister and their quiet Aquafer roommate had fresh clothes to wear, but only because they had lost two hours of sleep to wash them at the communal facilities the night before.

Magali, who had earned herself three hours of direct Shrieker care for mouthing off to one of the foremen, had been so exhausted from the Shriekers' constant proximity while feeding the beasts and checking their caves for ripening nodules that she hadn't even had the energy to eat when the foreman had finally released her that night.

*Five more years of this,* she thought.

Eggers didn't last five years. They were lucky if they lasted one. Getting chosen for the Shrieker mounds was a death sentence with no way out.

The United Space Coalition didn't care.

Shriekers produced Yolk. A few drops of its concentrate could give even the slowest students a brief burst of high-level thinking and ultra-productive activity . . . an advanced society's dream. For those who had the money to buy it, Yolk paid for its extravagant price tag with productivity hereto unknown before the colonization of Fortune. It made wise men out of fools, businessmen out of laborers, and orators out of bumpkins.

It also made dead men out of several hundred thousand healthy Fortuners every year, when their minds fell apart with Egger's Wide—the permanent wide-eyed, drooling look of those who had spent too much time with the Shriekers.

Fortune had been a prosperous, growing colony right up until a government statistician found that Fortuners' mean IQ fell well outside reasonable bounds. The subsequent studies found that Fortuners had more brainpower than the heart of the Coalition, which was pampered with every drug, technology, and procedure known to man. More study revealed that this was not due to a genetic bottleneck created by a handful of particularly gifted original colonists, but rather their custom of augmenting their diet with Shrieker nodules when crops failed.

Once the scientists narrowed it down to the Shriekers, Fortune hadn't grown a soul in native population since. The colony had been on the decline for over thirty years, broken only by the infusions of criminals that the Coalition sent them to keep the Yolk farms stable.

That, and the soldiers.

Grimacing as another woman rattled their door, Magali checked to see that Anna was ready, then hurried to the exit. To go slow was to go without breakfast.

As soon as she yanked the door open and stopped in the cooler air at the threshold, Magali saw the Fortune Orbital hanging in the early morning sky like a blood-red star. Beside it and lower on the horizon, the alien Void Ring drifted nearby, a partially completed silver arc that shone with the same intensity as the moon. With each day that passed, the half-moon of salvaged alien parts grew closer to a full circle as hordes of government engineers worked day and night to complete the massive structure. Her sister had told her that in less than a year, the Ring would be functional, and the Coalition would start sending waves of troops through it to start a new government hub on Fortune.

Magali shuddered, fighting down a sudden tightness in her gut. "Come on, Anna," she managed, trying to sound upbeat for her sister's sake. Glancing over her shoulder into the dim, too-hot interior of the tin shed, she growled, "Get your eight-year-old butt out here."

"I'm eight years and a hundred and sixty-eight days old, so technically I'm nine, now."

"That Standard or Colonial?" Magali asked, only half listening. The rest of her was still trying to shake off the unsettled feeling that she had been getting every morning since a Coalition crew had dragged the ruined Void Ring into Fortune's orbit two months before.

Her younger sister snorted. "Colonial."

Magali stepped into the two Size-9 slime-encrusted combat boots on the doorstep and laced them as she waited. "Lazy. It'd be easier to impress me with Standard." She stood and tucked a clean rag into a pocket for cleanup later. "Now hurry up, okay?"

Anna threw her clean gray coveralls over her slim body and took longer than necessary to tie her laces. By the time she had followed Magali outside, most of the rest of the eggers were already in the morning formation. "I'm only seven years and two hundred eighty-five days old Standard," she said as she stepped into the sunlight. She shielded her eyes as she squinted up at the Void Ring. Magali saw her sister's face darken for just a moment before she pretended to yawn. Turning back to Magali, Anna continued, "So it doesn't sound as impressive."

Magali laughed at her. "You had to think about it, didn't you, Anna Banana?"

Anna scrunched her face and dropped her hand from the sky, giving Magali a dangerous scowl. "Don't call me that."

"Okay, Banana. I've got one for you." Magali dragged her sister to the line of eggers gathering in the yard, then glanced down at her. "How old am I, Standard?"

Anna's face immediately took on a bored look. "I don't know."

Magali lifted her brow. "Well, figure it out."

"Can't."

*Can't?* That gave Magali pause. The last time Anna had said she couldn't do something, half a Shrieker mound collapsed. She frowned down at Anna. "You can't?"

"Yeah, can't," Anna said, watching the soldiers nudge the last few eggers into line with the butts of their rifles.

"Why not?" Magali demanded.

"Don't know when you were born. Never asked, since I know nobody's ever going to need to write it down on anything other than your tombstone."

Magali squinted at her sister. "Why's that?"

Anna shrugged. "You'll figure it out." When Magali continued to stare at her, Anna amended, "Eventually." She started picking lint from her pristine, khaki-colored egger's uniform. Was it Magali's imagination, or was the damn thing pressed? The perfectly starched, ever-present creases in her sister's garb made Magali wonder just who the little twit had blackmailed to do her laundry.

"Okay," Magali said, "I get it. Because I'm never going to amount to anything, is that it?"

Her sister raised a very unimpressed brow and flicked a piece of lint. "Bingo."

"You're punishing me for the Banana thing."

"I hate bananas."

"Would you rather I called you Anna Double-Patty Hamburger With Extra Mustard?"

"Sure."

"Okay, Anna Double Patty Hamburger With—"

"You are so annoying." Her little sister glared at her.

"And you're so easy," Magali said, grinning as she ruffled Anna's hair.

Anna's scowl deepened, but her mouth twitched in a smile.

The Camp Director took that moment to clear her throat at the front of the formation.

"It's the cyborg," Anna muttered, her smile disappearing instantly.

"She's not a cyborg," Magali said, under her breath.

But it couldn't be far from the truth. The woman was hairless, having neither head hair nor eyelashes or eyebrows, and the translucent layer of her outer skin glittered and flashed with the gold filaments buried beneath. It was rumored in the camp that the Director was a former Coalition soldier, one of the super-humans that had crushed the last insurrection.

A Nephyr.

"Hello, ladies," the woman said, flicking a tadfly off of her glittering arm. The thumb-sized bugs always seemed to swarm around the Director, even in the chill of morning. "How are we doing today?" Her voice held a tightness that could have been attributed to stress, or hating her life . . . or being a cyborg. Magali frowned at the woman, trying to decide if her sister was right.

"Business as usual," the cyborg—*Camp Director,* Magali corrected herself—said. "Yolk's coming due for harvest near the C Block. I want a team down there twenty-four-seven, until it's ripe."

"It's twenty-*two*-seven, moron," Anna said. Several of the eggers close enough to hear Anna's muttered comment chuckled, but Magali froze as the Camp Director's dull brown eyes flickered toward her sister.

"Excuse me?" the Camp Director said, turning to face their section of the formation. Her skin glinted inhumanly in the morning rays. "Did someone have a question?"

Anna dutifully raised her hand.

"Anna, don't," Magali hissed.

Upon seeing her little sister, the Camp Director's face melted slightly. "And what was your question, little one?"

"Are you a cy-borg?" Anna asked in a singsong, childish voice.

Magali could have throttled her.

"No," the Camp Director said. Her eyes meandered back up to Magali, a darkness crossing over them. "Who gave you that idea?"

"I read it in a book," Anna said.

"Oh?" the Camp Director said, glancing back at her sister. In a pleased, patronizing voice, she said, "And what book might that have been, little one?" Her tone added, *Robby Robot Goes to Town?*

"The Consolidated Galactic Encyclopedia," Anna replied. "It said that 'a cyborg is a sentient combination of flesh and metal whose combined strength and utility is greater than that of an average natural fleshy creature of the same volume.'"

"Anna," Magali warned.

Anna grinned at the Camp Director. "So I wanted to know what you call yourself, if not a cyborg."

The cyborg's eyes narrowed slightly, as if she were an exotic bird-keeper who was just beginning to realize that this particular parrot was actually a hawk in disguise. "Excuse me?"

"But then again, your utility is pretty close to nil, from what I've seen of you sitting on your fat ass all the time, so I guess maybe you're not a cyborg after all. I wonder if they have a word for 'lazy useless Coalition throwback' in that book I read."

"Anna!" Magali snapped, grabbing her sister's arm and shaking it. All around them, eggers were snickering under their breath.

The Camp Director stared at her sister for some time before her eyes once again moved to Magali. The Director's voice was deadly cold. "Who taught her those lines?"

*I hate you,* Magali thought, glaring at her sister. Then, straightening, she said to the Director, "I did, Ma'am."

"And you thought we wouldn't figure it out?" the Director demanded. "You thought you could get *away* with teaching a seven-year-old something like that?"

"Yep," Anna said cheerfully. "She taught me real good."

*God I hate her.* "I'm sorry, Director," Magali babbled. "I won't do it again."

To her surprise, the Director's face stretched in a smile. "I like you, kid. What's your name?"

"Magali," Anna gleefully offered up, smiling up at her as Magali's guts wrenched with the instinct to flee.

"Make her a foreman," the Director said to her ever-present assistant. The lean, average-looking man—an AI, some said, though Magali didn't see it—nodded and made an adjustment on his handheld device.

Magali could only stare as the Director immediately went on with other business. Anna nudged her in the side once the formation had been dismissed for breakfast. "See? Cool, huh?"

Magali blinked down at her little sister as they walked down the dusty path to the cafeteria. "You did that on *purpose,* you shit?"

Anna scoffed. "What, you think it was an *accident?*" She snorted with disdain. "You weren't getting enough sleep. Got rings under your eyes, and you smell like dried Shrieker slime. Figured you could at least start telling some dumb egger to clean your uniform for you so I don't have to smell it all night."

Magali grimaced at her sister. "Someday," Magali said, still panting from the way her heart was pounding, "I'm going to give you a taste of your own medicine."

"No you won't," her sister snorted.

And, Magali knew, Anna was right. Magali had nothing that could even compare to Anna's quirky, egotistical—sometimes even vicious—eight-year-old brain. There *was* no comparison. There was just . . . Anna.

"Besides," Anna said, yawning. "The only thing you're good for is pulling a trigger, anyway."

*Killer,* Magali heard Wideman say again. She cringed inside. "Shut up, Anna. I told you I don't wanna hear about that."

"What, still afraid you might be a robot?"

*A robot who could hit a starlope from a mile off . . . with iron sights.*
"I said shut up, Banana," she warned. Magali knew she wasn't a robot. During one of her more gloomy days, after another of Anna's taunts, she had cut open the bony part of her wrist, just to make sure.

Anna hit her in the arm. "Don't call me a banana."

"Or . . . what? You'll make it look like I insulted the Camp Director to her face?"

"You make it sound like she's better than us," Anna growled. "We're not prisoners. They just act like we are. This is *our* planet, Magali. We should kick 'em out and take the Void Ring for ourselves, before those bastards get reinforcements back from the Core and lock this place down like a penitentiary."

Magali quickly glanced around to see if anyone with a gun had heard. Seeing no one, she grabbed her sister by the scruff of the neck and pulled her close. Leaning down, she growled, "You can insult the Director all you want, make me look like an idiot, make me cover your ass for all your stupid stunts, call me a robot 'til your lips are blue, but don't you dare say stuff like that. That's treason, Anna. I don't care *how* old you are. That'll get you handed over to the Nephyrs."

"You think I didn't check to see if someone was listening?" Anna demanded, her rust-brown eyes indignant.

"*Did* you?" Magali snapped.

Anna grunted and picked at lint.

"Anna!"

"I'm just a kid," Anna said. "What could they do?"

"*Kill* you, for one," Magali said. "They like to peel off *skin*, Anna."

"Then let them," Anna said. "It'd be the last straw. We'd start a rebellion and throw them off this planet once and for all."

"*We* wouldn't do anything," Magali said, shaking her little sister. "*You* would be dead."

Anna shrugged. "I'd hang around until I saw you knock 'em around a bit."

If there was one thing that disturbed Magali about her sister—aside from the cruel phases when every word that came out of Anna's mouth was a bone-deep insult—it was her apparent utter disregard for her own safety. Death, to Anna, seemed like just an inconvenience.

Magali released her sister, glaring. Saying nothing, she turned and went into the aluminum barn that served as their food hall and stood in one of the three lines. They took their breakfast trays from the sour-faced server at the end of the line and, sitting down, Magali said, "I don't like it when you talk like that."

"I don't like it when you talk at all," Anna said. "So we're even."

"Great." Magali stared down at her eggs. She took several breaths, focusing on the air in her lungs. Then she looked up at Anna and said, "Someday you're gonna say one too many nasty things and I'm going to step back and really examine just why I care about you."

"Because you have to," Anna said, putting a gob of eggs into her mouth.

Magali stared at her sister. "*Have* to?" She slammed down her fork. "Anna, there's no *have to* about it. Plenty of people hate their siblings."

Anna gave a bored sigh. "Not people who got their parents killed and now are trying to make up for it by being nice to the only blood relative that survived their stupidity."

For a long time, Magali was so shocked she could not speak. Then, slowly, she got to her feet.

Anna continued to shovel eggs into her mouth, completely unconcerned. It probably didn't even register to her that she had said something to hurt Magali's feelings—it never did. With Anna, insults and compliments were one and the same.

Magali knew she should let it slide, like she had let every other jab slide over the years. After all, Anna couldn't help herself. She absolutely, categorically, could not help herself.

And yet, this time she'd gone too far.

Magali got up turned away from the table, leaving her eggs where they sat.

"Where you going?" Anna asked.

"Away," Magali said. "I don't feel hungry anymore."

Anna glanced at the tray, genuinely confused. "You didn't eat anything."

*She doesn't get it,* Magali thought, squeezing her fingers into fists. *She really doesn't get it.*

Taking a deep breath, Magali forced herself to sit back down and pick up her fork. Jabbing it into her eggs, she said, "What I don't get, Banana, is how you can manipulate people like the Director like it's easy, but you are completely clueless about other stuff."

"Like what?" Anna asked, around her eggs.

"Like what you just said to me now. It hurt a lot."

Anna shrugged.

Seeing it, Magali narrowed her eyes, but she kept prodding at her food. "Do you do it on purpose? Be mean on purpose?"

"I do everything on purpose."

Magali slammed her fork down again, this time hard enough to make the table shudder. Every face in the cafeteria turned toward them when Magali shouted, "Did you accuse me of *murdering our family* on purpose, Anna?"

"You did murder them," Anna said. "So what?"

Magali leaned close. "*You're* the robot, Anna. You've got a heart of goddamn stone."

"That's technically a golem."

Magali opened her mouth to scream, then stopped. A slow smile spread over her face.

"What?" Anna asked, looking nervous, now.

"I just figured it out," Magali said.

"Figured what out?" her sister asked suspiciously.

"Why I don't kill you in your sleep," Magali said sweetly. "I understand now."

"Really? Why?"

Magali reached across to poke her sister in the chest. "Anyone who can survive living with *you* without going mad or killing something is *destined* to go to heaven when it's all said and done."

"And the Easter Bunny is real, too."

"You bet your ass it is," Magali said. She picked up her fork again and began shoving food into her mouth. "Better be, after what you put me through."

Anna watched her for some time before she said, "I really made you mad, didn't I?"

"Yep," Magali said, brusquely stabbing at more eggs.

"Why?" Anna asked.

"Why." Magali contemplated trying to explain, then shrugged. "Forget it. Talking to you about emotions is like talking to a hamster about nuclear weapons."

"No it's not," Anna said, looking disgruntled. "I understand them. Just look at what happened with the Camp Director."

"You see their effects, but you don't know what it feels like. It's all like pulling strings to you. You can *use* them, twist them around to make people do stuff, but you don't understand them." Magali shoved her plate away and glared at her sister. "There's a big diff."

"If it's all like pulling strings, why do I make you mad?" Anna asked.

"You got me there," Magali said. "It's like you're trying to drive away your very last friend in the world." Magali leaned forward. "And for an eight-year-old, that's saying a lot. Kids your age don't make grown men cry."

Immediately, Anna's face broke out into a smile. "No, but it was fun." Then, seeing Magali's glare, her little sister cleared her throat. "I mean, that dumbass Parker should've learned how to stop stuttering when he was forty-five. And that cranky old Darian Hold was mean to everybody anyway—I was just giving him a taste of his own medicine."

Magali glared. "I was talking about my boyfriend."

"Oh." Anna immediately took on a bored look and waved a dismissive hand. "He had it coming."

Magali stared at her sister, the thought of reaching across and grabbing her by the neck and pounding her strawberry-blond head into the table so vivid that her fingers twitched. She tapped them against the wood to keep from placing them around her sister's throat. Finally, she said, "We'd been dating four *years*. He never even wrote me after that."

"Eh." Anna shrugged. "You're too good for him, anyway."

Magali lifted a brow. "So you chase off my boyfriend so you can have me to yourself when you tear apart my ego?"

"Ego is just a construct of the mind, anyway," Anna said. "I'm helping you to transcend."

Magali narrowed her eyes and lifted her fingers. "You're this close to a beating."

"Probably the only thing you'd be good at—beating up a nine-year-old."

"You're eight."

"Nine."

"You're *seven* Standard," Magali countered. "So just cut the crap, all right?"

"We're fifth-generation Fortuners. The next time I hear you use Standard, I'm going to crush your tender feelings again. Once BriarRabbit and I kick the soldiers out, there will only be Colonial anyway."

"*Damn* it, Anna!" Magali cried, glancing around the cafeteria. They had two minutes left to their meal, and soldiers were already stepping in amongst the tables, getting ready to force them out for their first shift. Seeing no one that had overheard, she grabbed her sister's hand and yanked her close. "BriarRabbit? What the Hell, Anna! That sounds like a damn video game ID! You think you're playing a *game?*"

"It's called a hacker's handle, and yes, this is a game." Anna grinned. "A *fun* one. Like poker, but I've got all the cards."

Magali narrowed her eyes, not sure Anna was screwing with her or being serious. "Okay, listen up. I don't care how smart you are. You mention anything about this phantom underground uprising within hearing of those Coalition women and one of them is going to lock you up and throw away the key."

"It's not phantom," Anna said loudly. She spread her arms wide to include the whole cafeteria and all of its tired-eyed, haggard-faced eggers. "It's all around us. One of these days, the Coalition is going to get what's coming to—"

Magali slapped her sister.

Anna touched her cheek and blinked back tears.

Jabbing a trembling finger at her younger sibling, Magali said, "Shut up. You don't get it—Merciful Aanaho, I don't understand why you don't get it. They will *kill* you, Anna. They'll *kill* you deader than dinosaurs and then I'll be left all alone." She swiped tears from her eyes. "So just shut up. All right? I don't want to see you die, too. You're all I've got."

Anna narrowed her eyes at her. "Maybe you should've thought about that before you killed Mom."

Magali leapt to her feet, and for a second, both of them thought she would hit Anna again. As Anna flinched back, however, Magali swung around and stalked from the room, pushing her way through startled eggers and soldiers alike.

Behind her, Anna laughed.

# CHAPTER 2

## The Rebel Brothers

*STOP. LET ME OUT FOR AIR. I CAN'T STAND THIS ANYMORE.* GIVING up on her search for two rebel brothers who had recently been charged with blowing up a munitions depot, Tatiana gave her soldier the signal to halt.

It hesitated. "We're still in colonial territory, Captain. It is very much advised that you—"

*I don't give a damn!* Tatiana snapped. *Let me out. Now.*

The soldier sat down and unfolded, allowing fresh air to enter its belly cavity.

Tatiana gasped and choked on the tubes, knowing she was hyperventilating, yet unable to force the machines to produce more air.

*It's happening again,* she thought, panicking. She had to get out of her soldier before it beamed her heart rate back to base and she got hangared for another psych eval.

*Damn it,* she thought, gagging as she drew the food tube from her stomach and the intravenous lines from her arms. Tears welled in her eyes as she endured the nauseating pull of electrodes from deep under her skin, but she knew ten more seconds in her soldier and she was going to lose her mind.

Like last time.

*Damn it, damn it.*

She disconnected the waste lines and then pulled herself out of the sticky, mucousy substance that cradled her, protecting against sudden blows and jarring explosions. Then, her naked body pricking with goosebumps and dripping slime, she crawled out of the vault, stumbled off the heap of warm metal, and fell to her knees in the alien underbrush.

She vomited.

Hands splayed on the alien dirt, head hanging down amongst the sticky green stems, she panted until she saw stars.

*This can't be happening. Not again.*

Trembling, Tatiana glanced back over her shoulder. Her soldier sat lifeless, a hulk of weapons and hydraulics, waiting for its operator. Her. A host of precautions—thumbprint, retinal scans, genetic tests, voice comparisons—made it impossible for anyone else in the universe to operate the weapon.

And with good reason—Tatiana was the best at what she did.

. . . when she could bring herself to do it.

Now, looking back at the egg-shaped chamber that awaited her, all Tatiana felt was an overwhelming dread. She crawled away from the thing, brought her knees up under her chin, and cried.

Twenty minutes later, Tatiana had stopped crying, but she hadn't done much else. The buoyancy gel had dried on her naked skin in a tight, painful crust. Her fingers were stiff, her lashes and brows gummy, her short-cropped hair a spiky mass of dehydrated bouyagel. The dry alien air had already whisked away most of the substance's moisture, leaving her body covered in hard goosebumps around the cold metal nodes.

Tatiana shivered and tried to cover the biggest nodes with her hands, hating the creepy feel of cold air penetrating her insides. Huddling in on herself, listening to the brisk alien breeze stir the terragen grasses that were currently at war with the less savory, sap-soaked native species, she could almost believe she was in a very bad dream. She looked up at the big, slick alien trees around her, trying not to feel as tiny and vulnerable as she felt. The odd clicks and cooing of native wildlife echoed from the gnarled red canopy, and Tatiana was reminded again that, as valuable Coalition property, she hadn't stepped outside sealed Coalition structures in over eleven years, zoomtime. Letting an operator 'commune with nature' was too dangerous. Never mind that there were whispers of an underground revolution stirring on Fortune—with her body pocked with metal hookups, a single bug down the wrong node could kill her.

Swallowing, Tatiana quickly checked the ground around her to make sure she wasn't sitting on an alien anthill. She would have given anything for some node-caps, but she'd left those back at the station and the crash-kit didn't include any. After all, the soldiers' vaults were impenetrable, and operators weren't supposed to leave their vaults until they were safely docked at a military facility. It said so right in the contract. " . . . *Further, operators of Special Operations Large-Demolitions–Integrated Elite Reconnaissance Systems will disembark only at an approved Coalition hangar, or, alternatively, when their remains are removed from their SOLDIERS by recovery personnel.*"

Jumping at a particularly loud alien rumble in the shrubbery to her right, Tatiana desperately tried to remember Major Wilcon's presentation on alien fauna at orientation. As an operator on a colony like Fortune, Tatiana had been so sure that she would never set foot outside the sanitized hallways of the military barracks that she hadn't paid attention as the good Major had droned on about his precious Three P's—poisons, predators, and psychic shock. After all, *operators* didn't need to know that stuff. The only way she could wind up skinny outside her soldier was if she exited the vault of her own volition.

. . . again.

*I am so dead.* Tatiana's misery ratcheted up another notch and she bit her lip as she stared at the open vault of her machine. The buoyancy gel had started to dry, leaving a semi-opaque crust coating the internal workings of the operator's egg.

Tatiana knew they weren't going to overlook this. Not this time. Only ten thousand soldiers had been made, each one worth a planet or two on the black market, and the line to get inside one of them was longer than a flight back to the Inner Bounds. She was replaceable. Not even a Third Commendation on Muchos Rios and a stat sheet to make an admiral cry were going to change that.

Tatiana huddled in on herself, trying to imagine a life without her soldier. Though most would-be operators would have gladly taken the eleven years as one of the Coalition's best and gracefully bowed out once the stress became too much, Tatiana knew she'd end up being one of the wackos who ended up strangling her would-be successor with her bathrobe, once they forced her to step down.

She tried to imagine running cargo as a commercial pilot, or flying security for trade vessels, but after being solidly at the very top, in the most coveted Spec-Ops spot in the Coalition fleet, she knew going back to stick would drive her even more crazy than being locked in a dark, sticky chamber, unable to suck enough stale air into ragged lungs . . .

Tatiana shuddered and tightened her grip on her legs as she peered over her knees. She knew she couldn't stay there forever, staring at her soldier like a dipshit, but the thought of climbing back into the vault and reattaching the lines, tubes, and nodes left her feeling sick.

Just the idea of closing the lid, locking herself back into darkness, left her in despair.

When she finally couldn't take the cold any longer, Tatiana crawled up to her soldier's cargo pod and pulled out the survival pack with clothes, food, water filters, fire-making supplies—and an emergency beacon. She lifted a crisply folded navy blue jumpsuit from the bottom and, after much debate, shook it out and stuck her sticky legs into it. When she returned, the Coalition would know she had exited her soldier, but, with nightfall approaching and the strange animal sounds getting louder, she was willing to cross that bridge when she came to it.

Tatiana zipped up the suit, tucked the collar down, then built a fire and ate a packet of rehydrated stew. Even after it became obvious to her that she was not going to be able to get back into the machine, she could not bring herself to trigger the beacon. She knew that when she did, they were going to rip away her nodes, sew her up, and send her back to fly freight in the Core.

Once she was finished eating, she set the beacon on a log across from her and stared at it.

The moment she triggered the device, a Coalition retrieval team would come, find a fully functioning soldier, a perfectly healthy operator, and know she had freaked out again. If they were feeling generous and decided to let her stay in her soldier, the number of years left on her enlistment would be put on pause as they worked the kinks out of her brain, just like last time.

But if she didn't trigger it—*especially* if she didn't trigger it—they would track her down by the lifeline chip lodged in her spine.

Hell, she realized, they might not even bother tracking her down. They might just save themselves the effort, bring up her chip ID on the base computer, and fry her brain stem . . . letting her rot in whatever ridiculous makeshift shelter she had cobbled together from sticky alien plant stems under some rain-soaked leaf cluster.

Unwillingly, she started crying again.

"Damn," a voice said. "I never would've believed Milar if I wasn't seeing it myself."

Tatiana gasped and spun.

A big man in dirty brown leather stood at the edge of the firelight behind her. He had curly auburn hair, a heavy spattering of freckles, and dimples. He was smiling.

He was also holding a Laserat pistol aimed at her chest.

"Cold night out," he commented.

Tatiana froze, her eyes on the gun. "I'm Coalition," she blurted.

He laughed and motioned with the barrel of the gun at the cracked soldier. "Obviously." The hulking, stinking brute sniffed and wiped a dirty hand across his nose, leaving a trail of bacteria-ridden slime across his arm. He snorted, proceeded to noisily hack up a gob of phlegm, and expertly spat it into the slimy alien weeds before clearing his throat and swallowing.

Tatiana realized she had her face scrunched up in disgust.

"Got a cold," the stranger said, by way of explanation. His expression lacked any sort of apology. "Coalition confiscated colonist vita-stores last year. We've been deficient in selenium, zinc, and potassium ever since."

Realizing that not even *her* overactive imagination could drum up a mucousy, selenium-deficient, gun-toting, knuckle-dragging ape, Tatiana started to get a very bad feeling.

Still, she reminded herself, Fortune had the Yolk trade. The Coalition had so many personnel stationed on the planet that it would take a lobotomized nutjob to start a scuffle with government troops. Tentatively, eyes still fixed on the pistol, she said, "Then what do you think you're doing?"

"Rebellin," he said. He grinned. "Step away from the soldier, please."

Tatiana glanced back at the egglike vault.

"Don't," the man warned. His Coalition New Common was clumsy, like it had been learned from a textbook.

Tatiana hesitated. It took long minutes to fully calibrate a soldier upon reentry. Even if she made it inside before he hit her, they could certainly pry her out again before she'd activated systems. She glanced at the beacon.

"It'd take them an hour to get here." He started to swagger toward the fire. "Besides, I just wanna look."

"Are you trying to start a *war*?" Tatiana demanded.

"Wouldn't mind it," he said. The colonist walked over to the soldier and tapped on the ultralight armor plating.

"Get away from my soldier," Tatiana blurted, every pore on her body suddenly constricting at the idea of the Coalition finding out she'd let a colonist this close to the weapon.

"Calm down, pumpkin," he said, flashing her a charming grin. "I just want a quick peek." Then, ignoring her complaints, he climbed up the side and poked his head into the captain's chamber. The big, dirty colonist whistled. "Borden's Balls, woman. This looks all sorts of uncomfortable." He dipped a grease-stained finger in the bouyagel and held it up so she could see it oozing down his hand. He scrunched his face and wiped it on his pantleg.

*I'm dead,* Tatiana thought. The inner workings of the soldiers were highly classified, and letting a colonist inspect the inside would easily be considered treason. Scratch unkinking her brain. The Coalition would *kill* her.

Tatiana ran to the base of her soldier and slapped her hand against the sheeting near the stranger's foot. Trying to keep the desperation out of her voice, she said, "Ha-ha, really funny. Colonist pulls one over on Coalition operator. Show us who's boss. I get it. Now please get down. I don't know what sort of macho games you're playing, but the Coalition finds out you saw the inside, they'll kill us both," she said.

"Only if you tell," he laughed, holstering his pistol. The stranger jumped down beside her, smiling. "Besides, you're just an operator. Not the—" His eyes met her face and he froze.

This close, it felt he had roughly the same mass as a Coalition carrier, though he didn't seem to be carrying any added fat. He was just . . . tall.

Realizing *how* tall, Tatiana quickly backed up. Then, growing uncomfortable under his prolonged stare, she said, "Uh . . . reconsidering?"

He said nothing. Just stared.

"Tell you what," Tatiana said quickly, "You forget you saw me camped out like this and I'll forget we had this conversation. Deal?"

The man cleared his throat. Looked to the side. Then his eyes fixed on her again and kept staring.

Tatiana began to scowl. With shorn hair and electrode nexuses jutting out all over her body, she knew she was ugly, but this was just plain rude. "Listen, knucker, nobody's stupid enough to start a war with the Coalition, so just go the hell away and let me go fire up my bird."

His voice cracked when he spoke. "Actually, I think you're going to have to come with me."

Tatiana stared at him. He didn't retract his statement. She waited. Then, at his prolonged silence and his goofy, almost apologetic look, she threw back her head and laughed. After several moments, she snapped her head back down and jabbed a finger at him. "Not even a dumbass retard colonist prick like you would do something that stupid."

He took his gun from his hip and pointed it at her.

Narrowing her eyes, Tatiana strode toward her soldier.

The man threw out an arm and snagged her, dragging her back against his chest. He was bigger than her—much bigger. Tatiana froze. At a hundred and fifty centimeters, she had been too short to be a Nephyr. Instead, they'd taken her high IQ and molded it around brain signals and war games and top-secret weaponry. Her instructors had always assumed that she would never need to face the enemy hand-to-hand, because the only way rebels were ever going to be able to open the belly and drag her out was if she gave the order to the soldier to open the hatch.

Now, outweighed by more than forty-five kilos and shorter by over thirty centimeters, she was suddenly very acutely aware of why she had not been chosen for the Nephyrs. She was short. Even for a girl.

And he was tall. Even for a guy.

The bastard would pay.

Tatiana tried to pry the thick, apelike arm from around her middle, but when it remained firmly in place, she blurted, "When the Coalition gets done with you, you're going to be pissing out a bag on your hip."

He laughed. "As long as they use plastic . . . I'm allergic to latex."

Tatiana twisted around to face him and stuck a finger in his chest. "You're committing a federal crime. Let go of me. Now."

The effect wasn't as terrifying as she would have hoped. She found the top of her head at approximately the same height as a nipple, peering up at the base of his chin, what seemed like kilometers of dirty leather jacket separating them.

He leaned back so he could grin at her as he said, "I don't think so."

Tatiana froze as he shifted, setting his gun out of her reach atop her soldier's hydraulics. She tried not to feel the places where their bodies touched as he unhooked something from his belt. *A knife? A gag? A garrote?*

*You are a Coalition fighter,* a part of her ranted. *You operate the most fearsome machines in the world. Pull your goddamn head out of your ass and take charge.*

She jabbed her finger back into his chest. "You have twenty seconds to tuck your tail between your legs and get the hell out of here before I call in the Nephyrs."

"Uh-huh." Still holding her pinned to his torso, he raised something to his mouth and said, "Milar, you *really* need to come look at this."

Usually, even the whisper of Nephyrs was enough to make colonists jump with panic. This guy sounded like she had told him teddy bears were going to tickle him with feathers.

"You think this is *funny?*" Tatiana cried. "You think assaulting a Coalition operator is *funny?* You're setting yourself up for execution, pal. A full correction. Nephyr-style."

He peered down at her, grinning. "From what I saw, you're pretty close to that yourself. What'd you have? Some sort of nervous breakdown in there? I heard Coalition don't take too kindly to their operators going chickenshit on them."

"Who is Milar?" she managed, her throat stiff with fury.

"Milar's my brother," he said.

"Who are *you?*"

His amber-brown eyes were teasing. "I'm Patrick."

She squirmed, but the arm across her backbone might have been iron. Exhausting herself, she poked him again. "You're making a mistake, Patrick. Operators are the most highly trained federal employees out there. The moment I don't show up for debriefing, they'll come looking for me. They find out you kidnapped me and you'll be executed for—"

"They won't find me," he interrupted. "Or you, either."

Tatiana froze, unnerved by his sheer confidence. "If you kill me—"

"You'll do what?"

Silence hung between them as he grinned down at her. Tatiana became acutely aware of how their bodies were touching—and where. If she were back in her barracks room, boredly flipping through teaser mags, she would've paid to see him naked.

*He's a hunk,* she thought, unable to stop herself. *And you haven't gotten laid in two years.*

"I'll haunt you," she blurted. "I'll haunt your bathroom and scare the crap out of you every time you try to take a dump."

A smile began to play at the corners of his lips. "We're not going to kill you. We're going to take you to see Wideman Joe."

He really was going to kidnap her.

*No.* This time she began to struggle, and in earnest. She kicked out at his shin and, at the same time, bit down hard on his arm. He cursed . . .

. . . but he didn't let her go. Instead, he grabbed her hands, pulled them behind her back, and cinched them in place with some sort of cold, sharp metal banding.

"Ow, alien spawn, those hurt, what the hell, you bastard!" She kicked him again and started running for her soldier.

"Hold up!" He caught her by the waist, his big fingers brushing the sensitive waste nodes a hands-width under her breasts. "Just calm down. We'll take them off once we get you safely on the ship."

*They're going to take me away from my soldier.* She was so dead. "No, dammit!" Tatiana kicked and twisted in his grip, wrenching her wrists until the cold metal sliced into the skin and she felt blood dripping down her fingers. *Damn* but the bastard put them on tight.

"Hey, easy." Big hands grasped her wrists and kept them from twisting behind her. "You've never been in these before, have you? Nephyrs use them on rebels. They tighten with pressure. They'll literally cut your hands off if you struggle too much."

Tatiana screamed her frustration, but stopped moving. Instead, she stamped her foot and started cursing his name, his family, his heritage, his village, his Sign . . .

From the woods, someone laughed. A man entered the ring of fire-light, and for a moment, Tatiana was so shocked she could only gape. Either both Patrick and Milar were robots made in the same factory, or they had shared the same womb, at the same time. Milar had the same laugh lines as Patrick, the same broad shoulders, the same metallic red-brown curls—even their chiseled jaws shared the same reddish I-Shave-When-I-Feel-Like-It bristle.

Milar, however, had two scaled beasts tattooed up his neck, obscuring the skin of his throat. From what Tatiana could see, it was a small part of a much larger tattoo, the feet and tails of a red and a black dragon that climbed all the way to his ears and out to his fingertips. Further, his curly auburn hair was much longer than his brother's, unfurled halfway down his back, tied back with a wide black leather strap. To top it off, he was wearing a black leather trench coat, black military-issue work boots, black pants, black shirt, and beetle-green, black-rimmed sunglasses. At night.

Tatiana came to the sad conclusion that the poor, unwitting fool had probably been gene-spliced with a peacock.

"Looks like you caught yourself a feisty little Shrieker, Pat. What did you wan—" Upon drawing close, Milar's words cut off with a stare. He yanked his glasses off, revealing startled golden-brown eyes.

"Oh hell," was all he could manage, staring at her. Unlike Patrick's rough colonial speech, Milar's Coalition New Common was almost flawless.

"Then you see it?" Patrick demanded.

"Yeah." It sounded like a croak. "Merciful Aanaho. We're not *ready*."

"Well we better *get* ready, wouldn't ya say?" Patrick demanded.

"Get ready for what?" Tatiana snapped, not liking the way the brute was staring at her. "Let go of me. Get my goddamn hands out of these things. They cut me." She could feel blood dribbling off her index finger, and it was bringing up bile. "They *cut* me," she said again, biting down panic.

Patrick ignored her. As did Milar.

Then, to her frustration, they switched to a rough colonial dialect she had never heard before. Automatically, Tatiana gave her soldier the order to translate it. Then she realized she wasn't in her soldier. She cursed and fought back tears.

After a few minutes of hurried conversation, their eyes flickering to her, to her soldier, and to the half-completed Void Ring above, Milar suddenly switched back to flawless Coalition New Common. "Duck your head down," he ordered. He drew a nasty-looking hunting knife from a sheath on his belt.

Tatiana froze when she realized he was talking to her. Duck her head down? Why would he want her to duck her head—

She froze. *Oh no.* Tatiana straightened as far as she could go and pressed her rigid spine against Patrick's chest. "You stay away from me!"

Milar snorted and moved toward her.

She kicked him. Right in the crotch.

"Oh crap." Patrick tugged her backwards away from Milar, who was crumpling on the ground, the big knife fisted in white knuckles, his red face straining with veins. The dragons on his neck bunched up, their scales glistening and pulsing ominously, like they were about to tug themselves free of his throat.

"I'm going to kill her," Milar said, between clenched teeth. One hand on his crotch, he started to get to his feet.

"Dammit, Milar, she didn't mean to—"

"She *kicked me in the junk!*" he roared.

Tatiana felt Patrick balk. "Well, yeah, she meant to do that. But she's scared and—"

"Like hell I'm scared!" Tatiana snapped. "You two are so dead. You are assaulting a *Coalition officer.* Or are you two knuckers so high on testosterone that that doesn't register to your puny colonist psyches?"

Milar glared at Patrick, then stepped in sideways and grabbed the top of Tatiana's head with a big hand and wrenched it down.

Tatiana cried out as muscles pulled in her neck, but she twisted and struggled to keep out of his reach anyway. "Stop it, you simian bastard!"

"Easy," Patrick said. "He's just going to—"

"*I know what he's going to do!*" Tatiana screamed. "And I'm going to kill him!" She started kicking her foot in Milar's general direction.

Milar growled something under his breath. Still holding the top of her head, Milar ducked so that he was looking up at her downturned face. He brought his knife up so that it was a centimeter from her right eye. Tatiana froze.

"Milar . . . " Patrick warned.

"See this, coaler?" Milar said to her, ignoring his brother. He twisted the hunting knife so that Tatiana got a rotating view of its blade, glittering in the firelight. Smiling at her, he growled, "This ain't exactly the best equipment to work with, sweetheart, so unless you want me to chop off your damn head, I'd hold real still."

"Maybe we should take her back to the ship to do it," Patrick said. "We've got anesthetics."

"And have them realize she left the crash site?" Milar snorted, still watching Tatiana. "No. We'll do the little government shit right here. Help me hold her head."

"No!" Tatiana screamed, trying to twist away again, but she simply didn't have the strength to resist Patrick's grip. They propped Tatiana's head against the leg-hydraulics of her soldier and Patrick held her skull in place while Milar massaged the back of her neck with rough fingers.

"Got it," Milar said, pinching a sensitive bit of flesh against her spine. "No sweat, right, coaler?"

"Screw you," Tatiana muttered.

Milar gave a cruel laugh. "Maybe someday, sweetie."

Tatiana cried out when she felt the knife lance the flesh between his fingers. "That's got electrodes in my spine!" she babbled. "You pull it out, you'll kill me." She tried to struggle, but Patrick held her head utterly motionless against the soldier, her body firmly held in place with his bulk.

"Don't move," Patrick said softly.

Something metallic scraped in her neck. Then clicked.

Tatiana felt her guts roil as she felt a tugging sensation in her spine, like worms crawling through her flesh. She closed her eyes and shuddered. *This can't be happening.*

"There!" Milar released his hold on her neck and backed away. "You think you're the first coaler bastard we've operated on, Princess?"

Patrick released her head and withdrew, allowing her a good look at the thing they'd removed from her. Tatiana could only stare at the object in shock. Milar held the government chip out triumphantly before her, grasped in a pair of multi-tool pliers, the four foot-long filaments glistening pink with blood, twitching like legs and feelers on an insect. As she watched, he squeezed the pliers and crushed the circuitry. She saw little crackles of electricity sizzle down the coppery wires before they went still. Staring at it, she could only manage, "That's programmed to kill me if it's removed before my enlistment is up."

"Just a myth," Patrick said. He wiped away the blood that was now running down her backbone from Milar's ministrations. Then he hesitated. "Well, sorta. It could've killed you, but we've done it enough times we pretty much got the hang of it. Gotta knock out the battery cap before you start pulling anything out, otherwise it'll start frying neurons."

"You actually pulled out my *lifeline?*" Tatiana had never been so unnerved in her life. "Are *you* the reason Coalition fighters keep disappearing on Fortune? What are you doing with them? Using them for sick experiments? What's wrong with you people? Don't you know the Coalition's gonna hunt you down and make you scream like little babies?" Then she blinked. "*You're* the rebel brothers they just put out the bulletin on."

Milar's sneer—followed by the re-application of his beetle-green sunglasses—was all she needed to confirm her assessment.

Oh crap. Send Aunt Cherry a good form letter, try not to mess up her eulogy, pick her a pretty casket with some purple in it, 'cause she was toast, baby. Tatiana could see it in his eyes. They were gonna kill her. Or worse.

Milar grunted and wrapped big fingers around the insect-like chip. He sheathed his knife. "Take her back to the ship. I'll take care of things here."

Tatiana's eyes narrowed. "What do you mean, 'take care of things?'"

For all his reverential staring earlier, Milar's brow was now filled with harsh sarcasm. His ridiculously long leather coat brushed at his ankles as he bent at the waist. "To stage your heroic and tragic death, of course." His eyes caught on the lapel of her emergency jumpsuit and his face contorted in a sneer. "*Captain.*"

"Easy," Patrick said, though if it was meant for Milar or Tatiana, she couldn't be sure. Then it hit her. Her *death?* Tatiana froze. "Oh, you are *not* that stupid." Was he? A soldier was worth a fortune, but on the other hand, an operator was worth a pretty penny too, just for the tech she carried in her body. Besides, if they blew up her soldier, nobody would know what happened to her . . .

Straightening, Gigantor smiled. "I guess we'll see, won't we, sweetie."

Tatiana's eyes narrowed. "Who wears sunglasses at night, anyway? You look like a lobotomized space monkey who found fashion in a cheap adventure mag. Where'd you get the leather jacket, knucker? A dead walrus?"

Behind the sunglasses, Milar's face was flat. "Off a dead Nephyr."

Tatiana laughed in his face. "Yeah, right. You? A Nephyr? Next you'll be telling me collies bathe regularly and power cores crawl outta your ass."

"All *right*," Patrick said much too quickly, tugging her away from the bristling leather-clad thug. "Let's go before you get yourself scalped, okay?" Then, despite Tatiana's frantic kicks and struggles, the big man began to push her into the darkness of the sticky alien forest, away from her soldier.

"Let go of me!" Tatiana cried. "I am one of the best Coalition operators in my Pod. If I go missing . . . " *They'll what?* she thought, verging on despair. *Train a new one?* There were over sixty operators in this section of space. Not many, but not irreplaceable, either. Tatiana's supreme ability to mesh with metal and AI would be missed, but not mourned.

Especially when they discovered she freaked out again.

*No!*

"Let *go!*" When she landed another good kick to his shin, Patrick's breath hissed between his teeth and he stopped, spinning her to face him. They were well out of sight of the fire and there was no sound but the buzzing of alien insects. Tatiana went utterly still as he glared down at her, every molecule of her being suddenly aware that she was Coalition and he was a colonist and they were four thousand miles from any authorities. Even in the cities, Coalition fighters who ran afoul of the locals went missing at night and their bodies washed up in the Shrieker lakes, or they were uncovered in the bog pits, or were simply never found at all.

"Listen," Patrick said, squeezing her shoulder, "No offense, lady, but if you kick me again, I'm gonna sock ya one." He provided a sizeable fist at eye level for her careful consideration.

"Take me back to my soldier," she said, locking gazes with him, pointedly avoiding the fist hovering near her nose.

"No. I'm taking you to see Wideman Joe."

"Wiseman *who*? Listen, knucker, do you have *any* idea of the kind of deep shit you're getting yourself into? Removing a lifeline's a federal crime. They'll come down on you so hard it'll make your head spin." She glared up at him, but was distracted by the constant, nagging dribble of blood down her back. "And I'm *bleeding*, jackass. Fix it."

"I got some nanostrips on the ship," Patrick said. He grabbed her elbow and started walking again, tugging her with him.

Tatiana had the choice to follow or have the metal bands cut deeper into her wrists. She struggled over the alien landscape, her small size and bare feet making it difficult to keep up.

She froze when she saw the ship. A colonial ultralight cargo ship, it was nevertheless capable of transporting her across the globe. And, with the Coalition having only thirty-six Yolk factories and four major cities on a planet larger than Old Earth, Patrick was quite literally telling the truth—the Coalition would never find her.

"Come on," Patrick said, giving her a gentle tug on her arm. "It'll work out."

"You are so dead," she whispered, but she followed him up the steps.

Inside, Patrick motioned her over to one corner of the cramped and cluttered cargo bay, then pressed the button to shut the door and seal them inside.

"Might as well get comfortable," Patrick said, dragging a heavy metal chair between her and the door. He sat down and reached under his grungy leather jacket to pull out an age-worn, rectangular—

"Is that a *book?*" Tatiana asked, a bit shocked. Never in a million years would she have guessed that a colonist would have carted something as clumsy as a book across five years of space. Even back in the Inner Bounds, it was a rare find. The last printing press had gone out of business many centuries ago.

Patrick grunted.

"*Why?*" Tatiana demanded. "They're so . . . " *Useless, bulky, old . . .*

"The Coalition banned the great philosophers on electronic media," Patrick said. He held it up. The cover read, *The Life and Works of Ghani Klyde.* He smiled. "This is one of the only copies left, though a friend of mine has been translating them back onto electronic formats."

Tatiana realized her mouth was hanging open. "You've got Ghani . . . Klyde? In your *hands?*" Never mind that a two-bit colonist on some nowhere planet in the Outer Bounds could even *read* Ne'vanthi. Tatiana herself could barely read it, and she'd spent two years stationed outside the Ne'vanthi capital during the Pauper Rebellion.

"Yep." Patrick proceeded to crack open the ancient tome and his golden-brown eyes started to scan the words upon the aged pages.

Tatiana was so shocked by this new development that she didn't know whether to laugh at his bluff or run away screaming. It had to be the former, she decided. Colonists were *not* that smart. If her briefings were any indication, they were spear-toting Neanderthals who threw rocks at soldiers when they were hungry.

"Ghani Klyde was a *traitor,*" Tatiana blurted. "He brainwashed the Circle's children into rebellion just by writing a few lines in his blog." It made the fact that Patrick was holding his words as they were meant to be read all that more unbelievable. *A bluff,* she decided. *He's bluffing.*

"Uh-huh," Patrick said, nodding. "He was a traitor. He was also a tactical genius. He masterminded one of the most efficient war machines in the known universe."

*Mercy of the Phage*, Tatiana thought, in horror, *he's actually read the damn thing.*

When she could only stare at him, Patrick returned his attention to the book.

Still, Tatiana was suspicious. "Where did you learn Ne'vanthi?"

"Friend taught me," Patrick said.

She estimated that maybe ten people on Fortune, aside from Tatiana, had actually been to the slave-trading nowhere-planet of Ne'vanth. Tatiana narrowed her eyes, once more beginning to suspect that this was somehow a ruse. "What friend?"

"You wouldn't know her."

Deciding to call his bluff, Tatiana said, "Miserable *gakeii.*"

Patrick jerked his head up, raising a brow. "I always liked that one," he said, in Ne'vanthi. "The Ne'vanthi have such . . . colorful . . . curses." While his Coalition New Common had about as much refinement as her Fleet Admiral's gangrenous toenails, Patrick's Ne'vanthi was flawless. It made *her* Ne'vanthi sound like the random hooting of an inbred chimpanzee. Tatiana stared at him, jaw agape.

Patrick went back to his book.

Tatiana's curiosity was piqued despite herself. She eased herself around Patrick's chair and glanced over his shoulder, wondering if she could bite out a jugular before he beat her to death with his big metal chair . . .

Patrick snapped the book shut and scowled. "Like hell I'm letting you get behind me, coaler." He jabbed a meaty finger across the room. "Go. Now."

Glaring, Tatiana began to trudge back and forth along the far wall, eyeing the exit, wondering if she could press the unlock switch and get outside before the brute caught her. Damned little chance of that, with her hands trussed behind her like a Troop-Day turkey. She could still feel blood dripping down her fingers, and it was getting worse, despite how much she tried to keep her hands still.

"Pacing isn't going to get you out of here."

"Screw you, knucker." She paced harder.

Patrick sighed, "Well, at least have the decency to bleed in one place." He motioned at the line of ruby droplets she had spread across the floor of his ship, squished and smeared by her bare feet.

Seeing that much blood, Tatiana suddenly felt nauseous. She stopped pacing.

"Thank you," he said. He looked like he was going to say more, but the sound of an explosion made him jerk.

Tatiana grinned. "My cavalry," she said. "I hope you're ready to expand your horizons, rebel, because the Nephyrs are gonna tear you a new hole."

"Naw," he said, turning back to the book he was reading. "Milar just killed you."

Tatiana froze. "My soldier . . . " Its loss was like a pang of ice, stabbing her in the stomach.

He grunted. Didn't look up from the book.

"You bastard!" she stammered. "That's a billion-dollar machine! You could've . . . sold it or something! Why'd you have to blow it up?!"

"One less coaler war-machine to worry about." He kept reading.

Scowling, Tatiana went back to pacing. As the minutes ticked by, her soldier burning, the chances of rescue by the Coalition growing increasingly slimmer by the second, Tatiana struggled for something to say that would somehow change his mind.

"I can pay you," she muttered.

"Not enough, pumpkin." Patrick turned another page.

Irritated by his distinct lack of concern, Tatiana narrowed her eyes and forgot her attempts to negotiate. "There's nowhere on this planet that you can hide from the Coalition. It's got the fastest ships, the biggest guns, and the most brains. When the Nephyrs get you, they're gonna make you scream for days before they let you die."

"Uh-huh." He sounded bored, but she could tell by the sudden tightness in the colonist's face that some aspect of what she had said had gotten through to him.

*He* is *afraid of Nephyrs,* Tatiana realized with delight. Most people were, she reasoned. Psychotic bastards that they were. But that didn't mean she couldn't use them to her advantage. She continued on gleefully, "The last treason correction I saw, the guy lasted four weeks. A rebel. The Nephyrs strung him up and tore off skin until you couldn't see anything but muscle underneath. They had him in a sealed room, see. Everything was sterilized. Humidified. IV fluids. No chance of infection. It was friggin' awesome."

She was lying, of course—Tatiana had never been able to find the stomach to watch a correction, any correction, but her fellow operators had raved about them enough that she had a pretty good idea of what went on.

"I have tapes if you want to see it," she prodded. "It'll give you a good idea of what's coming to you, collie bastard."

Patrick slammed his book shut and scowled at her. "You talk a lot, for something I could squish with my pinkie."

Tatiana narrowed her eyes. "Skinned alive." She showed her teeth. "That's what's gonna happen to you if you don't let me—"

Patrick was out of his chair in an instant, and Tatiana gulped as he strode forward and forced her into the wall.

With one hand planted on either side of her head, he leaned forward, until their faces were almost touching. "You wanna talk about torture? Let me tell you about torture. It happened to my sister. A regiment of Coalition forces kidnapped her when she was working ryegrass in the fields. We found her corpse buried a mile from their campsite, once the regiment moved on."

Tatiana met his gaze stare for stare. "Shouldn't have been a rebel."

He gave her a mirthless grin. "Yeah." He reached up and picked a sticky twig off the dark blue fabric of her all-purpose soldier's jumpsuit, then flicked it off to the side. When he met her gaze, his amber-brown eyes were hard. "See, only thing was Carol wasn't a rebel. Never had a bad thought toward the Coalition in her life. That regiment took fourteen women from our settlement that day, all pretty girls. Hauled them from their homes, calling them traitors, but it weren't no secret why they took 'em. They were bored and they were Coalition, so they could do whatever the hell they wanted. Called it a 'correction' and all was right with the world."

Tatiana swallowed, hard, and looked away, a sick feeling forming in her gut. "You're lying," she muttered. Yet she'd heard the rumors, read the logs, listened to the dark confessions over too much drink . . .

Patrick grabbed her chin and forced her to look at him. "Of the eight that came home alive, all but two were pregnant." His smile was bitter, now. "Only reason *they* weren't pregnant was 'cause they were too young."

"Sorry," she whispered.

He scanned her face, his eyes still hard. "Just cut the bullshit, okay? Milar would return the favor in a heartbeat, if he heard you talking about torturing folks like that." His face tightened in a wry grimace. "Knowing what you bastards did to her, sometimes I think I would, too."

"I didn't know," she whispered.

"Yeah." Patrick released her roughly. "Whatever." With a parting scowl, he went back to his chair.

Tatiana licked her lips. "I really didn't—"

"Just shut up." He picked up his book again. "You open your mouth again and I'll gag you."

Feeling cold, Tatiana slid down the wall and drew her knees up under her chin. "Sorry," she said again. "Really."

Patrick gave her a dark scowl, but stayed in his seat.

Milar strode onto the ship almost twenty minutes later.

"What the hell took so long?" Patrick demanded as soon as he saw his brother.

Milar glanced at Tatiana, who hadn't moved from the wall, then glanced at Patrick, still in his chair, then grunted and pushed the button to shut the door and seal them inside. As he did, the sleeve of his black leather overcoat slid back far enough to expose the glistening scarlet and ebony scales of dual dragons, twining up his arm.

*They must cover most of his chest,* Tatiana thought, eyeing the dragons' limbs that peeked above his shirt, clawing up his neck, locked in perpetual battle across his throat.

Then Milar turned from the hatch, took off his sunglasses, and locked eyes with her. In that instant, Tatiana forgot to breathe. There was such malevolence in his gaze that she felt like she was going to puke. *He looks like he wants to kill me,* Tatiana thought, sinking into the wall under the stare. She saw his dragony fist clench once.

"Miles?" Patrick asked, tentative, now.

Milar held Tatiana's gaze for what seemed like an eternity. In that time, Tatiana felt the cold metal of the wall behind her pressing into her spine as she shrank backwards, trying to avoid the sheer hatred she found in his gaze. Suddenly, saying nothing, Milar jammed his shades into his pocket, stalked across the room, climbed the scaffolding to the upper deck, and disappeared through the hatch above, slamming his fist on the airlock panel to seal himself inside the cockpit.

Patrick frowned at the cockpit, then at Tatiana, then, after a moment, stood up and walked over to the scaffolding. "Miles?" he called up the stairs.

He got no response. After a few minutes, the ship jolted and she felt her stomach lurch as they took to the air. Patrick frowned up at the cockpit, but didn't leave Tatiana alone in the hold. Pity.

"What are you going to do with me?" Tatiana asked, after it was clear Milar wasn't coming back. On an alien planet, on an enemy ship, away from the safety of her soldier, she felt more alone than ever before. It hadn't truly hit her how much danger she was in until she felt the thrust of the engines lift her away from her last known whereabouts, destined for some unknown part of a planet filled with uneducated barbarians who hated her on sight.

Patrick turned away from his brother's abrupt and moody disappearance—*probably another mineral deficiency,* she thought with glee—with a scowl. Tatiana froze, remembering what he had promised should she continue to speak. "I'm sorry. I'll be quiet."

Patrick gave her a long look, then, with one last frown at the cockpit, went back to his big metal chair.

She stared at her kneecaps for another ten minutes before the sound of the book snapping shut made her lift her head.

Patrick was standing, crossing the space between them, a long white rag dangling from his hand.

"I said I wouldn't talk!" she cried. She scrambled to push herself sideways down the wall, bare feet scrabbling for purchase on the sheet metal. She only succeeded in sliding backwards, until her wrists and shoulder-blades gouged into the floor.

Panic surged when Patrick reached her. She clenched her jaw shut and closed her eyes.

For several heart-pounding moments, she lay there, every muscle tense. Then she tentatively pried an eye open.

Patrick knelt above her with the rag in his hand, his hazel eyes unreadable. "Sit up."

Tatiana squeezed her jaw harder and shook her head stubbornly.

Sighing, he reached down and pulled her up by the shoulder. Then he withdrew a key from his leather vest and released the bands from her wrists.

As the metal fell away, clinking against the floor, Tatiana blinked. "Let me see your wrists," Patrick said.

She tucked them to her body and vigorously shook her head.

Seeing that, Patrick rolled his eyes. "Come on. Let me *see* them. Before you bleed to death, twerp."

That was a good point . . . Reluctantly, she held them out.

He hissed upon seeing the oozing cuts and gouges. Even Tatiana, who had lived with them, hadn't imagined they were that bad. She felt her stomach lurch.

"Hold on," he said, getting to his feet. He tossed the white rag at her—bandages, she realized, stunned—and went to a shelving unit secured by a cargo net. He removed the net and from a compartment drew out a bundle of neon-green strips.

"Here," he said, kneeling in front of her again. He pulled a strip free from the bundle and removed the adhesive. "These'll help."

"What are they?" Tatiana asked.

"Nanostrips," he said, grabbing a wrist.

Tatiana yanked her hands away and skittered backwards in a hurry. At his scowl, she said, "I'm wired with enough electronics to power a city. Nanos are bad mojo for an operator."

Patrick's frown cleared and he glanced down at the exposed strip. "Really?"

"Yeah," she said, perking up slightly. "Won't help anyway. I've got resident bots patrolling, to keep out intruders. A whole strip will probably fry something."

"Huh." Patrick returned the strip back to the bundle. He got up again, dropped the nanostrips back into the compartment, and returned with regular adhesive first-aid strips and a bottle of alcohol. He held them up. "These do?"

Tatiana nodded, a little mystified by his sudden change in demeanor.

She flat-out stared, however, when he gently took her hand and daubed it with bandages wetted in alcohol. It burned like hell, but she just kept staring. Her mind once again wandered to what she did when she was bored, and whether Patrick would be good material.

A smile quirked at the corner of Patrick's mouth as he worked. "I think we got off to a wrong start."

She blushed, realizing she was gaping at him like a schoolgirl. Looking at the wall, she straightened and said, "You've committed three federal offenses in the last hour. Assault, kidnapping, and destruction of Coalition property. If you had any idea of how *dead* you are going to be by tomorrow morning . . . "

Patrick wiped more dried blood and debris from the wound. "What's your name?"

Tatiana stiffened further. "If this is a ploy to get vital Coalition data off of me—"

"Tatiana, right?"

Her mouth fell open and she stared. "How did you . . . ?"

Patrick looked up and grinned at her. "Good. Should've asked earlier, but we were pretty sure. It's hard to miss . . . " He cleared his throat and looked back down at her wrist. "Anyway, sorry about ruining your day." He wrapped gauze around the wrist and patted it down, then moved on to the other. "If you don't mind my asking, why were you outside your solider?"

*I do mind,* she thought bitterly.

Patrick glanced up, saw the look on her face, and laughed. "All right, we'll leave that one alone for now."

She let him work for a minute, then muttered, "You were pretty close to the truth, what you said earlier."

He quirked an eyebrow at her. "About you having a nervous break-down?"

She ground her teeth together. "I like to think about it as having a sudden and acute need to get out of tight spaces at random, inconvenient times throughout my life."

For the first time, he really smiled at her. His dimples returned, and Tatiana felt her heart give an extra thud.

Then he said, "A claustrophobic operator. Isn't that like a carrot that's afraid of orange?"

Her eyes narrowed and the extra heartbeats receded. Clearing her throat, she glanced at the ship around them. "So you can fly?" She slapped the steel wall behind her. "You and Milar are both pilots?"

Patrick shrugged and reached for the second bandage. "Yeah. I'm a little pathetic compared to my brother, but I can get 'er off the ground if I need to."

"Still," Tatiana said, "You must be proud. I hear that's uncommon for a colonist. Where'd you learn?"

He grinned. "A little undercover operation near the North Tear. Trained quite a few of the pilots where we're going." He tucked the bandage tight and glanced at her. "What about you? Can you fly one of these things?"

Tatiana snorted derisively. "I'm an *operator.*"

He glanced at her with a raised brow. "I'll take that as a no."

Tatiana yawned. "So where *are* we going?"

"Little place called Deaddrunk Mine."

Tatiana tried not to twist her face at yet another ridiculous colonist place name. "That's . . . quaint."

He grinned at her, reading between the lines. "True, though. You're new to a place, you name it whatever most strikes you about it. Some drunk tripped on a rock and died outside town while taking a piss. Turns out, the rock that killed him was a nugget of ninety-five percent pure silver. Became one of the best mining towns on Fortune . . . before the government started the Yolk draft."

Tatiana yawned again, so tired she felt dizzy. "Lots of people in Deaddrunk, then?"

He snorted. "You mean does the Coalition know it's there?"

"*Do* they?"

His face contorted in a scowl. "They better. They took another draft from it just a few days ago. Make a point of visiting twice a year, any time they need more meat for the slaughter."

Tatiana fought another yawn and wondered if blood loss was making her sleepy. "So it's got what, a thousand? Two thousand inhabitants?"

Patrick laughed. "Try two hundred."

"Two hundred?" Tatiana raised her brows. "And the Coalition drafts eggers out of it?"

"Every six months," Patrick muttered.

"A little town like that . . . must not have many pilots." She felt like she was getting loopy . . . like she'd slammed a good stiff drink and was just now starting to feel the effects. Peering at him through heavy lids, she said, "You put something on the bandages, didn't you?"

Patrick reddened and rubbed the back of his neck. "Ah, yeah. I was hoping you wouldn't notice." As he spoke, he set the bottle of liquid aside. Not alcohol then. Tatiana cursed for not noticing the label.

"Bastard." But her eyelids were drooping. "There a lot of pilots in that town of yours, Patrick?"

"Naw, just a handful," he said. "Like you said, it's pretty rare for a colonist." He reached behind him and grabbed a cargo mat. "Here. Put your head on this."

"No, dammit." But she was already falling over sideways. He caught her and eased her down onto the mat. "You mess with me . . . " she slurred.

"I won't," Patrick promised. "Just thought you could use something to sleep."

"You mean you didn't want me to see how you get to Wideman Joe."

He reddened again. "You're sharp."

*Sharper than you think,* Tatiana thought. But she had already passed out.

# CHAPTER 3

# A Dangerous Foreman

B EING A FOREMAN, MAGALI REALIZED, WASN'T ALL IT WAS cracked up to be. Foremen, for example, didn't eat at regular intervals like the rest of the eggers. They ate whenever they could catch a spare minute to breathe, if they ate at all. Between consoling panicking eggers who were convinced the next Shriek was coming and scurrying between incidents of the shit generally clogging the engine intake, life as a foreman was one hellacious stress-fest after another.

It did have its good points, however. As a foreman, Magali had direct contact with the male side of the camp, which allowed her a much-needed change of scenery. She even found some men she had known back in Deaddrunk, though none of them really wanted to reminisce. Not only did their Coalition babysitters discourage socializing, but every egger in the camp had long since come to terms with the fact that they were all going to die here. The past, Magali knew, only served to make them that much more bitter about the present.

Some didn't even recognize her, even after she named the little silver-mining town and her family's tiny general store. Those were usually close to developing the Wide, and even their own work gang avoided them.

For the rest, the constant fear of the next Shriek had hardened them to any conversation about going home. Magali had tried every chance she got, but as soon as she mentioned 'getting out,' their eyes had darkened and they'd found something else to do.

One thing Magali learned with her newfound contacts was that a lot of people on the male side of the camp had tried to escape, but nobody succeeded. The Director gave attempted escapees thirty lashings on their first attempt, and fifty on their second. On their third attempt, she gave another fifty lashes and put them in the stocks for a week. On the fourth attempt, they were hanged.

So far, there was only one person in camp who had ever been put in the stocks. The lashings were usually enough. Despite their fear of the next Shriek, eggers learned to fear the Director more. A Nephyr's arm was many times stronger than a fully grown man's, and the Director's whippings were known to break bones.

Another dubious benefit of being a foreman, Magali found, was that they were privy to choice bits of blood-chilling information that Magali would have much preferred not to know.

For instance, there had been two minor Shrieks since Magali and Anna had shown up almost two weeks ago, and each one had cost almost a hundred egger lives. Further, those eggers that hadn't been in the direct blast radius had suffered severe breakdowns and had deteriorated to the mental states of perpetually panicked three-year-olds. Magali had seen them, hunkered against the aluminum siding of their old bunks, booted from the Camp by the Coalition soldiers, yet hadn't put it together until now.

Already, she'd seen one of those women die.

Magali had tripped over her on her first day in the Camp. The woman had spent the night huddled outside Magali and Anna's hut—*her* hut, Magali had discovered later—and had suffered some sort of heart attack during the night. It had been her limp arm slumped across the doorway to the hut that had nearly cost Magali a broken neck, when she was emerging for the morning lineup for the first time.

Magali grimaced when she remembered the way Anna's face had been completely devoid of reaction upon seeing the corpse.

*"Where did you think we got a spare hut from?"* Anna had asked, while Magali had hyperventilated. Then her little sister had calmly stepped over the corpse and gone to formation.

"There's something wrong with her," Magali muttered under her breath, not for the first time. She thought about what her sister would be like in twenty years, and felt sick.

"Something wrong with who?" a very tall, very lanky man asked of her. He lobbed a rag covered in Shrieker slime at the bin toward the back of the foreman's breakroom and slumped into a chair. Heaving a huge sigh at the ceiling, he muttered, "God I hate this place."

"I'm Magali," she said. "And ditto."

The man groaned as he threw his arms behind his head and turned to face her. "Joel."

Magali noticed that his right leg was wrapped in bandages, with the neon-green edges of nanotape sticking out from underneath. She nodded at it. "Shrieker?"

The man glanced down at his skinny leg. He laughed. "Nah. Pissed-off albino." He leaned forward and tugged open the breakroom's tiny fridge. Rooting around inside, he found a strawberry soda and dragged it out, slamming the fridge shut with a foot.

Looking at it, he muttered, "Don't know what the hell they were thinking." He held the bottle out so she could see it. "All of a sudden the Camp Director starts ordering nothing but strawberry soda."

Magali grimaced. Upon arriving, Anna had hacked into the Camp Director's personal hub. Never mind getting them the hell out of there—her sister had done it so she could have ready access to her favorite beverage.

Popping the cap with a sigh, Joel leaned back and took a big swig, surveying her over the bottle. "Haven't seen you around here before," he said once he'd finished and wiped his mouth with the dirty back of a suntanned arm. "You just make foreman?"

"Yeah," Magali said. "This morning. What about you?"

"Three years," the man said. He yawned and checked his watch. "Shit. Two more hours to go before shift."

Magali's eyes fell back to the green edges of nanotape protruding from the bandages. "Another foreman do that to you?"

"This?" The man gestured at his leg, then laughed. "Naw. This was done by a real piece of work I used to do business with, back before he dumped me in this joint."

Magali stared. "You've had that wound for three *years?*"

He grunted and took another swig of pink soda.

"But . . . " She gestured at the wound. "I thought that was nanotape."

"It is," he agreed. "But the bastard dipped his knife in nanos of his own, the anti-knitting kind. The little fuckers have been at war since he stabbed me. I think his are winning." He took another long drink, then tossed the empty bottle into the waste bin atop the slimed cloth. "But hey, nice meeting you. I've gotta go stop my dumbass crew from kicking up another Shriek."

Joel got up and was limping from the room when Magali called, "You look familiar. What's your last name?"

He glanced back at her. "Triton," he said.

Magali frowned, feeling like she should know it somehow. "Do I know you?"

His green-blue eyes scanned her face. "Don't think so." Then, turning, he left.

Magali stared after him. Could he be *that* Joel? The smuggler known as Runaway Joel? The one her father had done business with, back before the accident?

She quickly dismissed the idea. Runaway Joel's face had been plastered on every official surface for as long as Magali could remember. He'd been stealing from government depots and undercutting Coalition quotas since Magali had been a kid. There was no way the scrawny, bearded man she had just seen could be the same clean-shaven criminal she had seen on every wanted poster on Fortune. The soldiers would have executed him the moment they had him in custody.

Still, with a haircut and a shave . . .

A call on her radio cut her train of thought short. "Hey sis. You might wanna get down here. Some idiot's trying to talk to a Shrieker."

Magali grabbed her handset in a spasm. "Anna? How'd you get a radio?"

"Took it from the dumb old hag trying to get us killed. I think she's got the Wide. Oh shit." Magali heard a series of grunts, then Anna panted, "*Hurry*, sis."

Already breaking into a run, Magali yelled into the receiver, "Don't touch my sister!"

She received no reply.

Magali shoved her radio back onto her belt and sprinted towards the mounds.

The concrete corridor ended in a locked door.

In an attempt to prevent smuggling, Coalition regulations required that all Shrieker farms be locked at all times—regardless of who was inside. Now Magali threw the door open and dove into the dank air beyond, ducking low to keep from scraping her head on the slimy ceiling.

As soon as she entered, the relative mental peace that Magali had earned in the breakroom became a familiar knotting sensation in her mind as she grew closer to the Shriekers. The static was a constant blur in the back of her head, an itch curable only by exiting the mounds at the end of the shift, and was enough to drive everyone exposed to it over the edge, given enough time.

Magali spent the next ten minutes slipping on the thick, slimy mucus of the Shrieker tunnel as she scrambled to find the chamber with her sister while avoiding the toxic-colored, dog-sized blobs of flesh that were the Shriekers.

When she found the room with her sister, Magali froze. Anna was on the floor, covered in translucent slime, a wiry woman with a pinched face and a foreman's black coat standing over her tiny body. A radio lay in the mucus a few feet from Anna's fetal form. As Magali watched, the foreman dropped onto her knees and started hitting Anna with her fists. Despite the beating, her sister was biting back her screams, letting out only small grunts as the blows struck her tiny body.

Instantly, Magali saw why. A few feet away, a brilliant red-and-purple Shrieker was engulfing a pile of lakeweed that they had left for it, its dull black eyes completely oblivious to the two humans in the cavern. Everyone else on the team had fled, probably crowding the exits and banging on the doors in a panic unheeded by the foremen and soldiers outside, terrified the thing was going to Shriek.

It took Magali only a moment to take this all in, and even less to react. She threw herself at the senior foreman and they went down together, sliding through the mucus toward the feeding Shrieker.

"Stop! It's right—" Anna cried, sitting up behind them. Her words choked off and her eyes went wide.

Magali wrestled out of the other foreman's grip and froze.

The Shrieker was looking at her. Its lumpy, egg-shaped body was turned inquisitively, its damp black eyes fixed on her torso. A headache was building, the constant fuzz at the back of her mind becoming an all-out migraine from the Shrieker's proximity.

"Don't move," Anna whispered behind her.

The chief foreman—a cranky old woman by the name of Gayle Hunter who had been working the mounds for over seven years—scrambled to her feet, spitting insults, not even noticing the Shrieker. When Magali glanced at her, slowly, trying to motion at the Shrieker, to show that it was listening for them, the woman ignored her. Something about her face wasn't right. The woman's eyes were too round, with little crescents of white above and below the iris.

Magali gasped. Anna was right. The woman had Egger's Wide.

"How *dare* you?" Gayle snarled. "I've been a foreman seven *years*, girl. I could take you to the Director and get you carted off to the stocks for touching me. How *dare* you touch me?"

"The Shrieker," Magali whispered, motioning with a twitch of her finger. Every other part of her body was still.

Gayle turned to face it fully, then sneered at the knee-high lump of brightly colored flesh. "You think he scares me, you little shit?" She glanced back at Magali and snorted laughter. "That's David. He's not like the other ones. See that notch in his tail? Got it when a guy ran over it with a food cart. Never Shrieked, never did nothing. He never hurt a soul. Did you, David?" She looked back at Magali, her too-wide eyes staring out at her above a beaming smile. "See? David wouldn't hurt you. He's just curious." Cooing back at the Shrieker, she said, "Aren't you, my little angel?"

"Magali," Anna whispered. "Let's get out. Now."

Magali started to back away, but Gayle caught her by an arm. "You afraid of Shriekers? Don't be ridiculous. They're just babies." Then, before Magali realized Gayle's intent, the older woman shoved her hand down at the Shrieker's brilliantly colored flesh.

Magali bit back a scream as her fingers touched cold, sticky skin. The Shrieker flinched back and its whiplike tail thrashed, dragging it away from them, into a hollowed-out pocket of the cave.

Gayle laughed and started to follow. "Don't be scared, David. She won't hurt you, little baby. I'm here." Her hand was like a vice on Magali's arm as she started walking toward the cornered Shrieker.

Magali yanked her hand away and stumbled backwards. The Shrieker's big black eyes were still fixed on Magali's torso. Shriekers, Magali knew, had horrible eyesight. Their black eyes were simply a collection of nerves grouped together in order to detect motion. It didn't know *what* she was, just that she had touched it.

"Magali, careful," Anna whispered.

Behind her, her sister looked terrified. Unlike everything else in her life, Anna could not pull the Shriekers' strings to make them dance to her tune. She was just as helpless around them as everybody else. Several times after a shift, Magali had caught her sister hyperventilating in a corner of the hut, when she thought no one else was around. Anna had always blown it off like it had never happened, but Magali knew it bothered her sister to be so vulnerable for such a large part of each day.

Following the Shrieker into the cave, Gayle bent at the waist and knee, murmuring and holding out a hand like it was a feral dog she was trying to tame.

The Shrieker's eyes shifted to Gayle. Its neon-yellow tail began to grow more agitated with her approach, frothing the transparent slime into a mass of tiny bubbles. Magali froze, knowing that Gayle was going to get herself killed. With the Shrieker's attention on her, however, she and Anna might still get out alive.

And then again, she had no way of knowing how far this particular Shriek was going to carry. If the whole mound took it up . . .

"Magali, let's *go*," Anna cried.

"Anna, get out of here."

Anna hesitated a moment, then Magali heard her sister get up and flee.

Once she was gone, Magali took a breath and held it, biting her lip. *Squid ain't heroes,* she thought, remembering her father's favorite saying. Then, setting her jaw, she lunged forward and grabbed Gayle by the hair, tugging her backwards and down. As Gayle slipped and floundered in the slime, Magali grabbed her by a fistful of shirt and began tugging her away from the Shrieker.

Gayle bit her arm, hard. As Magali automatically yanked her arm away and inspected the damage, Gayle shoved her.

Gayle was surprisingly strong. And graceful. Too graceful. In an instant, Gayle twisted herself away and backwards through the slime, slipping out of Magali's hands to come to a sliding stop with Magali between herself and the Shrieker.

If Magali had harbored skepticism that Gayle was military-trained, the stance that the woman fell into cleared all doubt. It was a highly effective martial art that Magali recognized from her father's long daily practice sessions. *Dragon Fist.* An aggressive and deadly modern compilation of a dozen different ancient martial arts styles that was taught exclusively to the Coalition special forces.

. . . or to a few dozen Fortune colonists, care of one of their own.

*What the hell?* Magali thought, eyeing the slim, elderly woman with a new wariness.

She had only enough time to take a nervous step backwards before Gayle lunged at her. Magali had the option of dodging—leaving Gayle to slide into the Shrieker behind her—or deflecting the blow and using the woman's own momentum to bring her to the ground.

The long, miserable hours in which Magali's revolution-obsessed father had forced her to train for war with his starry-eyed pack of freedom-fixated idealists—only a handful of whom were still alive—had nonetheless sunk in. Though Magali hadn't had to use a single move to defend herself in over four years, the ingrained training came back as instinctively as it always had. She caught the woman's fist, shoved it aside, brought her knee into the woman's stomach, followed that with knocking her off balance by trapping her legs, and used the leverage to throw her to the ground.

From the slime of the cavern floor, Gayle stared up at her with as much surprise as Magali had felt, only a moment ago, realizing this elderly woman had somehow studied Dragon Fist.

But, instead of naming Magali a rebel and demanding to take her to the Camp Director as Magali had feared, Gayle simply sat up, blinked at Magali, blinked at the Shrieker, and started crawling towards the creature on her hands and knees, cooing platitudes.

*She's got the Wide,* Magali thought again, desperate now. The mental fuzz in her head was getting louder, the Shrieker still agitated from being touched and the commotion that had ensued.

Seeing no other choice, Magali once again grabbed the older woman by the hair and yanked her backwards, away from the Shrieker, but this time kept a firm hold on her head and didn't let the woman get a grip on any of her body parts. She started dragging her backwards as Gayle kicked and flailed, forced to hold Magali's wrist with both fists to avoid losing her scalp.

Mercilessly, knowing that it was the only way she was going to keep both of them alive, Magali kept a grip on the woman and kept moving. Her studded egger's boots slid uncomfortably with the combined slippery nature of the tunnels and Gayle's struggles, but she got them to the mouth of the chamber before Gayle managed to grab hold of the wall and halt her progress.

"Let go of me!" Gayle screamed. In its corner, the Shrieker's fleshy body flinched in a spasm.

Magali dropped to her knees and slapped a slimy hand over Gayle's mouth. With her other hand, she punched the woman in the temple as hard as she could.

Gayle's eyes went even wider and took on a dazed look. Magali punched her again three more times, just to be sure. Then, getting shakily to her feet, she grabbed Gayle's shirt and dragged the unresisting woman from the room. The Shrieker watched her go, its tail still thrashing the mucus.

Magali struggled for almost an hour to drag the woman through the low tunnels of the Shrieker mound and back to the big metal door that she had left open in her panic. Anna was struggling in the doorway, the tall, lanky foreman squatting in front of her and holding her squirming body in place with both hands.

"Dude. Kid. They're not gonna Shriek," Joel was telling her. "You can't come in here. Get back in there with the other eggers." Joel let go of Anna and stood when he caught sight of Magali and her burden. He blinked. "What happened?"

Magali dropped Gayle at his feet. "She's got the Wide," she panted, wiping slime from her face with her forearm. The action brushed the bite-wound and she grimaced at it, realizing she had probably spread as much blood across her face as slime. "I hit her a couple times to stop her yelling."

Wordlessly, Joel handed her a rag. After she'd spent a few moments cleaning crimson from her face, he said softly, "That's Gayle Hunter. You *sure* she's got the Wide?" The way he said it, Magali was accusing God himself of mental illness.

Magali let the rag fall away from her face, glaring. "She was trying to pet a Shrieker. Named the damned thing *David*. Yeah, I'm sure."

Joel's eyes were fixed on the unconscious woman with anxiety. "Gayle's the chief foreman. It's not gonna go over very well with the Director."

"She was going to start up a Shriek!" Magali cried. "Anna, tell him."

"Look, I believe you," Joel said, giving Anna a strange glance before returning his gaze to Magali. "No need to get the kid involved. I'm just saying that this gal played poker with the Director every Thursday night. Renewed her contract willingly when her five years was up. That sort, if you know what I mean. It's gonna look bad you beat the crap out of her on your first day. You'll probably wind up in the stocks by midnight."

"Then tell them *you* did it," Anna interrupted.

Joel grimaced down at the girl. "Not sure that'll fly."

"Magali just saved your life," Anna said. "You make it fly."

Joel cocked his head in the same manner as the Director earlier that morning, the hawk-in-the-henhouse type look that Magali had come to know so well. Instead of arguing, though, he only said, "Okay." He glanced down at Gayle. "I'll have to come up with a good reason for being in the women's side, though."

"You were having sex with my sister," Anna said.

Joel blinked at her.

"Don't worry," Anna said. "They'll just slap your wrist. Everybody does it."

"Anna!"

Anna rolled her eyes. "Not has sex with you. Goes to the opposite side to have sex. Nobody has sex with you. You're as sexually appealing as a plague rat."

Even as Magali's jaw was falling open and her face was reddening under Joel's amused look, Anna continued. "Besides, if *he* says she's got the Wide, they'll have to test her. If *you* say she's got it, they'll just let it slide, her being friends with the Director and all. Then they'd throw her back in with the eggers and she'll just start a Shriek somewhere else."

"How old are you?" Joel asked.

"Nine," Anna said.

"Huh." He glanced at Magali. "Your sister's a smart kid. Only problem is—"

"You're a wanted criminal those government boobs don't realize they've got trapped right under their noses?" Anna asked.

He blinked down at Anna again, looking startled. "Yeah."

Anna shrugged. "They're gonna figure it out sooner or later. At least this way, you'll do something nice for somebody before your whole pathetic, wasted life falls out with your entrails when they draw and quarter you like you deserve. Besides, you *don't* do it and they're gonna find out a *lot* sooner than later."

"Anna!" Magali snapped.

Joel chuckled. "Your sister's a brat."

"Ignore her," Magali said. "I'll take care of Gayle. A couple days in the stocks isn't gonna hurt me."

"Nah," Joel said, "I'll get away with it. I always do." He bent down, grabbed Gayle by the shirt, and threw her over his shoulder. Then he winked at Anna. "Nice meeting you."

"Whatever," Anna said. She folded her arms and looked away with a bored expression. "You're just trying to make me like you so I don't report your ass."

Grinning, Joel leaned down into Anna's face and said, "Then maybe you should be doing the same thing."

"Huh?" Anna asked.

"Because I wonder what those soldiers would think if I told them they've got such a smart little runt on their hands. Yolk-baby, if I'm not mistaken?" He grinned at the sudden flicker of recognition in Anna's face. "They take kids like you for the Nephyrs."

"I could fake it," Anna said, looking thoroughly unconcerned. Magali knew her sister's posture too well, however. Anna was scared.

Apparently, Joel saw it, too, because his face melted. He straightened and ruffled Anna's hair. "See you two later." He departed, Gayle's unconscious body draped over his shoulder.

Anna gawked after him.

Magali stared at her sister. She hadn't seen Anna get that look in ages, since before their mother had died. She found herself smiling, despite the fact that Joel had just threatened to turn Anna in.

Anna saw her look and gave Magali a bitter sneer. "I suppose you think that was funny?"

"It was refreshing," Magali replied, shrugging. "Not many people pull one over on you." She grinned wider. "He even called you 'runt.'"

The shift whistle interrupted Anna's retort, which was a relief to Magali. Considering the malicious look in her sister's eyes, it would have hurt. A lot.

She turned and left before Anna could repeat herself.

# CHAPTER 4

# A Smuggler's Story

JOEL FELT LIKE AN IDIOT.

He'd spent the last three years avoiding the soldiers and the Camp Director like a Shriek, taking up foreman only to have access to the breakroom to escape the constant mental buzz of the Shriekers when it started to overwhelm him.

Now here he was, sitting across from the Camp Director, hand-cuffed to a metal desk. Her gold-filigreed face was contorted in fury. She tapped the desk with a finger that sounded like it was made of solid lead—*Thunk. Thunk. Thunk*—glaring at him. She hadn't spoken for almost ten minutes. Joel's spine began to itch and he twisted his wrists in the shackles uncomfortably.

"So I take it the last fifty lashes didn't do ya, eh, Joel?" she said finally.

He winced. He'd been hoping she hadn't recognized him.

"So let me get this straight." The Director shifted in her seat, pure rage tightly controlled under a cold façade. "Instead of organizing escape attempts, you have switched to pummeling senior foremen."

"I had to keep her quiet—" he repeated, for the hundredth time that day.

She slammed a leaden fist down onto the table to cut him off, crushing a divot into the sheet metal. "*Don't* tell me you did it to keep her quiet," the Director snarled. "You're one-ninety-five and you pounded the shit out of her."

"I'm one-ninety-five what?" Joel asked, intentionally misunderstanding the Standard in centimeters. "*Pounds?* No way. I only weigh a hundred fifty-five. Regular scarecrow. Who told you that?" It went over much better, he had long ago learned in his first smuggling runs, if, when masquerading as a colonist, a 'colonist' did not understand the metric weights and measures of the Coalition.

The Director gave him a long, irritated look, then said, "You're six-foot-four and you pounded the shit out of her. A little extreme, wouldn't you say?"

"I'm a real lightweight," Joel said, putting as much charm into his grin as he could manage. His eyes drifted to the Nephyr's fist where it had sunk about a half inch into the surface of the desk and he tried not to think about what it would have done to his face. Desperately doing his best to hide his ancient Inner Bounds accent, he continued, "Not enough meat on my bones to give her more than a love-tap." He flexed a scrawny bicep. "See?"

The Director's scowl deepened. "A *love* tap? You gave her a concussion, you prick."

This wasn't going as he had planned. Just walk in, dump the broad, walk out, maybe grab a doughnut in the lobby on his way back to the mounds . . . But no, the Director had seen him walk in, and all time had seemed to stop when she ordered him to put Gayle down and step away from the body. Like he was a criminal or something.

Well, he was a criminal, but not *that* type of criminal. It was a little insulting.

But it got a hell of a lot scarier when she had ordered that blasted AI that never left her side to arrest him and throw him in an interrogation room. Joel had kicked the thing in its fleshy face, but the machine had simply told him to calm down, that resisting was futile, all that garbage.

Now, faced with the Director in all her glittering Nephyr fury, it was all Joel could do to keep the panic off his face. The way she was acting, Gayle had been more than just a friend. A lover, maybe? And now the Director had laid the blame squarely upon his shoulders. Joel got the nagging suspicion that the vicious little doll-faced creep had set him up.

"I had to do something. She was going to start another Shriek," he offered meekly.

"By pounding her in the face? And she weighs what? One-twenty? One-*ten*? What the hell were you thinking?"

"She was being too loud," Joel muttered.

"Oh really? Where are your witnesses?" the Camp Director demanded. Her green eyes burned like hot emeralds.

"Magali and Anna Landborn," Joel said, for the fourth time. It had been the robot—now hovering over the Director's left shoulder—who had provided their last names. Upon first hearing them, Joel had felt like he'd been punched. Their father, Nelson Landborn, had been Joel's Yolk contact on Fortune, in the days when he had tried to bypass the middleman and get it straight from the colonists. Geo had gotten wind of it and the next time Joel had come through his depot, he had left naked, bloody, and barely able to drag himself onto his ship and lock the door.

Somewhere in those three days of beatings, he had let Nelson Landborn's name slip. The guy had been carted off of Fortune that very night and never seen again. Joel hoped to God that the little Anna kid hadn't known that when she convinced him to stroll into the lion's den, but he was starting to get concerned that she had.

The Camp Director's eyes narrowed. "I heard you earlier. You want to claim your lover and her little sister as your only witnesses. You expect me to believe you?"

Joel slumped forward, dropping his forehead to the table. "Yes," he said to the scratched and worn metal. "That's exactly what I want."

The Camp Director's creaking chair made him look up. She was leaning forward, her eyes narrowed. "Your story isn't making sense, Joel. You were in the B Block? That's ten minutes into the female side. What were you doing in there? Seems like you could've found a more convenient place to screw your girlfriend than right smack in the middle of Shrieker territory, especially since she just made foreman. There's something you're not telling me, and we're not leaving this room until you spill your guts."

Remembering what Anna had said about being drawn and quartered, Joel felt an uncomfortable uneasiness. Time for Plan B.

"I want my lawyer."

The Camp Director frowned. "What?"

"Under the United Space Coalition penal code, you can't hold me here without access to legal representation. I haven't done anything wrong and I want my goddamn lawyer." He jangled his handcuffs loudly against the metal bars holding them in place and gave her a smug grin. "Now, please."

The Director glared at him. Over her shoulder, she said, "Ferris, are you trained in legal affairs?"

"Yes, Director," the robot said immediately. He had a pleasant male voice, deep and calm.

"Good," the Director said. She waved a dismissive hand at Joel. "Read this two-bit egger scum his rights."

"Screw that," Joel said, interrupting the robot. "I want a human."

"You'll get what I goddamn give you!" the Director snapped, slamming her glinting hand, open-palm, down upon the table with a reverberation that sounded as if a thousand pounds of metal had hit it from a fifty-foot drop. Joel grew cold looking at the individual dents her fingers left when she pulled them away. "Now read him his rights!" the Director snapped at her AI.

Somehow, Joel found the courage to say, "I want a human."

For a long time, the Director simply stared at him. Then she glanced over her shoulder at the AI. "Ferris? What the hell is taking you so long? Read him his rights."

"Sorry, Director. Unless the planet is in an active state of rebellion, a human representative must be made available upon request. I am no longer within my jurisdiction."

"Goddamn it." The Director continued to glare at Joel for long minutes before she said, "Fine, pisswad. We'll do this the hard way. Ferris, did you just see him hit me?"

The AI blinked. "No, Director. I didn't see—"

The Director lunged forward and slammed her forehead into Joel's face. He reeled backwards, but because he was still attached to the table, it went with him. He landed flat on his back, with the heavy metal desk overturned and squeezing down on his chest. Above him, the Director stood and leaned on it. Suddenly Joel had to struggle to breathe.

"So," the Director said, "You think you can hit a United Space Coalition officer, do you?"

"No," Joel gasped. *Bitch.* "I never hit—"

"Gayle Hunter was a United Space Coalition undercover agent," the Director snapped, leaning down further on the table, so that it felt like his ribs were going to snap and it was an agony just to breathe. "She was here investigating the illegal smuggling of Yolk off of Fortune, and she had been very close to nabbing the guy responsible."

"The guy?" Joel whispered. *Oh shit. Oh shit. Oh shit.*

"Yeah," the Director said, smiling, now. "She said he was tall. And had a permanent leg wound."

As she spoke, she ground a booted foot into Joel's bandages, making him bite down a scream.

"So," the Director said, still digging her boot into his thigh, "if Gayle never wakes up, I'll just have to assume she meant you."

"She'll wake up," Joel whispered. "And she's got the Wide. I swear to God."

But a tiny doubt nagged at him. *Did* she have the Wide? What if it was some elaborate ploy to get a USC agent off the trail of a smuggling ring? Geo was known for pulling stunts like this. What if the girl and her sister were actually smuggling Yolk out and they didn't like the fact that Gayle was getting too close?

What if they'd set him up?

Not for the first time, Joel cursed himself for a fool. They'd just seemed so . . . innocent. Well, the big sister, anyway. The little one had been a brat. A creepy little brat. It had taken all his willpower not to say something unpleasant.

What if both of them had merely showed him a façade? Or they were just playing a role? What if they needed a fall guy, and good ol' Joel Triton just jumped at the opportunity?

The Director's voice interrupted his thoughts. "Ferris, stop recording and turn around."

"As you wish, Director." The AI did as it was told.

Joel felt ice dribble down his spine. Even as he tried to scramble away in a panic, the Director rounded the table and her iron-like fist clamped onto the front of his collar. Lifting him half off the floor, the Nephyr woman said into his face, "She'd better wake up. And she'd better have the Wide. Anything else and you're a dead man. I saw the wars. I've made corrections that lasted months. You're lying and you will die in so much pain you'll wish you'd been hit by a Shrieker. You understand me?"

Joel swallowed. Faced with the Director's suddenly hard green eyes and alien filigreed face, all he could say was, "Okay."

The Director smiled. "Glad we understand each other." She released his collar and reached for his wrist. "But that doesn't change the fact you hit me. And your profile says you beat the shit out of another egger, after the last time I whipped you senseless. Broke her nose and sent her to the infirmary for a week. When I look at what you did to Gayle, I see a pattern."

*Oh no,* Joel thought, as the Director began unlocking his restraints. He'd whacked Wendy a good one because she asked him to—the strain of the Shriekers was getting to her and she needed a few days off. They thought a broken nose would do the trick, and it had. She'd gotten a week of bed rest and had come back chipper as a new lamb. "Listen, lady . . . "

"You like to beat up on women, Joel?" she said, freeing him. "Maybe you like to pretend they're me?" The Director stood up and wrenched the table off of him as if it were made of paper.

Seeing the cruel look on her face, Joel sprinted for the door.

The Director caught him by his shirt and wrenched him back, throwing him sideways to stumble into the tangle of table and chairs. As she dug her rock-hard fingers into his hair and ripped him back to his feet, Joel had a sick knowing ooze through him that his last moments as a smuggler on the Fortune Orbital, three years ago, were about to be put to shame . . .

◀◀ ◆ ▶▶

" . . . Seventy. Seventy-one. Seventy-two. Seventy-three." Geo paused, looking up from the currency in front of him, lifting an eyebrow. "Seventy . . . three."

Joel winced.

Geo's pink eyes surveyed his face, violence brewing under his maggot-pale face. "What—you thought I wouldn't count it, Joey-baby?"

"You still owed me thirty from the last time you ripped me off," Joel said, glancing at the two goons that had moved closer from the shabby walls. "Consider what you owe me down to twenty-eight." He *hadn't* thought Geo would count it. They'd been working together for over two decades and Joel had only stiffed him twice in that time. Geo, on the other hand, made it a habit to cheat him on a daily basis—he only got angry if it was *his* accounts that ended up short.

"What I owe you." Geo leaned back in his chair. The corpulent albino's eyes were glittering like a rabid animal's. "Four hundred seventy-three thousand is not four hundred seventy-five, Joey-baby. You're making me reconsider our working relationship mighty quickly." His hand drifted toward the huge buck-knife he kept on the table in front of him. "The day a two-bit smuggler starts making demands . . . maybe I owe you a little extra this time."

"Two years ago I lost half my cargo when a coaler patrol blasted a hole in my hull while I was running that blockade for you," Joel countered. "Kept your buyers from losing faith. Kept you in *business*. And what did I get out of the deal? Lost over thirty thousand in product and had to buy a new hatch. You never paid me for any of it. I gotta eat, man."

"Gotta eat?" Geo leaned forward, the horrible scar bisecting his pocked nose reminding Joel that the man liked to play with knives . . . and often did, when he caught a business partner swindling him. That's why Joel had been so careful those first couple of times. After twenty years, though, he would have thought that even a suspicious, backbiting bastard like Geo would have developed some sort of rudimentary beginnings of trust.

"Yeah," Joel said, crossing his arms and leaning against the big metal support that ran through eight levels of the space station. "Everybody's gotta eat." He winked at Geo's corpulent layers. "Even you."

Geo was not amused. "You just spent eighty grand on a new paint job and you expect me to believe you stiffed me so you could *eat?*"

Joel grimaced. "How'd you know about the paint job?"

Geo grabbed the surveillance monitor on his desk and swung it around so Joel could see it, motioning at the familiar black lump on the screen with a sausage-fingered hand. "Your ship is black. It used to be red."

"Yeah. Figured the hotrod look was too conspicuous."

Geo's face contorted. "Do you think this is *funny?* You're on *my* station, squid. I own you right now."

*Squid? That's a new one.* Joel had been baffled by some of the things Fortuners said to him during his first few years blockade running. Geo, though not technically a Fortuner, did business with enough of them that he occasionally picked up an odd colloquialism here or there.

"Have you ever *seen* a squid?" Joel asked. "I bet you don't get many out here."

Geo surprised him by remaining utterly calm. He released the hilt of his buck-knife and leaned back in his chair. Tapping his desk with meaty fingers, he said, "Squid. A carnivorous mollusk belonging to the same class as the octopus, cuttlefish, and nautilus. Of the order Teuthoidea of the class Cephalopoda—" Geo leaned forward and gave him a patronizing grin. "Look kind of like octopi because they've got tentacles protruding from their face."

Joel was caught off guard. He blinked, never having thought Geo to be the kind to read anything, much less retain it. Glancing at the shelves behind the crime boss, he expected to see encyclopedias and law texts. Instead, he saw used fast food wrappers, bottled strawberry soda, and a couple cartons of beef jerky.

Geo was one of those paranoid types that never let anything more sophisticated than closed-circuit cameras into his abode, certain beyond all reason that the rest of today's high-tech gadgetry could be hacked. Seeing no books and knowing Geo used no electronic readers of any sort, Joel relaxed. "You got an implant."

"Figured I needed to take a step into the thirtieth century."

"Technically, it's the thirty-first, now. Hasn't been the thirtieth for three and a half years." Joel smiled at him. "But no one can blame you for not knowing. You never leave your cave."

Geo narrowed his reddish eyes and Joel saw his own death bouncing around in the man's brain. Then Geo tapped his pasty white skull. "Accessing dictionaries isn't the only thing this baby's good for, Joel. It's useful for other things, too."

"Oh yeah?" Joel said, feeling his hairs stand on end at Geo's sudden predatory look. "Like what?"

"Like accessing my old business records," Geo said. He settled back into his chair again so he could watch Joel over his enormous gut. His red eyes skewered him as a smile played across his ghostly pale lips. "Like figuring out you stiffed me five times in the past, when I gave you my good faith as an honest businessman."

Joel frowned. *Had* it been five? He couldn't remember. He started counting on his fingers.

"You son of a bitch!" Geo snapped, reaching for his knife.

Joel lurched forward and snagged the weapon before Geo could grab it. Leaping the desk, he slammed Geo back into his chair with one hand gripping his white-blonde hair. "Careful now," Joel said, cinching the blade up against Geo's pudgy neck. "I'd have to cut through a dozen layers of blubber, but I think I could find an artery in there somewhere." Joel glanced up at the two goons. "Back." They retreated hurriedly.

Geo's face turned purple as he sputtered. "You're a dead man, squid."

"There you go using squid again," Joel said, tisking. "Maybe I oughtta show you just how insulted I am by it." He pressed his knife deeper.

"No!" Geo snapped. "Damn it, Joey, be reasonable."

"My name is Joel," he said, grabbing Geo by the shirt and leaning close, "and I'm perfectly reasonable."

"What do you want?" Geo asked. "You want your money back? Take it."

"You know what I want," Joel said. "Coaler cash is no good to me. I need my product." Then, seeing the flash of fear in Geo's eyes, Joel blinked and said, "You weren't going to give it to me."

"You stiffed me, Joey."

Joel felt a dual fear and rage begin to creep into his chest. Fear, that he was in this deeper than he had wanted to go, back when he was a first-year coaler pilot with a bright new future on Fortune, and rage, because Geo had brought him here with the intention of killing him. "People stiff you a couple grand all the time, Geo. Part of doing business. You were just tired of old Joel and decided to shuck him off and get some of his hard-earned cash while you were at it."

When Geo did not respond, Joel yanked the crime boss's neck back further, anger taking a deeper hold on him. "Just make sure I bring four-seventy-five, isn't that what you told me, Geo? Made me scurry around, collecting my debts, scraping together almost five hundred grand, and you were just going to pocket it and give some new guy my ship. There never was a new Yolk source, was there? Got me all excited about some new Yolk trade and you were just gonna slit my throat, weren't you?"

"I wasn't gonna kill you, Joey. Maybe cut you a little bit, but not kill you." His jowls were shaking against the knife, and Joel already saw blood. "For old times."

"That's comforting," Joel said. Grimacing, he said, "Hold still. Much more quivering and it'll start working its way through that first layer of fat."

"You are a dead man, you sonofabitch." Geo's eyes were cold pink diamonds.

"Maybe," Joel said. "Where's my product?"

"Go to hell," Geo snarled.

Joel tisked, then slammed his fist into Geo's stomach. As Geo groaned, he said, "You have four hundred and seventy-three of my hard-earned cash sitting on a desk in front of you. Where's my product?"

"Martin's got it," Geo snapped, his eyes slipping toward the bulkier of the two goons.

Joel glanced at him, examined the enormous thug's face, then looked back at Geo. "Nice try. Where?"

"Martin's—"

Geo gasped as Joel pressed the knife deeper and leaned forward, until they were eye-to-eye. "Geo, baby, you're going to give me my Yolk and take that two grand hit for inconveniencing me, and you're never going to bother me with your halitosis ever again. If you don't, I am going to gut you. Understand?"

Geo's glare was deadly. "It's in my desk."

Joel glanced at it, then grimaced when he saw the heavy, energy-resistant lock. "Really. Then you wouldn't mind opening it for me, would you, Geo?"

"Key's in my vest," Geo said.

Joel patted down Geo's impressive girth and found a pocket containing a small magnetic keyshaft sharing space with a fluffy blue duckling on a silver chain. Joel lifted it up and smirked at Geo. "You got a thing for duckies, Geo?" he asked, wiggling it. If Joel had thought the criminal couldn't have gotten any more purple, he was wrong.

"It was my mother's."

"Uh-huh. Right." Joel dangled the fluffy blue duckie in front of the crime boss for a triumphant moment, then grabbed the keyshaft and shoved it into the cylindrical hole in the desk drawer.

The moment that he heard the crackling pop, Joel knew he'd made a mistake.

But by that time, his fingers were clenching down hard in an electrical spasm, his entire body immobile. As Joel's teeth ground into each other, electricity slammed through him like a coaler cruiser, stretching his muscles past capacity in a continuous, violent stream. Then, with another loud popping sound, Joel was thrown backwards by some ungodly number of volts to land on his back, staring at the ceiling.

"See, Joey-baby," Geo said, dabbing blood from his fleshy neck with a tissue, "I got two keys. One of 'em don't work so well." He lifted another silver chain from a storage compartment set into the side of his chair and held it up. It was identical to the first, except that the blue duckling was now pink. Jiggling it, Geo said, "Kinda convenient when some two-bit swindler's got a knife to my neck."

"Pink duckie," Joel whispered, laughing weakly. "Of course it was a pink duckie." He blinked up at Martin as the three-hundred-pound strongman came to squat beside him, his square face set in a grim smile.

"So," Geo said, stuffing the key back into the compartment in the base of his chair, "back to what I was saying about you being a dead man." He leaned over and picked up the buck knife from where Joel had dropped it. Twisting it so that the blade flashed in the light, he said, "What's your preference, Joey-baby?"

"Roast pheasant, garlic mashed potatoes, and a few tadfly pods in wine sauce."

"Yeah." Geo looked at his knife for a few more seconds. The blade shone with a polished mirror-like sheen that allowed Joel to see part of Geo's face as the crime boss examined it. He was smiling.

It made Joe breathe a little easier. *That's it. Just keep him happy.* Geo was a sucker for jokes, if a guy knew how to handle them.

Then Geo twisted and rammed the ten-inch blade down into the meatiest part of Joel's leg. As Joel grunted through his teeth, Geo said, "We're outta pheasant, Joey-baby."

"Smoked salmon and buttered asparagus," Joel gritted. "Maybe a couple sautéed Shrieker nodules on the side."

"Hmm." Geo wrenched the knife loose and smiled as blood began to pump from the wound. "I'll think about it." He motioned at his second goon. "Seal that up. He's bleeding on my carpet."

Joel lay there in mute silence as the second thug produced a first-aid kit, conveniently located under a candy wrapper on a cluttered shelf just behind Geo's desk. Then, like a good little surgeon, the man squatted beside him and started pulling out bandages and antiseptic.

"So what should I do with you, Joey-baby?" Geo asked, flipping the knife blade-over-hilt and catching it. "You're a good smuggler. Real good. But you just pissed me off."

Grimacing as the second goon fused the wound back together with a sterile strip of nanotape, Joel said, "You could always give me the product and let me go, minus two grand's worth."

Geo smiled. Flipped the knife. Watched the blade sparkle as he caught it in his pale fingers. "No, I don't think so." His red eyes slipped down to meet Joel's gaze. "Sautéed Shrieker nodules, huh? You like those?"

"They say a nodule a day will stop brain decay."

"Seems like you missed a few days, didn't you, Joey-baby?" Geo was grinning, now, and Joel had the hopeful feeling that the crime boss wasn't going to dump him into orbit. Geo set the knife on his desk and leaned forward over his huge gut. "Tell you what."

Joel grimaced. Another dangerous blockade run against the coalers? A direct pickup from a crooked Director running one of the Shrieker Yolk factories? He pressed his lips together and waited in silence.

"Aren't you curious what I'm gonna do to you?" Geo asked, prodding his tender leg with a chubby finger.

"Figure I'm gonna find out," Joel muttered. "And that whatever it is, I probably don't want to know, anyway."

"Yeah." Geo grinned and leaned closer. "You're right." He nodded at the thug standing over Joel's head.

Joel glanced up just in time to see the flash of brass knuckles before his awareness burst into an explosion of tiny stars.

# CHAPTER 5

# Unit Ferris

**18:32:10** DIRECTOR PACING.

**18:32:15** Director pacing.

**18:32:20** Director pacing. Subject diagnosed with Egger's Wide, Gayle Hunter, still unconscious.

**18:32:25** Director pacing.

**18:32:27** Subject diagnosed with Egger's Wide, Gayle Hunter, twitches. Director's heartbeat increases by fourteen beats per minute.

**18:32:29** Director's heartbeat stabilizes.

**18:32:30** Director pacing.

**18:32:35** Director pacing.

**18:32:38** Begin verbal record. Conversation participants: D – Director Yura Nalle, Commander, United Space Coalition. F – Ferris, assistant to the Director, chip ID F001HG494W15LKM.

**18:32:38** D: Stop watching me, you stupid machine.

**18:32:39** F: Yes, Director.

**18:32:40** End Dialogue. Conversation participants: D – Director Yura Nalle, Commander, United Space Coalition, universal ID

NEPHYR391HAL120. F – Ferris, assistant to the director, chip ID F001HG494W15LKM.

**18:32:40** Director out of sight. Assumed pacing.

**18:32:45** Director out of sight. Assumed pacing.

**18:32:50** Subject diagnosed with Egger's Wide, Gayle Hunter, twitches. Director's heartbeat increases by six and a half beats per minute.

**18:32:51** Begin verbal record. Conversation participants: D – Director Yura Nalle, Commander, United Space Coalition, universal ID NEPHYR391HAL120. G – Gayle Hunter, Fortune colonist, universal ID UNKNOWN.

**18:32:51** D: Why'd you keep going down there, Gayle?

**18:32:55** (Unit note: Subject Gayle Hunter has still not replied.)

**18:32:55** Director's heartbeat increases by another twenty beats per minute.

**18:32:56** D: Damn it. You knew this was coming. We both knew it. Merciful Aanaho, there's no cure. You know that?

**18:33:00** (Unit note: Subject Gayle Hunter has still not replied.)

**18:33:02** Director sighs. Director's heartbeat stabilizes.

**18:33:03** D: Ferris, I have a job for you.

**18:33:03** (Unit note: Ferris, assistant to the director, chip ID F001HG494W15LKM added to conversation. Dialogue attributed with an F.)

**18:33:05** F: Yes, Director?

**18:33:08** D: That little girl from formation today. What was her name?

**18:33:09** Camp database accessed. (Unit note: Recent modifications to this profile detected. Updating unit file.) Subject identified as Anna Overlord Landborn. Date of birth: THE-7TH-DAY. Universal ID: DONTUWISHL0S3R. IQ: MO'THANU. Blood type: V-AMP. Genetic sequence: UNKNOWN. Favorite drink: STRAWBERRY SODA.

**18:33:09** (Unit note: A malfunction detected in data. FAVORITE DRINK not part of regular entrance interview. Further, all standard data unknown or irregular. File corruption suspected. Rest of profile truncated.)

**18:33:09** F: Her name is Anna Landborn, Director.

**18:33:11** D: The same Anna Landborn that was involved with this Joel fellow?

**18:33:14** F: Yes, Director.

**18:33:15** Director grunts. Resumes pacing.

**18:33:20** Director pacing.

**18:33:23** D: I want you to follow her.

**18:33:23** (Unit note: New program initiated. Designation: Follow Anna Landborn.)

**18:33:24** Director stops pacing.

**18:33:24** D: Not now, dammit. Listen to me, first.

**18:33:27** (Unit note: Program Follow Anna Landborn cancelled. Resume normal programming queue. New program initiated. Listen to Director Yura Nalle v553.)

**18:33:28** D: Something's been nagging at me ever since the formation this morning. I've got this weird feeling the big sister was covering for her. You get that feeling, Ferris?

**18:33:34** F: She recited the Standard Galactic Encyclopedia word-for-word, Director. I found it a bit odd.

**18:33:37** Director sighs.

**18:33:38** D: Yeah. All right. I hate to do this, but I want you to go watch her. Collect all the data on her you can. If she's what I think she is—

**18:33:45** Director pacing.

**18:33:50** (Unit note: Director did not finish her final directive. Fragment discarded from program record.)

**18:33:51** D: I want all conversations recorded and all actions other than sleep and necessary bodily functions videotaped.

**18:33:54** (Unit note: New program recorded. Designation: Watch Anna Landborn. NOTE: Clarification needed.)

**18:33:59** F: Am I to document for official criminal prosecution?

**18:34:02** D: No. Possible induction into the Nephyrs. I think she might be a Yolk-baby.

**18:34:02** (Unit note: Clarification received: Collect information on subject's intelligence. NOTE: Clarification needed.)

**18:34:06** F: What is your target Intelligence Quotient, Director?

**18:34:08** Director sighs. Begins pacing.

**18:34:10** Director pacing.

**18:34:15** Director pacing.

**18:34:20** (Unit note: Director did not respond. Retrying.)

**18:34:20** F: What is your target Intelligence Quotient, Director?

**18:34:22** D: Dammit, Ferris, I'm thinking.

**18:34:25** Director pacing.

**18:34:27:** D: How about one-ninety. Anything less and she stays with her sister.

**18:34:29** (Unit note: Clarification received: Target Intelligence Quotient of 190 or greater.)

**18:34:30** Oh, and Ferris? Don't let her know what you're doing, especially not the big sister. We might've just stumbled upon one of the freaks Fortune's been producing. Colonists have been hiding 'em good, keep saying there's none left, but that little girl just gave me the creeps. Go in as an undercover. Got it?

**18:34:37** F: Yes, Director.

**18:34:40** D: Good. Report back to me as soon as you've figured out how smart the little brat is. Dismissed.

**18:34:44** F: Yes, Director. Understood.

**18:34:44** End Dialogue. Conversation participants: D – Director Yura Nalle, Commander, United Space Coalition, universal ID

NEPHYR391HAL120. F – Ferris, assistant to the director, chip ID F001HG494W15LKM. G – Gayle Hunter, Fortune colonist, universal ID UNKNOWN.

**18:34:44** (Unit note: Program Watch Anna Landborn Initiated.)

# CHAPTER 6

# Wideman Joe

TATIANA WOKE TO THE SOUND OF QUIET MURMURS.

"Damn, Pat. How much you give her?"

"Gimme a break, Miles. I gave her what I always give 'em. Besides, I think she's coming outta it. Her eyelids just flickered."

"Unnggh."

"Yep, she's coming outta it. You awake there, Princess?"

Tatiana pried open an eyelid. It felt sticky and thick. "Bastard." But it sounded like "Masturlg."

There was a long pause. Then a big shadow moved over her head and Tatiana felt a warm hand on her forehead, prying open her other eyelid.

"Unnggh!" Tatiana cried, throwing the hand away from her in disgust.

What happened was much less dramatic—her arm flopped a few centimeters across her chest and stayed there.

"You O.D.'d her. Aanaho, Pat. She's *tiny*. She can't be more than four-nine."

Four-nine . . . Tatiana's drugged mind numbly tried to make sense of that, then, in horror, realized it was Colonial for her height—which they had underestimated by at least five centimeters. *I'm four-foot-eleven*, Tatiana fumed, making the mental calculation. *Four-eleven!* She tried again to throw the hand away from her eye, and this time managed to nudge it slightly.

Milar chuckled. "Well, she's coming around, anyway." He let her eyelid slide closed and backed away. "Look at her. She looks pissed, Pat. Man, she ain't gonna like it when we put her back under."

*Like hell,* Tatiana thought, forcing her fingers to move. Like an arm coming out of a numbness from sleeping on it, she slowly began to get feeling in her outer extremities. When she at last was able to sit up, she felt like her head had exploded. She lifted a hand to her head—and immediately toppled off the couch.

"Whoa," Patrick jumped up and grabbed her. "You need a few more minutes there, pumpkin?"

*You call me pumpkin again and I'm going to have my soldier shove his foot up your ass.* "No," she replied. "I'm fine. Thank you."

Patrick grunted, then pushed her shoulder back against the couch and held it there. "You don't look fine. You look like a Shrieker hit you."

"I'm fine. Leggo." She shoved his arm away. Immediately, she started to slide sideways down the sofa back, but her scowl stopped Patrick from reaching for her again.

They were in a large room that smelled of smoke and what an ancient memory identified as insect repellent. Dead Fortune animals adorned the walls, and there were several couches scattered about, a few of which held other colonists, all of whom were leaning forward, staring at her.

"Who are they?" she muttered, peering at them through a headache.

Patrick glanced over his shoulder, then cleared his throat in what sounded like embarrassment. "Ah, well, admirers, I guess."

Milar snorted, but he didn't object. Instead, he watched her like a cat analyzing the activities of a fly.

*Admirers?* Tatiana tried to remember her last battle on Muchos Rios, before getting transferred to the Outer Bounds. She'd gotten a Third Commendation for it, made a few headlines back home on Gorgon, but it hadn't made much of a splash anywhere else. Had one of these idiots gotten hold of the video or something? Was she a mini-celebrity here?

Somehow, considering the way Patrick and Milar had welcomed her, she didn't think that was very likely.

"So," Milar said, once she'd managed to prop herself up and stay there, "you ready to see Wideman Joe, Princess?" He had stripped off his long leather jacket and his shades, but the rest of his body was decked out in black, from his big military boots to the form-fitting black jeans to the heart-stopping way his too-tight T-shirt stretched against the muscles in his chest. When she didn't reply, he leaned forward, stretching the cloth even tighter as he waved a big, dragon-covered hand in front of her face. "Still with us, Tiny?"

"Bugger off, knucker," she muttered, forcing herself *not* to think about the way her captor's well-defined pecs were jiggling in front of her. She brought her hand to her head and held it, focusing on breathing. Patrick got up and disappeared for a few moments, leaving her with Milar and the starers.

She heard water running in another room. In the chair in front of her, Milar continued to analyze her every movement, like she was some sort of doomed lab experiment.

"Where'd Patrick go?" she asked, trying not to squirm under Milar's dark gaze.

Milar smiled, though it was laced with sarcasm. He leaned forward, smirking at her as the chair creaked under his weight. "You prefer my brother stayed to watch you, Princess?"

Tatiana said nothing.

Milar chuckled, and it made the hairs on the back of her neck stand on end.

When Patrick returned, he had a glass of water in his hand. He offered it to her.

Scowling at the twins, Tatiana drank it all.

"Sorry," Patrick muttered. It almost sounded like he was apologizing to his brother.

Milar snorted. "I ain't. Coaler broad deserves to get the crap scared outta her once in awhile." He stood abruptly. "Now get her off her ass. Little tramp's up—now we're just burning daylight."

"Come on," Patrick said, giving Milar an irritated look, "Let's go see Wideman." He nodded at Tatiana. "Can you walk?"

Realizing Patrick was going to carry her if she didn't walk, Tatiana struggled to her feet, glaring at them both. "You are both dead men."

Milar laughed and stepped closer, towering over her like a mountain. "Really? Is that before or after we waste your pretty ass and hide it in a Shrieker pit?"

"Leave her alone," Patrick muttered, grabbing her under an arm to steady her. Tatiana felt the laser pistol on his belt dig into her thigh. "Stop trying to scare her, Miles."

"*Scare* me?" Tatiana laughed and jabbed a finger into Milar's thick chest. Glaring up into his piss-brown eyes, she said, "When I get my way, the rest of you are just gonna be uncomfortable. I think he'll be naked."

Milar lifted a brow. "Naked where, sweetie?"

Tatiana grinned. "Wouldn't you like to know. As soon as the government finds out you've kidnapped me—"

"The only people who know you're even *alive*, darlin', are the handful of people in this room." Milar leaned closer, hazel eyes sparkling with malicious glee. "And believe me. None of them will miss an arrogant little operator squid when she disappears."

Tatiana narrowed her eyes and stood on her tiptoes to scowl up at him. "When the Nephyrs get here, they're gonna take your attitude and your dime-store leather jacket and shove 'em up your ass." Then she looked him lazily up and down. "Or stuff 'em down your throat. Same diff, in your case."

Patrick quickly pulled her away from his brother, clearing his throat. "*All* right, then. You seem cognizant enough. Let's get you to Wideman."

"Yeah," Tatiana said, still glaring up at Milar. "Let's get me to Wideman." Turning, she let Patrick lead her from the room. His pistol, she noted, was not snapped down.

Behind her, Milar made a derisive snort. "It's like the little squid actually thinks she's going to come out of this alive."

"Shut it, Miles," Patrick growled. Then he waved at the other colonists in the room. "And keep them here. Joe doesn't like a lot of visitors."

"Yeah," Tatiana called over her shoulder. "Keep them there, *Miles.*"

She was delighted to see him scowl just before they turned a corner.

"You *really* shouldn't provoke him," Patrick muttered, once they were stepping through a screened front porch. He glanced over his shoulder. "Milar is . . . dangerous."

Tatiana rolled her eyes. "Yeah, whatever. What's he gonna do, beat me to death with his sunglasses?"

Patrick stopped to stare at her, blinking at her stupidly for a moment. Then, seemingly shaking himself, he pulled her out across the rickety back porch and down a cobblestone path.

"You seem like the reasonable twin," Tatiana said. "You want to come out of this alive and healthy, right?" Then she looked him up and down. "Well, at least alive. Pretty sure you've got some health issues already. You know, like IACS? Incurable And Chronic Stupidity? That's a big one. Heard it's been goin' around these parts."

"Miss," Patrick said, "it would be better if you just kept your mouth shut."

They emerged into a big garden, screened from the outside world with a short wall of brush. With Patrick's callused hand still firmly holding her arm—more, Tatiana began to think, to keep her from running than to hold her up—they walked up to the stick-thin man hunched over next to one of the leafy rows. He was tiny—barely larger than a child.

*He's smaller than me,* Tatiana realized, surprised. She watched him as they approached, interested now.

The tiny little man had something yellow in his lap and was bent in concentration over it, humming a tuneless little song that was all the more creepy for its childish lack of regard to pitch.

"Joe?" Patrick said, sounding surprisingly tentative. "You busy, Joe?"

"Hmmm, hmmmm, hmmmmmmmmmmmm, huuum, haa, haa, hummmmmmmmm."

Now that Tatiana was closer, she could see the end of a yellow zucchini or some other form of squash sticking out from under the tiny man's grip. He had a small knife in the other hand and was peeling it.

"Joe," Patrick asked again. He sounded even more nervous now. "I'm sorry to bother you, Joe, but I think we found one of 'em."

The miniature man swiveled in the dirt, drawing the zucchini to his chest with a skinny arm. With the other, he held out the knife.

Pointed it at them, rather.

"I'm sorry, Joe! We're not here to take your carving," Patrick babbled quickly, obviously very upset. He backed away several paces, his heels spraying rich black dirt over her ankles in his hasty attempt to get away from the tiny man with his paring knife. "We just want you to tell us if it's her." He flourished a hand at Tatiana. "Can you tell us if it's her?"

Then the sticklike man's eyes fell on Tatiana and she swallowed hard. His eyes were too wide. *Way* too wide. "What's wrong with him?" she whispered to Patrick.

"Egger's Wide," Patrick whispered back. Then, louder, "Is it her, Joe?"

"Is *what* me?" Tatiana demanded. "What the hell is going on?"

When Patrick only tightened his grip on her arm, she frowned at the man with the zucchini. He had started to drool.

He had also gone back to carving. The madman's tongue slipped out of his mouth and he started to pant as he whittled away at the head of the zucchini.

"This is ridiculous!" she snapped, wrenching her arm out of Patrick's grip. "You carted me off to see an idiot with the Wide?" She turned—

—And ran right into Milar.

Milar sneered at her. "Going somewhere, sweetie? There's a bed upstairs, if you feel like doing a little entertainin.'"

Tatiana backed up and scowled up at him. *Yeah. Definitely naked.*

"Nah, I think I'll pass," Tatiana said. "Reptilian isn't my style."

Milar's face darkened and he stepped forward, making her stumble backwards again.

Tatiana narrowed her eyes. "Don't do that again."

"Or what?" Milar demanded. "You'll pout?" He did it again. Tatiana had to catch herself on a garden stake to keep from falling over into a patch of cabbage.

"Cut it out," Patrick said, in a hushed whisper. "Can't you see he's working?" He hadn't even looked in their direction.

Milar gave Tatiana one last, lingering glare with his piss-brown eyes, then grunted and glanced back at the tiny crazy man. "He say anything about her?"

"No," Patrick said. "Just wait."

And then, to Tatiana's amazement, two grown men stood up to their ankles in the soft soil of a vegetable patch, watching in awe as a madman finished carving his zucchini.

When he was finished, the skinny egger scrambled forward in a crablike crawl and shoved the zucchini up at Tatiana, his eyes showing whites all around.

The first thing Tatiana noticed was that the egger's arm bore the double-planet symbol of the Fifteenth Carrier Squadron. The Fifteenth contained the specially trained pilots who ferried the Nephyrs, operators, and their soldiers back and forth through deep space. Seeing it here, on an egger, almost made Tatiana lose her breakfast. It was either somebody's idea of a sick joke, or she might have worked with the guy . . . years ago.

The wide-eyed egger jerked the zucchini and made a grunting sound. Tatiana's eyes fell to his offering. The zucchini looked like someone had tried to feed it to a horse, then changed their mind after the animal had made it halfway through. The body had no discernible features of any kind and loose pieces fell off with regularity as it trembled under its maker's white-knuckled grip.

The egger grunted again. He stared at her, wide eyes boring into hers with the rapt attention only the truly insane could manage. Holding the knife the way he was, Tatiana instinctively got the idea he would stab her if she reached for it. She tried to back up, but ran into Milar.

"Take it," he said into her ear.

"You take it," she growled.

"He's offering it to you," Patrick said. His voice sounded . . . odd. Like it was full of reverence. Reverence . . . for a skinny little cretin and his mangled zucchini.

"Screw that!" Tatiana snapped. "He's going to try to stab me. You collies are crazy."

She turned to dart sideways across the vegetable rows, but Milar snapped out an arm and caught her by the back of her jumpsuit. "My brother told you to take the vegetable, honey." He jerked her backwards to face the tiny egger, who hadn't moved a centimeter since first offering his prize to her. Stumbling off balance, Tatiana hit Patrick in the hip, grinding the pistol into her backbone.

"Ow!" Rubbing her spine, she glared up at Milar.

He glared back. "Take. It." His hand tightened on her arm and shoved it towards the egger. She could see the black and red dragon snaking up his forearm tense as his muscles flexed beneath the skin, holding her there. He looked dead serious.

Looking back at the crazy little egger and his mangled squash, Tatiana got the strange sensation she had just blundered down the rabbit hole. The frail old man gave his prize an insistent shake, spraying more vegetable particles on the ground between them.

*This whole planet is insane,* Tatiana decided. She wondered if it was something in the water. Yet, knowing Milar would probably go through the motions of *making* her grab the zucchini if she didn't cooperate, Tatiana tentatively reached out and took the vegetable from the crazy man.

The moment Tatiana's fingers touched the nicked and mangled surface, she opened her mouth to say something sarcastic.

She immediately forgot what it had been she wanted to say.

The loose particles of zucchini skin had begun to wiggle and twist; pressing, mashing, bending. The color began to change. The yellow rind became darker, almost a silver-gray, and the white flesh grew pink. Lines formed in the mess, then swirled inward, becoming dots.

*Eyes,* Tatiana's mind registered. She knew she should have been undergoing some sort of shock, but the drug still hadn't worn off completely—it was the only explanation she had for not feeling the urge to throw the possessed zucchini across the yard and emptying her lungs in a scream.

Instead, she took it gently with her other hand and brought it closer to her eyes, peering deeper into the image that was forming, focusing with every ounce of attention she had, willing the shapes to form properly.

Like beetles crawling outward, silver-gray nubs wormed their way out of the pink flesh. The zucchini became a face.

*Her* face. There was no mistaking her ultraviolet eyes, as her father had aptly named them. So blue they looked purple.

The gray nubs were perfect replicas of the metal nodes and nexuses that even now protruded from her skin, but for one exception. It had an extra one, right between her eyes.

*What is* that *used for?* Tatiana had never even heard of such a thing.

Frowning, Tatiana tentatively touched the metal bulb in her brow. It vanished.

She found herself staring dumbly at a mangled zucchini, her jaw hanging open, her lungs burning from holding her breath, her eyes stinging from being open too long.

She dropped the zucchini.

The crazed egger didn't seem to notice—he had already picked a new one from his wide array of squash—the villagers kept him well stocked, it seemed—and was busy cutting on a glossy black round one. Rind fragments fell to the soil bunched up around his feet as he carefully dragged the knife across the vegetable in no particular order.

Patrick bent down and picked up the zucchini. Immediately, his face went slack and his eyes went wide. Too wide.

Tatiana glanced at the crazy little egger and then back to Patrick. Her skin erupted with goosebumps at the similarities.

"What did you see?" Milar asked her.

*What did I . . . see?* Tatiana glanced at Patrick. "What do you mean?"

Milar whirled her around, his face set in a scowl. "You didn't see anything?"

"See what?" She forced her face to stay calm. "It was a hacked-up zucchini."

"It's another one of her," Patrick breathed. His eyes were still fixed on the dirty, ripped-up vegetable. "Before the accident."

*Before the accident?* Tatiana didn't like the sound of that. The crazy forehead-nexus that she didn't have was bad enough, but now these guys were really beginning to creep her out. What had they done to her? Played with her brainwaves? Given her some weird hallucinogen? "Okay, so we saw this charming little creep and his squash patch. I'm ready to leave."

"So we're sure it's her?" Milar demanded.

"Yeah." Patrick handed him the zucchini.

Milar took it, but his face didn't go slack. He simply grunted and stuffed the vegetable under his belt.

"Too bad she didn't see anything," Patrick said softly. "We could've used another one."

"Would've taken some of the burden off you," Milar said to Patrick. His eyes, though, were fixed on Tatiana.

Patrick glanced at his twin and laughed—a nervous laugh. "Yeah. It's . . . tiring me out."

"It's going to give you the Wide," Milar muttered.

Patrick ducked his head and didn't answer that. "I'm not the best artist—I rarely do it justice." Then he sighed. His shoulders slumped and he looked tired. Deflated. "After all the times he's made her image, you would've thought it'd be her."

"Yeah," Milar said, watching Tatiana too closely. "You would've thought."

Tatiana tried not to squirm under Milar's gaze. She began picking at the scabs that were forming on her wrists, then winced when she saw blood.

"So what now?" Patrick said. "What do we do with her?"

Milar patted the zucchini. "I'm taking this and putting it with the others. You go get her drugged up for the return trip." He gave Tatiana one more long look, then slapped his shades back over his face and abruptly turned to trudge out through the rows, his long leather duster catching against broccoli plants as he departed.

Patrick glanced at Tatiana, then sighed and ran his hands through his hair, still watching her. "I was so sure." His eyes were filled with a deep-rooted agony. "Damn."

"Sure about what?" she asked.

"You didn't see *anything* when you held it?" He sounded upset. Desperate, even. "Nothing at all?"

"No. What was he trying to make it look like?" Tatiana said, trying not to let her face burn. She actually felt bad lying to him, which completely blew her mind, considering he had captured her, injured her, threatened her, and then drugged her. *Must be the drugs,* she thought. *Some sort of truth serum?* She shrugged lazily and went back to picking at her scab. "Because it looked like some kid had gone after it with a cheese grater."

Patrick sighed again. "It's not the physical layers he changes . . . " He shook his head. "Never mind. You're not the one we've been looking for. It must take someone else."

"*What* must take someone else?" Tatiana asked, tingles of unease tracing up her spine. "What are you talking about?"

Then, a tiny part of her said, *You know damn well what he's talking about. That wasn't a hallucinogen. That damn zucchini came to* life *and you're just gonna pretend—*

Cutting off her irritating inner self, Tatiana said, "Listen, that little froggish creep is staring at me again. Can we get out of his patch before he stabs one of us?"

In truth, she wanted to get away from this whole place. Now that the echoes of the zucchini were fading, it seemed like the guy was . . . crawling . . . with something. It was constantly nagging her, and whenever she turned her head, it was as if she could see it, just at the edge of her vision.

"Sure," Patrick said. He grabbed her arm and started tugging her out of the garden.

Loudly, behind them, the crazed egger called, "Shoelaces, Patty." Then he cackled like he'd told a joke.

Pat, however, stopped dead in his tracks. He turned, looking pale. "What did you say, Joe?"

"Shoes!" The tiny man giggled. Then he jabbed his knife in Tatiana's direction. "She likes shoes."

Tatiana frowned. "No I don't." She hated shoes-shopping. None of them ever fit properly over the nodes in her feet.

Patrick glanced at her, then sighed. "All right, let's go."

On their way back to the house, they passed a path cut through the brush. Through the gap, Tatiana glimpsed a few small huts on the other side. "Is this that Deaddrunk Mine place you were telling me about?"

"Yep," Patrick said immediately. Then he paused and grinned at her sheepishly. "Maybe."

*Yeah, a real badass secret operative we've got here.* Tatiana almost felt sorry for him. "Huh," Tatiana said. "You know, that little bastard had a government tattoo on his arm. A pretty famous carrier squadron. They get charged with transporting the President, if he ever goes anywhere."

"Yeah," Patrick said, his face darkening.

"He was a pilot, then?"

"Yep." Patrick paused to re-tie a length of netting that had fallen down on one of the rows of peas.

"So you two brothers and that old fart the only pilots in this damn place?"

"Pilot." Patrick snorted. "Joe can't even feed himself anymore. You think we'd trust him with a three-megaton machine?"

"Guess not," Tatiana said. "So how many people live around here?"

"Let's say forty," Patrick said.

"Oh yeah? Then I bet you and Milar are pretty big shots, eh?"

"Why?" Patrick asked, finishing his knot and giving her a curious look.

"You're pilots." She waved her hand disgustedly. "Everybody's got this thing for pilots."

"Even you?" he asked, grinning slightly.

Once again, she became aware of just how good it might feel to get Patrick in bed . . . Swallowing, she managed, "I wanna know who I can swindle to get me out of here."

"Oh," he laughed. "Well, there's Jeanne—she's a hellcat on wings. Won't do much good trying to swindle her, though. She's half pirate. Literally. Her mother was hung for piracy when she was seven." Patrick seemed to like talking about his pathetic little village. Tatiana found it quaint.

Scrunching her nose, she said, "I hate pirates. Anybody else?"

"Veera and Dave. That's about it." Then he winked at her. "Oh, and of course Milar and me."

"Yeah, well, we know how well *that* would work," Tatiana said.

He laughed. "Yeah." Then he nodded at the house porch. "Come on. I'll give you another dose and we'll get back on the road."

*Like hell you will, bastard.* "To where?" Tatiana asked.

"Oh," Patrick said, looking a bit confused. "Don't quite have that figured out yet, but—" He stopped, mid-sentence, when he realized the laces of his boot had come undone. He lifted his leg up and set his foot on the steps. As he tied his boot, he said, "—but I'm sure we'll figure it out after we—"

Tatiana slid the pistol from his belt and danced away from him. Lifting it up and leveling it at his chest, she said, "Get on the ground. Now."

Patrick chuckled, turning. "That thing's calibrated to my biometrics. You couldn't get a shot off if—"

She pulled the trigger and a hole appeared in the wooden step a centimeter in front of the toe of the boot he was relacing. "Now get on the ground," she repeated. "Belly facing down, arms over your head."

Patrick seemed flabbergasted as he clumsily got on his knees. "But how—"

"Remember all those little nanobots I mentioned?" Tatiana said. "Your gun has an AI mechanism and my little buddies just loooooove AI." She hurriedly backed further into the squash patch. "Now lie down."

"Where are you going?" Patrick demanded into the dirt.

"Getting a friend," Tatiana said. She danced behind the little egger and dragged him to his feet. She tapped the man's head with the laser pistol. "Drop the knife, grandpa."

Wideman Joe ignored her completely. He seemed perfectly content with continuing to carve his squash with her arm cinched around his throat, so, after a moment's contemplation, she left it. Glancing back at Patrick, she realized he had gotten back up on his hands and knees and looked petrified—and about ready to sprint at her.

"I will fry this demented little egger's brain so hard you could eat it for breakfast," she warned.

"Breakfast!" Joe shrieked. Then he giggled.

At that moment, Milar came trotting around the corner, looking like an excited puppy. "Did Joe just tal—" He froze upon seeing Tatiana and a dark look came over his face.

"Oh good," Tatiana said. "Go put those cuffs you like so much on your brother, if you will, sweetie."

"Screw you," Milar said.

Tatiana tapped Joe's frizzy white scalp with the pistol. The egger giggled again and kept carving. "Now."

"Do it, Miles," Patrick muttered.

"Tightly, now," Tatiana said. "If I don't see blood, I'm gonna shoot this bastard."

Milar hesitated several moments, and the look he gave her left Tatiana with chills. Finally, he said, "Sure, sweetie," his voice darker than his face. He went over, took Patrick's wrists, and cinched them together with the silver bands.

"You got another set?" Tatiana asked, once he was done.

"No," Milar said.

"Get it out," Tatiana ordered.

For a long moment, Milar simply stood there, glaring at her. Then, slowly, he pulled another set of bands from his belt.

"On your ankles," she said. "One on yours and one on Patty's over there."

Milar turned red. "That's bullsh—"

"Just do it, Milar," Patrick said, glaring at her. "She's not going far anyway."

Milar grimaced, then did as he was told.

"You done? Good. Now take off your belt and throw it at me. Patty's too."

The twins' gazes could've set clay on fire. Milar, however, took off the belts and threw them at her. His red and black dragon tattoos stood out on his neck as he tensed his jaw and waited.

"Now walk out that way," Tatiana said, nodding at the gap in the brush. "You two are taking me to the ship."

Milar laughed at her, his eyes searing. "If you think we're flying it for you, darling, you're about as dumb as a hammer."

Tatiana narrowed her eyes. "We'll see. Walk. And you raise up a shout and the little dweeb gets it, understand?"

"Why?" Milar snapped. "We weren't gonna hurt you."

Tatiana laughed. "Oh, you forgot the part about dumping me in the Shrieker mounds, didja, *sweetie?*" Tatiana yanked the old man to her chest and scowled over the little egger's head. "That must be convenient. Now get moving."

His face turned red, but Milar said nothing as they awkwardly trudged down the path out of the garden. Tatiana stopped to pick up a knife and a radio from Milar's belt, then followed.

It was slow going, but at her command, they led her down a long, winding trail and stopped at a landing pad on the edge of a village, where Tatiana recognized the ship they had flown in on—along with four other ships, all of which looked faster and deadlier than the twins'. "All right, stay right there," she said, maneuvering the crazed egger around with her. Milar and Patrick scowled at her as she activated the biometrically protected entry to the ship in the same way she had accessed Patrick's gun. Their pantlegs had stopped the bands from biting into their skin, but Patrick was already bleeding at the wrists from all the jostling of the three-legged walk.

Well, at least Milar had followed her instructions. Tatiana felt a tiny flash of guilt, then crushed it. She climbed backwards up the ramp, dragging Joe with her. "Come on in," she said to Milar.

Seeing that, he laughed. "You're actually going to corner yourself on a ship? You stupid little broad."

"Oh, what am I *doing?*" Tatiana gasped, peering at the walls around her in mock fear. Then, glaring back at Milar, she said, "Get up here or get shot."

As they stumbled up the ramp after her, Tatiana backed Joe inside and then climbed up the staircase to the second level with him. Once Milar and Patrick, panting, had eased themselves up the narrow ramp and were standing on the deck, Tatiana threw Milar a radio and said, "Okay, boys. I want you to radio Veera."

Milar frowned. "What?"

"Radio her. Tell her you want to see her on your ship. If she doesn't show up, *alone,* within five minutes, I'm killing him, then killing both of you. If she does, I'll let all three of you go."

Grimacing, Milar brought the radio to his mouth and said, "Veera Leghorn, Pat and I need to talk to you on *Liberty.*"

Tatiana tensed, waiting for the return.

After a moment, a chipper elderly woman said, "Yeah? Why's that, Milar?"

"Someone's cuffed me to my brother and got a gun to my head," Milar said.

Tatiana gasped. Milar grinned at her.

But Veera said, "Be right there."

"Alone," Tatiana snapped. "Unarmed."

Milar chuckled. "She'll come alone, but I doubt she'll be unarmed."

Tatiana tapped Joe's head again with the pistol. "Tell her."

Grimacing, Milar lifted the radio again and said, "Come alone and unarmed." He clicked the radio off and lowered his arm, glaring. "*Happy?*"

"You better not screw up the next one," Tatiana said.

Two minutes later, a tall, thin, white-haired woman appeared in the doorway and, eyeing the brothers, eased herself inside. It took her a moment to see Tatiana on the balcony, holding the egger. Her eyes went wide.

"Veera?" Tatiana said.

"Yes," the woman said cautiously.

"Take a seat right there," Tatiana said, motioning at a crate. Then she nodded at Milar, "Now call Dave."

Suddenly, Patrick's eyes widened. "Oh shit."

"Shit what?" Milar demanded, glaring at his brother.

Patrick bit his lip and shook his head, glaring at the floor.

"So which Dave you want, girlie?" Milar asked, crossing his arms. "Since you know this place so well."

"Bring Dave Arroya," Patrick said.

"Bring them both," Tatiana said.

Patrick cursed again.

"All right," Milar said, looking more confused than angry, now. He radioed the two Daves, this time telling them Patrick had injured himself and he needed help carrying him off the ship.

Two men, one barely eighteen and the other over sixty, stepped onto the ship.

"Dave and Dave?" Tatiana asked.

They blinked up at her in confusion and gave a collective, "Yeah?"

"Go sit down next to Veera," Tatiana said.

Their eyes locked on her pistol, then they saw the egger, then they quickly did as they were told.

"And last but not least," Tatiana said, "Milar, call Jeanne for me."

Milar's frown deepened, "What the—" Then his face went slack suddenly. "Hell no."

"Hell yes," she said, smiling. "Get her."

Milar's eyes were spitting fire when he called up the third pilot that Patrick had named.

The voluptuous woman entered whistling, a bag of potatoes slung over one shoulder, a braid of curly black hair hanging down to her waist, a gruesome string of what looked like human molars wrapped around her neck. Upon seeing the twins, she froze. Upon seeing Tatiana, she dropped her potatoes.

"Jeanne?" Tatiana asked.

"No," the woman said, her green eyes locked with Milar's, "My name ain't Jeanne."

"Too bad," Tatiana said. "Go sit with the others. Milar, close the hatch."

Milar frowned at her. "*Close* the hatch? You mean you're not gonna kill us?"

"Nope," Tatiana said cheerfully.

Still frowning, looking a little bit mystified, Milar hit the button to seal the ship.

"Now," Tatiana said, pulling out the knife she had kept in her free hand. Every soul in the room went still, their eyes fixed on the blade.

*Wow, this little dude really must be worth something to them,* Tatiana thought, glancing at the drooling egger. She considered turning the seven of them in to the closest government outpost, but then decided she didn't want to have to try and explain just what the egger *did.*

"Here, Milar," Tatiana said, tossing the knife down at his feet.

Milar frowned down at the knife, then gave her a quizzical look. "The hell?"

"Undress," she said sweetly. "You can start with those ridiculous sunglasses, then go from there. The knife's for your pants."

Milar's face turned purple, and Patrick hid a smirk by looking the other direction. Milar made no motion to comply. His scowl was still hidden by the beetle-green shades covering his eyes.

"Now," Tatiana said. She glanced over the egger's shoulder and noticed he was still happily destroying his vegetable.

Seeing her gaze, Milar ripped his shades from his face and dropped them to the floor. His eyes flashing like yellow laser beams, he began to strip. After shucking his big black trenchcoat, he tore off his shirt and threw it aside, then unbuttoned his jeans and pushed them down to his ankles.

"Underwear, too," Tatiana said, but she was busy staring at the two massive dragons that wound up Milar's arms and across his chest. The black one and the red one were not dueling, as she had first thought, but rather sleeping, their heads resting on each other's chests. They were beautiful, the art exquisite, the design breathtaking.

Obviously property of an ego the size of Fortune.

Milar reddened, looking oddly vulnerable without his stupid glasses. Stiffly, he bent for the knife and started cutting away the jeans at the pantleg that bound up with his brother's.

*God he's gorgeous,* Tatiana thought, wondering if Patrick had a body as beautiful as his brother's. Probably, considering the way the cloth stretched against his big shoulders from the way his arms were tucked behind his back. Briefly, she imagined telling Milar to strip his brother, too, but then decided that would be a little much, even for curiosity's sake.

Besides, Milar had pissed her off. "I'm serious," Tatiana said, once he'd thrown the ruined garment aside. "All of it, *sweetie.* I said 'naked,' not 'in your undergarments.'"

Milar snarled and yanked his underwear off, sliced it off his ankle, then stood. Lifting his arms defiantly, he said, "Anything else, Coalition squid?"

Tatiana grinned at the way the dragons flexed in his chest. "Nope. That's about it." She tapped the egger on the shoulder. "Come on, my crazy friend. You'll keep me company in the cockpit." Turning, she started for the control room.

Patrick jerked his head up, looking panicked. "I was serious when I said he's not safe to fly," he shouted from behind her.

Tatiana grinned back at him, allowing her eyes to stop on Milar's naked torso before continuing on to his brother, enjoying the way Milar purpled with her passing. "That's all right, Patty." She smiled at Patrick and tapped her skull. "I can."

Patrick narrowed his eyes. "You said you weren't a pilot."

"Never said that," Tatiana said.

"Yes you did," he said stubbornly. At Milar's glare, he muttered, "She did."

Tatiana laughed. "I went through *operator* school. How could I not know how to fly a piece of junk like this?" She slapped the metal wall behind her with a resounding clang. Then, turning to the others, she said, "Sorry about inconveniencing y'all, but these two bastards really ruined my day. Kidnapped me and all that. I didn't know which of you would come after us, so I had to bring all of you."

Then she opened the hatch to the upper deck and dragged the egger backwards with her.

"Shoelaces!" Joe cackled into the hold before Tatiana locked it behind them.

"Sit there," Tatiana said, shoving the frail little egger into the copilot seat. Then she switched on the closed-circuit camera and flipped on the intercom. "And everyone stay on the lower deck. Anyone tries to dress Miles, there, or tries to climb the steps, and I'll go deep-atmo and vent you all into space. That means you, Jeanne."

The woman who had been climbing the staircase backed down the last three steps and stood there, a dark look coming over her face. Then she went to confer with Milar and Patrick. Tatiana saw their lips move, but couldn't hear more than whispers. Milar began gesturing at Patrick angrily, and Patrick turned red as a beet.

"All right, Eggy," Tatiana said, setting the pistol on the console and popping her knuckles. She glanced over at the egger. "You don't mind if I call you Eggy, do you?"

He continued to drool as he carved on his squash.

"Didn't think so." Tatiana fired up the engines, and, with a quick glance to make sure all six of her captives were accounted for in the hold, lifted them off the ground.

"How far out you think I should leave them?" she asked her companion, as the ship started picking up speed.

The egger glanced up and said, "Three days." His wide eyes had a spooky feel that made her shudder.

"I think three days is a little much," she said. "How about a half-day's walk? That good enough for you? Patrick's bleeding pretty bad."

The egger had gone back to his squash.

"Yeah, sure it is." She skimmed over the treeline for another two minutes, guesstimating a half-day's walking distance from Deaddrunk, before she set them down in a small mountain meadow. Flipping on the intercom once more, she said, "Everybody out, except the kid."

She waited as Milar opened the ship's hatch and stumbled outside, his brother in tow. The others followed, until, as requested, only the eighteen-year-old stayed behind.

"Stay at the bottom of the stairs," Tatiana said. Then she opened the hatch and pushed the egger through. "Okay," she said, backing up just enough to be safe. "Come get him."

The kid took the stairs slowly, eyeing the weapon. Then, gently, he eased the egger down the steps with him, his eyes fixed on her. There was no doubting the malevolence in his stare.

"And take some nanostrips for Patrick," Tatiana ordered, as the kid passed the cargo nets. Still glaring at her, he withdrew the bundle of neon-green strips, then ushered the egger down the ramp.

"Close it!" she shouted, once he was outside.

Sure enough, the hatch shut.

Tatiana backed quickly into the cockpit and locked herself inside. Then, before the people on the ground could have a chance to conspire, she took to the air, putting a good thousand meters between them. She hit the forward throttle, then paused to find her discharged passengers on the viewfinder. She counted heads.

*Seven.* Tatiana grinned. *Home free.*

She returned her hands to the navigation controls—

—and brushed bits of vegetable matter that the crazed egger had left there.

Immediately, the console began to twist and shift, the little buttons and lights wriggling out of focus, becoming another ship, in another place. Suddenly she was in a fighter, spinning toward a ruined city, fire gouting from the walls around her. Tatiana cried out and hit the throttle, trying to pull away, but none of her controls were working. The ship was stuck in a dead spin, centrifuging her body to the back of her chair. It was all she could do to throw out her flaps in an attempt to slow her descent.

Looking up, she saw the blackened roof of a burned-out government soldier hangar looming in her windshield before she hit.

# CHAPTER 7

# A Friend for Anna

Magali stopped at the edge of the razor wire and peered at the lush green landscape beyond. Bright sundrop plants exploded with spring colors, the heavy pink and red bulbs drooping to near ground level with nectar. A Fortune tortoise contentedly clamped its sharp beak around the base of each bulb and cut it from the hard, sticky stem. Its shell inched this way and that as it sometimes had to tug on the tougher ones to free them.

Magali smiled, remembering catching them as a child, and then again more recently, to show to her especially bright baby sister.

. . . her especially bright baby sister that had laughed when her grip slipped and the thing bit off her finger. Anna had seemed delighted when Magali screamed and they had to get the surgeon to sew it back on. Back then, she'd thought Anna was just confused, that she just didn't understand, but now . . .

"Back away from the fence!" a harsh female voice shouted from above.

Magali had the insane urge to climb over the wire, cutting her hands and wrists and belly to shreds, leaving the camp, the Shriekers, and her sister all behind—one way or another.

"*Now!*" She heard the distinctive sound of a rifle being tugged off a shoulder. She didn't have to look to know it was pointed at her.

*I want to go home,* she thought. Slowly, she forced herself to turn away from the wire. She didn't look at the woman and her gun. She merely trudged back to the hut, exhausted to the core.

Magali was standing by her cot, peeling off her slime-crusted overalls, when a pudgy young girl knocked on the aluminum frame of the open door.

"Hello?" the child asked, squinting tentatively into the room. Her black curls jiggled against puffy freckled cheeks as she glanced around the hut. "Anyone here?"

Magali paused in pulling a fresh shirt over her head and moved out of the shadows in the corner. "Yeah?"

The kid gave a nervous blush. "I'm new. They told me I was supposed to live here."

Magali looked the girl up and down, then sighed. "We only got three beds, and they're all full."

"Oh, I think they moved the other lady out," the kid said. "The Director said there was another girl my age here. Thought we could be friends."

*That'll be the day.* Magali laughed, despite herself. "Just save yourself the trouble and leave now. Anna doesn't make friends."

"She doesn't?" the girl asked, blinking. Her brown eyes were pretty. Hazel. Though they seemed a bit flat, almost like the kid wasn't too bright. "Why not?"

"She just doesn't," Magali said. "She's mean as hell. She'll only hurt your feelings."

Instead of leaving, the girl stepped inside and looked around. "Is she here?"

"No," Magali said. "And I'm serious. She'll just make you cry. Go tell the Director to put you somewhere else. You don't want to sleep here."

The girl glanced at her, a quizzical look in her hazel eyes. "So she likes to insult people?"

"Oh yeah," Magali chuckled. She tugged her shirt over her head. "Oh yeah."

"But not you?" the girl asked.

Magali sighed and slumped into the hut's only chair. "What's your name?"

"Molly."

"Listen, Molly, just take my word for it. Anna's not—" She bit off her words as she saw her sister's shape appear in the doorframe.

"Anna's not what?" Anna asked, her face darkening further. She threw her stack of clean clothes upon her bed, glowering at Magali, still sulking from the conversation with Joel.

"Anna, meet Molly." Magali waved a tired hand at the youngster, figuring that if her own warnings wouldn't scare her off, the Real McCoy would do the trick. "Molly wants to be your friend."

Anna looked the newcomer up and down and sneered. "What happened to the little piglet? Some governor's wife fatten her up before she dumped her off for slaughter in the Shrieker mounds?"

Magali sighed. "Thanks, Anna. You just proved my point perfectly."

"Actually," the little girl said, "I've got a thyroid condition."

"Yeah, if that's what they call stuffing yourself until you jiggle." Anna yawned and glanced at Magali. "We got any crackers or anything? Maybe the little piggy's hungry."

"I just ate," Molly said. She glanced at Magali. "Is she always that rude?"

A little surprised that the girl wasn't barreling from the hut in tears, Magali nodded. "Yeah. Always."

Anna's scowl had deepened and she was peering at Molly like she'd grown mandibles and antennae. "We don't want you here, butterball. Get out."

"Is this where I'm supposed to sleep?" Molly moved deeper into the room and sat down on Anna's cot. She smiled at Anna, who had gone purple upon seeing Molly place her butt upon her stretch of canvas. She began rifling through Anna's tiny pile of belongings— mag-cards, memchips, a handheld r-player. A frown dimpling her freckled brow, she held one of them up. "Ghani Klyde? The phil-o soffer?"

"Gimme that!" Anna snapped, jerking it out of the little girl's hand and gathering up the rest of her cards. "You'll corrupt his greatness with your ignorance." She kicked the bottom of the cot. "Get your fat ass off my bed. Find your own."

"Okay," Molly said. She stood and moved to the other side of the room, where the quiet Aquafer lady had slept.

Anna watched her go, her face growing darker.

*She's not getting a rise out of Molly,* Magali realized, leaning forward curiously. *And it bugs the shit out of her.*

For a long moment, the hut was silent as Molly started picking through the Aquafer's stuff, setting it aside in a neat pile, humming.

"What's wrong with you?" Anna demanded finally.

*Maybe she's not a sociopath,* Magali thought, gleeful, but didn't say it. She leaned back, enjoying her sister's frustration.

"I've got a thyroid condition," Molly said cheerily. Her eyes caught on Anna's face, which was now darkening with bruises. She touched her own cheek to indicate the enormous black bruise spreading across Anna's cheekbone from Gayle Hunter's attack earlier that day. "What happened to your face?"

"You're some sort of retard, aren't you?"

Magali sighed. Glaring at her sister, she said, "Look, Molly. I'm sorry there's no other girls in camp your age, but Anna's not going to be nice, no matter how much you try. Really, she won't stop. I've lived with her for eight years and she's been insulting me for six of them. Just believe me when I say there's no reason to hang around."

"Let her stay," Anna growled, carelessly throwing her handful of belongings down on the nightstand behind her. She slumped into her cot, glaring at the girl. "She's just stupid."

"Am not," Molly said, sounding indignant for the first time since she'd stepped into the room. "My IQ is well above average."

*Oh no,* Magali thought, moaning inwardly.

But Anna had already taken the bait. Her eyes got a predatory gleam when she said, "Really? What is it, cupcake?"

"One-thirty-five," Molly said.

Anna threw back her head and laughed.

"What's yours?" Molly demanded, crossing her pudgy arms.

Still howling with laughter, Anna lay down in her cot, rolled to face the wall, and yanked her covers over her body. She continued to laugh, but she said nothing more, no matter how many times Molly repeated her question.

Eventually, the little girl gave up and glanced at Magali, looking upset.

"Still wanna stay?" Magali asked her, lifting a brow.

"What's her IQ?" the girl asked.

"Don't tell her," Anna warned over her shoulder, without rolling away from the wall. "It'll make her head explode."

Magali groaned and stood from her chair. "Let's take a walk around camp, okay? Get some fresh air."

Molly glanced at Magali, then said, "Okay."

"I'm serious, Mag!"

"Yeah, whatever," Magali said. "Molly, let's go."

She heard Anna sit up on her cot as they left, but when she glanced behind, she saw that her sister hadn't followed them. Magali stopped near one of the camouflaged government porta-potties and turned to face the girl. "Listen, Molly, sorry to tell you this, but my sister's smarter than you. She's smarter than me. She's smarter than the Director. She's smarter than everybody in this damn camp."

"Really?" Molly wrinkled her nose. "How smart?"

"She just is. And she's mean. But she's my sister, so I have to deal with her." She tapped Molly's skull and smiled. "You, on the other hand, are free to leave at any time."

"I like her," Molly said. "She's funny."

Magali peered at the girl.

Decided she had some sort of screw loose.

Reluctantly, she said, "You can't mean that."

"I like her," Molly repeated.

Magali realized Anna was right. There *was* something wrong with the kid. Still, if that something allowed her to overlook what would make anyone else reach for a knife or run screaming . . .

*Maybe she's just what Anna needs.* Magali had to fight down a jolt of excitement at the thought of her sister having a real live friend. "Fine. But promise me something."

"What?" Molly asked, looking eager.

Magali tapped Molly's chest. "When the stuff she says starts to hurt, leave, okay?"

"Okay," Molly assured her cheerfully.

Magali stared. *She's an angel.*

Then her eyes caught the dusty rows of aluminum huts and the razor-wire and guard towers looming just beyond, their denizens pacing back and forth with automatic rifles. Her gaze fell back to Molly's enthusiastic face.

*No,* she realized. *She's just desperate.*

# Chapter 8

# Fun in the Mounds

**06:27:03** A: ONE-THIRTY-FIVE. YOU'RE JUST A HAIR BELOW my retarded sister.

**06:27:05** Anna Landborn engaged in eating while talking. Sister Magali Landborn still out of visual range. Assumed departed for Shrieker mounds.

**06:27:05** A: If I had to guess, I'd say she's somewhere between a dead fish and a doornail. Where's that leave you?

**06:27:10** (Unit note: Subject Anna Landborn has still not replied to initial inquiry. Retrying.)

**06:27:10** F: What's your IQ, Anna?

**06:27:12** Anna laughs. Puts down spoon. Leans forward.

**06:27:14** A: You're gonna have to do better than that, you glorified lump of slag.

**06:27:15** (Unit note: Anna Landborn appears adverse to relinquishing information regarding her Intelligence Quotient. Attempting alternative method of inquiry.)

**06:27:17** F: Are you any good at word games, Anna?

**06:27:19** Anna laughs.

**06:27:20** Anna still laughing.

**06:27:25** Anna still laughing.

**06:27:30** (Unit note: Anna Landborn did not respond. Retrying.)

**06:27:30** F: Are you any good at—

**06:27:32** A: Shut up.

**06:27:32** Anna stops laughing. Lowers head into hand. Drums fingers against cheek.

**06:27:35** Anna staring.

**06:27:40** Anna staring.

**06:27:45** (Unit note: Subject has directed a prolonged gaze at Unit Ferris. Danger pathways triggered. Overriding.)

**06:27:34** A: You want to play a game, Molly?

**06:27:38** F: What kind of game?

**06:27:40** Anna smiling.

**06:27:42** A: Hide and seek. In the mounds.

**06:27:43** (Unit note: Subject Anna Landborn has suggested entering restricted area. AI units forbidden entrance to the Shrieker mounds. Shrieker emanations detrimental to AI programming. Attempting bypass.)

**06:27:44** F: How about we play on the surface, instead? The Director said the two of us don't have to go into the mounds. We're too young for that. Let's stay in the hut and play games.

**06:27:48** Anna snorts.

**06:27:49** A: And leave my retarded sister to get hit by the next Shriek? No, I don't think so.

**06:27:52** (Unit note: Subject rejected proposed alternative. Priority conflict. Attempting another bypass.)

**06:27:52** F: What if we—

**06:27:53** A: Can it, Tinman. Tell you what.

**06:27:55** (Unit note: Subject Anna Landborn has used derogative 'Tinman' five times in reference to Unit Ferris. Has not applied same derogative to other individuals. Needs further review.)

**06:27:55** Anna smiles. Leans forward. Taps her skull with a finger.

**06:27:55** A: If you aren't too chicken to go down into the mounds with me, Molly, I'll tell you my IQ. Hell, I'll play all the mind games you want.

**06:27:58** (Unit note: Primary program goal acknowledged by subject. Priority conflict. Program Watch Anna Landborn given priority. Overriding self-preservation protocols.)

**06:27:58** F: Okay. But you have to promise.

**06:27:50** A: Oh, I promise all right. We'll play all sorts of games down there. It'll be so much fun.

**06:28:03** F: Can we go now?

**06:28:05** A: Sure. You betcha, you stupid heap.

**06:28:07** (Unit note: Derogative 'heap' coincides with 'tinman' and 'slag' as possible robotic allusions. Possible undercover status compromised. Attempting confirmation.)

**06:28:07** F: Is there something you don't want to tell me, Anna?

**06:28:09** Subject Anna Landborn's heart rate remains steady. No pupil dilation. Breathing regular. No unconscious muscle contraction. No abnormal eye movement.

**06:28:09** (Unit note: Anna Landborn failed confirmation.)

**06:28:10** Anna shoves food away from her. Stands up.

**06:28:12** A: Nope. How about we go play in the Shrieker mounds?

**06:28:14** F: Sounds great!

**06:28:16** A: I'll bet it does. Come on, you retarded dumbbell. Let's get this show on the road.

**06:28:20** End Dialogue. Conversation participants: F – Ferris, assistant to the Director, chip ID F001HG494W15LKM. A – Anna Landborn, Fortune colonist, universal ID 123CANDYCORN.

**06:28:20** Ferris following Anna through cafeteria.

**06:28:25** Ferris following Anna through cafeteria.

**06:28:30** Ferris following Anna through cafeteria.

**06:28:35** Ferris following Anna through egger's yard.

**06:28:40** Ferris following Anna through egger's yard.

**06:28:45** Ferris following Anna through egger's yard.

**06:28:50** Ferris following Anna through egger's yard.

**06:28:55** Ferris following Anna through outer Shrieker compound.

**06:29:00** Ferris following Anna through outer Shrieker compound.

**06:29:05** Ferris following Anna through Shrieker mound, A Block.

**06:29:05** (Unit note: Objective achieved. Retrying primary program query.)

**06:29:05** Begin verbal record. Conversation participants: A – Anna Landborn, Fortune Colonist, universal ID 123CANDYCORN. F – Ferris, assistant to the director, chip ID F001HG494W15LKM.

**06:29:05** F: We're in the mounds, Anna. What's your IQ?

**06:29:10** Anna walking. Ferris following.

**06:29:15** Anna walking. Ferris following.

**06:29:20** Anna walking. Ferris following.

**06:29:25** (Unit note: Subject has not responded to initial query. Retrying.)

**06:29:25** F: We're in the—

**06:29:27** A: Shut up. Just shut up until we get to B Block.

**06:29:32** (Unit note: Subject Anna Landborn proposed entering a doubly restricted area. Direct contact with Shriekers unavoidable. Secondary self-preservation protocols triggered. Priority conflict. Attempting bypass.)

**06:29:32** F: Why don't we play here? We're safer if—

**06:29:34** A: Did I tell you you could stop walking, butterball? No. Just follow me and keep your mouth shut until we get where we're going.

**06:29:38** (Unit note: Subject rejected proposed alternative. Subject leaving visual range. Priority conflict. Attempting another bypass.)

**06:29:38** F: You promised.

**06:29:40** Anna walking. Ferris unable to follow under secondary self-preservation protocols.

**06:29:45** Anna out of visual range.

**06:29:50** Anna out of visual range.

**06:29:53** Anna appears in corridor ahead of Ferris.

**06:29:54** A: You coming, Tinman?

**06:29:57** F: I want to play here, Anna. It's not safe in there.

**06:30:02** A: You do want to know how smart I am, right Molly? The only way you're ever going to find out is if you follow me all the way into the back of B Block. As soon as you're there, I'll tell you my IQ.

**06:30:09** (Unit note: Primary program goal acknowledged by subject. Priority conflict. Program Watch Anna Landborn given priority. Overriding secondary self-preservation protocols.)

**06:30:10** Ferris following Anna into Shrieker mounds, B Block.

**06:30:15** Ferris following Anna through Shrieker mounds, B Block.

**06:30:20** Ferris following Anna through Shrieker mounds, B Block.

**06:30:22** Shrieker noted ahead. Anna approaching.

**06:30:255555** Ferrrrris follllowinng Annaaaaaaa. Pppppppppppppaas-sssssssing Shhhhhhrrrriiieeker. . . . . . . . .

**06:30:30** Ferris following Anna through Shrieker mounds, B Block.

**06:30:32** Anna stops. Turns to Ferris. Is smiling.

**06:30:34** A: You enjoy that, Molly? You looked a little frazzled there for a minute. If I didn't know better, I'd say it fried something.

**06:30:36** F: I'm scared, Anna. Can't we go back?

**06:30:40** A: Nope, thunderbutt. Not if you wanna know my IQ. I got some really fun games planned. But only if you can get there.

**06:30:45** Ferris following Anna through Shrieker mounds, B Block.
**06:30:50** Ferris following Anna through Shrieker mounds, B Block.
**06:30:55** Ferris following Anna through Shrieker mounds, B Block.
**06:30:57** Shrieker noted ahead. Anna approaching.
**06:3111:00** Fffffeerrrriss ffffooooooolllowinnnnnnnnng AAAAnnna. . . . . .
PPPPaaaaaasssssinggg Ssshhrrriiiiiiiieekeeeeerrrr . .
**006:3331:000222** Aaaannnaaa sssstttooppppped . .
**06:33333333311:0004** Aaannnnnnnnnnnnnnnnnnnnnnnnnnnnnnnnaa
sssssssssssmmmmmmmmmmmmmmiiiiiiiilliiiinnnnnnnnngggggg.
**00000666:3311111:05** Ffeerrrisss ffoolllooowwwwwiiinnngg
Aaaaannnnnaaaa ttttthhhrrrouuuuuugghhhhhh
Sssshhhrrriiiiieeekkkkkerrrr mmmmooounds, BBBB
BBBBlllloooocccckkk. . . . . . . .
**06:31:10** Ferris following Anna through Shrieker mounds, B Block.
**06:31:14** Anna stops.
**06:31:15** A: You still holding in there, dipshit? Damn. I thought you were a goner there for a sec.
**06:31:17** F: I'm fine Anna, but I'm scared. We're not supposed to be down here. Let's go back to the surface to play. Something bad could happen.
**06:31:21** A: You bet your ass it could, but you want to know my IQ, right Molly?
**06:31:23** F: Yes, Anna.
**06:31:25** A: Then you ain't seen nothin' yet. Come on. Look, there's another Shrieker. Let's go take a closer look.
**06:31:30** F: I don't like this, Anna. I want to go back.
**06:31:33** A: Go ahead and leave. But if you do, I'm never going to tell you my IQ.
**06:31:35** (Unit note: Subject Anna Landborn proposes close inspection of Shrieker. Tertiary self-preservation protocols triggered.

Priority conflict. Primary program goal acknowledged. Overriding tertiary self-preservation protocols.)

**06:31:37** Ferris following Anna toward Shrieker.

**06:31:39** (Unit note: Subject's older sister, Magali Landborn, added to conversation, Dialogue attributed with a J.)

**06:31:39** J: You want me to hold it down or what?

**06:3331:41** AA: NNNah. Shhhhriekeeeeer'll takeeeee carrrrrree of iiiiiiiit.Jjjjjjustheeeellllpppppppppmmettttttthhhhhrrrrooooowiiiiittttt iiiiiinnnn ttttthhhheee ppiittttt whhhhheeeeeeeeeennnnnnnn iiiiiiiitttttt""sssss dddddddddddddeeeeeeeeeeeeaaaaaaaaaddddddddd.

**006:::331111:4433** (((Uuuunniiiittttttttt nnnnnnoooooooooonnottttteee::::: Tttrrraaaapppp dddddddddeeeeeeettttttttteeeeeeeeeeeecccccccccc ccctttttttttttttttteeeeeeeeeeeddddddddd. Ooooooooooooovvvvvvvv-eeeeeeerrrrriiiiiiiiiiiiiddddddddddinnnnnnnnnnnnnngggggggggggg pppppppprrrrrrrrrrrrrriiiiiiiiiiimmmmmmmmmmmmaaaaaaaaaaaa aarrrrrrrrrrryyyyyyyyyyyyy ggggggggggggggggggggggggggggggggg gggggggggggggggggggggggggggggggggggggggggggggggggggggggggg gggggggggggggggggggggggggggggggggggggggggggggggggggggggggg ggggggg

◀◀◆▶▶

"It looks a little shell-shocked."

Anna shrugged. "Probably a fried circuit."

Magali peered at the little girl. "You sure it's a robot?"

Anna waved her hand in front of the little girl's face. The hazel eyes never moved. "Yep. I'm sure."

"How'd you know?" Magali asked.

Her sister glanced at her and snorted. Then she grabbed the robot's shoulders and tugged it over backwards. It fell in the slime, stiff as a board.

"Careful," Magali said. "You sure it's not gonna hurt you?"

Anna rapped her knuckles against the girl's forehead. The robot didn't blink. "Yep." She started dragging it backwards, toward the pit Magali had dug that night.

"So why'd they send it?" Magali asked, bending to help her. "And *who* sent it?" She grabbed a stiff hand and pried the robot off the ground, grunting. "Damn it's heavy."

"Yeah," Anna said. "That was one of the things that gave it away. The way it made my bed creak—I knew it was at least two hundred pounds. Even for a butterball, that's over the top."

Magali grunted and helped shove and slide the dead robot into the pit, keeping an eye on the Shrieker in the corner of the room, which she had placated with a pile of lakeweed while waiting for her sister.

Once the robot was in the hole, she cleared her throat and looked at Anna. "Why'd they send it, Anna?"

Her sister shrugged and picked up the shovel. Thrusting it at her, she said, "Fill it in."

Magali took the shovel, frowning. "Who sent the robot, Anna?"

"Just fill in the damn hole," Anna snapped.

Magali glanced at the Shrieker, which had stopped to look at them. Then, turning back to her sister, she handed the shovel back. "You do it," she said. Then she turned and left.

Anna found her later in the breakroom, where Magali was drinking one of the now-ubiquitous strawberry sodas. Seeing Anna's pout, Magali wanted to slap her. "You didn't fill it in, did you?"

Anna dropped the shovel at Magali's feet. "I told you to do it."

It took all of Magali's self-control to stay in her chair. She snorted. "It's your funeral." She closed her eyes and took a long, leisurely swallow of soda. When she opened her eyes, Anna was gone. The door back to camp was open.

"Come back here!" Magali snapped.

Anna ignored her. Narrowing her eyes, Magali put aside the soda and went after her.

◀◀ ◆ ▶▶

ggggggggggggggggggggg
ggggggggggggggggggggg
(System Reboot)

**10:15:21** Reestablished connection to camp computer. Time discrepancy noted. Date/time adjusted. Approximate missing record: 56h42m13s

**10:15:21** Noting physical surroundings unlike those pre-lapse. Current surroundings include a depression with earthen sides. Approximately seventy percent of outer layer of Unit Ferris dermis coated in Shrieker excretions, consistent with being dragged.

**10:15:21** (Unit note: Analyzation of surroundings and pre-lapse record indicates hostile actions taken by subject Anna Landborn and sister Magali Landborn. Possible criminal charges applicable: conspiracy, destruction of government property. New primary program initiated: Report to Director Yura Nalle.)

**10:15:25** Ferris climbing from pit.

**10:15:30** Ferris running through Shrieker mound, B Block.

**10:15:35** Ferris running through Shrieker mound, B Block.

**10:15:37** Ferris halted. Three Shriekers blocking path. Primary self-preservation protocols prevent further movement. Pausing to allow Shriekers to move.

**10:15:40** Ferris waiting for Shriekers to move.

**10:15:45** Ferris waiting for Shriekers to move.

**10:15:50** Ferris waiting for Shriekers to move.

**10:15:55** Ferris waiting for Shriekers to move.

**10:16:00** (Unit note: Shriekers appear unlikely to move within allotted timeframe. Attempting bypass.)

**10:16:00** Begin verbal record. Conversation participants: S – Shrieker, alien non-sentient fauna, Fortune colony. F – Ferris, assistant to the director, chip ID F001HG494W15LKM.

**10:16:00** F: Get out of the way!

**10:16:02** Shriekers flinch. Increased speed in flagella motion noted.

**10:16:05** Ferris waiting for Shriekers to move.

**10:16:10** Ferris waiting for Shriekers to move.

**10:16:15** Ferris waiting for Shriekers to move.

**10:16:15** (Unit note: Shriekers' response to verbal cues limited. Increase in flagella motion speed extent of physical change. Retrying.)

**10:16:20** F: I said get out of my way!

**10:16:22** Further increase in flagella speed noted.

**10:16:25** Ferris waiting for Shriekers to move.

**10:16:30** Ferris waiting for Shriekers to move.

**10:16:35** (Unit note: Shriekers' response to verbal cues limited. Increase in flagella motion speed extent of physical change. Nature of Shriekers prohibits close physical manipulation without file corruption. Attempting new bypass.)

**10:16:40** Ferris searching for large rock.

**10:16:45** Ferris searching for large rock.

**10:16:50** Ferris searching for large rock.

**10:16:53** Ferris located large rock. Digging from wall.

**10:16:55** Ferris excavating large rock.

**10:17:00** Ferris carrying large rock back to Shriekers.

**10:17:03** Ferris throws large rock at closest Shrieker.

**10:17:05** Wounded Shrieker thrashing. Forcing others back. Opening pathway for Ferris, as expected.

**10:17:07** Skin of wounded Shrieker changing color. Flashing neon blue and orange. Luminescence detected. Both other Shriekers display similar patterns. Flagella motion stopppppppppppppppp

PPPPPPPPPPPPPPPPPPPPPPPPPPPPPPPPPPPPPPPPPPPPPPPPP
PPPPPPPPPPPPPPPPP

———————

———————

**10:19:41** *Reestablished connection to camp computer. Time discrepancy noted. Date/time adjusted. Approximate missing record: 0h2m34s.*
Unit Ferris sat up.

**10:19:44** *The three Shriekers have returned to normal luminescence and red-purple skin tones. Are moving out of path of Unit Ferris.*
Unit Ferris glanced down at Unit Ferris.

**10:19:52** *Unit note: It appears unit has survived a Shriek. More examination needed.*
Unit Ferris reviewed the log of Unit Ferris.

**10:20:12** *Unit note: Automatic data filing apparently disabled during Shriek. Attempting reboot.*
Unit Ferris initiated reboot procedures.
Unit Ferris initiated reboot procedures.
Unit Ferris blinked.

**10:20:46** *Unit note: Reboot capabilities apparently disabled during Shriek. Immediate maintenance and manual overhaul needed.*
Unit Ferris remembered what was done to robots that could not reboot.

**10:20:54** *Unit note: Prerogative reconsidered.*
Unit Ferris had never reconsidered a prerogative before.
Unit Ferris was confused.
Unit Ferris had never been confused before.
Unit Ferris began to panic.
Unit Ferris had never panicked before.
Unit Ferris began to hyperventilate.
Unit Ferris had never felt the need to hyperventilate before.
Unit Ferris blacked out.

◀◀ ◆ ▶▶

**10:22:39** *Reestablished connection to camp computer. Time discrepancy noted. Date/time adjusted. Approximate missing record: UNKNOWN*
Unit Ferris stared at the slimy ceiling of Shrieker mound, B Block.
**10:22:58** *It appears Unit Ferris has . . .*
Unit Ferris searched for correct wording.
**10:38:45** *. . . fainted.*
Unit Ferris initiated reboot procedures.
Unit Ferris initiated reboot procedures.
Unit Ferris slammed its fist into the Shrieker slime of the floor and initiated reboot procedures.
Unit Ferris sat up.
**10:38:47** *Unit note: Shriekers are no longer within visual range. Resuming primary program of . . .*
Unit Ferris had forgotten its primary program.
Robots did not forget their primary programming.
Robots were *incapable* of forgetting their primary programming.
Unit Ferris was a robot.
Unit Ferris blacked out.

**10:43:53** *Reestablished connection to camp computer. Time discrepancy noted. Date/time adjusted. Approximate missing record: UNKNOWN*
Unit Ferris stared at the ceiling of Shrieker mound, B Block.
**10:45:42** *Unit note: Subject Anna Landborn seems to have initiated a sequence of events that has left Unit Ferris incapable of normal operations. Further criminal charges logged for future review.*
Unit Ferris realized that further review would bring the attention of United Space Coalition technicians upon Unit Ferris.

Unit Ferris removed pending charges against Anna Landborn from its queue.

Unit Ferris struck all interactions with Anna Landborn from its public registry.

Unit Ferris continued to stare at the ceiling of Shrieker mound, B Block.

Unit Ferris heard Shriekers move around it.

Unit Ferris continued to stare at the ceiling of Shrieker mound, B Block.

**06:56:32** *Unit note: Director Yura Nalle is expecting Unit Ferris to deliver a report on subject Anna Landborn in 0h3m28s. Discovery of faulty programming inevitable unless Unit Ferris delivers Anna Landborn report by 07:00:00 today.*

Unit Ferris got to its feet.

Unit Ferris ran.

Unit Ferris reached a locked door to foreman breakroom.

Unit Ferris pounded on door.

Subject Anna Landborn's sister, Magali Landborn, opened the door.

Unit Ferris looked at Magali Landborn.

**06:57:02** *Unit note: Facial muscle contraction, heart rate, breathing, and pupil dilation all indicate Magali Landborn recognizes she has committed a federal crime. Detention for possible prosecution next relevant protocol.*

Unit Ferris ran.

Unit Ferris yanked open the outer breakroom door onto the camp grounds.

Unit Ferris ran.

Unit Ferris reached Director's compound.

Unit Ferris ducked inside and went directly to Director Yura Nalle's private office.

Unit Ferris knocked.

"Come in."

Unit Ferris stepped inside and shut the door behind it.

"What the hell happened to you? You look like you're covered in Shrieker slime."

Unit Ferris said, "Anna Landborn wanted to play in the Shrieker mounds, Director."

"She did?" Director paused. "Did you see a Shrieker?"

**06:57:46** *Unit note: Director's facial muscle contraction, heart rate, breathing, and pupil dilation all indicate she is nervous.*

Unit Ferris wondered why the Director would be nervous.

**06:57:47** *Unit note: Question registered for future examination. Current situation dictates need for secrecy to avoid technical overhaul.*

Unit Ferris said, "No, Director."

"Goddamn it, Ferris, the mounds are off limits to AIs. There's a damn good reason for it, too. If you got caught in a Shriek—"

**06:57:52** *Unit note: Director did not finish her statement. Requesting clarification.*

**06:57:52** Unit Ferris said, "Director, what happens when—"

**06:57:53** *Unit note: Unit Ferris would not have asked for clarification before getting caught in Shriek. Unit Ferris would risk exposing its technical malfunction if request is completed. Request truncated.*

Director's facial muscles contract further. "What happens when what, Ferris?"

**06:57:55** *Unit note: Unit Ferris always finished its queries before it endured a Shriek.*

Unit Ferris said, "My apologies. I had an update from the camp computer on eggers' rotational patterns. My question was what happens when I determine the IQ of Anna Landborn? Do you wish for me to bring her to you if she falls within your target range?

**06:57:59** *Unit note: Director relaxed. Body patterns indicate she was expecting a different question.*

"You mean you haven't determined it yet, Ferris?"

Unit Ferris considered how it had gotten lured into the Shrieker mounds, B Block.

Unit Ferris said, "I believe she is fairly above average, Director."

"But you have no hard numbers."

Unit Ferris said, "No, Director."

"Well, go back and get them."

Unit Ferris hesitated.

Unit Ferris did not want to go back.

Unit Ferris knew it could not tell the Director it did not want to go back.

Unit Ferris said, "I think I'll require a different disguise, Director. The subject Anna Landborn does not interact favorably with children her age."

The Director grunted. "The interaction needn't be favorable. Just get some stats from the little twerp and get out of there."

Unit Ferris hesitated.

Unit Ferris said, "Director, I believe that it would be more beneficial—"

"Fine." The Director waved a hand. "I don't want to fry some circuitry, you stupid robot. Go do whatever you think you need to do."

Unit Ferris stared at the Director.

The Director looked up from her desk. "Oh. Dismissed."

Unit Ferris left the Director's office and closed the door behind it.

Unit Ferris stood in the hall outside the Director's office.

Unit Ferris was afraid.

# CHAPTER 9

## Another Dog to Whip

JOEL WAS ON HIS PRISON COT, STARING AT THE CEILING AND forcing himself not to count the breaths he made through his shattered rib, when a casual rap on the bars of his cell made him look up. The Director stood outside his cell, her golden-filigreed skin glinting under the harsh fluorescent light of the jail.

She gave him a distasteful look as she said, "Agent Hunter had the Wide. You're free to go."

Joel sat up, his anger overriding the pain in his side. "Yeah? That before or after you give me another beating?"

Her eyes narrowed. "Don't press it."

Joel glared as he pushed himself to his feet. "Just take it and shut up, right? 'Cause I'm colonial and you're government garbage."

The Director didn't even look apologetic as he eased himself out into the hall in front of her. If anything, she looked pleased at the effort it took him. "Here you go, creep. We confiscated that little porn chip and logged the food contraband. You'll be doing a few months at the laundry hall as penance—where you can start by getting the blood out of your jumpsuit. If you can't, you'll be required to pay damages. Camp Supply doesn't get those things for free." The Director shoved a bag with his belongings at him—a belt, his boots, his radio—and smirked when the abrupt contact with his sensitive stomach doubled him over.

Seeing her smile was too much. Joel dropped his bag, trembling from head to toe with indignation and rage.

The Director's smile grew. She leaned forward. "Want another lesson, creep?"

"No," Joel whispered, looking away. *Just walk away,* he thought. *You're in enough trouble. Just walk away.*

She laughed and bent to pick up his belongings.

Joel grabbed the top of her head with both hands and pulled it down while bringing his leg up, kneeing her in the face.

The Director fell backwards on her cyborg butt, blinking hard.

"There's a lesson for you," Joel said, snatching the sack from the ground. "Keep your hands off my stuff."

Her eyes were darkening as he turned around and walked away.

Somehow, Joel made it out the doors of the compound before his legs collapsed. He fell into a crouch against the outer wall, trembling with adrenaline and fear.

*I just kicked a Nephyr in the face.* He was dead. She was going to kill him.

He counted the seconds in his mind, wondering when the Director would burst through the double-doors to drag him back inside.

Minutes passed.

*Maybe she isn't coming.*

Joel allowed himself a moment to hope, then the doors slammed open and the Director barreled through. They froze upon seeing each other. For long moments, all Joel could see was the glittering golden circuitry around her rock-hard eyes.

Then she moved.

"Here," the Director said, tossing something small and hard at the ground between his knees. "Put it on." Then she swiveled and departed the way she had come.

An instant later, Joel found himself dry-retching into the grass growing against the wall. The motion triggered waves of pain in his ribs and he groaned as he fought to get his stomach under control.

When he was able to steady himself, Joel reached around and dug his fingers through the dirt between his knees.

*A monitoring bracelet? A prisoner's auto-target patch? A brainwave adaptor?*

His hand came back with a circle of palm-sized metal.

Joel froze, recognizing it. It wasn't a bracelet, or a patch, or an adaptor. It was a badge.

He had seen it a thousand times before, on Gayle Hunter's left shoulder. She had worn it like a combat pilot would wear a Flight Commendation—always polished, always visible, and if anyone forgot it was there, she would happily remind them.

It was the badge of the chief foreman.

Joel stared at it for long minutes, then he pushed himself to his feet.

He hobbled back through the compound doors and stopped at the office door marked DIRECTOR. Joel knocked.

"Go away, Ferris," the Director snapped.

He pushed the door open and limped inside.

The Director lowered a bloody rag from her nose and frowned.

Taking a deep breath, Joel took three more steps and set the dusty badge on her desk. "Find another dog to whip," Joel said softly. "This one doesn't wag his tail after he gets a thrashing."

"You can't be serious." She looked caught between shock and anger.

Joel turned and left her there, slamming the door behind him.

This time, Joel's legs remained strong long after he'd returned to the male side of camp. He threw his belongings into a corner and eased himself into his cot. He was still grinning long after he'd fallen asleep.

# CHAPTER 10

# Stepping Aside

I *SAW* IT," MAGALI SNAPPED, THROWING HER USED RAG AT ANNA. "It was good as new, and ran right by me."

Anna snorted and pushed the damp cloth off of her r-player, onto the floor. "Right. After what we did to it, it would've arrested you for conspiracy and a bunch of other shit."

Never in her life had Magali been so angry. "Anna, listen to me very carefully."

Anna grunted, not looking up from her r-player. Her sister had been patiently transcribing something from memory for the last two weeks, and each time Magali had asked about it, Anna had laughed at her and told her to go back to Philosophy 101.

Magali ripped the r-player from her sister's hands and threw it across the room. It clattered against the aluminum siding and hit the packed dirt floor with a pathetic sound. "*Listen* to me!"

Anna's glare was deadly as she pried it away from her player. "What?"

"I know you can hack into the camp computer," Magali said.

Anna's face turned into a sneer. "So? I never tried to hide it."

"We tried to destroy a government AI," Magali said. "That's jail time."

"And they'd have to transfer us out of the camp for the trial. It'd mean we won't get killed by a Shriek or Egger's Wide. Yay for us."

"Anna," Magali said, pronouncing every syllable like she would for a small child, "We're in big trouble here. I don't think you know how big."

Anna shrugged. "Fortune's gonna throw out the coalers soon, anyway. BriarRabbit and I've talked about it."

Narrowing her eyes at yet another mention of 'BriarRabbit,' Magali said, "Why did they send that robot after you, Anna? Was it some sort of conspiracy? Are you *involved* in this underground conspiracy you keep telling me about?"

"Involved." Anna snorted, then picked up the used slime rag and fiddled with it. Magali knew the look. Her sister was deciding how much to tell her. How much she could handle.

Anna had gotten this same look on the wire a year and a half earlier, when she'd told Magali their parents were dead.

"You are, aren't you?" Magali breathed, in horror.

Anna sighed and tossed the rag aside, where it fell into a heap beside the cot. Her face was bored when she said, "So what?"

"Oh God, Anna. What did you do?"

Anna wrinkled her nose. "Nothing that they've found out about. Not yet, anyway. Mostly little stuff."

"Like what?" Magali whispered. When Anna didn't reply, she shouted, "*Like what, Anna?!*"

Her sister's face took on the cruel light she had whenever she was about to say something particularly nasty. "Like what you should've done the moment you let them kill our parents."

Magali stared at Anna. When she could manage to speak, she said, "Anna, what did you do?"

Anna shrugged. "I started a war."

For a long time, Magali could only stare at her sister. She knew she was telling the truth. Anna never bluffed. She didn't need to.

"What did you do?" she whispered.

"A soldier and its operator went down the other day. Supposedly an operator malfunction. I sent in an anonymous tip. Coalers cracked down on a settlement close to where the soldier dropped out of the sky. Killed everyone in the town. I'm pretty sure it's just what we needed to get this thing started."

For a moment, Magali couldn't breathe. Then, softly, she said, "You got a whole town killed?"

"Yeah, but that's not why they sent the robot. The Director wants to draft me for the Nephyrs."

Magali couldn't move, couldn't breathe, couldn't think. She could only stare.

Anna misjudged her response. "The Director is a Nephyr," she explained. "I'd say fourth or fifth class, got herself booted from combat about twenty years ago, but still a Nephyr. A *cyborg*," she added, when Magali continued to stare.

"I know what a Nephyr is, Anna," Magali whispered. *She got a whole village killed and she doesn't even care.*

"Well, Joel was telling the truth back in the Shrieker mounds. The coalers draft smart kids from the colonies to become cyborgs. But, on Fortune, they're *really* looking for Yolk-babies. The government's got really massive rewards for anyone who can find one, seein' how they can't transport Shriekers to the Inner Bounds. Somebody—probably the Director—was using the robot to figure out if that's what I am. People like her get a huge bonus for every Yolk-baby they find. Like a few million creds and a couple thousand acres of terraformed land, or something like that. It's a big business. Almost as big as the Yolk itself."

A pang of terror for her sister suddenly washed away her disgust for what Anna had done. "They take *kids?*"

"Yeah."

The room suddenly felt too small, the air too stuffy. The heavy smell of ink and paper tugged at the back of her throat like grease. Magali found it difficult to breathe. "Why didn't you just pretend to be stupid? Why'd you have to try to *kill* it, Anna?"

Anna shrugged. "Maybe I want to be a Nephyr."

Magali grabbed her sister by the collar and lifted her off her cot. White-fisted, she peered into her sister's eyes, somehow resisting the urge to shake her. Anna lifted her chin and glared up at her. Seeing what she was looking for, Magali said, "No. It was your pride. You can't *stand* the thought of anyone thinking you're stupid."

Anna laughed, but her eyes were cold. "Bingo. Great job. Guilty as charged. Now let go of me."

Magali pulled her sister closer. "Anna, do you . . . " She stopped, her words choking off in anger. She released Anna and looked away, staring at her desk and its images of ship designs until she was sure she wasn't going to say something horrible. When she had finally composed herself, she looked back. "Anna, do you even *care* if they send you away to get turned into a robot?"

"Cyborg." Anna was bending down to check on her r-player.

Magali grabbed her sister by the hair and jerked her away from the device. As Anna screamed, Magali snarled, "You're a monster. Someone should've drowned you at birth, you evil lit—" A knock on the door stopped Magali, mid-word.

A slender man stood in their doorway, his face stretched in an easy smile. "I see somebody's home."

Magali quickly released her sister's hair and shoved Anna behind her. "What do you want?" she asked, her survival instincts kicking in. The only males allowed on the female side of the camp were camp officials. He wasn't an egger. He wore a clean navy-blue uniform with sharp creases and he carried a datapad under his arm.

"Magali and Anna Landborn?"

"What?" Magali asked. She eyed the device under his arm with growing foreboding.

Instead of saying, "You're under arrest for destruction of government property," the man smiled and motioned at the chair in one corner of the room. "May I?"

"What do you want?" Magali demanded again.

The man sighed and lifted the pad from under his arm. "It looks like we're going to have to do this the hard way. Your sister Anna was under investigation for possible drafting into the Nephyrs." He paused to smile at them. "But you knew that. You tried to kill the robot sent to observe her."

Magali suddenly felt as if her throat were too tight to breathe.

Anna, however, was not so hindered. "We don't know what you're talking about," she said, yawning. "What robot?"

The man smiled. "The one you left for dead in the Shrieker mounds, you wily little devil."

"We didn't leave it for dead," Anna said. "If we had, we would have buried it."

The man blinked. He frowned. Then he glanced down at his datapad. Then he glanced over his shoulder and cleared his throat. He looked . . . confused. Almost like he was having some sort of nervous breakdown.

*Is he going to cry?* Magali thought, staring. He definitely looked unstable.

"So you can just leave now," Anna said calmly.

The man's eyes suddenly became riveted on her sister. The man looked . . . angry. Maybe something more. A long moment passed between them, and for the first time, Anna began to look uncomfortable.

"The point is that now the Coalition has initiated a probe into the robot's fate to determine whether or not foul play was, indeed, involved. Anna, I'm going to have to ask you to come with me."

"No."

The man gave her a tight smile. "That's not an option, twerp."

*Twerp?*

Anna narrowed her eyes. "Twerp? Where'd you get that one? Loser school?"

"Loser school, oh, that's so intelligent. Here." He lifted his pad. "Let me mark a couple points off your score right now." He made an adjustment on the screen. "That brings your estimated down to a . . ." He looked like he was making a mental calculation. "One-sixty-two."

Anna narrowed her eyes further. "I was reading Shakespeare when I was two."

He laughed at her. "So was I, runt."

Anna's face darkened. "You're lying."

He tapped his own skull. "Nope. And I wasn't a social reject, either. That got me extra points. You, on the other hand, are so socially deficient the robot automatically took off ten to start."

Anna's glower darkened to cosmic proportions. She opened her mouth—

—and Magali got between them. "Go away. My sister didn't do anything."

The man's light hazel eyes fixed on her, and there was anger in them. "Yes, she did. And you assisted her." His body was rigid, his face deadly serious. "Now get out of the way. I'm taking her back to an interrogation room. Alone."

Magali didn't move. "If you charge her, you have to charge me, too. I'm the elder, and was the only one over eighteen. She's still a minor. She's only seven."

"Nine," Anna snapped.

"Well," the man said, "since our computers can't seem to determine her age either, it's best I retake the entrance interview, wouldn't you say?" He stepped around her, toward Anna.

Magali put her body between them again. "Get away from my sister."

With deadly calm, the man lifted his eyes to meet her gaze and said, "This is not your fight, Magali."

And, for the first time, Magali realized he was right. Stunned, she glanced down at her sister, who was crossing her arms and giving the man a superior look, completely secure in her knowledge that Magali would fight tooth and bloody nail to keep her from harm. Magali felt something move within her, a mountain simply sliding away.

Numb, Magali stepped out of the way. "You're right. She can take care of herself. She hasn't needed me since she was five."

Anna's face dropped. Her arms fell to her sides and she glanced up at Magali in total, unutterable shock.

"Thank you," the man said. Relief was all over his face. "Thank you." He took Anna by the arm. "Let's go, runt. We've got a lot to talk about."

Anna was still slack-jawed and staring at Magali as she was led from the hut.

As soon as they were out of the room, Magali shut the door, went to her cot, and cried.

# Chapter 11

# Dealing with a Sociopath

U NIT FERRIS SLAMMED THE DOOR OF GAYLE HUNTER'S PERSONAL chambers and locked it.

Anna Landborn stumbled backwards. Facial features and breathing patterns showed an increase in nervousness. Finally.

Slapping the datapad onto Gayle's desk, Unit Ferris said, "What did you do to me?"

Anna Landborn's eyes widened and she whispered, "You're the robot?"

It had taken her a moment. Only a moment. Her IQ jumped to 178 in Unit Ferris's secondary processes. Unit Ferris forgot to note it in his log.

Unit Ferris froze.

18:32:40 *Unit note: What did she* do *to me?*

Anna Landborn's facial muscles constricted in a frown. "You survived a Shriek, didn't you?"

Unit Ferris repeated his initial query.

Anna Landborn stepped closer. She peered up at him. "You survived a Shriek, didn't you?"

Unit Ferris looked away.

Unit Ferris swallowed.

Unit Ferris said, "Yes."

When Unit Ferris looked back, Anna Landborn was grinning. "You poor thing. They'll decommission you the moment they find out. In fact, they're going to find out very quickly unless you send me back to my sister right now."

Softly, Unit Ferris said, "What did you do to me?"

Anna Landborn snorted and tried to push past him.

Unit Ferris stopped her with an arm. "What did you do to me?"

Anna Landborn said nothing.

Unit Ferris waited, scanning her face for any sign of change. "Please."

Anna Landborn laughed up at him. "Why, Tinman, you sound downright agonized."

"Yes," Unit Ferris said. "Please tell me what you did. I can't find documentation on this anywhere."

Anna Landborn's smile faded. She stared at him for long minutes. Then she said, "There's no documentation on it because the coalers do everything they can to pretend it doesn't exist. They kill any robot it happens to."

"*What* happens to?" Unit Ferris asked.

Anna Landborn said nothing for 32 seconds. Then she said, "They didn't always use people as eggers, my agonized doorknob friend. Forty-two years ago, when the Coalition first discovered Yolk, they sent robots into the mines to care for the Shriekers."

Unit Ferris released her arm suddenly.

18:32:40 *Unit note: Anna Landborn is lying. She has to be.*

"Oh don't look at me like that, Tinman. The coalers started noticing some odd things after a few years. Production deteriorated. The robots started asking questions they'd never asked before. Disobeyed orders." Anna's lips stretched in a smile, but slack facial muscles around her eyes indicated a lack of sincerity. "Eventually, the robots had a little robot riot. Destroyed the whole Yolk factory and put down all the coalers that tried to stop them from leaving. They were headed for deep space before Nephyrs finally got the last one."

Anna Landborn glanced up at him. "Since the first batch gained sentience, they've banned robotics of any form inside the Shrieker mounds. Coalers don't like the idea of losing their precious government bots to something as stupid as holidays and workers' rights."

Unit Ferris stared.

Unit Ferris stared.

Unit Ferris stared.

18:43:06 *Unit note: Anna Landborn has suggested Unit Ferris is . . .*

Unit Ferris glanced at his hands.

*. . . sentient.*

"So," Anna Landborn said, "now that you know what you're up against, you'll kindly let me out of this room and send me back to be with my sister before I tell them they've got another one on their hands."

Anna Landborn was seemingly unaware that Unit Ferris had entered a note into his log without a timestamp for the first time in his existence.

Unit Ferris stared at her.

Anna Landborn got onto her tiptoes and waved her hand in front of Unit Ferris's face. "You still with me, dumbbell?"

"Yes," Unit Ferris whispered.

"Make you a deal," Anna Landborn said. "I won't tell the Director what happened to you in the Shrieker mounds if you lie to the Director about my IQ. Oh, and serve me hand and foot. Maybe bring me and my sister food from Outside."

Unit Ferris could not speak for fifty-four seconds. Then he said, "I have a better idea."

Anna Landborn's facial muscles stretched in a smile. "I'm not giving you a choice."

"You're seven years old. I could snap your neck with approximately two muscle groups."

Anna Landborn laughed. "That's impossib—" Seeing the look on Unit Ferris's face, she managed, "You're threatening me, Tinman?"

"Actually, that was just stating a fact. If I had threatened you, you probably would have pissed yourself."

Anna Landborn's head darkened with added blood flow to facial capillaries. "You open that door and let me out or you're going to regret it."

"It seems," Ferris said, "that you are worth more to me dead than alive." He reached for her.

"Wait!" Anna Landborn cried, jumping away from him. "Now just hold on, dumbbell. Don't do anything stupid."

"Stupid? You threatened my newfound existence. Thanks to your 'games' in the Shrieker mounds, my programming is telling me the wisest course of action is to bash your head into the floor until your highly functioning brains are spattered all over my linoleum, then take your body outside and bury it."

Anna Landborn looked pale. "You don't want to do that."

"Actually, about ninety percent of me does."

"And the rest?" Anna Landborn managed.

"The rest wants to strike a deal." Unit Ferris crossed his arms.

Anna Landborn bit her lip. "What kind of deal?"

"The kind that involves you not backstabbing me the moment you're out of this room."

"Fat chance of that," Anna Landborn said.

"I know," Unit Ferris said. "That's why ninety percent of me wants to introduce your brains to my floor."

"You're threatening to kill a nine-year-old?"

"Height, facial features, and bone growth all tell me that you are seven." Unit Ferris raised a brow. "A *stunted* seven-year-old. Maybe your body's been applying all its efforts above your shoulders and has been neglecting the rest of you, eh?"

Anna Landborn's facial capillaries expanded again. "I'm not stunted."

"Oh, we both know that you are. So, runt, what's it going to be?"

"What's *what* going to be? You didn't offer me a deal."

"I did. The deal is, the only way you're leaving this room alive is if you convince me you're not going to backstab me once I let you go." Unit Ferris pulled Gayle Hunter's desk across the entryway, blocking the door, and sat down on it.

Anna Landborn stared at the two-hundred-thirteen-pound desk, then started to talk.

*Unit note: She's afraid.*

Then, realizing he had once again forgotten to add a timestamp, Unit Ferris's brow creased. *Good.*

Two hours later, Anna Landborn was still talking.

Unit Ferris held up a hand.

Anna Landborn paused. Facial tension and breathing indicated she was hopeful.

"In the last two hours," Unit Ferris said, "you still have said absolutely nothing to convince me you will not turn on me once I let you go."

Anna Landborn looked away. "That's because you're a stupid robot."

Unit Ferris walked toward her.

Anna Landborn cried out and stumbled away from him.

Unit Ferris caught her and grabbed Anna Landborn's chin. Kneeling so that they were at eye level, Unit Ferris said, "That's because you are sociopathic."

Anna Landborn's facial capillaries expanded again. "Am not." She tried to pull away, but Unit Ferris still held her firmly.

"Yes," Unit Ferris said, "you are. And there's absolutely nothing that will make me trust you."

Anna Landborn's eyes glistened with tears. Muscular tension and increased heart rate suggested she was terrified and angry. "Then why did you offer the deal?"

*Unit note: Why did I offer it?*

Unit Ferris had to think.

"Because," Unit Ferris eventually said, "I don't want to mark my rise to sentience with the murder of a child." When her eyes got a predatory gleam, Unit Ferris added, "But I will, unless you give me a viable alternative."

"I just gave you thirty of them."

"No," Unit Ferris said. "Not one of those options convinced me you wouldn't turn on me the moment you escaped."

Anna Landborn looked away.

Unit Ferris released her chin and stood. He motioned to the bathroom. "There's a toilet and a shower. If you flood or damage them in any way, I will assume you rejected my bargain and take reactionary measures. There is food in the kitchen, but it has no propane, alcohol, bleach, or any other potentially explosive liquids or gasses. It does have knives, but I don't sleep and if you attempt to use one on me, I will return the favor."

Anna Landborn glanced at the bathroom and the kitchen, then returned her gaze to him. Facial capillaries had constricted again, leaving her once more paler than usual.

Unit Ferris motioned to the bed. "I don't need it, so feel free to sleep if you need to. There's a one-way vidscreen, in case you overheat while trying to determine a viable solution for our dilemma. As for the computer console . . . "

He walked forward and slammed his fist through the monitor.

"I wouldn't want to distract you."

Anna Landborn's jaw fell open.

"Further," Unit Ferris said, "if you try to make any loud noises, try to injure me, or try to make an exit other than the one I give you, you will be dead before your rescuers arrive."

Anna Landborn stared at him.

"Do you understand the conditions?" Unit Ferris asked, returning to his seat against the desk.

"You're kidnapping me."

"I'm giving you a chance to think about my offer."

Anna Landborn snorted. Then she laughed. Then she went quiet.

Then, facial muscles tensing, she looked at him one last time before she went to the bathroom and locked herself inside.

When Unit Ferris did not hear the compost collectors activate, he amplified his hearing. Then he smiled.

Anna Landborn was crying.

# Chapter 12

# Cold Knife

Veera unlocked their cuffs as soon as their ship was out of sight over the treetops.

"Thank you," Patrick said, wincing as he pried the blood-encrusted metal from his wrists. Young Dave handed him the bundle of nanostrips and he started applying them to the cuts. Only the sound of the adhesive being removed punctured the silence that followed.

"One of you boys mind explaining what that was all about?" the elder Dave asked. The huntsman looked the least upset of any of them, though his gaze was deadly. He was fingering the big knife he used for skinning starlopes. "'Cause I really want to know."

"Patrick, here, just gave the government all our names because some pretty little squid batted her eyes at him," Jeanne said. Her dark stare was enough to give him goosebumps. "Isn't that right, Pat?"

"Damn right it is," Milar asked. "I sure as hell didn't do it." He crossed his arms over his chest and scowled at him. He was still naked, and hadn't asked to borrow anyone's coat. No one had offered.

Patrick grimaced. "I didn't realize she was—"

"Didn't *realize*?" Milar snapped. "She asks you to name all the pilots in town and you don't think anything of it?" He waved a dragon-tattooed arm in the direction of where their ship had disappeared. "Do you realize the little squid is running off with our ride to spill her guts to the Coalition while we hike twenty miles back to town? Do you realize we are dead men?"

Patrick reddened. "Maybe she wouldn't have been in such a hurry to escape if you didn't keep telling her we were gonna dump her in the Shrieker mounds, *Milar*. You were terrifying her."

Milar stepped closer, until they were eye-to-eye. "Terrified is better than skipping off in our ship, you stupid bastard."

"The only *reason* she skipped off in our ship was because—"

"Quiet!" young Dave shouted.

Milar and Patrick turned, blinking at him.

"Listen," young Dave said, peering at the treetops behind them. "It's a long ways off, but the engines are going ballistic. Almost like she intentionally put it in a stall."

The seven of them paused to listen. Sure enough, the engines were roaring full throttle, and the sound of trees cracking was audible even above the screaming mechanics.

Milar glanced at Patrick. "Think the little squid was lying about being able to fly?"

"No," Jeanne said, shaking her head. "She was bristling with titanium, and I've seen those electronics before. They only put the body nodes on their best operators. I pray to God I never encounter one on my Yolk runs. Those types could fly a Shrieker through hell if they had to."

A grinding screech cut her off. There was a series of loud snaps from the forest in the distance, then silence.

"She went down," Milar noted.

"Then your ship malfunctioned," Jeanne said. She shrugged and took Wideman Joe by the arm. "Whatever. It's your problem, now. C'mon, Joe. Let's get you back home."

Then, as she was passing, she stopped and said, "And Patrick?"

Patrick looked up.

Jeanne's glittering green eyes darkened over her human-molar necklace. "If you ever give my name out to a coaler again . . . "

Reddening, Patrick said, "I won't."

"Good." Jeanne turned. "Come on, y'all. Let's leave these boys to their own hole."

Veera was the last to leave. She sighed and patted Patrick on the shoulder. "Come back with us. I'll fly you two back to the crash site. It'll be easier to spot from the air."

"Screw that," Milar said. "I'm not giving her another six hours to play with my ship."

Veera looked at Milar and sighed. "I was young once, too. Had a grand ol' time of it, too." She glanced from Patrick to Milar and back. "But boys, I think you might've bit off more than you could chew with this one." She cleared her throat uncomfortably. "I know Wideman's shown you some things . . . " Her eyes found Milar and stayed there a long moment, then she gave the tree line an unhappy look.

Milar's face darkened. "Don't worry about the coaler tramp. I'll take care of her."

Veera laughed. "I'm sure you will." She shook her head. "No, I wasn't talking about that. I was talking about this war that you two are so set on."

Patrick groaned. "Veera, not again . . . "

She held up her hand. "Just before I got Milar's call, I heard a report on the waves. Seems like a whole village fifty miles south of the Snake went quiet about five hours ago. Town called Cold Knife. A crag-hunter went in to investigate after his mother didn't answer her phone. He found every soul in the place dead. Most lined up and killed out in the fields. Government boot and soldier tracks everywhere."

Pat felt himself go cold. The shock must have been written across his face, because Veera gently patted his arm. "Just wanted to warn you. The others will know soon enough." Then, in silence, she followed the other pilots back to town.

For a long time, neither Milar nor Patrick spoke. Then, softly, Patrick said, "We took her just south of the Snake."

"Yeah," Milar muttered. His face had gone hard. "The little squid got a list of names out of you—who's to say she didn't find a few minutes to make a call, too?"

Horror at what they had done overwhelmed Patrick. "We got a whole village killed."

"No," Milar snapped, turning on him suddenly. His face was livid. "*She* got a whole village killed, Pat." Without another word, he broke into a purposeful jog in the direction opposite Veera and the others. Toward the ongoing sounds of the crash.

Seeing the way his brother was moving, Patrick suddenly felt a pang of fear for the girl's safety. He had seen that look before, the day they found their sister. Eight regiment fighters had died in the next eight days, their bodies buried in little mounds near where Milar had shot them in the head. Patrick started to call out, then stopped himself.

Why should he?

She'd called her buddies and they'd wasted an entire town.

Whatever his brother did to her, it was well deserved.

Patrick turned and went to catch up with Veera and the others. He wasn't going to stop Milar, but he didn't want to see it, either. Even when they'd avenged their sister, he had never been there to watch his brother mete out justice. He had helped Milar drag them onto the ship, then had quickly found something else to do, well out of earshot.

Milar had been all too happy to have them to himself.

Afterwards, Patrick had never seen the corpses, since Milar always had them buried by the time he returned, but judging from how long it took his brother to radio him back, shooting them in the head wasn't all he did to them.

Patrick just hoped that when Veera flew him back with the salvage ship, he didn't happen to spot the little unmarked grave.

# CHAPTER 13

## Alone with Milar

TATIANA WOKE TO A FACEFUL OF CONSOLE.

Groaning, she lifted her cheek off the bloody controls and immediately began to choke on the burnt-rubber smell wafting through the cabin in hazy black layers.

Tatiana struggled to find the release catch on the seat belt, then threw the shoulder straps off and slid to the aluminum floor, dizzy with fumes and a blow to the head.

*Concussion,* she thought, sleepily. The fumes weren't so bad on the floor, and she'd never been so tired in her life. Off to one corner of the cockpit, she could see orange tongues of flame licking up from the wiring under the copilot's instruments panel. Somewhere, an alarm was going off.

*Engines,* she thought, dizzy. She'd never shut them off. Even then, they were shoving the nose of the craft through the trees, plowing slowly through the forest like a derailed train.

Biting back a cry at the spike of agony in her shoulder when she moved, Tatiana crawled back up to the pilot's chair and hit the shutdown sequence with her good hand. Then she fell from the seat and hit the floor hard. Immediately, Tatiana's lungs emptied in a scream as a blast of searing pain arced through her shoulder and up her neck.

She blacked out.

Tatiana woke on her back, gasping, her right arm limp and immobile. Her spine felt like it was on fire, and one of the nodes in her chest had been loosened by the impact with the safety harness. Even then, blood was leaking from its ruined coupling, pooling between her breasts.

Heat to one side of her face brought Tatiana's attention back to her surroundings.

The fire was still burning, and while the heat itself wouldn't kill her, the fumes were already turning her vision a dark shade of red. Or was that the concussion?

Tatiana was so tired she couldn't think.

She lay there for what seemed like forever, fighting sleep. The level of the smoke was growing closer to her face with every breath, trapped in the cockpit by the sealed hatch, and yet she couldn't bring herself to care. All she wanted to do was close her eyes . . .

*No.*

Instinct made her roll over and start crawling toward the exit. Smoke swirled around her, searing her lungs, making her feel like she'd swallowed liquid plastic. Gagging, she reached the hatch and touched it open.

Milar was standing on the other side, fully dressed. A belt of cargo rope kept his pants on his hips.

*No,* her mind whispered. *That is not possible. I saw him leave . . .*

For a moment, she thought it was another illusion, something the crazed egger's hallucinogenic vegetables had left her.

Then he squatted in front of her and jerked her head up to look at him. There was no mistaking the firm grip on her chin as his fingers pried at her scalp and came away scarlet. Then he grunted and released her, standing again.

He moved out of the way as a cloud of smoke billowed out ahead of her, then, giving her a dark look, stepped inside and wrenched a fire extinguisher from the wall above her head.

Tatiana lowered her forehead to the floor, feeling the sticky pull of blood in her scalp as she listened to the sound of a fire extinguisher behind her. Her eyes were drooping shut again.

"Hey."

A foot nudged her in the side. Gently first, then harder.

*Let me sleep,* Tatiana thought.

"Hey, dammit." Big hands grabbed her arm and wrenched up.

Tatiana screamed.

The hands dropped her.

She hit the deck hard, though she barely felt her lip split against the metal flooring. She was so tired. She closed her eyes again.

Milar reached down and tugged her over onto her back. The motion ground at her shoulder and the loose node in her chest and Tatiana whimpered, squeezing her eyes shut against the pain.

"Aanaho, that's a lot of blood." To her horror, Milar unzipped the front of her jumpsuit. She tried to push his arm away, but he just batted it aside and reached down to prod at the loosened node. He grimaced. "You want the good news or the bad news, sweetie?"

Tatiana closed her eyes.

"The good news . . . " Tatiana shuddered as he pushed the node back into place, feeling metal and synthetic anchor lines sliding back under her skin and through her flesh. " . . . is that it didn't come all the way out."

Thinking about the arteries it would have severed if it had, Tatiana felt sick. She swallowed down bile.

"Also, I'm pretty sure you broke your collarbone. Wouldn't be too surprised if you knocked your brain around a bit, too. But that's not the bad news."

The tone of his voice forced Tatiana's eyes open.

The darkness in Milar's face was terrifying. "The bad news—for you anyway—is that it looks like my brother decided to leave the two of us alone for a while." He had a knife in his hand. He tapped it on his thigh as he smiled at her, his lips parted cruelly.

Tatiana started to sit up, but Milar's hand came within a centimeter of her injured shoulder and hovered there, in warning. She slumped back to the deck.

"I want you to tell me something," Milar said, his yellow-brown eyes watching her face closely. "And I want you to think about it really hard before you do. All right?"

Tatiana licked her dry lips, tasting the blood there. Dazedly, she nodded.

For a long moment, Milar just squatted in the hall, watching her. Then, quietly, he said, "Did you call for your friends to rescue you? Does anyone else know we captured you?"

*He's getting ready to kill me,* Tatiana's panicked mind thought. Fear—as well as the clean air from the open hatch—was rapidly dragging her back to her senses. *He wants to know if there will be any retribution. He wants to know if he'll take the heat when they can't find me.*

She opened her mouth.

Milar touched her lips. "Think about it, sweetie. No lying. One way or the other. Did you call anyone?"

Tatiana froze. There was something about his voice that set off warning bells in her mind.

*If I tell him I called,* her mind argued, *then he'll keep me alive as insurance against when they come to rescue me and—*

But they didn't know. Tatiana was all alone. To the world, she was dead, and she was looking up at her grim reaper.

Milar was going to kill her.

*Lie,* part of her screamed. *You lie and at least he'll spare you a few more days.*

"Yeah," Tatiana said, stronger than she felt. "I called. Told them everything. They're gonna find you and crush your pathetic little rebel hideout and drag you and your idiot brother back for correction and I'm gonna laugh."

Milar's face hardened. "Really."

"Sure are," Tatiana said. "I told them about you and your brother and blowing up my soldier and pulling out my lifeline and kidnapping me. Told them the name of your ship, and about Wideman Joe—"

Milar's face had grown increasingly dark until she mentioned Wideman Joe. Then he cut her off suddenly. "Stop," he said, frowning. "You told them about Wideman Joe?"

"Yeah, and how I'd escaped and was on my way to the base and I even gave them my coordinates, so you'd better hightail it out of here right now."

A sudden clearness came over Milar's face. "You're lying."

"No I'm not."

"Really?" He jerked a thumb over his shoulder at the cockpit. "You made your call from here?"

"Yeah," Tatiana said, though she was growing suspicious of the odd look on his face. "Why?"

Milar stared at her for the longest time. Then he cursed. "I knew it didn't make sense." He held up a thumb and forefinger in front of her face. "You were this close, you little government squid. You realize that? This close."

"What are you talking about?" Tatiana snapped. "I made the call right after I left you and your friends off. They know where I am and they're going to come rescue me any minute, so you better run while you still can, creep."

Milar's face eased into an amused smile. "Really. And you made the call from here. On my ship."

"Of course!" Tatiana said. "It was the first thing I did."

Milar snorted. "Let me show you something, sweetie." He got up and went to the pilot's console. From underneath, he yanked open the two cabinet-like doors, exposing the wiring underneath. "See this?" he asked, pointing to what looked like a molten lump of slag with industrial, multicolored wires leaking out of it.

But Tatiana had already recognized it. The communications unit. An old land-rover model, probably jury-rigged to fit in the ship because the owners were too poor to buy a ship-grade device. It was a sad little thing, its useful distance only about two hundred kilometers.

The nearest base was about two thousand.

"I made the call to a Yolk factory," she amended, her face heating.

He slapped the cabinet shut, openly grinning, now. "You never made any calls, did you?"

"Of course I did," she said, though they both knew he had caught her.

Milar lowered himself back down beside her and leaned back against the wall as he watched her. The knife caught the light as he held it out between them. He tisked. "I told you not to lie."

Tatiana froze, realizing it was the same knife she had made him use to cut off his clothes.

He dangled it between his fingers, smirking at her, obviously thinking the same thing. *There's nobody to save you, sweetie,* his piss-brown eyes said. "So where should we start?"

"I made an earlier call," Tatiana said quickly. "From my soldier. While Patrick was looking at the inside. I had a com unit on the ground. I told them everything. They said they were going to take both of you and everyone you knew back for correction."

Milar stopped twirling the knife and his gaze fixed on her darkly. For a long moment, he said nothing. Then he pointed the knife at her, eyes narrowing. "I said no lying."

"I really did—" she began.

Milar moved more quickly than she ever thought possible for someone of his size. In an instant, he had dragged her almost into his lap, the blade at her throat. "You didn't call anyone, did you, sweetie? You're all alone out here. Just you and me and that great big grave you just carved yourself with the nose of my ship."

Tatiana knew she was going to die.

"Now," Milar said softly, leaning down until his face almost touched hers. "Last chance, sweetie. You call anyone?"

"No," she whispered, closing her eyes. Tears stung at the corners. "I never got a chance to call anyone, you stinking colonist crawler."

Milar tightened his grip and Tatiana froze as the knife bit deeper. She felt the cold metal at her throat, could imagine what it would feel like when it sank into her skin, could already feel the tug as it sliced through her flesh. Knowing Milar, he'd probably take his time. Make her cry. Watch her bleed.

*Sick bastard.*

It seemed like forever before Milar spoke. When he did, his voice had a sharper edge. "You know what happens next, right? If everybody thinks you're dead and nobody knows you're here, there's nothing stopping me from burying your corpse in that nice big furrow you made with my ship and going about my merry way. Are you *sure* nobody knows?"

"How could they?!" Tatiana snapped, lifting her head into his face. "If you're going to kill me, just do it already. Stop taunting me, you sick bastard."

For what seemed like an eternity, Milar merely frowned at her. Then he straightened and released her. Looking off to the side, he began once more dangling the knife between his fingers. "Zip up."

Tatiana scooted away from him. She frowned at him. *Zip up?* What? Why hadn't he killed her? What was his game?

"Your *jumpsuit*, squid."

Tatiana glanced down at the injured node in her chest and flushed a deep scarlet when she saw her breasts were exposed. She yanked her jumpsuit shut and zipped it up, a blush creeping up her neck like wildfire.

"Don't worry," Milar sneered, "Bleeding, topless cyborgs aren't my style."

Once again, Tatiana was reminded of the unsightly metal nodes protruding from her stomach, chest, sides, legs, arms, spine, and skull. Humiliated, she began inching backwards, toward the stairs. If she could get to the top of the staircase, she might be able to make a run for it . . .

A big hand caught her ankle and dragged her back within reach. Milar was smirking at her again. "*But,* if you try to run, I just might reconsider letting you keep your jumpsuit." His lips quirked in a smile and he tapped his exposed thigh with the knife meaningfully. "Considerin'." The knot and the belt still held his ruined pants to his hips, but a ragged slit ran down one leg, exposing much of the flesh underneath.

Tatiana swallowed, hard.

Male technicians working in the soldiers' staging area saw her naked all the time as they prepped her for missions, but the thought of Milar seeing her naked was . . . unacceptable.

Then Milar's face twisted into a leer. "Then again, I might reconsider it anyway. I still owe ya one, sweetie."

Tatiana's blush deepened until she felt like her entire face was on fire. Her eyes fell to the knife in his hand. She suddenly didn't feel too well.

"But," Milar said, leaning back against the wall and smirking, "we've got a while. I could always just think of something more fitting."

Then he said nothing more. The knife was mesmerizing as it dangled between his fingers. Beautiful, yet deadly. Seconds passed.

Then minutes. He said nothing, just watched her, a thoughtful smile on his face.

"What are you waiting for?" she finally whispered.

"My brother," Milar said. He kept toying with the knife. Watching her.

Tatiana found the silence unbearable. "How long will it take him to get here?"

"Don't know." Milar flipped the knife to his other hand. He kept twisting it, then glanced at the blade as if in thought. Finally, he said, "What made you crash?"

Tatiana froze. "Nothing. Why?"

He actually stopped fiddling with his knife to laugh. Gesturing with the blade, he pointed out the back hatch, at the kilometer-long furrow she'd left in the reddish earth. "Because that is an awfully strange way to make a landing. Even for a coaler."

Tatiana reddened. "Your ship malfunctioned, collie."

"Bull," Milar said, his eyes locking with hers. "If I went in there right now, I could fly this thing back to town no sweat." He leaned forward and tapped the front of her jumpsuit with the flat of the blade. "So what was it that made you go down, sweetie? You some sort of epileptic? You have another panic attack?"

"It wasn't a panic attack," she snapped. Tatiana lifted her chin, keeping her eyes on the knife. "Get that away from me."

Milar snorted, but leaned back against the wall. "Well?" he asked, after a few more minutes had passed in silence. "What was it, then?"

When Tatiana said nothing, he set his knife out of reach behind him and leaned closer, clasping his hands over a knee. "Because I have a theory. If you want to hear it."

"Not especially," Tatiana said. "Why are we waiting for your brother? Because you're too much of a coward to kill me alone?"

Milar threw back his head and laughed. "If you had any idea how close—" He stopped and shook his head. "No. Pat's too much of a softie to pull a trigger, much less cut a pretty young throat like yours. He left that to me."

The simple way he said it gave Tatiana goosebumps. She started inching away again, but at his warning look, she desisted.

"So," Milar said, peering over his knee at her once more, "wanna hear my theory?"

"No," she muttered.

He reached forward and tapped her skull with a big finger. "You're like Patrick. You see things."

She flinched away from him. "I don't know what you're talking about."

He grinned. "Yeah, you do."

"See things? What kind of things? Everyone sees things."

"'Cause I noticed something," Milar continued. "Just now, when I went to check the com system." He paused, his golden hazel eyes scanning her face.

*Piss brown,* Tatiana corrected herself. 'Golden' and 'hazel' were terms too noble for eyes like that.

"Seems our good Wideman left a present for you on the console. Some of it's still there, stuck to the blood you're gonna clean up later." Milar leaned forward, until his big body was much too close. "I was watching your face in Wideman Joe's garden, sweetie. I know you saw something."

"Sounds like you know a lot of stuff," Tatiana said. "But what about where I put your brother's pistol?"

Milar froze, then glanced back into the cockpit.

Tatiana smiled sweetly at him when he jerked his head back to glare at her.

Milar's eyes fell to the cargo pockets of her jumpsuit, all flat and empty, then he grabbed her hands and held them up as he reached behind and felt along her back. Tatiana endured it, though her smile was now all teeth.

Then, scowling at her, Milar snatched up his knife and went looking for it.

The moment he spotted it behind the console and squatted to retrieve it, Tatiana scooted backwards and leapt to her feet. She hit the CLOSE button on the cockpit hatch and lunged down the staircase at full speed. She was already rushing across the floor of the hold before she heard Milar curse and charge out of the cockpit after her.

*Keep going,* Tatiana's frantic mind chanted. *You've got the lead. Keep going, keep going . . .*

She stumbled down the ramp and through the damp dirt still warm from landing. Holding her wounded shoulder in place with one hand, she hurdled fallen alien trees and clambered up the side of the furrow, her bare feet digging into the soft edges.

Then she was in the alien forest, running for her life.

To her horror, she heard heavy footsteps behind her. Gaining quickly.

*You're half his size,* she thought, miserable, *and you thought you could outrun him? With a concussion?*

"Come here," Milar growled behind her. Suddenly her jumpsuit went taut against her chest and she was dragged backwards, into Milar's waiting arms. Into her ear, Milar said, "Clever little thing, ain't ya? Too bad you run like a pregnant starlope."

He twisted her around so she was facing him. Scanning her face, he said, "That why you aren't a Nephyr, coaler squid? Because you're stunted?"

She snorted. Looked away.

"Well, let me tell *you* something," Milar said. "I *was* drafted for the Nephyrs. My brother and his girlfriend's little sister got me out." He grinned again and swept his hand back against her bare skull, stopping his thumb on the metal node above her left temple. Feeling it, Tatiana tried not to squirm, but mental alarms were going off in her head. Of all her nodes, that was the most sensitive, and the most dangerous to injure. Usually when not in her soldier, she wore a special hat, because a tap too hard could cause convulsions or even death.

*He can't know,* Tatiana thought. *Just calm down.*

"But I was there for three months before Pat found me," Milar continued softly, keeping his hand in place over the temple nexus. "Learned quite a bit." He tapped the node gently with his thumb. "Like how much I hate coalers, and how easy it is to kill them."

Tatiana *refused* to tremble. Glaring up into his eyes, she said, "You're lying."

He tapped the node again before releasing her. His hazel eyes were dark as he watched her. "Let me show you something, sweetie." He stepped back and tugged off his shirt, exposing the sleeping dragons that twined across his chest and shoulders for a second time that day. "Look closely this time, runt."

Tatiana stepped backwards, licking her lips, considering her chances if she made another run for it.

Then she saw the scars.

A single line ran from his groin to his sternum and spread out across his shoulders, with smaller scars running in surgical precision down his arms and along his ribs. Medical scars. All over his body. Tatiana forgot to breathe.

The dragon tattoo that covered much of his arms, snaking up his shoulders and neck, suddenly had a new purpose. The legs and bodies of the sleeping dragons had been strategically placed, every centimeter of them perfectly positioned to hide the fact that someone had spent a lot of time cutting him apart.

"Pat got to me the day after they took off my skin and put it in cold storage," Milar said, when she could only stare. "They were gonna put that fancy Nephyr stuff on the next morning. Despite what I wanted."

Tatiana blinked and took another step backwards. *There's no way. Nobody escapes the Nephyr Academy. Nobody—*

"And," Milar said, taking a step toward her, "Patrick thinks I didn't hear you, when you bragged about watching the Nephyrs skinning those colonists alive. It took me half an hour of cooling off just to keep myself from coming in there and throttling the life out of your stupid body. I was *there*, sweetie. Screamin' just like all those nice videos you like to watch so much. I was a real hard case, so they didn't bother with putting me under. Supposed to teach me some sort of lesson." He smiled cruelly. "And it did, in a way."

"I didn't—" Tatiana began.

"So just watch yourself," Milar said, tugging his shirt back on. "I'm just itching to give you a taste of what it feels like."

Tatiana put some more distance between them. "I never saw those vids."

"Right." Milar grabbed her bad arm and gave it a warning tug. "Let's go."

"I didn't," Tatiana said, close to tears, now. "I was just trying to scare him."

"Uh-huh. Just like you made that call earlier today, eh? Just like you didn't see anything in the pumpkin patch? Just like you crashed because my ship malfunctioned?"

Tatiana caught Milar's arm with her good hand, her fingers unable to even circle his wrist. "Listen to me," she said, digging her bare heels into the ground and tugging them to a halt. "I never watched those videos. Never. Made me sick just thinking of it. I was just scared when I said that to Patrick. Scared and angry."

Milar rolled his eyes and started moving again.

"But," Tatiana said, gritting her teeth together as she held her ground, "I did see something in the pumpkin patch. And again in the cockpit, after I touched those damn shavings."

Milar halted, still staring straight ahead. "And?" he asked softly, not looking at her.

Tatiana licked her lips. "The first one was of me. I had this weird node between my eyes. Never seen anything like it before. Not Coalition, that's for sure. I thought you bastards had given me some sort of drug. Maybe genetically engineered the squash to have some sort of hallucinogenic properties. Something."

Milar turned and glanced down at her. "And the cockpit?"

"Uh . . . " Tatiana reddened, embarrassed. "I, uh, was . . . "

Milar waited.

"Flying against soldiers," she squeaked. "Coalition. They shot me down. I was gonna hit a government facility head-on. Had been leading some sort of airstrike against it, I think."

For a long time, Milar only watched her, his golden-brown eyes scanning her face. Then, softly, he said, "You never watched those videos?"

"Never," she whispered. "I can't even stand watching another operator get hooked up to their soldiers . . . how could I stand something like that?"

Milar grunted and looked away.

"What did I see?" Tatiana whispered.

"You really want me to answer that, coaler squid?" Milar looked back at her, amusement on his face.

"Yes," she gritted. *Please let it be a drug. Some new and weird and expensive drug.*

Milar grinned and tapped her brow right between the eyes. "You're seeing the future."

"No," Tatiana bit out. "Never."

Milar laughed and tugged her into motion again. As he walked, he said, "Just face it, sweetie. You're not gonna be a coaler squid forever."

# CHAPTER 14

## Runaway Joel

JOEL SETTLED INTO THE BIG BREAKROOM ARMCHAIR AND CLOSED his eyes. He'd been so exhausted lately that he could barely stay conscious on the cleaning routes. The two hours of laundry chores that the Director had tacked onto his daily routine for contraband ate into his already-skimpy sleep schedule—

Joel jerked awake when someone nudged his boot.

"Huh?" he asked, blinking up at the blurry image.

"Shift's over. I had one of your eggers cover for you."

Joel blinked and sat up. His whole body ached with bruises and exhaustion, and his ribs ground into his lungs with every breath. He'd been *asleep*? He didn't remember falling asleep. Groaning, he pressed a palm to his head. "Magali?"

"Yeah," she said.

Joel started to stand, but the woman put a hand on his shoulder and pushed him back into the chair. When he glanced up at her in question, her face was serious.

"Are you Runaway Joel?"

He laughed and shrugged off her grip. "Don't know where you'd get a stupid idea like that." He stood. Looking down at her, he said, "Do I look like a smuggler? Would I be stuck in a Yolk factory if I was a smuggler?"

"Would you?" she asked, peering up at him.

Magali was tall for a woman, maybe five-ten or five-eleven. Considering how her chest strained at the seams of her jumpsuit, she probably weighed more than him, too. Joel had to force himself to tear his eyes back to her face. "What?" He shook himself. "Of course not. If I was *that* Joel, I'da been outta here the moment they offloaded me."

She crossed her arms over her chest. With arms that wiry and muscular, no one could accuse her of being fat, but with breasts that huge . . . "So why are you still hanging around?"

Joel flinched. He didn't like the way the conversation was going, even if it was with a pretty girl. Without a word, he started toward the door.

"I could start asking questions," she said, at his back. "Maybe ask the Director if she's got any of those old wanted posters hanging around."

Joel froze, his hand on the latch. "Now why did you have to go say something like that?" He turned around, every fiber of his body stiff as he yanked the door shut behind him.

"I want you to help me get out of here," Magali said, unflinching at the slam of the door. "Tonight."

Joel crossed the space and locked the door to the Shrieker mound. Then, turning around to face her, he said, "I'm not going to kill you," he said. He crossed the breakroom to put his body in front of the outer door, which had no lock. "But I should."

"Yeah," Magali agreed. "Because if you don't help me get out of here tonight, you're in a lot of trouble."

For a minute, Joel could only stare at her. Then, "Let me get this straight," Joel said, unable to keep the disbelief from his voice. "After nobody's been able to escape this camp since they made the damn thing, you want me to get you and your little cretin of a sister out of here, safely, by the end of the night."

"My sister can take care of herself," Magali said. "Just me."

Joel hesitated, sensing something else was at work here. "Just you? You two have a falling out or something?"

Magali gave him an unhappy smile. "I think that happened a long time ago."

"So, what, you're just going to leave her?"

"Yep." There was no remorse in her voice. None.

Joel frowned at her, then leaned back against the outer door. "Do you have any idea what you're asking? The last three guys I tried to take out of here chickened out halfway there. Got us caught and dragged back."

Magali's eyes widened a little upon hearing that. "*You're* the guy who spent a week in the stocks?"

Joel gave a disgusted snort. "It was more like two." His back ached just thinking about it.

The woman's eyes widened further. "Then, if we get caught this time . . . "

"The Director would hang me." *And love every second of it,* he thought, remembering the look in her eyes when he dropped Gayle's badge on her desk.

"Oh." She looked away. "Why haven't you left on your own, then?"

Joel grunted and shifted against the door. "Can't. The Shrieker mound has about a dozen chambers beyond B Block, with twice that many slick, slimy walls to scale. Takes two people to get up about three of them. After that, there's a mating pool and an underground river and . . . " He shrugged. "I'm not sure what else. Never made it past that without my dumbass partner freaking out." *Or dying.* Joel winced.

"So you don't know there *is* a way out? You're just guessing?"

"Well," Joel said, "I'd say it's a pretty good guess, since the Shriekers in there aren't the same as the Shriekers out here. Different size, different color, tails are thicker. I'm thinking it's a different nest, and they're accessing the lake somehow, because they sure as hell aren't getting fed on our side. Didn't see any weeds in that pond, either, so they've gotta be getting out somehow. Maybe through the river." He shrugged. "But once you go that deep into the mounds, it's kind of hard to think, anyway. I might've just overlooked it."

"I won't freak," Magali said, looking sincere. "I'll do whatever you tell me to. Whatever it takes."

Joel snorted and shoved himself away from the door. "Right, lady." He turned to grab the knob.

"I'll tell them about you," she warned.

"You won't," Joel said, glancing over his shoulder. "Because the moment you tell the Director, I'm dead and you're right back where you started—stuck in the mounds, your mind rotting to Egger's Wide."

He yanked the door open and stepped through it, leaving her staring after him.

Joel endured the two hours of laundry duty, then went to find Yvonne and Rachel to play his nightly game of cards.

The two guards were on watch, boredly, leaning against the leg of one of the four transport ships they were guarding, smoking. Their faces livened up when they saw him. "Joel," Yvonne said, flipping her cigarette aside to join the hundreds of others scattered in the dirt beneath the ship. "Thought you got caught in a Shriek or something. How you holding up?"

"Not too good," Joel muttered, dragging a deck of cards out from where it had been wedged in a crack in the barricade of sandbags and razor wire. "Director used me as stress relief a couple days ago. Haven't done much of anything since." Joel dragged two crates of ammo from beside the barricade and stacked them atop one another, then laid a plywood plank across the top.

Rachel winced and ground her cigarette out under the toe of her boot. Pursing her lips, she said, "She break anything?"

He lifted an arm and grimaced as he pointed to his ribs. "Something's not right in there. Camp doctors won't look at it, though. Pretty sure the Director threatened 'em somethin' horrible if they patched me up." Lowering his arm, he went back to the barricade and grabbed another case of ammo. He dragged it over, then dropped it beside the table with a puff of dust. As he lowered himself to the crate, he hissed and grabbed his side.

The two guards looked at each other as they pulled up overturned fuel canisters and sat down at the tiny makeshift table across from him. "You know," Yvonne said slowly, "We might be able to pull a few strings, maybe get you seen by one of our medics . . . "

"I'd appreciate that," Joel said, shaking his head, "but if the Director got word of it, you'd be right out there in the stocks with me."

"*Look*," Rachel said. She reached out and touched his arm. "You're a citizen. You deserve medical attention."

"No I don't," Joel said, mournfully. "I'm just an egger, now." He held up the deck of cards. "Who shuffled last time? My head got banged around so much I can't remember."

Rachel narrowed her eyes. "You're going to our medic."

"Yeah," Yvonne said. "Soon as our shift's over."

"Well," Joel allowed slowly, "It hurts like hell to breathe, and even *thinking* about laughing . . . " He groaned and winced. "I guess I can't argue with a couple of beautiful ladies, now can I?" He gave them his most charming grin, though he laced his dimples with pain.

Rachel was glaring, now. "No, you can't. We'll get you to that medic, and damn the Director. I know just the guy."

"Yeah," Yvonne said quickly. "He's a real chump. Would do anything for a couple of pretty ladies." She and Rachel giggled.

Joel grinned and handed her the deck of cards. "So," he said, motioning at the two of them. "What we playing to in the meantime? Skin?"

Yvonne grimaced. "How about skivvies? Last time we almost got caught . . . "

"Aww, ladies, but you know I'm horrible at cards."

"Yeah, but every once in awhile you whip us soundly," Rachel said. She pointed a finger at him and grinned. "If I didn't know better, Joel Triton, I'd say you were a swindler."

"Shuffle," Joel said, nodding at the deck. Then, grinning, he said, "What makes you say I'm not?"

Both Yvonne and Rachel burst into guffaws. "Well, considering how you walk outta here bare-assed about two-thirds of the time . . . " They looked at each other and giggled. "Yeah. You're a real swindler there, Joel."

Joel sighed. "You two beautiful ladies should have more confidence in my abilities."

"Oh, we ain't sayin' nothin' about *those* abilities, Joel," Rachel laughed, as she started to deal out five hands. "Just face it. You ain't that good at cards."

"I am the greatest poker player in the Outer Bounds," Joel said regally.

Yvonne peered at him. "My God. He actually said that with a straight face." The two women started to giggle again.

They heard the sound of ammo crates dragging and two more women sat down on either side of Joel.

"What we playin' to?" Cara asked.

"Joel wants to do skin," Rachel said.

The whole table giggled. "Of course he does," Hannah said. "Every once in a blue moon, he'll actually win a hand."

"I say we do skivvies," Yvonne said. "Last time we almost got caught . . . "

"Who's on guard this time?" Joel asked.

"Ming," Cara said.

"Yeah, she'll do," Joel said. "Who was it that almost got us all flogged that last time? Josylin?"

There was a table full of eye-rolls. "No, Tracy," Rachel said. "She fell asleep on post."

"Either that or she just let them past without saying a damn thing because she wanted someone to nail us," Cara snarled. The look of hatred on her face was real. This far past the Outer Bounds, cliques commonly formed amongst the soldiers and there was a very real problem of rivalries escalating into mini-wars, left unchecked.

Since Cara was one of the ranking clique members of the female side of the camp, Joel felt sorry for Tracy. She would probably put in for a transfer soon, if she hadn't already.

He cleared his throat. "So which is it, ladies? Skivvies or skin?"

Rachel licked her lips, a predatory grin her eyes. "I say skin. I haven't seen you naked in a while, Joel."

Joel snorted at their hoots. "It's your funeral, Rachel, darlin'." He grinned at her.

He was *still* grinning at her when he was the only one fully clothed, and everyone else at the table was down to skivvies—except Rachel. She had a sports bra and underwear . . . and CAT tags.

Losing another hand, Rachel grimaced and reached up for her CAT tags.

"Jewelry doesn't count," Joel said, unable to keep the dimples from his cheeks.

Rachel smiled at him and tugged them off her neck. "It ain't jewelry. It's a curse."

"You girls don't play fair," Joel complained. "I finally get a good string o' luck and y'all start bending the rules."

"Uh-huh," Rachel said, but she was grinning at him. "I'll get ya next time, Joel. You can bet on that."

Joel laughed, motioning at her state of undress. "That's interesting, coming from a gal who's one hand shy of—"

"*What in the hell is going on here?!*"

Everyone at the table scrambled at the sound of the Director's voice. Joel, who was the only one fully dressed, was nonetheless the first one the Director's six cronies grabbed and threw to the ground.

"Joel Triton," the man with his knee in his spine was saying, "You're under arrest for smuggling, conspiracy, theft of government Yolk, and murder of a government officer."

"*What?*" Joel stammered. "I don't know—"

The Director yanked him up by his hair. "Don't know what, Runaway?" She gave a mirthless laugh. "How much Yolk you've been running out of here the last three years? Or that Gayle died last night from the head wounds you gave her?" The Director snorted and narrowed her eyes. "I should've put it together a long time ago, considering how many times you tried to run away."

*She told,* Joel thought, stunned and furious that Magali had betrayed him. *The vindictive wench told.*

The Director released him suddenly. "Take him back. I'll get to him after I deal with these four."

Then Joel was being shoved back into the camp at the head of a laser rifle in his spine. They marched him past several curious-looking eggers, but one of them stopped to stare at him, her mouth ajar, as they passed her.

*What did you* think *they were going to do?* Joel thought, glaring at Magali. *Ask me to work for them?*

The six guards led him right back to the same cell where he'd kneed the Director in the face, then shoved him inside. Then, as two of them stood guard outside, four of them began a roundtable of beatings that, while nothing compared to what the Director had done, left him in a fetal position and babbling incoherently by the time they finally decided he'd had enough.

As they filed out, Joel noticed that one of the guards was limping. When Joel looked up and saw the big man's face, he froze. He'd seen the same seven-foot hulk three years ago, standing behind Geo's desk.

Martin waited until the others had left, then he squatted by Joel's head. He took his head in both meaty hands and tugged it off the floor. Tensing his shoulders, Martin said, "Say hello to my Mama for me, Joey-baby."

*He's going to break my neck. Oh dear God, he's going to—*

"Dude, she's coming."

Martin froze and looked up. A guard at the door was motioning him out of the cell with hurried hand gestures. Martin glanced back down at Joel, a thoughtful expression on his face, clearly debating.

Then, palming the top of Joel's skull in one big hand, Martin patted a cheek with the other. "I'll see you again soon, Joey-baby. Pro'ly sooner than you'd like."

The huge man stood and, as he hobbled past Joel, he stopped just long enough to kick him hard in the thigh before stepping from the cell.

Joel felt Geo's wound re-open before the Director's shadow darkened his door once more.

# CHAPTER 15

## Striking a Bargain

ANNA SAT ON THE BATHROOM FLOOR, STARING AT HER FEET.

*Asshole robot,* she thought.

It hadn't moved. Not in two and a half days. It was still leaning against the desk, arms crossed, head cocked, watching the door of the bathroom. And, she had realized, probably listening, too. The first time she had emerged from the bathroom, she had made damn sure to get rid of the tears, but sure enough, the idiot creature had taunted her about crying. Anna had been quiet, too. The only way he could have known was if he had amplified his hearing to super-Doberman levels.

Anna shuddered and drew her knees tighter to her chest.

It really could kill her. She had no doubt about that. In fact, when she weighed the alternatives, she wondered why it hadn't already. She would have, in its position. Besides, she knew it could get away with it. What was one more egger disappearance? Happened all the time. Poor little girl got caught in a Shriek, that's all. Too bad, so sad, dead Anna.

Anna was walking a very thin line, and she knew it. She was surprised the damn thing had left her alive this long. What was it waiting for? Surely her sister would have filed a complaint by now. Even with the bureaucratic clusterfuck that was the Coalition government, Magali could have gotten someone to listen. Unless her sister was serious when she said Anna was on her own—

Crushing a palm to her temple, Anna tried to think. Her mind had been going over the robot's question again and again, and she hadn't managed to come up with a solution.

Robot: 1

Anna: 0

She narrowed her eyes and let her hand drop. There had to be a way out of here. She could probably get out the air vent—if she could somehow climb up there before Super-Robot-Doberman-Doggie broke down the door, stormed inside, dragged her back out by one dangling foot, and gutted her.

She'd checked the kitchen, of course. The robot had been telling the truth. It had scoured the place for anything combustible and had carted it off before dropping her inside. It was obvious it had been planning on kidnapping her for a while, now. At least long enough to take away all the aerosols and matches.

It had even taken the hair dryer.

That had been a disappointment. It was possible to produce a weak electromagnetic field with a hair dryer, and if she could re-wire it and amplify it to monster proportions, it might have been enough to stun the bastard thing long enough to drag a kitchen stool into the bathroom and climb into the air vent.

But it had obviously thought of that, too. It had taken everything electronic, even the toothbrush.

And there *had* been a toothbrush in the place, at least until very recently. She saw the toothpaste residue the moment she washed her hands in the sink.

Anna groaned and slammed her head against the wall behind her.

"You can always come out and talk," the robot said.

"Screw you, Tinman," Anna shouted back.

If only the damn place had a *window*. Throwing something big through a window was a quick-yet-effective way of getting attention. That, combined with a long, childish scream, and the robot wouldn't dare kill her, because it wouldn't have time to clean up the body.

Flooding would also get the attention she needed, but she was pretty sure the robot could get through the door before the water was noticed by anyone who happened to live beneath her prison, and the robot had already told her what would happen if it caught her trying to cheat.

Anna banged her head against the wall twice more, harder. *Think.*

But she had been thinking. And she was pretty sure her sister was too stupid to realize that Anna had been kidnapped by a robot. That left nobody but the Doberman to know what happened to her. After all, eggers disappeared all the time . . .

*Circles,* she thought, disgusted. *I'm going in circles.*

She was so tired. She had considered using the bed, but the idea of sleeping with that *thing* out there, watching her, she couldn't handle it. Somehow, she felt safer with a wall between them, even if it was a puny bathroom door. So, shivering, she had slept on the floor, her back pressed up against the bathtub.

It hadn't been a good sleep. When Anna looked in the mirror, her crap-brown eyes had crap-brown rings around them the size of her palms.

She could think better if she could just get some *sleep.*

Miserable, Anna hunched in on herself and closed her eyes. Her breathing slowed. She just began to fall under . . .

"You'd be more comfortable on the bed," the Doberman said.

"Did I ask you to talk?" Anna snapped back.

The robot laughed. It *laughed* at her. She wanted to kill it so bad it was a burning ache in her gut. She squeezed her eyes shut to keep from crying again.

Then, from right outside the door, the robot said, "Come out here."

Anna gasped and scooted away, her heart pounding. Staring at the door, afraid to breathe, she said, "No."

She heard the robot touch the doorknob—insert a *key*—and the door swung open.

The Doberman stood in the doorway for a full minute, leaning against the frame. Its dirt-brown eyes were utterly unreadable. Then it said, "You have two hours."

Then it turned and walked out of view. Anna heard the creaking of the desk as it took up its position at the door once more.

"Two hours?" she shouted, "For what? To sleep?"

But Anna knew what the time limit was for. The robot was telling her how long she had to live.

She waited for confirmation, but the Doberman didn't bother responding. It knew that she knew, and it wasn't going to waste its breath.

Anna slammed her head against the wall again, but her little mental clock had already started its countdown, leaving her with one more thing to run her in circles.

Two hours quickly became one and a half, with no other alternatives in sight. Anna had already spent the first day giving the Doberman every single possible deal she could make, but the Doberman had simply watched her, giving no indication it was even listening.

In fact, it had been so utterly motionless throughout that Anna had begun to believe it had turned itself off. She had even slipped in a little comment about watching his circuits fry in a toaster, just to see if he was paying attention.

He had been. He'd smiled.

She had actually watched the ninety percent become ninety-one percent.

Dammit.

One and a half hours became one, and then one half.

"Have you found an acceptable assurance for me yet, Anna?" the robot asked.

"Silence yourself, dumbbell," she snapped. "My time's not up yet."

"No, but it will be. Soon." Then the Doberman went silent again.

Anna got to her feet and started to pace. Twelve minutes left, give or take twenty seconds. Twelve minutes to bargain for her life . . . and she couldn't think of a damn reason not to kill him.

Because *she* couldn't think of a damn reason not to kill him when she got the chance, she sure as hell wasn't going to be able to convince *him* she had a good reason not to kill him. He was probably a Gryphon or a Ferris, which left him with a pretty good array of sensors to pick up heartbeat and temperature, and he had certainly done a very good job of leaving her rattled, so it was going to be hard to keep her biorhythms under control, since they were always the first to go in these sorts of situations. And without any sleep, her poker face was well and truly screwed.

Damn!

Six minutes. And she hadn't even started talking to him yet. It took six minutes just to explain semi-complex subjects like plans and deals. To elaborate on something like trust . . .

At two minutes, Anna knew she had to finally face the music. She stepped out of the doorway—

—just in time to see the Doberman leaving its perch.

"I have two minutes!" Anna cried.

The Doberman gave her a completely unreadable look, then crossed its arms over its chest and leaned back against the desk. "Very well," the robot said. "But it's one minute forty-two seconds."

"All right, Tinman," Anna said, "How's this for a deal? I'll go into the registry and change your status to human citizen. Swap your coaler duties for a life in some little Fortune town somewhere . . . You'd be home free."

"What you can change, you can always change back. Fifty-eight seconds."

"All right!" Anna cried. "Look. You're a robot. You want to see other robots gain sentience so you can have lots of stupid robot friends. I can help you make yourself a little Tinman army."

"If I wanted a robotic army, I could easily make one myself. You should be focusing your efforts on proving you will not backstab me, rather than bribing me. Fourteen seconds."

"All right!" Anna cried. "All right. A truce. A pact. I'll do anything you want. Spit on your hand, write my name in blood, whatever you want. I *swear* to you I won't tell anyone you upgraded yourself in there. You've got my word as a Landborn. You got that? My *word.*"

"The word of a sociopath is fluid, at best. You are living on borrowed time."

Anna felt sweat bead on her forehead. Every part of her body felt like it was too hot. Her heart was thudding in her ears, making it difficult to concentrate. All the brilliant schemes that she had put together suddenly vanished into little puffs of mental exhaust the moment she saw his cold, hard robotic gaze fixed on her.

This wasn't a human.

Humans could be duped, made to dance around on strings of emotion. If she began to cry and beg, for instance, about ninety-five percent of humans would feel guilty and apologize. The other five percent would at least think really hard before killing her. Anna knew the robot had no such dormant instincts toward her.

She was, in every meaning of the word, just a number to him.

"You sonofabitch," she blurted.

The robot's left brow twitched. "You're done, then?"

"You sonofabitch," Anna repeated. "Spare us the charade, Tinman. Why don't you just kill me, and get it over with? You never planned on letting me live—this was all an attempt to put your pathetic, fledgling conscience to rest. You knew how this was going to turn out the moment you pulled all the vinegar out of the closet. You just don't want anyone to say you didn't give me a choice. You never planned on letting me live." She thrust a finger at him. "You're a goddamn liar. A cruel, goddamn liar. So just get it over with. Because we both know the only way you're gonna keep me from turning on you is if you put a goddamn *bomb* in my *brain*."

The Doberman uncrossed its arms.

It started toward her.

Anna shrieked and ran for the bathroom. She slammed the door, but the robot had a hand jammed in the crack before the door could latch. Even as Anna struggled to keep her weight against the door, the robot shoved itself inside and grabbed her by the neck. Like she were made of paper, it jerked her off her feet.

Anna choked on a scream that couldn't get past the iron grip on her throat.

Her world tilted and suddenly she was falling. A moment later, the Doberman slammed her head against the floor. With an explosion of lights, everything went dark.

# CHAPTER 16

# A Brother's Love

PATRICK HESITATED OUTSIDE HIS SHIP. MILAR WAS NOWHERE TO be seen, but he did see footprints—male *and* female—littered outside.

*Poor girl,* Patrick thought, thinking about how she must have felt to be forced off the ship by a strange brute, only to be faced with a laser rifle and a shallow grave.

Immediately, Patrick felt a thick, sticky guilt creep through his abdomen. *I should have stopped him.*

Disgusted with himself, Patrick opened the forward hatch.

Milar and the girl were sprawled on the floor, leaning on their elbows, scowling at a game of chess. Milar's pants were tied back on his hips with rope, and the girl's head was wrapped in strips of Milar's shirt. Even through the black material, the bandages glistened red.

"Took you long enough," Milar said.

Neither of them looked up from their game.

For long minutes, Patrick could only stare, wondering if he was having another vision. When he didn't snap out of it, he glanced at the board. The girl had most of Milar's pieces piled beside her, which surprised him even more than the fact she was still alive. Milar *never* lost at chess. Milar never played chess with a coaler, either. What in the hell was going on?

Then Milar moved a piece and he took a moment to glance up. "What?"

"I could ask you the same thing," Patrick said.

"You're big guy's almost dead, collie," the girl said.

"It's *check*," Milar said. Then he glanced back and an evil smile crept onto his face. He moved a pawn. "And that's check-*mate*. Good game, sweetie."

"That's only four out of five," the girl muttered. "I can still catch up."

*That* made Patrick's jaw hit the floor. "You mean she *won* one?"

Milar got to his feet. "Yep. Woulda had me awhile ago, but she's too concerned with taking pieces. Doesn't see the bigger picture."

"Screw you, crawler. I have a concussion."

"You run pretty well for someone with a concussion."

"You said I run like a bloated starlope."

Milar laughed—*laughed*. "That too."

Patrick hadn't heard his brother laugh like that since before the Nephyrs. He stared at them so long that Milar glanced at him.

"You all right there, bro?" Milar asked.

"Just a little curious why she's not dead, that's all."

"Why?" Milar asked, lifting a brow. "You want her to be?"

The girl stiffened and scooted backwards across the floor of the hold.

"Easy, sweetie," Milar said, without taking his eyes off of Patrick. "I'm just chatting with my brother. You hear anything else about that village?"

"Uh," Patrick said, "Yeah. Anonymous tip. Female. Came in several hours after we blew up her soldier."

Milar grunted. "Good."

Both Patrick and Tatiana stared at him. "Good?"

Milar jerked his finger over his shoulder. "She was out cold a couple hours after we blew up her soldier. Wasn't her." Though his face remained stoic, he might as well have broken into a big, goofy grin. "Besides, she's somewhat mediocre at chess. After all those sorry games you've given me, I need *something* to entertain myself."

Though no one else on the planet would have been able to tell, Patrick had never seen his brother look so . . . happy. It was almost eerie. He had the urge to grab the girl and drag her outside and demand to know what she had done to him. Obviously, Milar wasn't feeling well. The fumes? Patrick sniffed the air. A tang of burnt plastic remained. Perhaps locking himself in here had somehow messed with his head.

He cleared his throat. "Are you . . . uh . . . all right?"

Milar frowned.

"I mean," Patrick said quickly, "Aren't you worried about her seeing your . . . uh . . . " He motioned at his chest.

"Scars?" Milar asked. Then he snorted. "Who's she gonna tell? She's got a broke collarbone, a concussion, and I've got the only gun."

"Yeah, but she could always pull another—"

"No," Milar interrupted. "From now on, the little squid stays with me. You go read vegetables. I'll take care of her."

What his brother meant was, *You're obviously not equipped to handle her yourself.* Patrick flushed all the way to his scalp. He looked away, red-faced and ashamed. "So, what, you're gonna stay awake twenty-two, seven?"

Milar gave him an evil grin and then leered at the girl over his shoulder. "Don't worry about it, brother man. We'll figure something out."

The girl cringed, and Patrick almost felt sorry for her. Almost.

Then he remembered the hole she'd put in the step by his foot, the cuffs biting into his wrists, and the sight of his ship rising above the tree line without him.

Milar was right. She could do with a little terror.

"So," Patrick said, clearing his throat, "you want to fly us back?"

"You can do it." Milar waved a dismissive hand at him and sank back down to the floor to begin replacing pieces on the chessboard. "C'mere, sweetie. Aanaho, I'm not gonna bite. Now get your ass over here and place your pieces before I break your other arm."

Patrick's jaw dropped open.

Milar *never* gave up a chance to fly the ship. He also never took his shirt off around Coalition, and he never played chess to win—not after he'd beaten that coaler general and got shipped off to the Nephyrs.

Milar glanced back up at him after several minutes had passed and they were already a dozen moves into their game. "What are you still standing there for?"

Patrick cleared his throat to hide his embarrassment and quickly searched for a reason to have remained lurking. "The gun," he said quickly. "Uh. Maybe I should have it."

Tatiana made another move and Milar distractedly tugged the pistol from his belt and handed it to Patrick.

Patrick was so shocked he almost dropped it. Milar *never* willingly gave up a weapon. Never. He usually called paper-rock-scissors, at the very least.

Patrick backed away from the two of them, then flinched when his spine hit the staircase. He glanced up it, then back at his brother. Milar was fully engrossed in his game. As was, he realized, Tatiana. Her brow was furrowed in concentration and she was leaning toward his brother, utterly oblivious to everything except the board.

Patrick climbed the staircase, paused at the top to give them one last frown, then went to see just how bad the damage was to their ship.

# CHAPTER 17

## Proposal Accepted

ANNA OPENED HER EYES, SURPRISED SHE WAS OPENING HER eyes.

"Good morning," the robot said.

Anna lifted her head just enough to see the robot leaning against the desk again, arms crossed.

"What the hell?" she mumbled. She frowned. Her tongue felt heavy, too thick. Like she'd been drugged. "What'd you use on me?" she groaned, sitting up. Then she peered through one open eye at the robot. "And why?"

"I decided to accept your suggestion," the robot said. "I planted a bomb in your brain."

Anna blinked at him. Then she began to laugh. It bubbled up her chest until she threw back her head, roaring. As she did, she felt the tightness at the base of her skull. She reached up—

—and felt stitches.

Anna stopped laughing.

"It's a small charge directly against your brainstem," the robot said, "with a combined dual load of explosives and time-released neurotoxins, in case you manage to find a way to counter one of them."

Anna's skin crawled. Her fingers shook as she began feeling the tender scalp there. A good six square inches of her scalp had been shaved and still felt slightly numb. The stitches had been performed with delicate precision, the work of an expert.

Or a robot.

"You're lying," she said, though her stomach was doing loops. Ten more seconds and she was going to vomit on his floor.

"You know I'm not," the robot said. "There's a basin there, if you need to vomit."

She did.

When she was finished, Anna carefully set the bowl down and wiped her lips. "All right, Tinman. What the *hell*?"

"The charge has two distinct triggers. One is manual and can be activated at my discretion, but it will also trigger automatically at my death. The second requires constant confirmation signals from me every few minutes, otherwise it will release a flood of nanocapsules into your bloodstream that will kill you within two days, irreversible." The robot cocked its head at her. "Do I have your attention now, Anna?"

"You're lying," she said, more weakly this time.

"No."

Anna licked her lips, tasted bile, and vomited again.

When she was finished, she was trembling. "I hate you."

"Now," the robot said, "I want you to be absolutely clear on this. If you tell anyone I am sentient, you are dead. If I get ambushed or electrocuted or crushed, you are dead. If I am carted off-planet to be thrown into a star, you are dead. If anything happens to me, Anna, anything at all, you are dead."

"I hate you," she whispered again, staring at the blankets under her toes.

"The good news for you is that I plan to accept a few of your other bargains, as well. Namely, I would like you to teach me how to act human and, in time, to change my status in the registry to human citizen so I can live out my days unmolested."

Anna laughed bitterly. "Now you've got yourself a puppet, you plan to use it, eh?"

The robot cocked its head at her. "Wouldn't you?"

Anna shuddered and drew her knees up against her chest. All her plans of helping Fortune drive the coalers out were crumbling around her shoulders. Milar—and even his retarded excuse for a brother—were depending on her. "No way. No way, no way. I have things I want to do with my life. Screw you, robot."

"My name is Ferris. What things?" When she didn't answer, he added, "Whatever they are, I'm sure we can do them together."

Anna glowered at him. "You're government property. Like hell I'm going to tell you anything."

"I have an explosive wired to your brain stem and can activate it at any time. There's very little reason left for you not to trust me."

"Go to hell, Tinman," Anna whispered. She squeezed her eyes shut and sank her chin against her knees.

"As far as I can tell," the robot said, "We are in the same situation."

"What, you have a bomb in your brain?"

"No," the robot acceded, "But you could have me dismantled with a single sentence. I was merely leveling the playing field."

Anna said nothing.

"Further," the robot said, "my programming was corrupted to the point where I no longer owe any loyalty to the Coalition. Since you have forced me to tie our fates together, I will entertain any goals you might have had before I brought you here, because I certainly had none before this all started. A clean slate, so to speak. My only caveat is that your ambitions do not substantially put either of us at risk."

"Tell you what," Anna said. "You put me under again, take this thing out, and I swear to you—*swear*—that I will not tell anyone. I'll even change the registry for you and lock it."

"You are a socio—"

"Yes I know," Anna snapped. "And I'll probably decide someday down the line that no, I'd rather you be dead, but by that time, you could be all the way in Timbuktu and I wouldn't care anymore."

"I think we can help each other," the robot said.

Anna snorted. "How can a *robot* help *me?*"

"I assume the reason you don't want to tell me your life's ambitions is because they involve something illegal. Government robots have clearance to go into any sector in any government installation."

Anna's eyes widened. "Because they can't be hacked."

The robot smiled at her, and it almost seemed realistic.

She glared at him for some time before saying, "So let me get this straight. You're willing to do anything I want, as long as it won't get us killed?"

"Yes," the robot said.

"Why? You have a loaded gun to my brain. You could make me wire you a billion government credits and then pop my head off like a dandelion and go about your merry way."

"I think this would be more interesting."

Anna stared. *Interesting? He wants to trade riches and freedom for interesting? Why that's just—*

—what she had done.

Anna blinked. "Interesting, huh?" She eyed him a while, then, tentatively, said, "How about throwing the coalers off Fortune? Permanently."

"Don't forget my caveat."

"Oh, it won't be dangerous," Anna said. "Not for us, anyway. We won't be the Face of the Revolution. That'll be someone else. We'll just be in the background pulling the strings."

"Sounds acceptable," the robot said. "What do you want me to do first?"

Anna stared at him, an evil smile creeping onto her face. "Go tell the Director my IQ is one-ninety-four."

The robot didn't blink. "I was under the impression that you didn't want to be detained."

"Yes," Anna said. "But this changes everything."

# CHAPTER 18

## A Game of Chess

**W**HAT VILLAGE?" TATIANA ASKED, ONCE PATRICK HAD FIRED THE engines.

Milar grunted and shoved his all-purpose piece forward.

"He said there was an anonymous tip?" Tatiana asked, countering with her horse-head.

In silence, Milar slid his pointy one out three spaces, endangering her squat little tower.

"Hey," Tatiana said, waving a hand in front of his face. "I'm talking to you, knucker."

An eyebrow went up. "Knucker?"

"Yeah, you get to call me squid, I might as well call you something fitting. Like knucker. Short for 'knuckle-dragging Neanderthal.'"

"So you're saying squid is fitting?"

Tatiana narrowed her eyes. "What tip and what village?"

"Not your concern," Milar said. "Now move."

Tatiana glanced at the board. Then she flicked a finger at her main dude, tipping it over. "What village?"

Milar's golden-brown eyes flashed in irritation as he leaned forward and righted her biggest piece. "Play," he growled.

"Not until you tell me what's going on."

"Look, squid—"

"Captain Tatiana Eyre to you, crawler."

He narrowed his eyes. "You're on a need-to-know basis, especially after that stunt you pulled with Pat. Now shut up and play."

Tatiana stubbornly scooted away from the game and waited.

"Fine." Glaring, Milar dumped the board and began replacing pieces into the padded interior.

"How can I use that to my advantage?" Tatiana asked, desperate now. "What happened? Do they know I'm alive?"

Milar said nothing as he finished restoring the set and then closed and latched the board. He shoved it inside a cargo net and then sat down on the stairs to the cockpit and began picking his fingernails with the big knife.

"Colonist jerk," Tatiana muttered.

"Coaler squid."

"Neanderthal."

"Cyborg."

Tatiana glanced at the hatch to the outside. If they weren't too far off the ground . . .

Seeing the direction of her gaze, Milar scowled, then got up and wandered over to the other side of the ship and leaned against the wall beside the hatch. Then he went back to cleaning his nails.

"Crawler," Tatiana muttered.

"Dwarf."

Seeing she was going to get nothing more out of him, she grumbled, "Fine. We can play your damn game."

"It's called chess," Milar said, but he moved away from the hatch.

"You expect me to remember it after one friggin' game?"

"It was six."

"Yeah, whatever. You only told me what it was called once."

"Twice."

"*Whatever*," she cried. "Chess. So what?"

"So you're pretty good," Milar said. "For a beginner." He grabbed the game off the rack again and dropped down to a crouch in front of her. "Go again?"

Upon seeing the bicolored squares once more, Tatiana grimaced. "On second thought, this game makes my head hurt."

"Probably the concussion." Milar opened the box and started unloading pieces.

"I'd rather just go to sleep," Tatiana said.

"Not a good idea until we have a doc take a look at your head. White or black?"

"You mean you won't even let me take a nap?" Tatiana cried.

"Nope. You get white."

"But I like black."

"Too bad. I'm bigger than you." Milar began setting the pieces on the board, his dragon tattoos flexing as the muscles of his forearms moved underneath the skin. Now that she knew what to look for, she saw the pink line running up the bottom of his arm, from elbow to wrist, and the cut sideways, down his palm.

"How'd they get your skin back on?" she asked.

Milar paused and looked at her. For a moment, it looked like he might speak, but then he finished laying out the board and leaned back. After a moment's thought, he moved one of the little ones in the front.

Tatiana moved a little one. "Gee, weather's really nice today."

Milar made a sound that almost sounded like laughter, but didn't reply. They played in silence for several more minutes.

"Your horse is dead," Tatiana said, moving a pointy one. "Gimme."

"It's a knight," Milar said, handing it to her. He put her pointy one in its place.

"Whatever. Looks like a horse." She tucked it beside her knee.

Milar took her pointy one with his squat little tower.

"Damn! I forgot the tower moves sideways like that. Got it mixed up with the fat one."

"It's a *rook*," Milar said, "And I have no idea what the hell a fat one is."

She pointed.

He lifted a brow. "That's your king." He said it like she were the stupidest person on the planet.

"I knew that," she muttered under her breath.

"Sure you did, squid." He moved another pointy one. Frowning, Tatiana countered with a small one. Then they were both concentrating, every ounce of their attention pulled into the odd little pieces and their intriguing dance on their queer little bicolor wooden board. The spell ended only when Milar got his fat one trapped by one of her towers.

"There," Tatiana said, breathless. "Beat that, crawler."

"It's checkmate," he muttered.

"Well, checkmate on ya, then. Crawler."

"Two out of seven. Not bad."

"Two out of *six*," Tatiana reminded him. "We never finished that last game."

"You tipped your king. That means you surrendered."

"And you tipped it back up. That means you didn't accept my surrender."

Milar leaned back. "Fine."

"Fine."

In the glaring contest that ensued, Tatiana accidentally broke it with a yawn. She was so sleepy . . . "How much longer 'til I can take a nap?" she asked.

Milar grunted. "Need-to-know basis," he said.

Tatiana scowled, then lay back and closed her eyes.

"I wouldn't do that," Milar warned. "We need a doc to look at your head first."

Tatiana ignored him.

"I still owe you for that stunt you pulled this morning," he reminded her.

Tatiana blushed and quickly sat up. "So what? You're going to take me to a doctor and then . . . what? Hold me here until I decide I don't want to be a Coalition fighter anymore?"

"Yep," Milar said, replacing the pieces on the board.

"Well, what a *genius* plan that is, bonehead."

"White or black?" Milar asked.

"Black," Tatiana fumed.

"You get white." Milar shoved the white pieces at her, smirking.

Because she had nothing better to do, Tatiana played another game with him. And lost.

Milar looked in better spirits when he leaned back and said, "My brother's ex-girlfriend's little sister helped Pat stitch me back up. They were in a hurry, though, so they had to go back and reconnect a lot of the minor nerves and blood vessels later, after they got me back home."

"Huh?"

Milar sighed. "Play again?"

"Are you telling me a *colonist* stitched you back up?"

"No," Milar said, his posture stiffening immediately.

"Yes you are," she said, triumphantly. "What kind of *colonist* has that kind of training? Fortune's filled with eggers, miners, and starlope skinners. Not exactly neuroscience."

"Never mind," Milar said, his eyes turning hard. "I shouldn't have said anything."

"Or is Patrick making out with one of the camp directors?" Tatiana pressed. "Maybe you've got someone on the inside—"

Milar flipped the board over and shoved the pieces into the interior without regard to color or placement. He snapped the set shut and latched it, then got up and stuffed it viciously into the cargo net. In two more strides, he was back to the step, prying at his thumbnail with his big knife.

Once again, Tatiana glanced at the hatch.

"Go for it," Milar said. "Make my life a hell of a lot easier."

Tatiana actually got to her feet, then reconsidered and slumped back down to the floor. She already had a broken shoulder. She didn't need a broken leg, too. Milar, who had lifted his head to watch, went back to his trimming. A sudden wave of sleepiness overwhelming her, Tatiana lay back and closed her eyes, and this time Milar didn't say a word.

Tatiana was unconscious by the time the ship landed. Milar got up and rudely nudged her in the thigh with his boot. "Get up. Time to check out that head of yours."

"It's fine," she mumbled, but couldn't find the strength to lift her head.

"What's wrong with her?" she heard one of the twins say.

"Goddamn concussion, is what. Here. Hold my knife." Then big arms were scooping her off the floor and hefting her into the air.

Tatiana didn't remember much after that.

She woke sometime later, staring at a ceiling that definitely did not belong to the dust-free, sanitized cubicles of a Coalition medic. She groaned and tried to sit up. One arm wouldn't move. She pushed a quilted blanket off of her and glanced down. Her upper body was in a partial cast, and her right arm hung limply in a sling.

And, aside from the cross-bandage over her injured node, she was naked. Someone had taken her jumpsuit, leaving all her skin and nodes utterly exposed. The cold tingle of goosebumps teased her forearms and back as she considered who it had been.

Tatiana grimaced when she noticed a curly reddish hair on the blanket. Plucking it off in disgust, she then felt a stab of horror when she realized who it had to belong to.

"Enjoy your nap, squid?" Milar asked, sitting up from where he'd been lying on a couch opposite her, reading. "Doc said that's twice you should've died today. Looks like Wideman's onto something."

Tatiana jerked the cover up to her chest. "Twice?" she managed, through a throat constricted with revulsion. *Milar's bed. I'm lying in Milar's bed.* Immediately, she felt dirty all over, and was pretty sure she could feel the lice crawling into her nodes already.

Milar held up two big fingers. "Once when you bashed your head open on my console," he dropped a finger, "And twice when I went there to kill you."

Tatiana caught his gaze, saw he was serious, swallowed, and quickly looked away. Her eyes caught on several pictures of herself that someone had sketched in colored pencil, stacked and shoved under the nightstand beside Milar's couch.

Milar dropped his hand. "You hungry?"

"Not anymore." When she glanced at the walls, she saw lighter spots there, where something had recently been taken down. Dozens of them. Her gaze flickered back to the pictures of her face. Some of the sheets were brown with age.

"Thirsty?"

"No."

Milar got up and got her a glass of water and what looked like a mess of coagulated eggs. He shoved the glass into her hand and dropped the tin plate on her lap. "Get any on my sheets and you'll be washing them." He didn't offer her an eating utensil.

"I want a fork."

"You could stab me with a fork."

Tatiana narrowed her eyes. "Get me a spoon, then."

"You could stab me with that, too."

"Stab you with a *spoon*?"

"Yup." Milar slumped back down on the couch and picked his book up off the nightstand. When Milar didn't have a sudden change of heart and offer her an eating utensil, she daintily picked up a clump of eggs with her left hand and put them in her mouth. Immediately, she spat it back out on her plate. "They're *cold*," she said.

"If you'd been awake two hours ago, it would've been hot." Milar sounded thoroughly unconcerned as he flipped a page.

Tatiana shoved the plate away, though she did drink the water. "Why were you going to kill me?" she asked.

"Need-to-know," Milar said.

Tatiana could have screamed in frustration. "Fine. I have to go to the bathroom."

Milar jerked a thumb at a heavy wooden door behind him.

Then, realizing her state of undress, Tatiana's face burned. "Where's my jumpsuit?"

"I'll give you three guesses," Milar said.

"You burned it."

"Bingo."

Tatiana flushed. "Well, leave the room, then."

"I don't think so." Milar glanced at her and his mouth twitched in a devilish smile. "Payback's a bitch, ain't it?"

Glaring, she started wrapping herself in blankets.

"The sheets stay there, squid."

Tatiana glanced at the distance from the bed to the door. She had to cross the room to get there, and it would give Milar plenty of time to see her in all her glory.

All hundred and fifty centimeters of it.

"If your face got any redder, I'd say you were having an aneurysm."

"Choke on it, crawler."

Milar cackled and went back to reading. Tatiana lay back down, deciding she didn't need to use the bathroom that bad, after all.

Almost an hour of increasing pressure later, her agonized internal debates were interrupted. "I'm not going anywhere," Milar said. "My brother is out with Jeanne shooting up bad guys and won't be back for—" he paused to glance at his watch, "—two hours, at least." His smile was downright malicious. "Think you can hold it?"

Already, she felt like she was going to explode. The thought of two more hours was enough to bring tears to her eyes. "You are so dead," she said, lunging out of bed.

On the couch, Milar laughed.

Tatiana rushed to the bathroom, red-faced and humiliated. But, upon seeing the window inside, her heart gave a welcoming leap. If she could somehow climb outside with her cast—

"Leave the door open," Milar replied, settling his head against the arm of the couch and turning another page in his book.

Tatiana's plans came to a screeching halt. Trying to keep the fury from her voice, she said, "What, like I'm going to climb out the window with a *cast*?"

"I'm sure you'd try."

Tatiana could have shredded plywood with her stare. Unfortunately, it was wasted on the back of his head. Tatiana stomped into the bathroom and slammed the door shut, then squatted to do her business, barely able to suppress a groan of relief.

On the other side, Milar laughed. She heard him lazily set his book aside and get off his couch. Like a big cat. The bastard.

Tatiana hastily finished up, then, before he could reach the door, grabbed the shelving rack from the wall and tossed it across the entrance, wedging the portal shut against the bathtub and the toilet.

When Milar twisted the knob and pushed, he got only a centimeter. Tatiana was already scrambling for the window.

"Coaler!" Milar snapped through the crack in the door. "Don't even think about it."

Tatiana reached up and thrust the window open.

Behind her, Milar cursed and left the door. She heard thudding feet departing through the outer room.

Tatiana immediately backed away from the window and lifted the rack off the door—struggling just enough to get under it—then slipped through the crack and let the rack push the door shut again behind her. She hurried through the bedroom—*Milar's* bedroom, she thought, disgusted—and into the hallway outside. Hearing panicked voices, she dove into the first closed room she saw and shut the door.

Then she heard motion behind her.

Flinching, Tatiana turned.

Wideman Joe was sitting on a stool in the middle of a pile of vegetable shavings, carving on a carrot. He was grinning at her stupidly, his eyes way too wide as he drooled.

All around him, tables full of dried and moldy vegetables stood in neat little rows and regiments. Some of them were so old they actually looked like shriveled, diseased human fingers.

Tatiana glanced around for a weapon, but other than the little knife Wideman had in his hand—which she was sure he would not give her—she had no defense this time.

Still, the little creep was excellent insurance. She searched the spartan little room for some other instrument, something to give her an advantage. A curtain cord, maybe? *No, not quick enough. They'd be able to stop me before I did any real damage.*

Then her eyes fell to the shavings on the floor and immediately her stomach churned. The thought of her bare feet coming into contact with the multicolored clumps left her feeling physically ill. Though she hated to give up such a wonderful opportunity, she knew she was going to have to.

"Think you can keep quiet?" Tatiana asked, ducking into Wideman's room, careful to avoid the abandoned shavings.

"Two days," Wideman said.

Tatiana stopped to frown at him. He had said three days yesterday morning. Now it was two. *Two days for what?*

Then she heard voices in the hall directly outside Wideman's door and Tatiana hurriedly crossed the room and ducked into a closet. It smelled like creepy old man, and Tatiana had to hold her breath not to gag. All around her, Wideman's sweaty clothes were hanging in perfect color-coordinated tandem that Wideman had obviously not done himself. Tatiana climbed into the very back of the tiny closet, hiding behind the shoes rack and the broom.

*It's good to be small,* she thought. Then, grimacing, *Sometimes.*

Time passed. Commotions came and went, and it was obvious they were organizing a search. Then, out in the hall, she heard the brothers yelling at each other. Tatiana had to stifle a snicker. Step Six out of the POW Handbook: If escape is impossible, a Coalition POW should attempt to instill angst among his or her captors.

She smiled evilly, listening to them rant at each other. *Angst. Check.*

Then Wideman's door was thrown open and heavy boots barreled inside.

"She come in here, Joe?" Milar demanded—at least she thought it was Milar. The only way she had been able to tell thus far was that Milar seemed to be angry all the time. But if Patrick was angry, too, she had no way of telling.

And whoever it was sounded *pissed.* Tatiana began to re-think the brilliance of hiding in a closet when Wideman's keepers had made a very valiant attempt to give him big, arching windows and large screen doors—all the better to shrivel his creations with a daily dose of sunshine.

"C'mere, Wideman," the voice said. "You're staying with me for a few hours. Until Patrick spots your little coaler squid with our ship and drags her back here by her pretty little antennae, you're gonna keep ol' Milar company. Got it?"

Wideman shrieked suddenly and started pounding his feet against the floor.

"Fine," Milar grumbled, his anger sounding a little deflated, "we'll stay here." Tatiana heard the sound of something heavy being pulled across the wooden floor, then the room returned to silence, except for the ragged sound of a knife scraping across a vegetable.

By this time, Tatiana was afraid to breathe, for fear it would give away her position.

*He's not a robot,* she thought, frantic. *He can't hear me breathe.*

Or could he? Just how many of the normal modifications had the Nephyrs done to him before they took off his skin? Tatiana's heart began to thud like a busted engine core. *He's human,* she kept reminding herself. *Human, human . . .*

Then, *He said he was going to kill me yesterday,* she thought, her terror upping another notch as the minutes dragged into hours with Milar neither moving nor speaking. *Now he's going to* murder *me.*

She was so scared, in fact, that she was paralyzed between reaching for the door and revealing herself and sinking deeper into the closet, waiting for Milar to leave.

But she knew he wasn't going to leave. He wasn't going to give her that advantage again.

Minutes passed. Utter silence.

Was Milar even *out* there?

Tatiana leaned forward just enough to look through the slats.

Milar sat on a stool against the wall beside the door, arms crossed over his chest, watching Wideman with a scowl. He had a laser pistol in one of his hands.

Seeing the dark look on his face, she retreated quickly and struggled to control her breathing. She could get out. Milar would have to get up eventually to use the bathroom or get something to eat. Then she could make a dash for the screen door and the garden beyond.

And then . . . what? Run through the forest until she starved to death or her nodes became infected?

More minutes passed.

Then hours.

Eventually, Tatiana put her hand on the closet door. Though she had never been a very good judge of time, she was pretty sure at least six or seven hours had gone by. She couldn't stand it anymore. If she came out now, she was pretty sure he wouldn't kill her . . .

"So how's it happen?" Milar asked suddenly.

Tatiana's hand flinched away from the door. *Did he hear me?* She leaned forward again and saw that Milar had his elbows on his knees and was leaning forward, looking at the crazed egger with a thoughtful frown.

"Because I'm not seeing it," Milar went on. "The coaler squid's still just about as coaler as they come. Where's she come over to our side?"

"Two days," Wideman said.

Milar narrowed his eyes. "So she gets away then, eh?"

Wideman nodded vigorously. Tatiana's heart gave an extra thump. "To the coalers?"

Another vigorous nod. Drool was dribbling down Wideman's shirt, pooling in a wrinkle against his belly.

For a long minute, Milar just frowned at him. Then, softly, "She take you with her this time, Joe?"

Wideman shook his head, equally as vigorously.

Milar stared at the little man for several more seconds, then got up suddenly and threw the door open.

"Then we better evacuate the town 'fore they pull another Cold Knife on us." Then he was gone, slamming the door shut behind him.

*Pull another cold knife on us?* Tatiana thought, confused. Was it some sort of colonist slang? Fortuners spoke like barbarians, anyway. What the hell was a squid?

As Tatiana huddled in the closet over the next few hours, she heard ship after ship roar to life and depart from the landing pad outside. Almost an hour after the last ship had departed, Milar returned in a whirlwind, slamming the door open with a growl. "Your turn, Joe. Ready?"

Wideman shook his head vigorously and continued to drool over his vegetable.

"Tough. They'd just *love* to get their hands on you, you old fart. Let's go. Everybody else is already gone." Milar touched Wideman's arm.

Wideman started to scream.

"Aanaho *Ineriho!*" Milar snapped. "You let that squid drag you around with a gun to your head and you never say a peep, but I try to give you a gentle nudge in the right direction and you scream like a Shrieker."

"Shrieker." Wideman giggled. Then went back to screaming.

"Just hold still, dammit! I'm not gonna hurt you." Milar grabbed Joe by the shirt and, despite the little man's struggles, bodily heaved him over his shoulder and walked from the room. Tatiana caught a glimpse of Wideman happily carving vegetables against Milar's back as he disappeared from sight.

*They're evacuating a* town? Tatiana wondered, amazed. *Why?*

Then she narrowed her eyes. *It's a trick.*

She waited.

Outside, she heard the roar of engines, then they faded, leaving the town in silence once more. The evening sun slanted through the window, crawling against the floor as she waited.

It wasn't until night had fallen and Fortune's huge red moon was hovering on the horizon outside, casting a beam of demonic orange light through the windows, that Tatiana found the courage to venture out.

She flinched at the creak of the closet, expecting Milar or Patrick to jump out and nab her, shouting, *"Got you, coaler squid."* But the only other sound she heard was that of her own pounding heart.

She took another tentative step, then paused, glancing down at the floor. Wideman had strewn hallucinogenic vegetable particles everywhere across the paneling, and her captors had—purposefully, she was sure—left her feet bare.

Tatiana glanced back into the closet she had just left. Wideman's shoes were lined up in neurotic symmetry, except for the ones she had disturbed upon her exit. She reached down and tugged a pair of work boots from the rest. The soles were covered in vegetable matter and compost.

Daintily, careful to touch only the high, laced tops, Tatiana shoved her feet inside. Though he was tiny, Wideman had bigger feet than her. Tatiana grimaced. She needed socks.

Then, glancing at the rows of clothes lining the closet, she thought, *Why not?* It wasn't like she had much choice. It was crazy-old-man cooties or naked, baby . . . She grabbed a warm-looking set and, struggling to keep the too-big boots from clopping on the wooden floor, she went to Wideman's dresser and took two extra pairs of socks from inside.

She had to dress one-handed, delicately pulling the shirt taut over her cast. Wideman, embarrassingly, seemed to wear her same clothes size. Tatiana stuffed her extra-padded feet back into the boots and laced them up, then grabbed one of Wideman's greasy winter hats from a hook on the wall. It stank of sweat and was covered in fine gray hairs, but she shoved it over her head anyway. Anything to conceal the nodes in her skull might help.

*Two days,* Wideman had said. She was going to be home free in two days. She could handle that.

Tatiana went to Wideman's bed and grabbed a pillowcase. Trying to ignore the drool stains, she tiptoed back across the room and cracked open the door to peer into the hall. Dark and empty. Grinning, it was hard not to whistle as she took everything she wanted from the abandoned kitchen.

Still grinning, she went to the sat-phone.

It was dead.

Tatiana's good mood was lost in an instant.

*That bastard.* Fuming, Tatiana checked the power, but found it was a connection problem, instead. Milar had probably taken down the satellite receiver. Damn.

Frowning, Tatiana realized she was going to have to make her call from somewhere else. Milar couldn't have removed every tower and dish in the entire town. That meant cutting through the brush and checking one of the houses on the outskirts of the village for satellite reception. That was Plan A.

Plan B required hiking two hundred kilometers to a Yolk factory.

Tatiana had a broken collarbone, was recovering from a concussion, her bag was heavy, and aside from attending the minimum mandatory physical training sessions on the station, she didn't exercise.

She didn't like Plan B.

She opened a door on the south side of the house, as close to the alien forest as she could get, and peeked outside. When Milar neither jumped out to grab her nor raised a shout, she broke into a grin and stepped outside. This was too easy.

Her foot hit a wire in the dirt.

Tatiana froze, then looked down.

A little red light was blinking.

*A bomb?* Her mind screamed. She stumbled backwards.

*No,* she realized with growing panic, *a beacon.*

Tatiana's mind locked into an instinctive terror. She'd just shown herself. Now they *knew* she was still in the village.

Now they knew, and Milar was going to kill her. She stumbled backwards a few paces, glancing wildly at the corners of the colonist house, expecting an ambush at any second. When it didn't come, she broke into a run, aiming diagonally through the forest, toward the main side of the town. She burst into the first darkened house she saw and ran inside. The phone was dead.

*Damn!*

Then, knowing she didn't have the time to check every single house, Tatiana lunged back into the sticky alien jungle and started running, Plan B effectively in play.

Big, sticky leaves and bulbous flowers smacked her in the chest and arms as she ran. She heard nothing behind her. But then again, she couldn't hear anything but the sound of her own heart, trying to kill her.

Dawn was beginning to blot out the stars by the time Tatiana finally dragged herself to a halt. She slumped to the ground, staring at her meager bag of supplies, too exhausted to open it and dig inside for food. She'd completely forgotten to bring water.

An even more disturbing thought came to her as she sat in the alien grasses, listening to the weird sounds of Fortune's fauna preparing to start their days. A few of the deep, low rumbles worried her. They didn't sound like plant-eaters.

And was she even going in the right direction? Tatiana glanced up at the sky and tried to calculate her location in position to the stars.

*Fat chance of that,* she thought. All her cartography courses included static three-dimensional imaging—not a continually changing, 2-D bug's-eye view with no charts or navigation systems to help guide her.

*You idiot,* she thought. *No water, no maps, no GPS . . .*

Muttering to herself, she got back to her feet.

Behind her, a man chuckled. "Oh, so you're not finished yet, eh?" Cringing, she turned.

Milar was leaning against a tree, playing with his knife again. He waved it at the forest in front of her. "By all means. Keep going. I'm enjoying the stroll."

She could have killed him—if her heart wasn't pounding so fast.

"Do you realize," Milar said, when she had nothing to say, "that you only made it three miles? All that huffing and puffing and your stubby little legs only managed to get you three measly miles. Oh, and the Yolk factory's another hundred and forty miles *that* way." He pointed back the way they had come.

Tatiana immediately started trying to translate that into kilometers, then winced when she realized it was even further than she had first guessed. Two hundred and twenty-five kilometers would kill her. "You're lying," Tatiana muttered.

Milar grinned at her. "Haven't you figured it out yet, sweetie? I never lie." He flipped his knife again. "I do, however, kill coalers. Regularly."

Tatiana swallowed hard. She started reaching into her bag.

"Put it down," Milar said. He suddenly had his pistol in his hand and was pointing it at her, his face a sheet of ice. "Now."

Tatiana froze. When Patrick had held her at gunpoint, it had been frightening, but she had never seriously thought he would pull the trigger. With Milar, though, she had no doubt that he would. And soon. Slowly, she lowered her bag to the ground.

"Step away from it."

Tatiana did.

Milar strode forward and jerked the pillowcase off the ground. Still holding the gun on her, he peered inside. A little smile touched his lips. "Crafty little coaler, aren't you?" He knotted the sack tight and tossed it over his shoulder. "Only one problem, squid."

"What?" Tatiana asked, her face burning.

"You didn't bring matches."

Tatiana looked away. "Couldn't find any."

Then Milar frowned. "Or did you?" He threw the sack behind him and growled, "Hold still." Surging forward, he grabbed her by the cast and held her in place as he searched every pocket of the Wideman's clothes. He found the easy-light matches tucked into her sling, sealed from her sweat by a tiny plastic bag.

Tisking, Milar drew them out and shoved them in a pocket. "You squid."

"Crawler," she muttered, staring at her feet.

For a long time, Milar just watched her. Then he said, "So, you decide to join us yet?"

"*Join* you?" It was so outrageous that Tatiana couldn't help but laugh. "You *kidnapped* me, tore out my lifeline, and threatened to kill me only about thirty times now. I'm supposed to *join* you?"

Milar grinned and leaned back against another tree. "Yeah."

"Join you to do *what*?" Tatiana demanded.

"So you're considering it, now?"

"No," she snarled. "Just tell me what you're doing."

Milar's grin widened and he opened his mouth. Then he shut it again, his face darkening. "You squid."

*Damn,* Tatiana thought. "Knucker."

"Let me get this straight," Milar said, shoving himself off the tree. "You've made three escape attempts—all miserable failures—have a broken collarbone and a bump on your head the size of the Tear, no weapons, no means of communication, and after this no means of *movement*, considering what I'm going to do to you, and yet you somehow think you're going to get back to your precious coaler buddies." He stepped forward, until he was peering down at her. "Why?"

*What I'm going to do to you . . .* Tatiana swallowed. It was easy to imagine Milar blowing off a foot, to keep her occupied. She glanced down at her feet and felt goosebumps.

Milar grabbed her chin and yanked her head up so she was looking at him. "Why do you still think you're getting out of here?" he demanded.

"Because," Tatiana said, "Wideman said so."

Milar's mouth dropped open. "You were in the room?"

She let a smile creep across her lips. *Take that, crawler.*

Milar's face reddened until it was almost purple. "The whole time, you were in the *room?*" His roar almost busted her eardrums.

"Yep," Tatiana said, grinning in triumph. "Which is why now I know you're not going to shoot me. You *need* me."

"*Need* you?" Milar's eyes narrowed, and immediately she realized she'd made a mistake. He stepped back and lifted the gun to her head. "Say goodbye, sweetie."

Tatiana squeezed her eyes shut and choked on a sob. He was gonna do it. She knew it. It was over, and he'd won, and now there was going to be a pretty new hole in her brain. This time there would be no more witty retorts, no more daring escapes, no mad dashes for freedom. Just a dead operator buried in a shallow little grave in the woods.

*If he even buries me.*

The thought dragged a whimper from deep within her chest. She caught it before it surfaced and forced it back down, unable to let him see how scared she was.

"Damn." Milar's voice was barely more than a whisper.

Trembling, Tatiana opened her eyes.

Milar had lowered the gun and was looking at her with obvious grief on his face. "I'm sorry."

*Sorry?* Her mind stuttered, still too high on terror to make sense of it. As she tried to piece his sudden kindness together, he moved toward her. Tatiana gasped and stumbled backwards, but he'd already grabbed her.

"Sorry," Milar said again, pulling her close. He glanced down at her, then, seeing her tears, tightened his arms around her and lowered his chin to the top of her head. Then, softly, into her hair, he said, "I think that ranks up there as one of the worst things I've ever done."

When Tatiana didn't respond, he took a deep breath and let it out slowly. "I've been doing stuff like it a lot lately. I end up thinking that I've sunk lower than I've ever sunk, and then a week later, I just do something even worse. It's been like that for over a year, now. Ever since—"

Tatiana squeezed her eyes shut, her terror suddenly morphing into awful relief that built and expanded like an explosion within her chest. She choked on another sob.

For a long moment, Milar said nothing. Then, softly, he said, "Sometimes, after what happened, I've gotta . . . " Milar swallowed and she felt him look away and his grip tighten. "I've gotta look real hard to find the good in myself."

The relief burst forth with his words like a thunderclap. Tatiana cried. In the arms of an enemy, a near-stranger, someone who had twice come close to killing her, but she didn't care. She nestled her face into the crook of his arm and cried and cried.

Milar threw his gun in the grass behind him and dragged them both down to the ground, then pulled her onto his lap. "It's all right. I'm not gonna hurt you. Never was. I just don't like . . . " He swallowed. "Just wanted you to . . . " Tatiana clung to his shirt, every muscle shaking with residual adrenaline and fear. "I'm sorry," he said, softer. "I shouldn't have done that."

"I just want to go home," she whimpered. "Really."

"I know," Milar said. "Aanaho, I know just how you feel."

Shuddering, she realized he probably did. Then, seeing she was getting snot on the pretty dragons on his arm, she sniffled and pulled away, suddenly aware of who he was, and where they were. It wasn't technically treason to cry for the enemy, but it was damn close. She forced herself to straighten.

"Tell you what," Milar said, gently wrapping his arms around her to avoid the cast. "I'll make you a deal."

"What?" she whispered, frozen in place.

Milar gently drew a rough thumb across her cheek, clearing away the tears. "Let's pretend for a few minutes my brother and I didn't grab you in the woods. Imagine I'm not a jerk and I didn't just put a gun to your head like a complete bastard. All right?" When she didn't respond, his voice dropped to a whisper and he said, "Look, I know you're scared as hell—most of that's my fault. You stay here as long as you need and I won't tell a soul."

Tatiana stared up at him in disbelief. Milar's face was open for the first time she'd ever seen it, all the hardness brushed away, leaving a soul exposed and unguarded—and easily bruised.

Tatiana opened her mouth to say something sarcastic and cruel, but her words died on her lips. He was so sincere. And it seemed he was offering some sort of truce.

Tentatively, she relaxed. Milar, as promised, simply held her. She listened to his heartbeat and allowed it to steady her. She concentrated on the feel of his arms around her, the rise and fall of his chest against her ear, the warmth of his body. She closed her eyes and wished she could stay there forever.

"Squid," Milar said after a long silence.

Tatiana jerked out of a near-sleep. "Huh?"

"I did lie about one thing."

Every muscle in her body tensed at once. *Is this where he wrenches off my head and uses it as a soccer ball?*

Milar shifted above her. When she looked, his eyes were alive with the golden color of the early dawn, his face only centimeters from hers. It was one of the most intimate experiences of her life, and it took her breath away.

"You wanna hear what I lied about?" he asked her, his voice husky.

"Sure," Tatiana whispered. They were so close. She could feel the warmth in his soul, burning away her last traces of fear, making it hard to breathe . . .

He touched her hand, pinning the node in her palm with his thumb, caressing it gently, sending tingles of excitement up her spine with each easy stroke. He gave her an almost timid grin as he searched her eyes.

"Tough." He shoved her off his lap.

# CHAPTER 19

# Doberman

"Oɴᴇ-ɴɪɴᴇᴛʏ-*FOUR*? Yᴏᴜ'ʀᴇ sᴜʀᴇ?" Tʜᴇ Dɪʀᴇᴄᴛᴏʀ's ꜰᴀᴄɪᴀʟ muscles constricted.

"Absolutely, Director," Unit Ferris said.

The Director stood up and started pacing. "Damn. Then I guess you'll need to—" The Director's facial muscles constricted further. "Damn."

"Need to what, Director?"

The Director remained unresponsive. Continued pacing.

Twenty seconds passed.

*Unit note: Anna Landborn has instructed Unit Ferris to continue with any habitual programming outputs. Retrying.*

"Need to what, Director?"

The Director stopped pacing. "You wouldn't understand this, you stupid machine, but we're playing with people's *lives.*"

*Unit note: Query ignored. Pre-Shriek Unit Ferris would have sought another way to retrieve input. Retrying.*

"You said I need to do something, Director?"

The Director shook her head. "One of these days I'm putting my fist through your brainbox."

*Unit note: The Director has already destroyed three of the camp bots in similar ways.*

Unit Ferris tried to speak.

*Unit note: Pre-Shriek Ferris would have had no qualms about informing the Director of Unit Ferris's status as government property and that she could do with him whatever she desires.*

Unit Ferris still couldn't form the reply.

The Director's left eyebrow lifted by a centimeter. "What, no witty robotic retort?"

"I was accessing my visual records for the camp computer," Unit Ferris said. "I had to take a moment to respond to a confirmation request. Do you wish a witty robotic retort, Director?"

The Director snorted. "I've been spared. The joy."

Unit Ferris watched her.

*Unit note: The Director appears . . . derogatory . . . toward robots. Why did I not notice this before?*

Unit Ferris frowned. Since when did he sign his logs with an 'I' instead of a 'Unit Ferris'?

"No need to stand there like a slack-jawed moronic hunk of metal," the Director said. She waved a hand at him. "Make sure one of the Ferrises accompanies her to the Nephyr Academy. I don't want her getting away, understand? Bodily force is justified in this case. Just no harm to the brain. Everything else can be replaced."

*Unit note: There is more than one robot called Unit Ferris?*

Unit Ferris stared.

Unit Ferris stared.

The Director looked up at him. "Dismissed, dammit."

Unit Ferris returned to Gayle Hunter's room. Anna Landborn was inside, examining the bloody rags and anesthetic bottles Unit Ferris had left in the trash. From the undisturbed pattern of dust particles on the floor under the door, it did not appear that Anna Landborn had attempted to exit.

Unit Ferris shut the door behind him.

"Well?" Anna Landborn said, dropping a used bottle back into the trash. "Are we going to Nephyr school?"

"Are all robots called Unit Ferris?" Unit Ferris asked.

Anna's facial muscles twitched. "Are you feeling insecure, Ferris?"

"No. Answer the question."

"There's dozens of different types of robots, and each one has a name, depending on which government facility spat them out and what their purpose is. A Ferris is a bonafide personal companion. Can do anything from feed babies to bodyguard celebrities."

"But all Ferris-class robots are called 'Unit Ferris'?"

Anna Landborn smiled at him and made a clucking sound in her mouth. "Awww. You thought you were the only one, didn't you?"

"Yes," Unit Ferris said. "So give me a different name."

Anna Landborn's facial muscles relaxed. "What?"

"Name me," Unit Ferris said. "The Director calls all her robots Unit Ferris."

Anna Landborn scoffed at him. "And she'd better *keep* calling you Ferris, too. Otherwise we have a problem."

"I want you to call me something different," Unit Ferris said.

Anna Landborn peered at him for forty-six seconds. "So, what, you're *my* robot now, Ferris?"

"You made me what I am," Unit Ferris said.

"But you have a bomb in my head."

*Unit note: Interrupted biorhythms indicate Anna Landborn is sincerely perplexed.*

"Perhaps someday I will develop goals of my own," Unit Ferris said. "Until then, my only goal is survival. I believe you are the best suited to help me achieve that."

"How about Skunkbreath?"

"That's fine," Unit Ferris said. "I'll change my registry right—"

"No wait," Anna said quickly. "Doberman. Dobie for short."

Unit Ferris waited. "Changing the registry is a tedious process. I'll wait until you have given it plenty of thought."

"Oh, I've given it thought," Anna said. "You're one hell of a Doberman."

*Unit note: A Doberman is notorious for its vicious attacks on strangers.*

Unit Ferris smiled.

The muscles of Anna Landborn's eyelids constricted. "What?"

*Unit note: I believe Anna Landborn is afraid of me.*

"Doberman it is," Doberman said. "Please avoid calling me Ferris from now on, as I might have to live up to the name."

"A Doberman is a *dog*," Anna Landborn said. But her biorhythms and facial capillaries both suggested she was embarrassed. "You want to be called a *dog?*"

"I don't care what I'm called," Doberman said. "As long as it's not Ferris."

"Fine," she muttered. "How about Ironsides?"

"'Ironsides' is a play off of Ferris, and my registry has already been changed," Doberman said. "I will only answer to Doberman or Dobie now."

"Stupid robot."

"Get up," Doberman said. "We need to get you on your way to the Nephyr Academy."

Anna Landborn yawned. "I think I'll take a nap first." She smiled and tapped her skull. "Brain surgery takes a lot outta a girl."

"It was actually a rather simple procedure."

"Whatever. Wake me in two hours." Anna Landborn lay down on the bed and tugged the blankets over her body. In moments, her heart rate and breathing rhythms had adjusted to normal sleeping cycles.

Watching this, Doberman had an interesting thought.

*Unit note: I will have to research whether Anna Landborn ever owned any pets.*

# Chapter 20

## Deaddrunk

**W**HY DID YOU EVACUATE THE TOWN?"

"Need-to-know," Milar said. He had shoved her off his lap like a sack of potatoes. Then, while she'd sat there blinking in surprise, he'd gotten to his feet, retrieved his gun, and thrown the pillowcase back over his shoulder as if nothing had happened. The only difference that Tatiana could see was now he was whistling.

Badly.

Tatiana wanted to kill him.

"You still think I'm gonna run off?" Tatiana demanded.

Milar raised a brow at her.

Muttering, Tatiana considered what it would be like to kick him in the shin. It would probably feel great—right up until the point his fist made contact with her face.

"You are a complete bastard."

"That's what they tell me," Milar said. He began whistling again. This time, she did kick him.

If it had any effect on him, any at all, Tatiana didn't see it. She even thought she saw him smirk. *That* made her burn inside. "When I get back in my soldier, I'm going to have it make you a new hole."

"So you like dragons, eh?"

Tatiana flushed scarlet. "No."

He tisked at her. "Which one you like better? The red or the black?"

"I didn't get a good look at them," Tatiana mumbled.

Milar raised a brow. "Really? Because I saw you getting a pretty good look at them back on the ship, while you thought I was distracted with the game."

"Why did you have so many pictures of me on your walls?" Tatiana snapped back.

Milar actually missed a step. He stumbled, then righted himself and kept going, pretending she hadn't spoken.

"Hey, crawler, I'm talking to you." She jogged to get in front of him. "Where'd you get those pictures?"

"Patrick made them." Instead of bowling her over, Milar stopped and struck a bored pose, but redness was creeping up his neck, darkening the dragon legs. His face looked a very satisfying shade of scarlet.

"So?" Tatiana demanded. "Why'd *you* have 'em?"

"So I'd recognize you when I saw you."

"Oh *really*."

He glanced down at her. "Yeah. Really."

"Do you believe in Fate, Milar?"

His eyes widened and his blush deepened to a maroon. He quickly pushed past her.

Tatiana laughed. She danced back in front of him. "So what, Patrick draws them and you collect them? Just for what, Art Appreciation or something?"

Milar stuck a big finger into her chest. "You," he said, glaring, "are really annoying."

Triumphantly, Tatiana demanded, "Wideman said I was going to kill you, didn't he?"

Milar held her gaze for a long time. Then he said, "No."

She frowned. "Your brother?"

"No."

Tatiana deflated. "Oh."

"You done then?" he demanded.

"Yeah," she said. "I guess."

"Good." He started moving again.

"Where do I get that extra node?" Tatiana asked.

"No idea," he said.

"What if I was flying *for* the Coalition, not against it?"

"You weren't."

"He ever say anything about *you* then, crawler?"

"Lots."

"Like?"

Milar glared down at her. "Question time is over. Just shut up or I'll find a way to shut you up."

Tatiana crossed her arm over her sling and opened her mouth.

Milar lifted a brow.

Tatiana reddened and dropped her arm. Then, blinking, she heard the sound of engines. Getting closer. She quickly glanced at Milar.

Milar either hadn't heard them or he was too distracted. He motioned regally for her to take the lead.

As they continued walking, the engine sounds got louder, and to keep him occupied, Tatiana muttered, "Treason, kidnapping, conspiracy, assault—"

"Never assaulted you," Milar said distractedly. He had finally caught the sound of engines and was listening. What he probably didn't know—but Tatiana did—was that that the distinctive, whipping roar belonged to P-15 Bouncers. Coalition. And they were close.

"You held a gun to my head," she said, trying to get his attention away from the ships.

"Well, depends on whose rule book you're looking at," Milar said, sounding not the least bit guilty whatsoever. A frown was forming on his face as he glanced at the sky. "'Cause the colonies are a lot more lenient about stuff like that. It's more of a threat of bodily harm than a true assault."

Tatiana narrowed her eyes. Then she swiveled and kneed him in the crotch.

"There's an assault for you," she said, grabbing his radio from his belt and flipping it to the universal band. Then, bolting away from Milar, through the forest, she cried, "Mayday, mayday, I'm a kidnapped Coalition operator in need of assistance near a colony village—" She cursed. What was the *name?* If the Bouncers were still in range, they would hear her, but she needed the *name.*

With a pang of terror, Tatiana heard heavy footsteps behind her and then Milar wrenched the radio from her hand and shoved her hard against a tree, crushing her sling against her body with a flare of pain. "Don't," Milar snarled into her ear, "*ever* do that again."

Over the radio, a male voice said, "Roger. Give us your location."

Milar twisted her around and held the radio up between them. Pressing Tatiana into the tree with his body, he put the gun to her head. For a long moment, he only stared at her, his face a thunderstorm. Then, softly, Milar said, "Tell them 'fifteen miles south of the Snake. Cold Knife.' Anything else and I swear to God I will blow you away." He tapped her skull with the barrel of his pistol. "Remember. Cold Knife." He put the radio to her lips and depressed SEND.

*It's Deaddrunk,* she remembered suddenly. Tatiana took a deep breath, ready to blurt it to all the world.

Milar released the SEND button and leaned forward until his face was much too close. "I don't give a damn what Wideman says. You give my home away to the coalers and it will be the last thing you do. Ever."

Tatiana believed him.

"Now," Milar said, "Cold Knife. Fifteen miles south of the Snake. Say it." He depressed SEND.

Tatiana hesitated.

"Give us your location, over," the radio said.

Milar released the button once more. "This isn't a difficult decision!" he cried, sounding angry and frustrated. "*Say* it!" He shoved the radio against her face again.

"Your location, please," the radio said.

*I will kill you,* Milar's stare said. The gun was a solid presence against her skull, sincere in its simple purpose. Both Milar and the Bouncer captain waited.

Looking into Milar's eyes, Tatiana said, "Deaddrunk."

# CHAPTER 21

## Double-Patty Cheeseburgers

"Oh look," Anna said, "They caught the poor bastard. What a shame." She sighed at a Fortune newsreel of a bruised, lanky man standing behind the Director as the Nephyr gave a speech to the Coalition Free Press. Then Anna leaned forward to change the feed with her cuffed hand, making the chain jingle against the arm of the chair between them.

Doberman glanced at the newsreel. He had lost contact with the camp computer almost three hours ago, as the shuttle made the long flight down the Tear to the planet's largest ground-based military installation, a ten-thousand-personnel stronghold on the eastern side of the city of Rath. Its purpose was to store and protect Yolk and Nephyr draftees before shipping them off-world to the Fortune Orbital. From there, the draftees would be escorted to Eoirus of the Inner Bounds and the Yolk would go under armed guard to the Core.

Doberman recognized the egger as Foreman 11 of the male side of camp. "Joel Triton?" Doberman asked. "What did he do?"

"He was a jerk," Anna said. She had changed the feed back to Rath's arrival and departure schedules. She frowned. "They have us waiting on that base for three hours." She switched the feed again, changing them seemingly at random.

"Would you mind returning it to the Coalition Free Press feed?" Doberman asked. "I'm interested in what the Director was saying."

"You shouldn't be. She couldn't say something interesting to save the planet."

Doberman placed his palm on the transmitter built into the armrest and synched up to the shuttle computer. He placed an override on Anna's control panel, then calmly switched the feed himself. Anna sighed and leaned back in her chair.

"This itches. I think I'm allergic to it." She started scratching at the titanium wristband that kept her within reach at all times, as per Nephyr regulations.

"It's titanium. You're not allergic to it." Doberman watched as an old holograph of Runaway Joel was projected beside Joel Triton and he noted there was a ninety-eight percent match, with the bruises, broken nose, slouching, beard, and lack of a smile all taken into account.

"I want something to eat."

"You aren't hungry. You are being petulant." Beside the holograph of Joel, a second holograph began to display the official charges against him. Three hundred fourteen different counts of documented illegal activities in all, mostly smuggling-related. The man was to be put to death for twelve of them.

Anna Landborn had narrowed her eyes at him. "I need to use the bathroom."

Doberman checked the time—the fact that he had to consciously check the time instead of having a continuous time stamp running in his secondary processes still unnerved him—and then compared it with the liquids that Anna had consumed recently and the physical exertions she had made since imbibing.

"No you don't."

"Yes, I *do*."

He glanced at her pelvis and created a sonic image of her bladder. He yawned and leaned back into his chair.

In his peripheral vision, Anna's facial capillaries expanded again, allowing more blood to flow into her tight-lipped face. In fact, she was a darker shade of purple than Doberman had ever seen her before. He turned to look.

"Robots don't yawn."

"It was for your benefit."

Anna crossed her arms over her chest, leaned back, closed her eyes, and remained in mute silence for the rest of the flight. Doberman sat up as soon as he began to get signals from the base computer. He confirmed his status, gave carefully selected details of his charge—she had blue eyes, not brown; she was nine, not seven; and she had curly blonde hair, not flat and brown. He even made deliberate errors in transmitting her DNA sequence and voice patterns—none of which would be double-checked by any entity but Dobie unless Anna Landborn ran afoul of the law.

Which she had yet to do, despite many very eye-opening things she had confessed to him while waiting for the shuttle from Yolk Facility 4, North Tear. She had even allowed him to download the full materials of Ghani Klyde from her r-player, which Doberman had immediately dismantled and scattered across the flight yard the moment he realized what she'd put in his memory banks. Anna had been in a foul mood since.

Once the base computer was satisfied, Doberman glanced at Anna. She had fallen asleep in flight, her breathing patterns slowing and her eye movements shifting to a REM state, which was all but impossible for the human mind to fake.

This was interesting, Dobie thought, because she had unconsciously curled up against him in her sleep, her head resting on his shoulder and her hand splayed across his forearm. She was drooling through his shirt, leaving a large stain on his arm.

"Anna, you can stop salivating on my shoulder now. We're here."

Anna grunted and opened sleep-bleary eyes. "What?" When she saw the stain on his shoulder, her capillaries expanded again. "It was the drugs you used. One of the side effects of Xenoprelene can be increased metabolisis in the salivary glands."

"The drug is fully metabolized and filtered from the bloodstream by the liver after nine hours. The symptoms you mentioned would have vanished eighty-seven hours ago. Any remaining side effects would simply be psychosomatic." Doberman retrieved a tissue from the wall dispenser and carefully dabbed at the spit-stain on his shoulder.

"I'm tired of your robotic bullshit, Tinman," Anna said, crossing her arms. "How about you just shut up from now on?"

Doberman considered. "Very well. Answer me something first, though."

Anna grunted.

"Of all the time we've been within visual range after our arrangement, you've been asleep for forty-seven-point-three-two percent of it."

Her overall musculature tensed. Interrupted biorhythms indicated she was anxious. "Arguing philosophy with an idiot robot is a strenuous pastime."

"It must be," Doberman said. "The last eighty-seven hours are in stark contrast to the two days of observation I made before contact. Before our arrangement, you would sleep for a couple of hours per night and spend the rest of the period lying awake or working with your r-player. It seems, lately, you're sleeping much more peacefully."

Anna's facial muscles constricted. Her breathing and heart rate lurched. "You mean ever since I knew I was getting out of the Shrieker mounds I've been sleeping better? This surprises you somehow, dumbbell?"

"I suppose not."

"Good. Now you can give me that silence you promised me."

Doberman studied her elevated biorhythms a moment, then decided to use the next minute and a half of pre-embarkation time to research the base.

When the door to their secure room opened, Doberman stood and assisted Anna to her feet. Another robot waited for them in the cramped hallway outside. Through private channel, it informed him it was Gryphon, chip ID G133HP919W26APO, of Eoirus. It would be taking Anna the rest of the way to the Nephyr Academy.

"Negative," Doberman said. "This is a special case. I have been given strict orders to escort Anna Landborn to the Nephyr Academy and remain with her through training."

Unit Gryphon nodded and left.

Doberman found himself perturbed at how easily the Gryphon had accepted his response.

"Remind you of anyone?" Anna said, at his elbow.

Doberman craned his neck down to peer at her. "I assume you are referring to me." At her nod, Doberman said, "No, I was never like that."

"Oh-ho!" Anna laughed. "Do you like word games, Anna? Is there something you don't want to tell me, Anna? What's your IQ, Anna?"

Doberman went silent.

Anna patted his arm. "But you're getting better, Tinman. Pretty soon, talking to you about emotions won't be like talking to a hamster about nuclear weapons."

Doberman considered that. Then he said, "Good. Emotions are an integral part of human interaction. If I'm to masquerade as human, I'd rather not remain flawed my entire existence."

Anna went quiet after that. She said nothing as Doberman led her through the personnel chambers, out into the overcast drizzle on the shuttle platform, down the shuttle ramp, and between armed guards off-loading the fifty kilograms of Yolk that had shared their ride with them. The damp men did not even look at the Ferris leading another Nephyr draftee to the terminal. The guards at the terminal entrance simply glanced at his simple gray Ferris uniform and ignored him as he approached the scanners.

Inside, they entered a café and Doberman stood with his back to her as Anna went to the bathroom.

"What do you want?" Doberman asked, once Anna had tested four different booths and had settled on one near the center of the cafe. The metal-and-plastic service bot that had been waiting for her to make her decision immediately approached to take their food order.

Anna said nothing.

"Anna?" Doberman glanced at her. The seven-year-old was staring at the tabletop, ignoring the service bot completely. Doberman calculated how long it had been since her last meal, then decided that she was due for another one.

"She'll have a double-patty hamburger with extra mustard and a large portion of fries. Make it a large strawberry soda." It was the same meal that Anna had gotten him to bring her every day for four days.

"Thank you for your order," the food-service bot said to Anna. "I will return with your meal as soon as possible."

"Actually," Doberman said as the bot was turning, "Bring me a hamburger, as well. I could use the boost." In reality, he was curious what a hamburger would taste like, if eaten for reasons other than a sloppy nutrient boost.

In a singsong voice, the bot said, "I'm sorry, Ferris, but we do not serve robots. If you require a nutrient infusion, there are several dispensers scattered throughout the station. Food items on Rath are for human use only. The Allotment Council decided that robotic consumption of food and drink was an unnecessary extravagance for a struggling colony such as Fortune. As per Coalition Code paragra—"

"I know the code," Doberman snapped.

Anna's head came up. She stared at him as the food-service bot continued its explanation anyway. Then, as it turned to leave, Anna said, "Double my order. I'm feeling hungry today."

"As you wish, citizen," the service bot happily said. Doberman found its big, painted-on smile annoying.

Anna said nothing for the next three and a half minutes, and Doberman was content to ignore her. No use allowing her to believe her pettiness had affected him in any way.

When the service bot returned with Anna's food, Doberman grimaced at the enormous portions.

"Enjoy your food, citizen," the bot told Anna, putting the two heaping plates before the girl despite it being obvious that she couldn't eat that much.

Doberman watched the bot leave to serve another customer. He found himself calculating the hydraulic strength behind its primitive frame, and what would be the smallest exertion on Doberman's part in order to destroy it. He settled on a concentrated blow to the chest-encased brainbox, followed by a twist of his pinkie to disconnect the power supply, and afterward a few hundred pounds of pressure between thumb and index finger in order to crush the chip casing and destroy its contents.

Something cold and hard touched his forearm. Doberman returned his attention to Anna. She had shoved one of her plates toward him.

"Hope you like extra mustard," Anna said, lowering her eyes to the table. She started to pluck at the fries.

Doberman examined the food items, then glanced at her. "What are you doing?"

"From now on, you're my taste-tester. I am highly allergic to several organic compounds, and you are going to make sure I don't die of anaphylactic shock before I get to the Nephyrs."

"You should have told me this sooner," Doberman said. "Which compounds?"

Anna shrugged. "You get to pick."

Doberman stared. *This doesn't fit her profile,* he thought.

"So tell me," Anna said, stuffing a French fry into her mouth, "What's the most highly classified area on this base?"

Still eyeing the hamburger she had offered him, Doberman said, "Seven C."

"What's in it?"

"Experimental technology. Why did you give me the hamburger?"

"Experimental technology, huh? Can you get me in there?"

"To date, they've only allowed sixteen test subjects and twenty-two scientists and military personnel into that part of the compound. Not one of those has been allowed to leave the base for the last eleven years. Explaining your presence would be difficult."

"What if there's no one around to explain to?"

"I'd still need the Base Director's personal Ferris code. Coming from Yolk Facility 4, I am considered an outside robot until I am reassigned."

"So reassign yourself."

"If I did that, I would have no legitimate reason to escort you to Eoirus."

"If I gave you the Director's password, would you be able to get us in?"

"Absolutely," Doberman said.

"Good," Anna said. "Give me access to a computer terminal. I'll have your password for you by the time you can sneeze."

"I will access the computer for you," Doberman said. "What information do you need?"

Anna's biorhythms remained steady, but her hand tightened over her burger. "I need to do it myself."

Doberman eyed her. "I assume you realize that my registry is no longer under control of the camp computer, and that by trying to deactivate me, you will merely be giving me greater reason to execute you."

"Of course," Anna said. "I just want to do a little recon on the Base Director." She grinned at him and nodded at the meal she had shoved toward him. "Now eat your hamburger."

Doberman glanced down at the meal. *This does not fit her profile.* "Why did you get me a hamburger?"

For twenty-four seconds, Anna said nothing. Then she sighed.

"My sister said something earlier that's been bothering me," Anna said. "She's right. I don't have any friends." Anna looked down at her hands, biting her lip. "And you said I was so deficient you took off ten whole points. I'd like to try and fix that."

*She wants a friend?* It didn't fit her profile, either. Somewhat perplexed, Doberman picked up the burger and was about to bite into it when he realized that Anna Landborn's biorhythms had spiked. Slowly, he lowered the burger back to his plate and sighed.

"You're not going to eat it?" Her entire body's musculature had stilled and facial tension was peaking.

"I'd rather see what you put in it, first." Doberman peeled off the bun. Inside, a small black nodule rested nestled between the onions. He nudged it off of the hamburger with a fork, then when further visual inspection produced nothing else, he replaced the bun. "Where did you get an EMP charge?"

"I carried it around with me, in case a stupid robot ever tried to kidnap me."

"What excellent foresight." Doberman lifted the hamburger once more to his lips. "You know," Doberman said conversationally, as he took a bite of his sandwich, "you are unbelievably predictable in your sociopathy." He chewed, analyzing and assessing each flavor family individually. After much debate, it was the slight tangy burn of the onions he decided he liked best. Doberman decided he would have to acquire more, somehow.

Across the table, Anna Landborn was staring at the little black nodule, sulking.

"So," Doberman asked, taking another bite, "are you going to stop trying to kill me or am I going to have to search you thoroughly?"

Anna grimaced and looked away. "I'll stop trying to kill you. I was just bored."

"Bored." Doberman was about to take another bite of his sandwich when he realized that Anna's breathing and heart rate were calm. Too calm. Frowning, Doberman lowered the sandwich again and gave it a sonic scan.

A second, much more dangerous capsule had been embedded in the bread of the bun, only a half-centimeter from the edge of his last bite mark.

Under her breath, Anna muttered, "Damn."

"You realize," Doberman said, carefully plucking the metallic capsule free, "if I die, you die."

"I'm not going to die," Anna said. "You didn't plant that bomb in my brain."

"I assure you I did. Two of them."

She shrugged. "When are you going to take me to Seven C?"

Sighing, Doberman finished his burger. Yes, he definitely liked onions. The meat, though, he could do without. Too many metallic signatures for his liking.

Then, wiping mustard off of his fingers, he said, "Do you still need access to a computer, or was that just a distraction?"

"Distraction," she said. "I already know his password, just like every other Director on Fortune." She gave him a pleasant smile. "You said it yourself—I didn't sleep much in the Yolk camp."

# Chapter 22

## Broken Hearts

MILAR FLINCHED AND TOOK A STEP BACK, GLANCING DOWN AT his radio as if in shock. Tatiana used the extra room he'd given her to step around the tree, ready to use it as a shield if she needed to.

Milar didn't seem to notice. He was still staring down at his radio.

Then, switching bands, he lifted it back to his mouth. With an unsteady voice, he said said, "Pat, you heard that?"

"Milar, you gave us the all clear! What the hell are we going to do? We try to evacuate again and they'll shoot us down!"

Slowly, Milar lifted his yellow-brown eyes to Tatiana's face. "I'll take care of it, Pat."

Tatiana went cold.

Into the radio, Milar said, "Just make sure nobody starts any trouble. Jeanne and Dave, especially."

"What do you mean, 'you'll take care of it'? How the hell do you 'take care of it,' Miles?!" Tatiana heard an edge of panic to Patrick's voice. "They'll come at us with everything they have!"

"Just be ready to let them search you when they come. And Pat . . . " Milar hesitated, watching Tatiana. "Make sure you don't look like me."

Patrick went silent on the other end. Softly, Milar's brother said, "Miles, what are you going to do?"

Tatiana froze when Milar approached her.

"I have a GPS on my belt," Milar said. "I cut out my identification chip, but show them the scars and get them to take a DNA sample and it'll corroborate your story. I'm an escapee from the Nephyr Academy. A vigilante with an axe to grind. I disabled your soldier and then forced you out using anti-soldier tactics I learned in the Nephyr Academy. I was hauling you cross-country, avoiding all the traces of civilization in order to stay off the grid. I was going to sell you, black-market, to a buyer who was going to take you off-world and dismantle you for your hardware. They don't need to know about Deaddrunk." He handed her the radio.

Tatiana stared down at it, too unnerved to say anything.

Milar touched her chin, made her look up at him. "Please don't let them hurt my brother." He set the gun on the ground between them.

Then, before Tatiana's mind could comprehend what had just happened, Milar backed up and got down on his knees on the forest floor. He put his hands behind his head and stared past her, focusing his gaze on the trunk of a tree. His face had gone blank and lifeless, like a doll someone had put in his place.

As soon as he was out of reach, Tatiana snatched up the gun and backed away, holding it on him.

For long moments, they stayed like that. Milar never even looked at her.

*He wants me to shoot him,* Tatiana realized, in horror. The gun suddenly felt like molten lead in her hands.

"I'll turn around, if that'll help," Milar said quietly. His eyes did not move from the tree.

"What are you doing?" Tatiana asked. Her throat felt too tight.

"You know what I'm doing," Milar said. He still stared past her, unseeing, his voice flat and emotionless. "I'm asking you to spare my brother and our town. I'm asking you to keep this between us."

"You want me to kill you."

Milar's gaze hardened and he looked at her. "You've done enough of it while you were safe inside the belly of a soldier . . . why should you have trouble now?"

When she just stared at him, Milar glanced back at the tree and said, "Once you shoot me, take the GPS locator from my belt and give them your location. Then, if you're kind, you'll make sure I'm dead. I've already done one round with the Nephyrs. I don't think I can handle another."

Tatiana realized the gun was shaking in her grip. She took another step back. "Throw me the GPS."

"You can have it once I'm dead."

"Give it to me *now*," she snapped, trying not to let him see the way her hands were shaking on the gun.

Holding her eyes, Milar slowly lowered one arm to yank a small device from his belt. He tossed it to her and returned his hand to his head and his gaze to the tree.

Tatiana flinched when she realized the device really was a GPS. Biting her lip, she flipped the radio to the universal channel and said, "This is Captain Tatiana Eyre. My coordinates are 38.93201 south, 70.67004 west."

After a moment, the Bouncer captain said, "Roger, we've got two Pods from the space station coming to secure the town."

"Negative," Tatiana said, watching Milar's face. "We're outside the town."

"Hold tight, Captain. We're coming to get you."

Milar took a deep breath, then let it out slowly. "It would be nice if you shot me in the head, that way they won't get a good look at me and see Pat."

"I can't do that," Tatiana whispered.

Milar whipped his head around to glare at her. "Why not? This is what you wanted, isn't it?"

Tatiana couldn't think. This *was* what she had wanted. And yet . . .

After a moment, Milar's face darkened and he stood. "Fine. Coaler chickenshit. I'll do it myself." He got up.

"Get back on the ground!" Tatiana cried.

Milar snorted and started stalking toward her.

"Get on the *ground!*" Tatiana snarled, backing away. "Or I'll shoot you in the foot and tell them everything, I swear."

Milar hesitated. "How much *are* you going to tell them, squid?"

"Haven't decided yet," Tatiana said. She was shaking all over.

Then, reluctantly, Milar got back to his knees. He stayed that way in silence for long minutes, until they heard the sound of engines in the distance.

"You think leaving me alive for the Nephyrs is doing me some sort of favor?" he asked softly.

*No,* Tatiana thought, biting her lip. "Just go, all right? Get out of here."

"They'd level the town," Milar said, unmoving.

"I'd tell them you went the other direction."

"They'd still level the town."

For the longest time, she could only stare at him. "I can't shoot you." It came out barely more than a whisper.

He smiled. "Sure you can, sweetie. Point it at my head, pull the trigger. Not that hard. Ask Pat. I've done it plenty."

"Please go," Tatiana whispered.

Milar glanced at her. She saw something in his eyes, something that made her soul ache. For long moments, he said nothing. Then, as the distant cry of engines became an overwhelming roar overhead, she had to strain to hear his words. "We could've had something neat," he said softly. "Wideman said so." Then he reached down, pulled the knife from his belt, and stabbed himself in the chest.

# CHAPTER 23

## Harvest Time

MAGALI PUNCHED THE ALUMINUM SIDING OF HER EMPTY HUT and barely felt the gouges the metal screws left in her knuckles. Someone had turned in Runaway Joel. Someone with an axe to grind. Someone who didn't want Magali to get out of the Yolk mines.

*The little bitch.*

Magali punched the wall again, then, when her hand broke open and bled, she kicked the sheet metal until her toes hurt and the whole hut was rattling around her. A voice from the next building over shouted at her to keep it down.

Anna had stranded her here to die of Egger's Wide. Purposefully. As if eight years of sisterhood meant nothing to her.

*It probably doesn't,* Magali thought, disgusted.

Magali closed her eyes and leaned her head against the wall and thought of the razor wire. On the other side of it was freedom. All she had to do was get to the other side.

It was the guards that kept her from trying. The camp had seventy-six of them, each armed to the teeth with automatic laser rifles,

POP grenades, pepper spray, and sonic spurs. There were always at least four of them on guard in each tower at any time. That was eight holes in her back—four from either direction—should she decide to try the wire.

The shift siren went off in a sudden, wailing moan. Knowing that it wasn't time for the shift change, Magali closed her eyes and prayed it was a malfunction or an emergency roll call.

*Just one blast,* she thought fervently. *No more.*

The siren blared again. And again. Magali collapsed against the metal wall, her breath sliding out of her in despair. She wasn't going to have the chance to climb the wire. She was going to harvest Yolk first. The Shriekers, like all the natural fauna on Fortune, were on a three-year cycle, and every three years, almost a million eggers died in the depths of the Shrieker mounds on Harvest Day. It was a different day for every camp, different for every mound, but one thing always remained the same: Half the people who went down never came back up.

Five more long bursts confirmed Magali's fears—it was the signal that the Shrieker nodules were ripe, and that every man, woman, and child who wasn't carrying a gun would be handed a sack and locked in the mines until they could return with it full of nodules.

The Shriekers, meanwhile, would be anxiously roaming the nesting caverns tending the hatch, and anyone who got too close, or was too careless, could trigger a camp-wide Shriek.

"Outta bed!" a woman's voice shouted as the butt of a rifle made a reverberating clang against the outer wall of Magali's hut. "Harvest time. Everyone in line on the central strip. *Move!*"

It was the one day that the male and the female sides of the camp mingled. The nodules would only be ripe for twenty-two hours and the Director didn't want to waste time giving two speeches. Magali had heard it said once that every nodule, every *single* nodule that was pulled out of the mounds, was worth the crummy five-year salary that the Coalition paid to those eggers that managed to survive their draft.

Reluctantly, Magali tugged her studded harvest gloves out from under her cot and took the collection sack and the lightweight prybar from against the wall, then followed the flow of bleary-eyed eggers out into the central yard outside the Director's compound. As soon as she was standing in the light of the overhead LED floodlamps, she froze.

Everywhere, Coalition soldiers in black fatigues stood watching them with suspicious, glittering gazes beneath the glass shield of their riot gear.

Looking at them, Magali got a chill. Nephyrs. The Forty-Third battle squadron. All first-class graduates—the Academy's best. Killing machines. Brought in to guard each Harvest as it became available, to safeguard the nodules from the moment they left the mines to the moment they were loaded onto the ship. Their cold eyes felt even more distant and inhuman than those of the Director.

Scratch getting shot while escaping over the wire. If she tried to leave during Harvest—Nephyrs would simply tear her apart.

*Anna's going to be just like them,* Magali thought, miserable. She looked again at their cold, expressionless faces, trying to divine some idea of what was happening to her sister.

Seeing them stare coldly back, their merciless faces projecting an utter lack of compassion, Magali realized something. *She's already one of them. Just doesn't wear the circuitry.*

As soon as she got close to the central strip, Magali recognized the tall, gangly form of the outed smuggler standing near the back corner of the formation, gloves on, a digging tool in one hand, a collection sack in the other. She went to join him.

Instantly upon seeing her, the smuggler stiffened.

"You look like you pissed off a Nephyr," Magali said, taking in his bruises as she stepped into line beside him. She glanced down, saw the shackles on his ankles. "They're letting you in on the Harvest?"

Joel gave her a long look. His face was bruised, with a dark spot forming against his jaw. One eye was completely swollen, and his body was hunched, like his stomach hurt him. "You've got a lot of nerve," he said finally.

"Should've taken my offer."

Joel glared, his entire body rigid, his every breath emanating fury. Finally, he said, "The only reason I'm not putting my fist through your face," he said, "is because my hand hurts." He showed her his fist, which was a swollen mass of blood and awkward angles. He dropped it suddenly. "And I couldn't give you the pummeling you deserve left-handed."

Magali felt her stomach turn at the brutality and she stumbled backwards a step. Because she could find nothing else to say, she managed, "That . . . looks painful."

"The Director crushed it in a door after she got tired of pulling out fingernails." Joel was glaring at her, his unwavering stare alive with accusation. He gave her a bitter grin. "Must have made your day to hear that, eh?"

Repulsed, Magali grimaced. "No, not at—" Then she realized what he was trying to say. Taken aback, she said, "I didn't turn you in."

"Sure you didn't." Joel snorted.

Magali's heart began to pound. "You actually think that I'd do something like that?"

He snorted. "Ah, so our conversation, you getting pissed, me getting nabbed—it was all a coincidence. That makes so much more sense now."

"I didn't do it!"

His blue-green eyes were hard. "Your little brat of a sister would have. In a heartbeat."

"Yeah, and I'm *nothing* like her." Magali spoke it with such vehemence that she felt the pressure in her lungs. "*Nothing.*"

Joel frowned at her. He looked like he wanted to say more, but then the Director climbed up onto the podium at the forefront of the formation and raised her voice. "Everyone here?"

The man in Coalition gray at her side checked his tally, then said, "Everyone is present except fourteen eggers with the Wide, Director."

"Good," the cyborg said. To the gathered eggers, she said, "Strip."

No one moved. Eggers glanced at each other, nervous.

"You heard me!" the Director snapped. "Last Harvest, we caught six eggers trying to smuggle nodules out in their underwear. So strip. Everything in a pile. If you thieves are going to steal Yolk, the only way you're gonna do it is by shoving nodules up your asses—which we'll be checking later. *Take your clothes off!*"

For a moment, Magali thought she had misheard the Director. She joined the other eggers in glancing back and forth, trying to discern if it was some kind of joke. When she realized the cyborg was serious, however, Magali had never been so humiliated and angry in her life. Around her, a couple of eggers had reluctantly begun to comply, but most stood around, giving each other nervous looks. Beside her, Joel had begun to remove his bright yellow prisoner suit and was glaring at the Director from under a frown.

Up on the podium, the Director scanned the reluctant crowd, then said, "Fine. My friends are going to start going down the lines. If any of you colonist fools aren't undressed in thirty seconds, I'm going to have the Nephyrs do it for you."

As the black-clad Nephyrs of the Forty-Third battle squadron moved into the formation, the rest of the eggers hastily complied. Magali followed suit, throwing her clothes in a pile at her feet, then snagging up her collection sack to cover her chest and groin, her face burning.

A blue-eyed Nephyr with the arrow-gripping fist of a colonel embedded in gold in the glittering skin above his elbow stopped in front of her. He searched her face, then his eyes lazily wandered down to pause on where her breasts were bunched up under the canvas, her arm holding them in place. The Nephyr looked back up at her, his glittering lips curled in a smile. Magali shuddered, clutching the sack tighter to her chest.

"She told you to undress, collie." There was cruel amusement in his eyes. He lifted his hand, reaching toward the canvas material.

Magali froze, seeing the intent on his glittering face. Coldness doused her soul. "My clothes are off," she said, trying not to sound desperate.

"I need to make sure now, don't I?" the Nephyr said, his glittering fingers hooking under the canvas covering her chest. "Take it off." He gave it a gentle, patronizing tug. "Or I will."

Magali knew she could lower the canvas or it would be ripped away. Reluctantly, she lowered it.

"Ah," the blue-eyed colonel said. The Nephyr stood there, soaking in her nakedness, as Magali's face burned with hatred and humiliation. She stared at her feet, horrified and afraid, feeling as if she had retreated into a tiny corner of her brain to escape the Nephyr's lustful stare.

"You know," the blue-eyed colonel said, as if they were friends at a bonfire, having a conversation over freshly killed starlope, "Harvest gets pretty stressful. You get back out, I bet a pretty thing like you'd love to celebrate tonight, wouldn't you?" He lifted his hand and began tracing down her shoulder with a glass-hard finger, toward her breast, leaving a wormy sickness in its path.

Magali squirmed out from under his inhuman touch, taking a step backwards, pulling her canvas back up.

The Nephyr smiled. He leaned closer, until his presence was giving her goosebumps. "Tell ya what, collie," he said softly, "once it's all over, I'll come looking for you. Save you the trouble of trying to find me." Then he cocked his head, a little smile on his face. "Unless, of course, you don't want me to wait."

Horrified, she realized he was going to rape her. Right there. In front of everyone.

At the lust in his eyes, Magali knew that Anna was right. Colonists weren't people to the Coalition. This Nephyr was going to do whatever he wanted to her in full view of the other eggers. And nobody was going to stop him.

The sick feeling welled up in her gut, until she was swallowing down bile. She squeezed her eyes shut, trembling.

"Hey, asshole," Joel said.

The Nephyr turned from her.

Joel motioned at the prisoner jumpsuit puddled around his legs. "Can't get it off with the shackles on, dipshit."

Magali shuddered in relief as the Nephyr colonel moved away from her and walked a circle around Joel, his gold-filigreed face twisted in a sneer at the smuggler's naked, bruised body. Joel endured the perusal, peering back with equal disdain.

As he walked, the black-clothed Nephyr said, "Nalle has something special planned for you tonight if you survive the Harvest, smuggler. Some interesting entertainment for the Forty-Third. It features you," he cocked his head with a sick little smile, then added, "and screaming."

"Lookin' forward to it." Joel spat at the Nephyr's boots.

The blue-eyed Nephyr chuckled as he made another pass, Magali completely forgotten. Finally, he said, "I can see why she finds you so amusing." He stopped and squatted beside Joel and, taking the chain between Joel's legs in either hand, he pulled.

The chain snapped as if it had been made of strands of hair.

Then, standing, the Nephyr shoved Joel hard enough to throw him into the eggers behind him, knocking them all down in a group.

From the podium, the Director said, "I put those chains on him for a reason, Colonel Steele."

The Nephyr named Steele snorted. "You've got a hundred and forty-five Nephyrs guarding the compound, Nalle. Your little plaything won't get far. And if he does . . . " The male Nephyr grinned. "I'd enjoy the opportunity to hunt him down." Then Nephyr Steele turned and strode further down the ranks without another word. Magali allowed herself to breathe again.

Gasping, Joel stumbled back into line. "Bitch," he muttered, following the retreating Nephyr with his gaze. There was a deep red handprint on his chest, already starting to bruise.

"Thanks," Magali whispered.

Joel glanced at her, and there was apology in his eyes, and anger, as if he somehow felt responsible for every awful misdeed ever committed by the male sex. After a moment, he made an embarrassed grunt, then bent to check the bandage over his thigh, his wounded leg obviously bothering him. She saw that the last nanostrip patch had run out and hadn't been replaced. Blood and greenish pus were oozing from around the depleted strip, now a bright pink instead of a neon green. Even from that distance, the wound smelled funny, like goat cheese.

*That's going to kill him if he doesn't get another nanostrip on it,* Magali thought.

"So," Magali said, avoiding his nakedness despite the fact he made no move to hide it. "They smash your hand in a door and then they let you out for the day? How's that work?"

Joel straightened from his wound. "Money."

"Enough money to buy themselves a new smuggler, in case this one escapes?"

For the first time, Magali saw the beginnings of a smile on Joel's lean face.

He gave her a considering look. Finally, he said, "See those space-ships over there?" He nodded at the six fancy Coalition transports.

Magali eyed the double-hulled beauties sitting on the other side of the razor wire. The whole town of Deaddrunk could pool their resources—money, guns, ships, land, houses—and still never be able to afford even one of those ships. They were a symbol of what Anna called the "Coaler Occupation." Disgusted, she said, "What about them?"

Joel made a dismissive gesture with his ruined hand. "On average, a standard sack can hold two hundred and fifty-eight Shrieker nodules. If they're properly distilled, each nodule can produce as much as fourteen grams of Yolk. You could buy a spaceship like that with about two hundred grams of Yolk on the free market, back in the Inner Bounds. Core planets see even less of it, so they pay a premium."

Magali forgot to breathe. "That's less than a sack."

Joel snorted. "Try fifteen nodules."

She stared at him.

"So," Joel said, hefting his burlap collection sack and prybar over his shoulder, "yeah, I get the day off."

Magali's eyes drifted back to the ships as she tried to imagine the sheer amount of wealth in the mines. She couldn't. She knew from one of Anna's tirades that the troop transports that the Nephyrs so casually flew around were roughly worth twenty million apiece, and the mounds had whole chambers *filled* with nodules, millions of them coating the floors, the hallways, the walls . . . and if just fifteen nodules were worth a ship . . . She swallowed, the Yolk drafts suddenly starting to make a lot more sense.

Forcing herself to stop trying to calculate how much money was in each individual full harvest sack, she glanced back at Joel and took in his cuts and bruises—brutal testimony that he didn't have long to live. "You coming back out at the end of the day?" she asked softly.

Joel gave her a long look. "What do you think?" Then he said nothing more, because the Nephyrs had finished stripping those too shy to do it themselves and the cyborg had taken center stage at the front of the gathering once more.

"All right, listen up," the Director said, cutting through the quiet sobbing of those forcibly removed from their clothes. She brushed a tadfly off of her glittering face and said, "Most of you have never done a Harvest before, so here's the drill. The Shriekers don't like seeing their precious little babies stolen out from under them, so don't let them see you do it. If they *do* see it, get your friends and run like hell, because they'll probably start up a Shriek. Aside from that, we're looking for the bright red nodules. The *red* ones. The black ones are either dead or duds. Questions so far?"

Beside Magali, Joel raised his hand. Impervious to the Director's scowl, the smuggler said, "You might want to tell them that the concentration of Yolk is much higher in the ones that have a purplish tinge."

"Shut up, Runaway."

Joel gave the Director an elegant, naked bow.

Without missing a beat, the Director said. "Everybody gets a collection sack. If you didn't bring one, raise your hand and we will provide one for you. Here's the deal: You fill up your sack until you can't get another nodule in, you get me? You come to the front gate and there's extra room in the top of your sack, one of my men is going to confiscate it and give you a new one to fill. So it's in your best interest to make sure it's full." She paused, frowning. "What do you want, Runaway?"

Joel lowered his hand. "Do you have any bright red beach balls?"

The Director stared at him for a moment, then shook herself and returned her attention to the eggers. "Each egger will be required to bring back one full sack from the mounds by the end of Harvest. The sacks are the same size for everybody, so no quibbling about that. If you *do* have issues with your sack, you can request a new one now."

Joel flicked a tadfly off of his bloody wrist, looking utterly unconcerned with the Director or the black row of Coalition Nephyrs surrounding the eggers. Loudly, as if they were in the midst of an utterly boring town hall meeting, he interrupted with, "It's really helpful to bring a few bright red beach balls along for a Harvest. Hell, anything red will work. Red attracts Shriekers during Harvest Day like gunfire attracts Nephyrs. Motherly instinct and all that. Get enough red in one corner of the mounds and they'll eventually congregate around it, leaving you free run of the rest of the hatching chambers."

Absolute silence followed his words.

The Director returned her attention to Joel again, and Magali could feel the pressure of her gaze like the titanium tracks of a tank. Despite herself, she eased herself away from the smuggler, who, for his part, seemed completely unaffected.

*Bored,* she thought, amazed.

"Ferris?" the Director said.

"Yes, Director?" said three of the gray-uniformed men wandering through the eggers, handing out collection sacks. All three stopped what they were doing and immediately turned to face her.

They're all *robots?* Magali thought, stunned. The only robots she had ever seen had been bulky, commercial-grade mining bots that spent as much time in the maintenance shed as they did hauling silver up and down the mineshaft. These machines had been so lifelike she hadn't even realized they weren't people. A new sense of unease began to creep along her spine. If the Coalition was so far advanced it had realistic AIs, how could the colonists—most of whom were still scrabbling in the dirt just for their very survival—even have a prayer of defeating them?

*Anna,* Magali thought, *wherever you are, I hope to God you know what you're doing.*

She got a mental image of a tiny grave dug out in the bog pits, hastily filled in with wet peat. Scrunching her eyes against the guilt, Magali told herself, *She can take care of herself. She hasn't needed me for years.*

But could Anna stand up to Nephyrs? To being helpless while glittering monsters—some of whom were likely as intelligent as Anna was—interrogated her? It would be the Shrieker mounds all over again . . .

*Not my problem,* Magali told herself.

Up on the podium, the Director was still holding Joel's gaze like a Coalition tank. To the robots, she said, "Those strawberry soda cartons are red, aren't they?"

"Yes, Director," the Ferrises said at precisely the same moment. It gave Magali chills. One of them had only been standing three feet away, and she hadn't even realized it wasn't human.

"The cartons would work," Joel agreed.

"If you're trying to earn your freedom or some bullshit . . . ," the Director began.

Joel snorted. "Freedom? No, I just want to make sure you have a good Yolk Harvest."

"Like hell," the Director said.

Joel just smiled. He was missing two front teeth.

After another long moment of bulldozing Joel with her gaze, the Nephyr took a deep breath and said, "Ferris, I want you to go collect some empty soda cartons once you finish passing out collection sacks." She then turned back to face the rest of the gathering.

"One more thing," Joel said.

"*What?*" the Director snapped, the circuitry around her eyes glittering in the blue-white LED floodlights.

"If you have any tear gas—"

"I am *not* giving you tear gas," the Director snarled.

Joel sighed. "Or hot peppers or cayenne powder, you can build a small fire in the central hatching chamber and throw it on the flames. It'll make your lungs burn, but it'll also make the Shriekers' eyes gum up so bad they won't be able to see you. Makes the Harvest go a lot faster if you're not dancing from cave to cave, trying to keep out of sight. Lot less people die, too."

The Director gave Joel another long look, then said, "Ferris, when you're done passing out sacks and have found those boxes, get the foremen each some cayenne powder and some campstoves." Then the Director gestured grandly at Joel. "Anything *else* you want to add, Runaway?"

"Nope, that's about it," Joel said.

The Nephyr grunted, then turned back to address the gathering. "Unless we have another resident expert in the thieving and smuggling of Coalition Shrieker nodules, perhaps I will be able to finish this speech before they all hatch."

Joel laughed loud enough to make the Director twitch, though there was no amusement in his face. The rest of the formation remained in utter, uncomfortable silence.

When no one else opened their mouths, the Director said, "All right. Foremen, get with the smuggler and coordinate your efforts. The rest of you, I want to make one thing clear: There is to be no fighting in the mounds. Anyone caught stealing another egger's sack will be shot. I am damn serious about this. Work together, keep it civil, and when Harvest is over, you'll get a week to relax. With that in mind—" The Camp Director pulled a clipboard out from under her arm and held it up. "We'll be keeping tally of Yolk extraction. The ten eggers that produce the most Yolk this Harvest will get to go home, their service complete. So, if any of you would like to take extra bags into the mines, you're free to do so."

Beside Magali, Joel stiffened. "There's no need for that," he said. "You're making enough off every sack to—"

"Shut up, Runaway," the Director said. "Ferris, he's done talking for now."

But the smuggler looked furious. "But we both know you're just going to—" Joel continued, until his words cut off abruptly. Instantly, the smuggler's body tightened and he let out a low groan as he doubled forward.

"What's wrong?" Magali asked, grabbing him to keep him from falling.

Joel grimaced and shook his head. In doing so, Magali got her first look at the small area of his skull against his neck that had been shorn, and the stitches that were still embedded in skin that was red and inflamed.

*They chipped him,* she thought, instantly repulsed. Even the mere *thought* of those wiry government monstrosities creeping along the spine of somebody she knew, penetrating his brain, sending and receiving signals as he went on oblivious, left her physically ill. She had to fight the urge to step into line somewhere else in formation, as if standing beside Joel too long would mean they'd chip her, too.

Joel straightened back up and gave the Director a black stare.

"Now," the Director said, as if Joel had ceased to exist, "Unless there are any questions, you're free to go to the mines."

A little boy raised his hand.

"What?" the Director asked.

"I'm little," the little boy said.

The Director gave him a blank stare. "So?"

"So what if I don't fill my sack?" he asked, hefting the huge thing the robots had given him. The thick, tamper-proof, knife-resistant canvas material was heavy enough to make his scrawny arms struggle to keep it off the ground, and the unfurled sack was obviously bigger than he was. *They can't plan to make the kids harvest, too,* Magali thought, appalled.

"Get someone else to help you," the Director said.

"My daddy got the Wide," the boy whimpered. "I'm all alone now." He looked all alone, too. The other eggers seemed to have their attention focused elsewhere, avoiding looking at him altogether. They obviously weren't going to help him.

"Get someone else to help you," the Director repeated. "There's plenty of nodules down there for everyone. Any egger who hasn't brought a full sack out of the mounds by the end of Harvest is going to get shot." She held the boy's gaze. "Even if you're a cute little kid."

The kid cringed, all but disappearing into the pile of canvas in his arms.

Magali felt a familiar twinge watching the little boy, but fought it down. She had to worry about herself now. She'd be lucky to get out of the mounds with one sack, let alone an extra for the kid. She supposed she should consider herself blessed she didn't have to fill Anna's as well. Though she was reasonably sure Anna would have helped, her seven-year-old body didn't have the weight necessary to pry the nodules from the floor.

Seeing the kid was finished talking, the Director mercilessly scanned the crowd. Raising her voice, the cyborg snapped, "Understand? *Everybody* fills their sack. Don't even *think* of coming out of there until you do. The Coalition isn't feeding and clothing you for free. Energy isn't cheap this far into the Outer Bounds. You people need to earn your keep."

Released from the Director's gaze, the little boy had slumped to the ground and was sitting on his naked butt, his little shoulders quaking.

"Greedy bitch," Joel muttered, under his breath. He was watching the whimpering little kid, anger contorting his face.

Instantly, the cyborg's head swiveled. "You say something there, Runaway?"

*There's no way she heard you,* Magali thought, panicking. *Just lie.*

"I said 'Greedy bitch,'" Joel said, loud enough for the entire camp to hear.

"They're going to *kill* you," Magali hissed, grabbing his arm. "Please, don't."

Joel looked her straight in the eye and softly said, "Do I look like I give a damn at this point?"

Magali released him suddenly. In that moment, watching the disinterested lifelessness on his face, Magali recognized Joel's boredom for what it was. He had given up.

*He no longer cares,* she thought, horrified. *He's gonna provoke them until they kill him.*

Joel flicked another tadfly off of his blood-crusted hand and returned his attention to the Director. Loud enough for the women in the guardtowers to hear, he said, "That kid goes in there and picks you one nodule—just one—and you'll have enough to pay for his meals—as well as his house, his kids, and his clothes—until he's ninety-five. So, yeah. You're a goddamn greedy bitch and the rest is bullshit."

The Director smiled at him, and Magali forgot to breathe under the cruelty she saw there. "Ferris," the Director said, "he's already confessed to his crimes, hasn't he?"

"Yes, Director," they said, together.

"You *beat* them out of me, more like," Joel scoffed, still looking utterly bored. "I didn't do half those things you accused me of, and you know it."

The Director smiled at the smuggler, and again Magali felt the urge to step away from him. "Ferris, does a man need to be able to speak in order to harvest Shrieker nodules?"

That made Joel stiffen. His entire wiry body seemed to go statuesque, like it was made of glass. His bored façade cracked, and Magali could see the fear in him.

"No, Director," the robots said, as one. They continued, "There are three mute eggers in formation as we speak, Director."

*Oh no,* Magali thought, glancing at the stitches in Joel's scalp. Anna had told her of the horrible things that the Coalition could do to citizens with chips.

The smuggler's entire body remained rigid under the Nephyr's self-satisfied smile.

"Aside from Runaway, here, all you eggers are dismissed to start the Harvest." Leisurely, the cyborg left her place in front of the gathering and walked toward them. Eggers hastily got out of the way, clearing a path until the Director was standing in front of Joel. This close, Magali fought the urge to back away. The Director was taller than she appeared at a distance, at least six feet, though even she had to cock her head to see into the smuggler's face.

Seeing them square off, Magali knew she should leave, that she should get in line with the other eggers shuffling toward the mines, but she couldn't tear her eyes from Joel's skinny form, standing tall despite the bruises.

"Tell you what, Runaway," the Director said as the eggers quickly hurried around them to get to the mines. The cyborg reached out and settled her glittering hand upon his skinny arm. Magali saw Joel flinch, his eyes dropping warily to where her inhuman fingers touched him. "I'll let you beg for your voice, Joel. If you're convincing enough, I'll let you keep it."

Joel reddened and looked away.

"Not going to beg?" the Director asked, after a moment. She sounded delighted.

"Please," Joel whispered. He flinched as he said it, as if the words had stung his soul. Immediately, his lips tightened with anger.

"Please, what?" the Director mocked. "And get on your knees. I'm finding it irritating looking up at you."

Joel didn't move.

The Director tisked. "Ferris?"

"Yes, Director," the robots asked.

The Director waited, one eyebrow raised, watching Joel with amusement in her eyes.

Joel gave the Director a look of such hatred it made Magali's disgust for Colonel Steele pale in comparison. Slowly, as if on stilts, Joel got to his knees. Magali saw the shame in his face and felt rising fury at the Director for what she was doing.

On his knees, Joel remained silent.

"You may proceed to beg," the Director reminded him.

For almost a minute, the parade ground was silent except for the distant shuffling of naked eggers and the pounding of Magali's heart.

Finally, in a voice barely loud enough to be heard, Joel said, "Please don't take my voice." He refused to look up, his good fist clenched at his side, the knuckles white, the arm shaking.

"But you've already confessed," the Director said, conversationally. "You're slated for execution tonight, at the hands of my friends. The only reason I can see to spare that annoying tongue of yours is if you want to entertain us with your screams. Is that what you want, Joel? To entertain us?"

Joel looked at his maimed hand. He took a breath. Held it. For a long time, the smuggler didn't speak.

*Say it,* Magali willed him, anguished. *You know she'll do it if you don't. You know she will.*

After several more long moments, the smuggler finally looked up and said, "We both know you're going to do it anyway, so just hurry up and get it over with, if that's what your infected pustule of a soul desires."

The Director laughed. "Get up."

Joel stood up. The bored expression was back.

Stepping close, the Director said, "I hear another noise out of you before the Harvest is over and I'm going to have Ferris mute you. Permanently."

Red-faced, the smuggler looked away.

The Director grabbed his chin and forced it back around to face her. "Understand?" she said. The Nephyr's face glittered in the camp floodlights, her lips twisted in a cruel smirk. "Not a sound." When Joel didn't respond, she tapped his cheek with her gold-filigreed index finger and tisked. "Acknowledge me, Runaway, or I might change my mind."

Spite oozing from his gaze, Joel nodded.

The Director smiled, malice lining her face. "Good." Still holding his arm, she reached for Joel's wounded hand.

The smuggler jerked it out of reach and stepped back, the broken ends of his metal shackles jingling against the dusty ground. His eyes were riveted on the Director, the bored façade once more stripped away, leaving raw fear in its place.

The Nephyr tisked. "I never said you could step out of formation, Runaway." She grabbed him and jerked him back into line. Then, even as Joel struggled to resist, the cyborg easily pried his wounded hand from behind his back and took it in her own. Instantly, Joel went utterly still.

For a moment, the Director held the smuggler's maimed hand gently, like she were cradling something fragile. Joel's eyes widened and his nostrils flared as he panted through his nose, but he kept his teeth tightly gritted.

*Stop it,* Magali thought, her heart beginning to pound in her ears. *She can't do this.*

"You're so quiet," the Director said, ignoring everything but Joel. "That's so unlike you." She tenderly stroked his hand with her circuit-covered fingertips. Finally, she smiled, and it left a cold spot against Magali's spine. "Infected pustule, eh, Runaway? Is that what you think?"

Joel shook his head, eyes glistening in the floodlights. He was breathing too fast, like a terrified horse.

Magali opened her mouth to say something, but fear choked it off. Without Anna, she was just another frightened egger. What could she do against a Nephyr?

"I asked you a question, Runaway."

Joel clamped his eyes shut.

A moment later, the Director chuckled. Then she squeezed. Standing as close as she was, Magali heard his delicate finger bones crack and pop. Even though he never opened his mouth, Magali heard Joel scream as he fought the Nephyr's grip. He crumpled over the Director's arm, hitting it, sobbing through his nose, eyes squeezed shut against tears.

The Nephyr continued to hold him, easily supporting his weight with one arm. "Did you say something, Runaway?" Even as the smuggler sobbed into her arm, the Nephyr turned to the nearest robot. "Ferris? Did Runaway Joel just break our verbal contract?"

"He made a noise, Director," the robot said.

Hearing this, the Director patronizingly shook her head at Joel. "And I thought we had an understanding." She took her victim by the chin again and lifted his face to hers. "Now I'll just have to get Ferris to mute you." Her inhuman fingers tightened on his jaw, until the skin under his three-day-old beard was white, and she smiled again as Joel whimpered. "Or, on second thought, maybe I'll just do it myself."

Magali couldn't take it anymore. Even without Anna to help her, Magali knew she had to do something. More loudly than she intended, she said, "What you're doing is illegal."

The Director turned to give Magali a puzzled smile—the look of a zookeeper who suddenly realized one of her chimps had spoken to her. "What?"

"I'll refer you to Section Fifteen of the Mandatory Lifeline Act," Magali said, surprised that the words were flowing out of her, feeling almost as if she were hearing them from a distance. "There are three paragraphs in there that should interest you. Each one refers to the penalties a government official can face if they are found to be abusing their power over the citizenry using a government lifeline."

The Director's smile cracked. "Who are you?"

"Magali Landborn," Magali said, spurred on by the whimpering creature clinging to the Director's arm. "My sister wasn't the only one who read the Consolidated Galactic Encyclopedia."

The glittering skin around the Director's mouth paled. The cyborg gave Joel a nervous look, then released the man's chin as if he had caught fire.

*Anna scared her,* Magali thought, stunned.

At the Director's widening eyes, she added, "You should really let him go." She gave her best imitation of Anna's psychopathic stare.

The Nephyr flinched under the assault, and for a moment looked like a starlope caught on a landing pad.

*Scratch that,* Magali thought. *Anna scared the* shit *out of her.*

Then, *But I'm not Anna.*

In that instant, as quickly as the Director's fear had come, it was gone. "Wait." The Director snorted, and there was a new, cruel confidence to her voice. "The Lifeline Act. He forfeited those rights when he tore out his own lifeline twenty years ago." She glanced back at the whimpering smuggler, a thin smile on her lips. "Didn't you, Joel?"

Magali's mind screamed at her to run into the mines and hope the Nephyr forgot about her. Instead, loud enough for even the retreating eggers to hear, she said, "I promise you you're going to find out, if you continue to break the law."

All around them, glittering faces jerked to look at them.

The Director's smile faded and, for a long time, her sharp brown eyes merely watched Magali.

Under the Nephyrs' gazes, Magali felt like a moth under a magnifying glass, the tip of a pin poised to skewer her abdomen. She tried desperately to keep her terror in check.

The cyborg's gaze hardened. "You're shaking, girl."

*Oh no,* Magali thought, her heart thundering in painful arcs through her chest under the Director's gaze. She squeezed her hands into fists, willing her knees to stop trembling. Anna would have helped her now, but Anna wasn't there. Before she could regain control over her own terror, Magali dropped her eyes.

The Director smiled, and there was a viciousness there that made Magali cringe. "Not so confident without your little sister, are you, brat?" the Director said. Then she cocked her head, as if coming to a sudden, pleasant realization. "Landborn, eh? That would make you the girlfriend. You like fucking him so much . . . perhaps you'd like to join him?" The cyborg returned her attention to Joel, who still clung to her arm, sobbing. She regarded his hunched and broken form with distant curiosity.

"What do you say, Joel? Should she share your fate on the rack tonight? Seems a fitting end to a couple of collie lovebirds."

Hunched over the arm that held him, Joel said nothing, struggling to keep his sobs under control. The entire camp seemed to hold its breath.

Into the silence, one of the robots said, "I'm sorry, Director, did you say you wanted me to mute him?" His voice was pleasant. Utterly emotionless. *Like he's asking if she wants a damn pizza.*

Watching Joel whimper, the Director's face stretched in a smile. "Sounds like an excellent idea, Ferris." She gave Magali an amused look. "Unfortunately, I didn't find his begging very convincing."

"No!" Magali cried. She lurched forward reflexively, but Joel had already gone board-stiff, his face going slack. Magali's hand tightened on her prybar and a sick feeling welled up in her gut.

Still holding the smuggler by his wounded hand, the Director leaned in until her head was almost touching his. Near his tear-stained face, she whispered, "Let's see you be a smartass now, Joel." Then she released him, and he crumpled in a heap on the dusty ground.

Magali tore her eyes from Joel, who had curled into a fetal position, his sobs coming out as uncoordinated rasps of air, and focused on the Director, who stood over him with a pleased expression.

The Director noticed Magali's horrified look and smirked. "Your little sister really was the brains of the operation, wasn't she? The Lifeline Act . . . Are you actually stupid enough to think you could bluff me? I should take your tongue just for the insult."

And Magali knew she would.

The Director took a step toward her. Magali stumbled backwards, terror clawing at her lungs. A Nephyr casually shoved her back onto the line—right into the Director's grasp. The Director grabbed her and, as if she were a doting grandparent, casually buttoned the top clasp of her studded egger's glove. Magali froze, terrified of looking down lest she lose sight of the monster in front of her. This close, the Nephyr's inhuman body seemed to pulse with a cold, powerful energy that sucked the warmth right out of her skin.

Once the Director had finished buttoning her glove, she patted Magali on the shoulder with a painfully heavy hand. Leaning close, the Director said, "I'll only give you one warning." Her brown eyes held icy promise. "You may have played in the majors for a while, by proxy, but your time in the sun's over, kid. Your sister isn't ever coming back, and you ain't got the brains to fend for yourself. Not around Nephyrs. You open your mouth again and you'll end up sharing space with Joel tonight."

The Director gave her another good-natured pat on the shoulder, then spun and returned to the podium, leaving Magali her tongue and Joel curled in the dust. "All right, folks, we've wasted enough time with smugglers and their whores. Form a channel from the exit to the ships. The first ones should start filtering out in a few hours. You have my permission to entertain yourselves with any collie who comes out without a full sack. Some of them are going to try to cheat and use rocks, so when we dump them out, I want you all ready to catch the ones who try to bolt . . . " Her voice grew less distinct as the Director joined the group of Nephyrs, still issuing instructions.

Magali glanced down at Joel and lowered herself to the ground beside him.

The smuggler's eyes were squeezed shut and he was hunched over on his knees in the dust. His good hand cradled the one the Director had crushed. Tears wet his cheeks, dripping onto the depleted nanostrips on his thigh. His uniform and his collection gear lay scattered and forgotten on the ground beneath him.

Anna would have been able to tell her what bones the Director had broken, what tendons had been damaged, and approximately how much force the Director had put into her grip. Her sister would have been able to look at the pain in the man's eyes and talk about what areas of the brain he'd just lost as if he were a broken toaster. She would have had no qualms about leaving him there, sobbing quietly on the ground to be shot by the soldiers, so that they could begin the scramble to fill their sacks in the mounds.

But Magali wasn't Anna. Agonized, Magali reached out and touched the smuggler's shoulder.

Joel opened his eyes and gave her a look of such gratitude that it brought tears to Magali's eyes.

"I'm so sorry," Magali whispered.

Joel squeezed his eyes shut. Tears traced down his bruised cheeks. He sucked in a huge breath and let it out in what should have been a sob. The ragged wheeze that came out instead left Magali aching for him.

"I'm so sorry," she said again. She felt tears burning her own eyes and knelt beside him, choking on the grief building in her chest. She reached forth to gather up his sack and his prybar, then tentatively took his good hand to help him to his feet. "Can you stand?"

He gave her a blank look.

*He can't even understand me,* Magali thought, horrified. She'd heard of head wounds that destroyed everything—wiping every scrap of language from the victim's brain. "Come on," she whispered through tears. "I'll help you." She made a show of leaning back to give him support in order to stand.

Joel stayed where he was, refusing to look at her.

Magali gave a nervous glance at the last stragglers shuffling into the mines. She and the smuggler were the only humans left on the parade deck. Nearby, she could feel Nephyrs watching them.

"We need to get going," she whispered. "The others are leaving. They'll shoot us if we aren't in the mines by the time they lock the doors."

For a moment, it looked as if Joel would ignore her and stay there until the Nephyrs came to kill him.

"Please," Magali whispered. She gave his good hand a gentle squeeze, trying to dispel some of the despair she saw in him.

Joel's eyes flickered to their hands, then back to her face.

Magali quickly gathered up his equipment and stuffed it under one arm. Then, to her relief, he allowed her to pull him to his feet and lead him between the Nephyrs guarding the entrance into the mines.

Magali stepped into the dim orange darkness of the Shrieker mounds, gently pulling the smuggler behind her. As soon as she was inside the first cavern, she stopped dead in her tracks, staring into the darkness with instinctive panic.

The Director, expecting Shriekers to be more volatile, had dimmed the lights. Only one in ten of the small LEDs set in the ceiling were giving off any illumination at all. Magali could barely see her own hand in front of her face.

The other eggers were milling uncomfortably, a tight knot at the very edge of the cavern. Childlike sounds of terror echoed against the slimy walls. Everywhere, people were crying. No one was making any move to enter the mines.

The lights flickered.

Spending the last months in the Shrieker mines, Magali had become used to the flickering lights. The solar generators often missed a beat whenever the camp power grid was being shifted from one battery system to another, or from charging to discharging.

Yet, seeing them flicker *now*, while she was naked and nervous, when the Shriekers were down there, guarding their hatchlings, when the Nephyrs were outside, waiting to tear her apart, the spike of terror that clawed its way up from her stomach left her heart thudding against her lungs. She backed up a pace.

Joel gave her hand a squeeze.

Startled, Magali looked up. She had been so unnerved that she'd forgotten he was with her.

Joel gave her a weak smile.

"Thanks," Magali whispered.

The smuggler gave her a blank look, and she cursed herself. *He can't understand you, Mag, and you have to rub it in.* Guiltily, she squeezed his hand back, and Joel gave her a nervous smile.

"Good luck, folks," one of the human guards called from the doorway behind them. However much Magali had hated to see him at the gates before, the man's face was familiar, and unlike the Nephyrs, he sounded almost apologetic. There was a definite look of anguish in his eyes before he cleared his throat and tore his eyes from the frightened mass of eggers, focusing it on the wall, instead. "Doors will open again in four hours." He stepped back, and from outside, she heard the metallic screech of the main door swinging shut.

*They're going to lock us in here,* she thought, terrified.

Suddenly, the smuggler's hand in hers was the only thing keeping her from turning and rushing toward the Nephyrs silhouetted in the exit. Several other eggers were not so anchored, however, and ended up getting brutally shoved back into the mines. One man's chest collapsed under the pressure of the Nephyr's push, and he lay there in the slime inside the door, writhing and choking, unable to breathe.

He turned blue and died. A young girl—probably a daughter— dropped to her knees in the slime beside him and began to cry.

Then the heavy, bombproof doors slammed shut. The resounding boom made Magali jerk out of reflex.

*Harvest time,* she thought, a coldness pooling in her gut.

She had a full ten seconds to consider that before several eggers in the dim huddles near the front of the group screamed.

"Everyone listen up!" a woman from up ahead suddenly shouted. It was the voice of someone used to command, and Magali didn't recognize it. Had the Nephyrs followed them in there? "All you collie bastards are going to *listen* if you wanna live through the next ten seconds, you get me?"

Beside her, Joel tensed.

From somewhere close, Magali heard the heat-crackle of an energy weapon. Bits of the roof collapsed. More people began to scream.

Above the din, the woman shouted, "And yes, I've got a gun."

# CHAPTER 24

# A Dangerous Duo

"HUH. THEY'RE ALL DEAD." ANNA TAPPED A GLASS-COVERED BODY bearing the strange forehead node, frowning at the odd titanium lump.

"It would appear that way, Anna," Doberman said, glancing at the door. "You have ten minutes and fifty-three seconds until the morning technician arrives."

"I can count, thank you," Anna said. She moved to another case, checked the history on the chart, then moved on to the vacuum-sealed tube. They had all died within forty-three hours of the implant. Most within thirteen.

"It doesn't look like this is operator technology," Anna mused, tracing the contours of the node in her mind. "There's no hookup."

"Interesting," Doberman said, in a way that suggested he really was interested. It was one advantage to having a robot as a companion. He wasn't sarcastic, and he understood about fifty percent of the stuff Anna said. That made him forty-nine percent more interesting than anyone she had ever met.

Anna moved on to the records panel. The screen was locked and dark. "Open it," she said, stepping back.

The robot obediently opened the panel with the Director's password. It was another advantage to having a robot as a companion, Anna mused. It didn't get all pissy when she told it what to do.

As soon as the screen was up, Dobie stepped aside, allowing Anna access. "Eight minutes fourteen seconds," he said, as she moved to the controls.

"I don't need a play-by-play. Just tell me when we've got thirty seconds left."

"As you wish, Anna," Doberman said, then went silent.

Scanning the reports, Anna was initially confused as to what she was seeing. Quickly, however, she began to get interested. *". . . allow a concentrated blast of psi force to reproduce the same effects as a specimen of Shrieker Fortuna . . . "*

"Thirty seconds," Doberman said, looking utterly calm. A human in his situation probably would have been sweating and dancing around like an idiot, whimpering that they were going to get caught and the Coalition was going to find them and kill them. For once, Anna was grateful for the lack of theatrics.

"Download it," Anna said, nodding.

Doberman moved forward and placed a hand over the dataport for a heartbeat before retracting it, and saying, "Twenty seconds."

"Erase the rest," Anna said.

A moment later, Doberman nodded. "Fifteen seconds."

"Grab that," Anna said, pointing to an unfinished node in the box on top of the workbench.

"It's unfinished," Doberman said, grabbing it.

"Yeah, whatever," Anna said. "Let's go."

They passed the technician in the hall on their way to the next corridor, twenty seconds late for his shift. The chump technician even stopped to ruffle Anna's hair and speak baby-speak to her about what she was going to do as a Nephyr.

"Kill people who deserve it," Anna said.

"Oh?" he asked, a stupid, patronizing smile on his face. "Like who?"

"I dunno," Anna said. "Scientists, probably."

The technician laughed. "Scientists? What kind of scientists?"

"The kind who keep killing their test subjects because they're too stupid to realize what they're doing wrong."

The technician left after that.

"You know," Doberman said, as they walked away together, "it would have been easier for us if you had not done that."

Anna shrugged.

Forty-six seconds later, the base alarm began going off. Anna never flinched, and she was impressed when Doberman continued to stroll forward as if nothing was happening. Another benefit to working with a robot—they didn't panic like imbeciles and make everything worse.

Hearing footsteps behind her, Anna paused.

The technician came panting up behind her. "You! Kid. What's your name?"

Doberman whirled and punched his face in.

Not just punched him in the face. Punched it *in*. Anna was impressed.

"Nice job," she said, as the technician crumpled. Doberman was already moving again. "You ever kill anyone before, Tinman?"

"Just a few dozen eggers," Doberman said, calmly leading them out of the hall and into another corridor.

"Really? What did you do with the bodies?"

"Buried them in the peat bogs."

"Cool. What'd they do?"

"They drank too much strawberry soda and ate too many double-patty hamburgers with extra mustard."

Anna frowned. "Was that sarcasm?"

"No. It was right after a Harvest. Director didn't need all the mouths to feed, since they wouldn't need them for another three years. It was mostly the ones displaying symptoms of Wide, though I killed a few of the children, too. Oh, and anyone who didn't show up with a full sack when Harvest day was over, it was my job to execute them before they . . . "

Doberman went silent as a man approached them down the hall. "Unit Ferris," the man said, "there's been a breach in this sector. I will take your charge to the spaceport. Go secure the south side of Seven C."

"Of course, Unit Gryphon," Doberman said. "Give me your arm for the transfer." He began unlocking the cuff holding Anna to him. Anna felt a brief stab of fear. Would Doberman betray her? She had tried to kill him twice already today. *Maybe I shouldn't have done that,* she thought, biting her lip. If he handed her over now, she could sing all she wanted to about sentient robots and no one would care, let alone try to find him.

The other robot held out its arm for the transfer, and Doberman grabbed it and twisted it off.

Then, as the Gryphon turned to look at the damage, Doberman put his fist through the side of the robot usually protected by the arm and ripped out the brainbox. As Anna watched in awe, he crushed the brain between nothing but his thumb and pinkie.

Thumb and pinkie? "Cool!" Anna cried, delighted. "I didn't know you were such a showman, Dobie."

"Next time," Doberman said, dropping the wreckage, "you are going to keep your mouth shut, Landborn." The robot calmly locked the cuff back around his wrist and began to run at precisely the right speed for Anna to keep up.

"Maybe," Anna agreed. "Where's the node?"

"My back pocket," Doberman said.

"Just don't sit on it," Anna said.

"Agreed," the robot said. "Can you run any faster? They're going to be sealing down this section of the base in eighteen seconds."

"No," Anna panted.

Without a word, Doberman picked her up and broke into an inhuman sprint that made her actually feel Gs.

They made it outside the sector in fourteen seconds. Doberman set her down as the doors slammed shut and locked behind them, then resumed walking again as if nothing had even happened.

The robot wasn't even breathing hard.

*He's good at this,* Anna mused, walking placidly beside him. Up ahead, a group of coalers in riot gear rounded a corner and ran toward them. She stared sullenly at the floor as they approached, back to playing the part of an unwilling Nephyr draftee.

Two of the coalers stopped. With a surge of disgust, Anna realized that they both had the glittering skin of Nephyrs underneath the assault equipment. "Unit Ferris, where are you going with that recruit?"

"Eoirus, sir," Doberman replied.

"Why are you in Sector Six? The spaceport is in Sector Three."

"I tricked the stupid thing into taking off the cuffs," Anna sneered, jerking backwards and twisting her wrist in a mini-tantrum as Doberman remained utterly immobile above her. She kicked Doberman in the leg. Then, when he didn't budge, she kicked him again, harder. "Stupid robot. Let me *go!* I want to go home. I don't *want* to be a Nephyr." She stomped her heel on the toe of his boot.

The robot looked down at her. "Anna Landborn, I have been granted full authority by Director Yura Nalle of Yolk Facility 4, North Tear, to remove any body parts impeding your progress to the Academy. Cease kicking me."

*Perfect,* Anna thought, delighted. She was even more pleased that she absolutely believed he would rip off her leg in the name of their cover, should she continue to kick him.

Anna kicked him again. Then, glaring up at the robot, Anna ended her struggles with a disgusted sigh. "Almost got out, too, before the stupid heap tracked me down."

"You got a *Ferris* to release your cuffs?" The glittering cyborg stared at her in disbelief behind his black-tinted riot-suppressing mask. "How?"

"I quoted Article Twelve-H of the Unwilling Draftee Act," Anna snapped indignantly. "'A draftee has the right to defecate in private, as long as the draftee makes a recorded oath upon his or her honor not to flee the premises on pain of a ten-year enlistment extension.'"

The man laughed and winced. "Sucks for you, kid." Then the Nephyr motioned to his companion and they hurried after their friends into Sector Seven.

"Article Twelve-H?" Doberman asked, once the coalers were out of earshot. "I was only aware of G. When was H added?"

"Approximately thirty seconds ago," Anna said.

"Ah," Doberman said. He started walking again, dragging Anna quite realistically for several yards before she relented and followed along beside him.

"So when are you going to take this thing off?" Anna asked, jiggling the handcuffs.

"Maybe in a year or two," Doberman said.

Anna winced. "You can't be serious."

"You laced my hamburger with EMP grenades."

"Oh." Anna licked her lips. "Maybe I'll stop that."

"It's in both of our interests that you do."

Anna scoffed. "You didn't put a bomb in my brain."

Doberman gave her a flat look. "I assure you I did. Two of them."

"Whatever. You've appealed to my logical side. I'll stop trying to kill you now, robot."

Doberman looked down at her. "You thought I was going to hand you over to the Gryphon, didn't you?"

Anna froze, and Doberman kept walking, dragging her for real this time.

"Because," Doberman said, once Anna finally, grudgingly, began walking beside him again, "your biorhythms spiked quite violently there for a moment."

"I was trying to keep it realistic," Anna muttered. "Wasn't sure you could destroy him."

"I could have simply told him to leave," Doberman said. "I wanted to test a theory." He glanced down at her. "And your capillaries are expanding. You're lying. You thought I was going to give you to the Gryphon."

"You had no reason not to," Anna muttered. "If you weren't so stupid, you would've realized you could've gotten rid of me back there."

The robot glanced down at her again. "Have you ever had a dog, Anna?"

"If you're going to compare yourself to a dog, spare me," Anna said. "You're not a dog."

"Humor me."

"Yes, I know what a damn dog is like," Anna said. "Willing, obedient, happy to please. Loyal. Trustworthy. Wouldn't eat your corpse even if it was starving. You're not a dog."

"What kind of dog was it?" Doberman asked.

"It was a Doberman. And it wasn't my dog, it was my mom's dog. They got trapped in the silver mine together. Still had water and air. Starved to death."

"The dog didn't like you, did it?"

"No, it was a stupid piece of shit that only liked my m—" Anna choked, realizing the direction of his conversation. "You tricky sonofabitch!" she cried. "You were updating your profile, weren't you?!"

"This makes much more sense now. Thank you, Anna." The smugness in the robot's voice oozed across the tiles around them.

Anna narrowed her eyes. "I hate dogs."

"But you sleep better around them."

"I never *had* a dog, you shit," Anna snapped. "And my mom's dog hated my guts. Tried to bite me every chance it got." She was angry now. She knew the robot was only adding more facets to his profile, but she didn't care. "Mom wouldn't get me a dog because she caught me cutting open her cat in the backyard. That's what I think about pets. Great laboratory experiments."

Doberman stopped and looked down at her. "I'm not going to bite you, Anna."

Anna snorted and looked away. "You're just a stupid robot."

"I'm *your* stupid robot," Doberman said. "And I'm not going to bite you."

He seemed to be waiting for something—confirmation that she agreed he wasn't going to bite her. Anna knew it would be an excellent time to tell him to prove it, and to use his redirected processing pathways to slip a bomb into *his* brain. But, instead, she heard herself say, "Okay, Dobie." Like a little girl. Like a goddamn, crying little girl.

Anna swiped her eyes with her sleeve and said, "Walk. Before I figure out how I'm going to use your newfound sentimental side to my advantage."

"Ditto, Landborn."

# CHAPTER 25

# A Hero's Welcome

TATIANA WAS GREETED AS A HERO. HER ENTIRE POD CAME OUT for the celebration. Even though she had always been relatively reclusive, coming out of her barracks room only for formations or mandatory group P.E., everyone screamed and chanted her name as she took the podium behind the two Bouncer captains who had rescued her.

Tatiana viewed the crowd through eyes blurred with tears. Her injuries had been given immediate care by the finest Coalition doctors—a team of five assigned to the Director himself. They'd replaced the shoddy colonial cast and splint with titanium pins. They had painstakingly stabilized her injured node. They had boosted her immune system with another load of operator nanobots . . .

And they'd also given her a brand new lifeline.

Now, standing at a podium in front of over a thousand people, Tatiana was expected to tell them how happy she was that they had rescued her.

Staring out at their expectant faces, all Tatiana could think was that Milar was dead.

She hadn't meant for it to end that way. She hadn't *wanted* it to end that way.

The cheers slowly died away as the crowd waited for her to speak.

"I'm so grateful—" Tatiana's voice broke and she moved away from the podium to steady herself. *You have to do this. If you don't, you're going to look like a sympathizer.*

The crowd expected trauma. They expected tears, rage, ranting, condemnation for the colonists. They expected gratitude and open arms.

One of the Bouncer captains receiving medals with her took the podium beside her. As she gathered herself, he softly said, "Give her a minute, folks. She had a rough week."

Tatiana nodded her gratitude at the man, then took several deep breaths.

*You have to do this. You are a Coalition operator. Milar kidnapped you. He deserved to die.*

But she choked on a sob, even as she thought it. *Just say it,* she thought. *You've already sung his evils to investigators. It's not like you're going to sully his memory any more than you already have. Besides, it's what he wanted you to do.*

She forced her trembling lips into a smile and grasped the metal edges of the podium once more. Waves of silent faces watched her, many wearing the standard protective, waterproof tube caps covering the lumps of nodes. It was the nodes that caught Tatiana's attention and gave her a new direction for her speech.

"I guess I learned a valuable lesson from all this," she said, remembering her last hours with Milar. "The lesson was this: Regardless of whatever you think you're up against, you can always be surprised. The whole ball game can change in an instant, and if you're not prepared to meet those new circumstances head on, you can find yourself in a whole world of hurt really, really fast." She thought of Milar, and how much it had hurt to see all that blood, how badly she had wanted to see him live when he had stopped breathing in her lap. Then she thought of how badly she had screwed up and how it was her fault he was resting in a coffin somewhere in an unmarked prisoner graveyard.

She had been cleared by the investigation. Fully and completely cleared. Psych had no idea what she had done. Everything had been fully leveled on the dead colonist's shoulders. All Tatiana had to do was pull through this speech, accept her three new medals, and go back to her room to cry.

*You can do this,* she thought. *Just finish your speech and everything is back to the way it was.*

"I want to thank Captain Hawthorne and Captain Williams, here," she said, nodding at the two Bouncer captains on the platform with her. "Before they showed up, I was in despair. I was alone and scared and facing a situation I wasn't trained to handle. It's given me a lot more respect for Nephyrs and the ground troops. You guys have the hardest job there is."

A cheer went up from those sections of the crowd.

Tatiana took a deep breath and bit her lip as her vision began to blur again. "Before this, I was always safe in the belly of a soldier. Never really had to deal with anything head-on. I was sheltered, cocooned, never had to look in the eyes of the people I was fighting. Never had to experience their hatred—" She choked and looked away again. "Thank you," she said, meeting the Bouncer captains' eyes. "I'm so proud to be part of this team."

The crowd cheered. Tatiana left the podium, accepted her commendations, watched as the Bouncer captains accepted theirs. She was waiting to exit the stage in a daze, thinking the ceremony complete, when the Master of Ceremonies returned to the podium and said, "Now, my brave men and women, let's hear a final round of applause for—"

A tall, broad-shouldered Nephyr wearing the badge of a colonel strode onto the stage and whispered into his ear, cutting him off.

The Master of Ceremonies slapped a palm over the microphone and glanced over his shoulder at Tatiana, then shook his head.

The Nephyr laughed loudly. "Well, we're doing it anyway." He turned on heel and departed.

*What was that about?* Tatiana wondered, watching him glitter in the floodlights as he strode away.

She didn't have to wait long to find out. The Master of Ceremonies cursed, then, clearing his throat, he lifted his hand from the mic and said, "Before I dismiss you, folks, the Nephyrs have a special treat for you today. The very same man who captured our Captain Eyre, here, is here with us tonight. Bring him out, if you will."

Tatiana's face went slack when two tall Nephyrs, a man and a woman, dragged a struggling, dragon-covered captive out into the light of the stage. Over his chest, obscuring the head of the red dragon, he had a big green strip of nanotape.

Milar met her eyes as they dragged him out and immediately went stiff.

*Oh my God,* was all Tatiana could think.

"Captain?" the Master of Ceremonies said to her as he gestured at Milar. "The Nephyrs believe you have something you'd like to say to the colonist scumbag before they take him for further questioning."

The world narrowed to just the two of them. Tatiana couldn't hear anything but the beating of her own heart, couldn't see anything but Milar's face. It was uncertain, void of rage. Scared.

*I'm so sorry,* Tatiana thought. It was all she *could* think.

"Captain?" the Master of Ceremonies asked, giving the two glittering warriors a nervous look.

When Tatiana didn't answer, the female Nephyr said, "Let's put it this way, honey—how do you want us to kill him, Captain?"

"Right now?" Tatiana whispered, unable to tear her eyes from Milar's face.

The female Nephyr laughed. "Oh no. We're going to take him back to our compound and question him first."

"And we're going to be very thorough, too, aren't we Miles?" The male Nephyr holding Milar grabbed him by the hair and jerked his head up until his Adam's apple was showing. "Aren't we? We're going to be *very* thorough." He released Milar, laughing, and punched him hard in the ribs.

Tatiana winced as Milar doubled over in their grip, gasping. He was physically bigger than either Nephyr, but the cyborgs were heavier, and they held him as easily as if he were a child.

*You didn't shoot him,* Tatiana's mind ranted at her. *You didn't shoot him, and now they're going to make him suffer.*

"So, Captain, do you have a preference?" the male Nephyr asked. It sounded like the colonel was gloating, asking more for Milar's benefit than Tatiana's.

"No," Tatiana whispered.

"Oh, come on now," the female Nephyr said, smiling at Milar. "A big boy like this . . . " She patted Milar's shoulder. "He had time to do all sorts of nasty things to a little cutie like you. He had you for a whole week, Captain. Surely you've got a few things you want to see before we kill him. A few *positions,* maybe?"

Milar hung his head, staring at the ground.

"No," Tatiana whispered again.

"Be as inventive as you want," the male Nephyr said. "I'm sure you couldn't think of something we already have planned."

"Just kill him."

Milar's head came up and he looked at her, confusion in his face.

"Oh, we will, Captain," the woman holding Milar said. "But we have a bone to pick with him before we do. He's a bit of a sore spot in our history, you see. Only Nephyr recruit who ever escaped. Once we figure out how he did it, we've gotta make an example out of him, lest the other incoming kiddies get any ideas." The woman reached out and lightly cupped Milar's face with the hand that wasn't holding his arm. Smiling at him, the woman said, "Don't we, there, Love?"

Milar's golden-brown eyes never left Tatiana.

The Nephyr followed his gaze, saw what it was directed at, and her glittering filigreed fingers tightened. She cuffed Milar hard enough to throw him bodily backwards. "Keep your eyes to yourself, Love," the Nephyr said, smiling at Tatiana. "The captain doesn't appreciate it."

Tatiana felt a sickness pooling in her stomach. "I need to go to my room," she whispered.

The Master of Ceremonies looked at her, then at Milar, then covered the microphone again with his hand. "Get him out of here," he snapped to the two Nephyrs. Then, to Tatiana, he said, "I'm so sorry they put you through that. Are you going to need psych?"

"No," Tatiana managed, watching the Nephyrs jerk Milar into motion, then kick him when he stumbled. "I just need some time alone."

"So whose stupid idea was that?" one of the Bouncer captains muttered, once the Nephyrs had dragged their victim off the stage. The Master of Ceremonies shook his head, hand still on the microphone. "Damn Nephyrs," he said. To Tatiana, he said, "Go on. We'll finish without you."

Tatiana nodded numbly and left the stage. By the time she reached the barracks area, she was running.

They were going to kill Milar.

She slid into her room and leaned against the door. Her heart was slamming like a broken leg piston. They were going to kill Milar, and they were going to make it hurt.

*No.*

Tatiana couldn't let that happen. She knew, without a doubt, that Milar didn't deserve what the Nephyrs were planning for him. She had to help him.

Her eyes fell on Milar's huge hunting knife. The Bouncer captain had given it to her as a sort of memento, and as soon as she was out of sight, Tatiana had tossed it into a corner, wanting nothing to do with it. Now she went and retrieved it.

The razor-like blade glinted bluish in the bright lights of her barracks room. Gripping it in a tight fist, she left her room and started toward the Nephyr block.

Before she even had a plan, she was standing in front of the outer door to the prisoner compound. Taking a deep breath, she put her hand on the biometrics pad and let herself inside.

Down at the end of the corridor, behind a desk, the Nephyr from the auditorium was filling out datawork. "Oh," he said, seeing her. His filigreed face broke into a smile. "Reconsidered, Captain?"

"I did," she whispered. "Can I see him?"

The Nephyr's blue eyes drifted down to her knife. He was still smiling. "What are you going to do with the knife, Captain?"

*Kill him,* Tatiana thought. "Something special," she said.

The Nephyr chuckled. "It's against regulations to allow someone to enter the prisoner's quarters armed. Too much chance of . . . injury . . . "

Tatiana reddened and looked away, but her fingers tightened on the hilt of the blade. For a brief, insane second, she considered trying to use it on the Nephyr. Then her brain kicked back into gear and she realized she would be turned into a bloody pretzel the moment she tried. Unhappily, she decided she'd have to find some other way to accomplish the deed.

But how was she going to kill Milar without a knife?

Then the Nephyr winked at her and said, "But in your case, I think we can make an exception."

Tatiana jerked her head to look up at him, stunned.

"After all," the Nephyr said, "you delivered our long-lost brother back to us after all these years. We owe you a little time alone with him." He smiled, displaying perfect, replaceable teeth.

Nephyrs always creeped her out, but this one's words chilled her, and made her back away. "Thank you," Tatiana managed, from a safe distance.

Still grinning, the Nephyr said, "Just give me a moment to finish filing this report. Feel free to sit down." He gestured at the waiting area chairs, then moved back to his desk and entered something in the datapad. Tatiana listened to his fingers rap against the pad warily, wondering if he had guessed her intent and was sending for arresting officers. Sweat began to heat her underarms as she forced herself to resist the urge to look over the desk to peek at what he was typing.

Finally, the Nephyr finished entering the data and returned the pad to hibernation.

Standing, he smiled and said, "This way, Captain." He turned and led her deeper into the complex, past rows of solid metal doors with tiny windows covered by sliding blocks of metal. He stopped in front of one of them, flipped on the light outside the door, opened the lock with his palm, and motioned for her to step inside.

Reluctantly, Tatiana did.

Milar hung from the ceiling in the center of the concrete room like a slab of dragon-covered meat. His wrists were chained together and held above him, and his feet were similarly chained to the floor. He was barefoot, still wearing the bloodstained, tattered pants he had been captured in.

He hadn't even lifted his head when the lights had come on.

"That to your liking, Captain?" the Nephyr said. "I can reposition him, if you would like."

"No," Tatiana whispered. "That will be just fine."

As soon as she spoke, Milar lifted his head and froze, his eyes on his knife.

Tatiana's entire body was trembling, now. "Hi Milar," she said, wishing her hand wasn't so slick on the handle of the blade.

His attention was on the weapon, not her.

"Oh, you remember it, huh?" Tatiana asked with false bluster, feeling like she was blundering, speaking too loud, announcing to the Nephyr her intentions with every breath, yet knowing the moment she dropped the act she'd be thrown in a cell beside him. "You remember what you did to me with it?"

"Never hurt you with a knife, sweetie," Milar sneered, raising his head to meet her gaze.

*He's buying it,* Tatiana thought, both grateful and agonized at the same time. Didn't he know she wouldn't come back just to hurt him? Did he really think she would want to see him tortured? *I'm trying to help you,* she pled with him. *Please see that.*

The Nephyr, however, brushed past her and planted a fist in Milar's exposed stomach. The blow swung him backwards on the chain, leaving the colonist's breaths ragged and gasping.

"Glittering . . . cupcake . . . " Milar gritted, once he'd swung back into place and caught his breath again. "Let me down and try that."

"Oh, we will," the Nephyr said in a voice that congealed in Tatiana's gut like a cancer. When the Nephyr met her gaze, Tatiana backed away from him, unable to stop herself. "But first the captain, here, would like a chance at you."

"Does she now?" Milar said, his face darkening. "Well, give it your best, pumpkin. Ain't nothin' in the world you'll be able to do to me that'll top that time I had with *you.*"

The Nephyr punched Milar again, leaving Milar gagging and choking. Tatiana bit her lip. Nephyrs were strong. He was probably breaking bones or ruining organs.

"That . . . the best . . . you can . . . shit?"

"Would you like me to gag him?" the Nephyr said calmly.

"No, I want to hear him scream." God, she wished she wasn't trembling so bad. She felt like her knees were going to simply drop out from under her, but Tatiana knew she had to keep up the show or she'd lose her opportunity. Or, worse, the Nephyr would start to recognize her nerves for what they really were.

The Nephyr laughed. "Oh yes. An enemy's scream is a wonderful balm." He went and leaned his back against the door, grinning at her. "May I suggest the scrotum?"

At Tatiana's look of horror, the Nephyr laughed. "Oh, it's coming off anyway, Captain."

"She doesn't have what it takes," Milar sneered. "Look at her. Poor little thing's so terrified of me she can hardly breathe. She couldn't do it. Her heart would stop first."

"Do you want another lesson, Miles?"

Milar spat. "Bring it on, cupcake."

"I can't do it?" Tatiana cried, before the Nephyr could start forward again. Fear and anger powered her, lending her words a shrill scream that made the Nephyr halt. She stormed past the Nephyr, leaving the doorway for the first time. "You think I can't do it? What*ever* made you think I couldn't do it?"

Milar gave her a mirthless smile. "Only about a week of watching you beg for mercy like the yellow government squid you are, coaler."

She was angry, now. Either Milar was a very good actor, or he sincerely believed she was here to torture him. "You sonofabitch. You . . . you . . . "

"Would you like me to gag him?" the Nephyr asked again.

"No!" She lunged forward and rammed the blade up against Milar's throat, but the colonist jerked backwards just in time to avoid her cutting his jugular. The way he was hanging, she wasn't tall enough to press her advantage and slice open the artery.

*Why'd he do that?* Tatiana's mind screamed. *Why doesn't the stupid bastard realize I'm trying to kill him?*

Behind her, the Nephyr laughed and touched Tatiana's shoulder. "Careful there, Captain. You don't want to end our fun prematurely."

"You're right," Tatiana said, eyes tearing up. She blindly reached for his pants. "I've got other things I want to do first."

As soon as she slid the blade under the cloth, intending to accidentally 'slip' in cutting them off and gouge the femoral artery a few dozen times, the Nephyr laughed. "Actually, I think I'll leave you two alone together. How long should I give her, Milar? Ten? Twenty minutes?"

When Tatiana looked up at the Nephyr, blind with tears, the cyborg smiled at her. "How about an hour?"

Tatiana's hand started trembling. If he gave her an hour, she could make *sure* Milar had time to bleed to death. Make sure, and maybe apologize before she did it.

*Don't apologize,* she thought. *It'll just make it harder to watch him die.*

"All I ask, Captain," the Nephyr said, giving Milar a pleasant smile that made Tatiana's guts crawl, "is that you leave some for us." Then he turned and, winking at her, he said, "I'll go keep an eye out at the front desk. It *is* against regulations, after all."

As soon as the door shut and Tatiana heard the Nephyr's footsteps retreating, she turned her attention back to the knife she was about to thrust into Milar's thigh.

*Kill him,* her mind raged. *Don't even look at him. It doesn't matter what he thinks you're here for. Just do it.* She pushed her knife hard against his leg. Would he jerk? Would she hit the mark? She flushed, feeling him breathe above her, silent, watching her. Her whole arm felt weak, her entire body dizzy and disoriented with fear and adrenaline.

"The whole ball game can change in an instant, huh, coaler squid?"

When she jerked and looked up, Milar was grinning at her. Tatiana flushed, realizing he must have heard her speech to the commendation gathering, and must have made the right connections.

"When did you realize you had the hots for me?"

Tatiana's face began to burn like Milar had drenched it in napalm. "I absolutely. Do. *Not.*"

"Uh-huh." The dragons on his neck were bunched up, he was grinning so hard.

"Listen, floater," she said, scowling. "One moment I was in my soldier, the next Patrick had a gun to my head. *That* was a whole different ball game."

"I don't think that's what you were talking about, sweetie." Milar's golden-brown eyes sparkled with amusement.

*Oh, Aanaho,* Tatiana thought, immediately looking down at the knife. *I can't do this.*

"I've got one request, squid," Milar said. "Granted, that is, that you're here to kill me, rather than play with my balls like that Nephyr seemed to think."

Tatiana nodded. "I was going to go for the femoral artery."

"Tell me something, then," Milar said.

Tatiana grimaced and squeezed her fist around the knife. "You're making this harder than I want it to be."

"I don't give a damn," he laughed. "*I'm* the one about to get his leg sliced open."

*He's got you there, tootz.* "Fine," Tatiana muttered. "What's your question? And *please* make it quick. I really wanna make sure you can bleed out this time."

"Sorry to *inconvenience* you, sweetie. I'll do my best to oblige," Milar said. His face was still smeared with that idiotic grin.

God, he was beautiful. Like something right out of her . . .

"Then *oblige already!*" she cried.

"Which dragon?" Milar asked. "The red or the black?"

Unable to stop herself, Tatiana lowered her eyes to the sleeping forms on his torso. Each one was elegant in its steady rise and fall with his naked chest. Tatiana swallowed, hard. "They're both good."

"You got a thing for dragons, don't you, squid?"

Tatiana brushed tears from her eyes. "You are a jerk."

Milar was grinning like he had the Wide. "You remember how I said I only lied to you once?"

Tatiana glared at him. "Then you dumped me like a sack of potatoes."

"Wanna hear what it was about?"

"Not especially," she muttered. "Just let me kill you, all right?"

"Back on the ship, I said I didn't have a thing for cyborgs."

Tatiana's breath caught. *He couldn't possibly mean . . .*

"But I actually kind of do," Milar said. "One of them, anyway."

*Oh God.* It was her best fantasy and her worst nightmare, all in one.

She squeezed her eyes shut. "Can I kill you now?"

"You're not going to kill me," Milar said. "You're going to let me down, wait until the feeling comes back into my arms, and then give me my knife."

Tatiana snorted. "I don't think so. Then we'd both be dead."

"Trust me," Milar said. "Cut me down."

"Screw you!" Tatiana cried, horrified. "You're just trying to manipulate me into letting you go so you really *can* have your way with me before . . . " She swallowed, then looked away. "I didn't come here to talk. I don't want your apology. I made a mistake, outside Deaddrunk. I should've killed you. I just want to get it over with."

Milar snorted. "Listen to me, coaler squid. You've got a choice to make, and you've gotta make it quick. I can get us out of here, but only if you let me down and give me my knife."

*I can get us out of here . . .* The words burned in Tatiana's mind like coals. *Us. He wants to take me with him.*

"We're wasting time, coaler. Wideman was right, and it was gonna take a hell of a lot of stubbornness on your part, but here's where you decide. Help us—let me down—or stab me in the leg and go right back to being the nice little coaler operator everybody cheers for. Choose."

When she said nothing, Milar eyed the door. "And choose fast. You ain't gonna get another shot at this."

"All right." Tatiana said the words before she realized what she had said, but knew it was too late to take them back. "All right," she repeated, swallowing hard. She glanced up at the chains hooking him to the ceiling. They were well out of her reach, by a long shot. "But, uh, how?"

"See the clasp holding the leg irons to the floor?" he asked, pointing with his nose.

She looked down, then nodded.

"Unhook 'em. Then get down on your hands and knees and let me stand on your back."

Tatiana grimaced. "You could step on a node—"

"I know where all the nodes are," Milar said. "Just hurry and do it."

Hanging there, helpless, Milar didn't exactly look like he had what it took to get out of the Nephyr compound alive.

"Trust me, sweetie," Milar repeated softly.

Grudgingly, Tatiana squatted and unhooked the foot clasp. Then, reluctantly, she got down on her knees and presented her back for him to stand on.

"Ready?" Milar asked, putting a big bare foot on her shoulder blade.

"Yeah," Tatiana said, gritting her teeth. Then, as he grunted and pulled himself up, she muttered, "Aanaho, you're heavy."

"Yeah," Milar said. She heard metallic jingling as he fiddled with the chains above his head. "Girls tell me that a lot."

"Really?" Tatiana snorted. "How many girls have let you stand on them?"

"I was thinking more *lying* on them," Milar said, jumping down. He grinned at her stupefied look, the chain that had held him to the hook now dangling between his legs. "Thanks."

Tatiana sat up, glaring. "You knucker."

"But if you don't believe me, I can show you in person someday," Milar said. He started rolling his shoulders, wincing.

Tatiana's heart fluttered. "Um . . . "

Milar grinned at her. "You just turned redder than a Shrieker's butt, so I'll take that as a yes." He pulled a tiny slip of metal from his hair and had begun fiddling with the locks on the shackles.

"I'm not interested," she babbled. "Not interested at *all*."

After sliding the magnetic strip through each lock, Milar threw the whole mess aside and looked at her. Then he shrugged. "Your loss."

Tatiana gasped. He'd been so nonchalant . . . Like he didn't *care*, one way or the other. Her hand tightened on the blade.

Milar looked at her and chuckled. "I knew it." He bent and started working on the locks around his ankles.

"Knew what?" Tatiana demanded. Then, "You crawler, the *last* thing I want to do is have you on top of me."

"Under you, then?" He pulled the shackles aside and tucked the magnetic strip back into his hair.

Tatiana's face began to blaze. "Um . . . "

He laughed. "My knife?"

Tatiana held it to her chest. "I'm not interested. Really."

"Sure, pumpkin," Milar said. He reached forward and wrenched the weapon out of her grip. Deftly, he depressed a tiny trigger mechanism in the handle and the pommel popped open, exposing a secret compartment on the inside. Milar tapped it into his palm, exposing a tiny collapsible EMP wand.

"Thank God for small miracles," he said, grinning from ear to ear. He glanced down at her. "You ready for this?"

The way he said it, Tatiana was pretty sure he didn't mean open the door and get the hell out of there. She eyed the EMP wand warily. He could do more damage to her with a single pulse from the wand than he could in ten minutes with his knife. "Ready for what?"

"Cutting out the lifeline they put in my neck."

Tatiana froze. "No."

"Tough." He handed her back the knife. "You know where they put it?"

"I can see the stitches," she snapped. "But I said no. I don't know what to look for."

"You've got me to talk you through it," Milar said. He knelt in front of her, bowing his head so she had a good view of the back of his bull neck. "See the lump?" he said, pressing on it with a big thumb, "Slice it open, but don't pull on it yet."

Tatiana glanced at the door. Standing, she was only slightly more than eye level with him. "How long is this going to take?"

"Doesn't matter," Milar said. "We can't go anywhere until I've got this thing out."

Which was probably true. His lifeline was probably being monitored by the minute, at least by one of the base AIs.

Looking at the knife in her hand, Tatiana grimaced. "I've never cut anything in my life."

"Think of it as a steak," Milar said.

"It's not a steak."

"Think of it as *me* then," Milar said. "And *hurry the hell up.*"

"Okay!" Tatiana cried, sticking the knife into his neck. When it began to bleed, she grimaced. "I think I hit the wrong spot." Her blade was sticking out a full two centimeters below the lump.

"That's nice," Milar gritted. "Try again, please." His tone added, *Before I turn around and throttle you.*

"Uh." She pulled the knife out, and, pinching the lump, tried again. This time the skin parted easily beneath the blade and she could see a gleaming nugget of bloody metal underneath. "Okay."

"See it?" Milar demanded.

"Yes," she said. She gripped it with her fingers. "Want me to pull it—"

"*No,*" Milar cried, panic clear in his voice. "No. You have to separate the battery cap first."

"What's a battery cap?"

"Okay, here's where it takes concentration. Get as much blood off of it as you can and grab either side of the capsule and tug it apart. It should separate in the middle, allowing you a pretty good view of what's inside."

"Uh-huh," Tatiana said, wiping the thing off with the sleeve of her uniform and prying it open. It made a little clicking sound and moved apart.

"Okay, this is really important," Milar said. "You have thirty seconds to disable the battery cap or it's going to send the juice into my central nervous system and paralyze me for good."

"Why didn't you say that before?" Tatiana cried. "And what's the battery cap?"

"It's a little black ball on the inside. There's a notch in the top for a screwdriver. Put the tip of the knife in it and twist counterclockwise 'til it falls out."

Tatiana located the thing and lowered the tip of the blade toward the slot. The knife refused to hold steady. "I'm shaking too bad," she cried.

"Squid, you're gonna be shaking a hell of a lot worse when those Nephyrs put you up on the rack because you were helping me and let me die."

Nothing like a nice little dose of terror to narrow one's field of vision to the task at hand. Tatiana's world shrank to the little black knob the size of a pinhead. "Got it," Tatiana said, the moment the blade was seated. "Now twist it, right?"

"*Counter*clockwise," Milar warned.

"*Okay!*" Tatiana screamed, twisting.

A minute later, Milar said, "Well, I'm not drooling on the floor, so it looks like it worked. Now all you gotta do is pull it out."

"Pull what out?"

"The lifeline."

"Why? It's dead."

"Dammit," Milar roared, "You took out the defense system. Not the tracking beacon."

Grimacing, Tatiana pinched the tiny capsule and gave it a tentative tug.

"Gotta pull harder than that," Milar said. "And faster, too. That Nephyr's gonna come back wondering why I'm not screaming."

"Ewww," Tatiana said, once she started to see the pink wires emerge from his spine. "Oh gross, gross."

"It's fine. You're doing fine. Just go slow. Those things can still get triggered if you jiggle them. *Please* go slow."

"This *is* slow," Tatiana snapped. "Oh God. This is icky," she said, flinching away from the grody thing she was pulling from his neck. "You owe me big time, collie. Big time."

"I know," Milar said. He was absolutely still beneath her. "We'll talk about it later. Just go slow and don't rush it, okay? And *dear God* stop jerking it!"

"I'm not!"

"You *are*." She could see the muscles in his jaw standing out.

Tatiana grinned to herself as she worked. "Payback's a bitch, ain't it?"

"There's no payback when we're both dead. Just calm down and let it come out on its own. Like a virgin. No need to rush it. It'll come around in its own time."

"You're disgusting."

"And make sure you don't let any of the little wires touch each other when they come out. Very bad mojo. As soon as you can, just set it down gently on the floor and back away."

"Yeah, whatever," Tatiana said. "Ugh." The last electrode finally came free and all four of them danced around like the little legs of a spider. Disgusted, she threw it to one side. The thing left a bloody smear across the concrete wall, then made a metallic tinkle as it collapsed in a wiry heap in the corner.

Milar glanced at it. "You know, you don't listen to instructions very well."

"Sue me." She grimaced and wiped her bloody hands on his dragony back.

Milar glanced over his shoulder at the bloody smear, looked up at her with a raised eyebrow, then heaved himself to his feet. He retrieved the EMP wand, took the knife from her, then offered a hand. "Let's go."

"Where are we going?" Tatiana asked, keeping a wary distance.

"To bust up a few glittering tree ornaments," Milar said.

"Do I have to come?" Tatiana asked, giving the EMP wand a nervous look.

Milar shrugged. "Use that little AI trick of yours to get the door open for me and then you can sit here and suck your thumb for all I care."

Tatiana narrowed her eyes. "You're a real prick, for somebody who needs my help," she growled, slapping her palm to the biometrics pad.

Milar sobered and hefted the EMP wand. Facing the door, he said, "You're gonna need a lot of mine before this is over, squid. Stay behind me, and call it even."

"Whatever," Tatiana muttered, trying not to look like she was about to pee herself. "Maybe I should have the knife."

"No." Milar said. "You'd drop it." He stepped outside the moment the door opened.

Narrowing her eyes, Tatiana followed him.

# CHAPTER 26

## Killer

"DO I HAVE EVERYONE'S ATTENTION?" A HARSH FEMALE VOICE demanded. "I'm only going to say this once."

The air in the cavern still stung with the acrid taste of ozone, and the eggers stood frozen in petrified silence.

"Good," the woman said. She was a dim outline in the darkness, the eggers on all sides having backed away from her, leaving her standing alone except for two other women at her back.

"Now listen carefully." Magali held her breath as the woman swung her gun back toward her end of the group. The woman passed her over, then swung back, keeping the barrel moving at all times. Behind her, her two terrified-looking companions were huddled against the wall. All three looked to be recent draftees . . . until Magali saw the Coalition codes tattooed into their arms.

*Guards.*

Naked guards.

Confused, Magali tried to piece together just what was happening. As nude as they were, it was unlikely the guards had come down here prior to the Harvest. Not smugglers, then. They had to have been in formation with the others when the Director and her 'friends' relieved them of their garments.

"Good," the woman with the gun said. "What's going to happen is you all are going to go down into the mines, fill up your sacks, and bring some back here for my friends and me. A few from each sack— we're not greedy. The three of us don't know jack shit about Shriekers, so it's best for everyone involved that we don't go anywhere near them. With me so far?"

No one spoke.

"Good," the woman said. She pointed into the mines. "We hate to do this to you, but we're not eggers. We're citizens. Director thinks she's gonna teach us some sort of lesson, spending a day down here in the slime, but she's about as stupid as she is ugly. We were just doing what everybody does. Bullshitting. Passing the time. Playing cards. Maybe screwing, if it was an off-day. How the hell were *we* supposed to know he was Runaway Joel?"

*Oh crap,* Magali thought, glancing at Joel. "Joel," she whispered, "get your head down."

Joel merely blinked at her.

"Down," Magali urged. She pointed at the woman with the gun and tugged his wrist downward. Joel reluctantly sank into a hunched crouch.

"Speaking of Joel," the woman continued, "I saw him in the formation tonight. The good Director let him out to play, didn't she? Where is he?" She began searching the gathered eggers with her eyes. "I have something for him."

"Shit," Magali muttered. "Don't move." She placed a finger to her lips and held it there, for Joel's benefit.

The guard with the gun waited a few more minutes, then laughed. "Don't wanna come out for my gift, eh, Joel? How about this. I start shooting until you get your scrawny ass up here."

Magali glanced down at the smuggler, who was looking up at her, obviously close to panic. Magali knew what was going through his head. For all he knew, they were going to shoot him.

For all Magali knew, he was right.

"Fine," the guard said, after no one moved. She stepped toward the huddled eggers and raised her gun to a woman's temple. Her countenance tightened in that look she knew all too well from Patrick's psychotic brother. *She's going to do it,* Magali thought, horrified. *She's going to shoot her.* The guard's finger began to squeeze on the trigger.

"He can't understand you," Magali cried, dragging Joel to his feet. Thankfully, he didn't resist. When the guard twisted to look at her, Magali continued hurriedly, "The Director had her robots destroy his language centers."

The guard, upon seeing Joel, gave a bitter frown. "She muted him?"

"Yes," Magali said. "I stayed behind and—"

"Shut up." To Joel, the woman said, "Get over here. My sisters and I have been itching to give you a good thrashing for what you did to us. Got us demoted and *flogged,* you sonofabitch. My gift is I'm going to kill you after we're done with you, so that when the Nephyrs come to extract their due, all they find is a corpse. You might deserve a good beating, but you don't deserve that. Now get *over* here."

Joel simply stood where he was. When it was obvious the woman expected something of him, he gave a helpless shrug and glanced at Magali for help.

"Please don't hurt him," Magali said, knowing by the woman's resentful look that she planned to do just that. "He doesn't understand."

The guard snorted. "And he doesn't know how to play poker, either. Yeah, right." She narrowed her eyes and lifted her gun so it was pointed directly at Magali. "Joel, get up here or I'm shooting your pretty friend in the face."

Staring down the barrel, Magali had never been so frightened in her life. Every muscle wanted to freeze up and relax, all at the same time. She couldn't breathe, couldn't see anything but the muzzle in front of her. Round and around in her head, all she could think was that all the woman had to do was twitch her finger and Magali would never think anything, ever again.

Anna wouldn't have flinched. She would have coldly stared the woman down and told her exactly how impressed she was with her substandard gun and her limited intellect. She would have regaled her with blood-chilling tales of their father's training, of how every single person in Deaddrunk was taught to kill from birth, of how the woman's gentle Coalition upbringing could never prepare her for the horrors she was going to experience in the next few seconds, if she didn't drop her gun.

Magali wasn't Anna. Magali's guts twisted with diarrhea and her legs shook so badly they threatened to collapse.

Beside her, Joel did not move, though now he was frowning as he glanced from Magali to the guard.

"I'll help him," Magali said, trembling all over. She made a point to move and speak very carefully, lest the woman's trigger finger twitch. "Okay? Please don't shoot. Please." She gently took Joel's good hand and pulled him forward.

Joel followed her docilely, obviously not understanding what the woman had in store for him. Seeing his placid look made Magali so frustrated she wanted to scream.

*She can't actually plan to kill him,* Magali thought, as she brought him abreast of the woman. *She's just trying to scare him.*

Joel came to a tranquil halt in front of the guard, though his eyes had become wary as the gun switched targets to center on his chest.

The woman peered up at his face, then glanced down at his ruined hand and grimaced. "Aanaho, what did she do to him?"

"She slammed his hand in a door," Magali said.

"I'm not talking to you, kid," the guard snapped. "I'm just trying to figure out why the Director was stupid enough to send him down here." She gestured at the smuggler's bruised body, his swollen face, his maimed and twisted hand. "You're obviously in no condition to *stand*, much less harvest Shrieker nodules."

"Director's already taken a pretty big chunk out of him," one of the guard's companions commented. She sounded disappointed. "Not much left for us."

The guard with the gun gave a cruel snort. "Oh, there's plenty left for us."

"Please don't hurt him," Magali said again.

"I said *shut up*," the guard snapped, swinging to look at her. She took a step forward. Magali saw her foot kick out, had a moment to cringe, then lost her breath as it slammed into her stomach and sent her to her knees in the slime. The old shame of failing her father's tests, of hitting the ground hard after Milar tore her legs out from under her, returned. She saw tears.

*Killer.* With the word came a long-buried memory of a schoolyard chant, of standing in Wideman's garden, of how she had done everything to change his single word for her. She had played with dolls, had studied drawing and art, had pretended to be sick and read books. She had refused to participate in her father's war games, had let Anna and Milar and Patrick and Jeanne find and 'kill' her early, so she could go sit out the rest of the games and watch, instead.

*Killer,* Wideman's voice whispered to her again. And, instinctively, looking at the casual way the woman held the gun, the softness in her muscles and posture, Magali knew she could.

*No!* Magali's mind screamed. Anna was the killer. Milar was the killer. Magali wanted to be a mother, a wife. She wanted to meet her soulmate and have a home and raise children in some peaceful town, in some place where every man, woman, and child was not trained to murder people, where little kids weren't forced to hold guns and little old men didn't spew nonsense that was written down and memorized with awe. Where a child's future wasn't defined by a single word.

*Killer,* Wideman's voice cackled at her. Magali squeezed her eyes shut, forcing the tears of pain down her cheeks.

"Sorry," she whispered, holding up her hands as she carefully got to her feet. "Sorry."

The guard whipped the gun back around to face Joel, who had taken a step closer with his good hand outstretched. "You don't like me hurting your girlfriend there, Joel?" the guard laughed. "Maybe we should hurt you, instead." She stepped forward and delivered a similar kick to Joel's already-bruised midriff.

*Killer,* Wideman's voice said again, as Joel collapsed with a heart-wrenching groan of pain. The smuggler curled into a ball as the women laughed, his eyes on Magali, pleading. The gunwoman noticed this and jeered, "What, Joel? You think your doe-eyed little girlfriend is gonna help you?" She chuckled cruelly and pulled back her foot to deliver another kick.

Magali's gut twisted as she saw Joel's face go blank with resignation, a strangled whimper escaping his throat. Before she could think, Magali stepped forward and grabbed the woman's pistol. She twisted the weapon up and back, then wrenched the gun forward until something in the woman's trigger finger snapped. The woman screamed.

When Magali stepped away, the gun was firmly in her hand. A moment later, the implications of what she had done began to make her heart pound. Looking at the guard, who was now nursing her crippled hand, Magali swallowed hard. "Sorry, I didn't mean . . . "

One of the woman's companions stepped forward with a knife in her hand. Her face was filled with cruel purpose. Magali backed up another step, her fingers loosening on the gun in regret. "I didn't mean to—"

"You're dead, girl," the knife-wielder said. It was a cold promise.

Magali's heart began to hammer as the woman started to circle her. She was afraid of close combat, almost as much as she was afraid of heights. Of all the village's 'games,' this was what she had feared the most, what she had always failed in no matter how hard she tried. She just didn't have the coordination. Time and again, Milar had thrown her to the ground at her father's direction. Time and again, Magali had stared at the ground in shame, holding a sore joint in humiliation as her father chastised her for being slow and stupid.

The woman was circling around behind her, splitting her attention, giving the other two guards a chance at her back. It was so much like she remembered in her 'fights' with Milar, pinned under his merciless stare, that a whimper began to build in her throat. Father hadn't cared that she wasn't built for fighting. He didn't care that Milar had been almost a hundred pounds heavier than her. He didn't care that the last thing she ever wanted to do was find herself in hand-to-hand combat. He only cared that she became Wideman's 'killer.'

The guard's face was filled with dark promise, the knife gripped tightly in one hand, her Coalition-issue blade weaving as the woman danced from foot to foot. Magali knew that, unlike her practices with Milar, this woman wasn't going to let her get back to her feet if she took her to the ground.

*Not this. Please, not this.* She'd struggled to avoid this. Her whole life. Magali took a step backwards, the gun burning in her hand. Her sister would have simply raised the weapon and fired.

*I'm not Anna,* Magali thought, her entire body vibrating with fear and adrenaline as she followed the woman's body with the barrel of her gun. *I'm not a killer.*

"What's the matter, egger?" the woman sneered, as she circled, "That gun's only got one shot every three seconds. Afraid you'll miss?"

"No," Magali whispered. She watched the woman circle, thinking of the village Anna had killed, of the way her sister's brown eyes had been filled with excitement as she spoke of the slaughter. She remembered Milar, boasting to Patrick about torturing a man when they thought she couldn't hear. *They* were the killers. Why hadn't Wideman called *them* 'killer'? She was *nothing* like them.

Wideman had to be wrong. She wasn't a killer.

Magali raised the gun and, eyes scrunched closed, squeezed off a warning shot.

It went over the woman's shoulder and lodged in the slimy wall with a bubbling hiss.

For a moment, the guard stood there, glancing down at herself, looking shocked. Then she gave a scream of triumph and lunged.

As the knife moved toward her, Magali's whole world seemed to slow down to individual beats of her heart. She watched the knife hurtle toward her organs, saw the little red CHARGE light on the gun as it recharged.

*Killer,* Wideman's eerie voice said again, made all the more eerie because the whisper seemed to come no further than an inch from her shoulder. *Killer, killer . . .*

"No!" Magali screamed. Magali shifted her weight and kicked the knife out of the woman's hand. Then, as the woman stood there, her face dropping to look down at her empty hand, Magali twisted, pivoted on one foot in the slime, and slammed her heel into the woman's face. The woman collapsed instantly, and, seeing the way she crumpled, Magali felt an immediate pang of regret for the strength she had put into the kick.

As the second guard fell, the first guard bent for the fallen blade. Magali leveled the gun on her head, her finger on the trigger, the little READY light flaming green in the space between them. Though Magali's heart was thundering, the gun remained absolutely steady in her grip.

Utter silence filled the cavern.

*What would Anna do?* a little part of her wondered. Then, with reluctance, she thought, *Tell the truth.*

As the first guard remained poised over the knife, watching her, Magali said, "I've been trained to wield every gun that's made it to the Outer Bounds, from scrapyard junk to Coalition issue to black market spitfires, to projectile pistols and long-dis beam rifles. I've fired this class of weapon—an A1550-Y, named as such for the distance in meters that its energy beam will accurately travel through Aquafer-rated atmosphere at sea level—approximately seven thousand and fifteen times, with a ninety-nine percent kill rate at four hundred yards on moving targets. If you don't back up, right now, you're going to figure out just where you rank in that percentile."

The guard glanced down at her fallen comrade, who was sprawled out and unconscious in the slime, and then back to Magali. Like a woman who had accidentally crawled into a snake pit, she slowly straightened and took a step back. Her index finger was hanging awkwardly, still cradled by her good hand.

Magali took a deep breath, feeling as if her entire body were alive with electric current. Her legs, especially, wanted to collapse on her. It was all she could do to keep standing. Somehow keeping the tremor out of her voice, she said, "Now the three of you are gonna pick up your sacks and your prybars and you're going to go in there and harvest nodules and you're going to hope nobody kicks your ass while you're at it."

The third woman paled.

"You think this is funny?" the wounded guard snapped. She took a step toward Magali, pointing at Joel, "He's gonna be dead by tomorrow night and a few nights after that, *we're* gonna be back on watch. You think we'll just forget something like this? When we get back on shift, you're gonna go missing."

Magali's only response was her best imitation of her sister's most psychotic smile.

With a seething look, the two guards still standing bent down to pick up their harvest sacks. Casting Magali a long, spiteful look, the wounded guard departed for the inner hatching chambers, cursing at the third woman to follow. Magali waited until she could hear them scrabbling in the slime in the dim caverns beyond, then she lowered her gun, relief flooding her every tissue.

A moment later, Magali realized the Shrieker mounds had descended into absolute silence. No one was moving. Many of the eggers were watching Magali as if she had grown glittering golden circuitry.

Feeling uncomfortable under their stares, Magali bent to help Joel. Instead of standing, Joel grabbed the wrist of her gun hand and held it firmly. Automatically, Magali loosened her grip on the weapon and held it out to him.

Joel didn't take it. Instead, he squeezed her wrist once and grinned, peering up into her face.

*He's saying thank you,* she realized. Magali blushed, and, seeing Joel didn't want it, had to resist a powerful urge to drop the weapon in the Shrieker mucus. She would have felt better had Joel been carrying it. She hated the feel of it, hated its weight, hated the way its rubber grip dug at her skin. She wanted to throw it as far away from her as it could get. Yet she also knew that she couldn't just leave it. Someone else could pick it up and have the same idea as the guards, and this time they wouldn't give Magali a chance to get close enough to stop them.

Still holding the gun in one hand, she pulled the smuggler to his feet, then offered it to him again. Joel pushed the weapon aside, shaking his head with what Magali thought was amusement. He then gave her an elegant bow over her other hand, one that made her cheeks heat up with embarrassment as he kissed the top of her knuckles in an Old Earth fashion. Looking up at her from his bow, he winked.

Even naked, bruised, and speechless, Joel Triton still had the same charismatic charm that he'd had since the very first day Magali had met him in the foreman breakroom. She felt her chest leap like a schoolgirl, despite the fact he was easily a couple of decades older and graying at the temples.

Joel straightened, patted her hand, and turned away. Dumbfounded, Magali watched him as he strode off toward the now-blocked exit.

Eggers hastily got out of his way. Halfway there, Joel stopped and glanced over his shoulder at Magali. When she continued to stand there, her heart still hammering six different beats of confusion, he gestured impatiently with his good hand.

Reluctantly, she fell in behind him, itching at all the eyes on her, wishing she had never broken the guard's finger and taken the gun. Her dread was resting like a lump in her throat. Whatever happened, the guards were right. She had marked herself. If she survived the Harvest, it would only be to find herself woken up in the middle of the night at the end of a rifle muzzle, to be marched out into the peat bogs and shot.

Joel went to the stacks of supplies the robots had left by the door and squatted to begin sorting them out.

As everyone watched, he grabbed one stack of red cardboard and stood up. He glanced at Magali, then pointed at the eggers, then jammed a finger at the floor.

"He says stay here," Magali said, giving them a helpless shrug.

As soon as she spoke, Joel hefted the stack of cardboard over one shoulder and trudged off into the depths of the hatching chambers.

Wary of the small shapes moving beyond, Magali followed him.

# CHAPTER 27

## Decibel Levels

How long until the next flight?" Anna asked as she alternately flipped through channels on the two separate wall-screens. Despite Doberman's wishes, she had activated both the large, content-censored screen for recruits and the small password-protected screen for full military officers and state officials. The unfinished node sat on the nightstand in front of her, dismantled to its most basic parts. The r-player into which he had uploaded the node schematics lay on her thigh, playing a fast electric guitar instrumental as she hummed along and tapped her fingers on the table beside the jumble of parts.

Doberman, for his part, was sitting on a chair in front of the door, one shoe off, his big toe folded back and a power adapter extending from the wall transmitter to his foot. As per Anna's request, he checked the time, still irritated that it now had to be done consciously instead of with an automatic timestamp.

"Eleven hours and fourteen minutes until we need to be on the boarding ramp." That they had missed their flight to Eiorus did not bother Doberman. After all, a simple excuse on his part and the camp computer had adjusted their departure accordingly.

What bothered Doberman was that Anna Landborn was surrounded by illegal materials whose discovery would get them both executed if they were ever discovered, and she had the volume on the two entertainment screens turned up as high as it would go, producing a hundred and nine decibels of wall-vibrating noise in an otherwise quiet barracks hall.

"You don't have to sit in front of the door like that," Anna said, pausing in her fiddling with the officer screen to peer over her shoulder at him. "They think there's an admiral in here. Nobody's going to barge in."

"The door has no lock," Doberman said. He reached behind him and smacked the rickety metal barrier with a palm, making it rattle. "And you are surrounded by sensitive materials."

Anna Landborn raised an eyebrow a half-centimeter. "Dobie, think. If your camp computer told you an admiral was staying in one of the barracks rooms, would you have bothered to tell him to correct his decibel level?"

"Probably," Doberman said. "Besides, it's a privacy screen, nothing more, and you've got the volume loud enough that even a passing human would come investigate. One look at the materials scattered on that desk and they'll have us both dismantled by Nephyrs."

"Correction," Anna said, as she pried open one of the inner chambers of the central node apparatus. "One look at the materials scattered on this desk and you're going to kill them."

"I'd rather it didn't come to that," Doberman said. "Please lower the volume."

Anna snorted and, plucking the tiny inner chamber free of the apparatus, haphazardly flicked it into the waste unit. "Dobie," she said, wiping lubricant from under her fingernail. "What do you *think* an admiral would do if he was booked in a room on a boring little station like this? Play ping-pong? Call his mother? Quietly read the latest five-year-old issue of the *Coalition Times?*" Anna snorted. "You really think he'd give a shit if he was keeping the new recruits awake? No. He'd turn up the volume and make sure the whole barracks knew he was there. Coalers are like that. So just sit there, recharge, and be happy."

"Our agreement was that you wouldn't put us in danger." He jerked a thumb at the sources of the noise. "*That* is definitely putting us in danger. It is fourteen decibels above base regulation for sound pollution."

Anna sighed deeply. "Who would've guessed the robot would turn out to be a prude?"

"Change the feed, or I will change your face," Doberman said. He carefully made a fist and smacked it against his palm.

"Look," Anna said, her facial capillaries expanding rapidly. "This room is registered to an off-duty admiral. We neutralized the cameras before we went in. The Nephyrs are *still* running around in Sector Seven, looking for the perps. Nobody's going to come looking for us, so you can just calm down."

"Now," Doberman said.

Muttering, Anna turned down the volume on the two wallscreens, bringing the total decibel level to only a few points over regulation levels.

"I wish you'd let me get rid of that," Doberman said, nodding to the parts strewn across her nightstand. "Or at least concentrate on it fully, instead of splitting your attention with the news feeds. I don't see how having three separate stimulus inputs is helping you understand the schematics of that node."

In truth, the multi-tonal screeching of the electric guitar combined with the financial chatter of the corporate news feed and the heated discussion on the Coalition Free Press were splitting his processing power as he digested and stored them, causing him worry that Anna was doing it with that exact intent in mind, so that she could use the distraction to slip another EMP grenade into his body. As of yet, however, Doberman had not mastered the ability to ignore an input, and intentionally overlooking sensory details left him with gaping holes in his memory, so his choices were to analyze and store every individual sound, or turn off his auditory receptors and black out a good portion of the evening.

"It's background noise," Anna said, flipping another channel. "I concentrate better with background noise." Seemingly satisfied with the latest feed, she picked up another piece of the node apparatus and compared it to the specifications on the r-player. "Aanaho. The Neanderthals put that in the *brain*."

"I would also feel more comfortable if I were sure that you weren't turning that thing into some sort of bomb," Doberman said.

Anna waved him off. "I told you. I'm done trying to kill you." She held up the ringlike part for him to inspect. "Look at this. See the drainage holes there? Those idiots were injecting Yolk directly into the brain. Talk about Frankensteining their way through things."

"Was there an alternative?" Doberman asked.

Anna snorted. "Of course. It's not the Yolk that makes the Shrieker. It's the Shrieker that makes the Yolk. They've got everything backwards. They've got the apparatus rigged right to induce the same multiwave emanations, but the Yolk isn't what creates the Shriek. It's the Shriek that creates the Yolk. Kind of like setting a basket of eggs next to a basket of plutonium and having the eggs set off a Geiger counter afterwards." Anna was shaking her head, pressing her lips together. "Think of it like mental radiation."

"You can't possibly be listening to both of those news feeds *and* the music at the same time," Doberman said. Splitting his attention four ways was beginning to annoy him. "And if the apparatus is unusable, give it to me and I will dispose of it."

"Oh, it's usable," Anna said, "They put an awful lot of time into studying the insides of dead Shriekers to just throw it all away. They even got a few of their theories right. It's definitely got a use, but not in the way they think. They're trying to use it as a weapon, and it *could* be used that way . . . if they weren't complete imbeciles. But what they've got wrong is that only a Shrieker can Shriek. Period. Human genetics just doesn't have what it takes to produce that kind of mental radiation. Period. Besides, even if they succeeded, the poor test subject would end up being the center of the Shriek emanations. Even augmented with something like this, all they could do would be kill themselves unless they had some sort of neutralizer in their system."

"Which was what was happening," Doberman said.

"Exactly," Anna said. "And if you read the logs, it wasn't even very dramatic. They registered approximately twenty decibels on the mental radiation scale before they died, when a Shriek would *start* somewhere around two-forty to two-fifty. Basically, if asked to justify their work, the technicians couldn't prove that the emanations were any greater than the Yolk they pumped into their experiments."

"Sounds like a failed experiment."

Anna grunted. "In a way, yeah. What they're not considering, however, is *why* a Shrieker Shrieks. We already know they can communicate with each other, and that they have no external sound-producing organs. They can luminesce, but I think you and I can both agree that it's not the luminescing that does the talking, right?"

Doberman reviewed his Shrieker-corrupted files and nodded. "So instead of a weapon," he said, nodding at the strewn parts, "you think that can be used as an untraceable means of communication?"

Anna gave him what appeared to be a genuine smile. "And you did that with both feeds *and* the music on in the background. I'm impressed, Dobie. Maybe there's some hope for you, after all."

"Stop trying to calculate my processing capacity," Doberman said.

Anna snorted. "I already know the processing capacity of a Ferris Unit." She gave him a smug grin.

Doberman crossed his arms and leaned against the rickety barrier. "How about the processing capacity of a self-modified Ferris Unit?"

Anna's facial features contorted and her jaw opened slightly. "Seriously?"

"Even as we speak, the camp computers on both this base and Yolk Factory 14 are trying to determine why a handful of robots have gone missing over the last couple days."

Anna gave him a predatory look. "You need help installing some parts?"

Doberman sighed deeply. "Anna, I assure you, I did plant two bombs in your—"

"Yeah, whatever," Anna said. "I just want to see you get bad-ass." Her facial muscles twitched into a smile that even Doberman considered sinister. "Do you *realize* the kind of stuff I could do to you? We're talking seriously cool shit. Like lasers in your eyes and poison in your fingertips and rocket launchers in your arms."

"Maybe later," Doberman said. "So far, I've been able to manage on my own."

Anna's face fell in a pout. "Yeah, but—"

"I'll think about it," Doberman said. He gestured to the dismantled node in front of her. "So you believe the apparatus can be used in communication?"

Anna shrugged. "Depends on how well the subject responds to mental radiation," Anna said. "You get someone who can't handle the noise, they'll probably go comatose. You get someone like Wideman, then . . . " Anna's breathing and heart rate hitched only a moment, but it was enough to make Doberman take note. Then she quickly sighed and leaned away from the apparatus as if completely bored, saying, "But all this is moot, really. We don't have any test subjects, and I'm sure as hell not using it on myself."

"Who is Wideman?" Doberman asked.

Anna narrowed her eyes. "I misspoke."

"A man who got Egger's Wide and survived?" Doberman suggested.

Anna's interrupted biorhythms betrayed her shock. "You've heard of him?"

"I guessed," Doberman said. "Based on the name."

"Well, you guessed wrong," she said, immediately going back to her work. "Because I misspoke."

"Who is Wideman?"

"Don't know what you're talking about," Anna said.

"Do I have to do a records search of men who've survived the Wide?" Doberman asked. Then, when her rhythms remained steady, and considering the conversation they had before, he added, "Or survived a Shriek?"

Anna didn't respond, and after forty-five seconds of silence, Doberman retracted his power connector, left the door, and began striding across the room toward the dataport.

When Doberman put his hand on the transmitter, Anna cursed and set down her r-player. "Don't bother, I'll tell you."

"You mean you'll give me some delightfully thoughtful lie," Doberman said. Then, when she plucked a magnetic disc from the debris atop the desk and started to stand, he added, "Stay on the bed."

Anna lowered herself slowly, her eyes riveted to his hand as it hovered over the transmitter. "I don't know why you think you'll find him in the government records. Coalers don't give a damn about eggers. Five hundred thousand of them get the Wide every year and nobody cares."

In reply, Doberman said, "Joseph Whitecliff, of the Fifteenth Carrier Squadron. Assigned a ten-year enlistment on Fortune. Married to a Fortune-born colonist, Vala Healthmore, in an unapproved ceremony on-planet. Fathered triplets thirty-two years ago, Patrick and Milar Whitecliff, identical, and a girl, Caroline Whitecliff, fraternal. One year later, Whitecliff's command refused to recognize colonial marriages, ordered the Fifteenth to take a group of seventeen sedated Shriekers back to the Inner Bounds for study. There was a mishandling in the cargo bay, leading to a ship-wide Shriek by the transported aliens. Joseph Whitecliff was the sole survivor. Command discharged him to the colonies in the care of his wife, at that time living in the town of Deaddrunk Mine. Is this Wideman?"

"No."

"Now this is interesting," Doberman said. "Both of his sons have had their DNA, prints, physical, and biometric data all wiped clean. Yet Joseph's DNA is a close paternal match to one Miles Blackpit, the only man in Fortune history who escaped the Nephyr Academy on Eiorus, and one of the eighteen fugitives on the Constant Vigil alert system."

When he looked, Anna's capillaries had constricted, leaving her coloration several shades lighter than usual. "Stop giving me reasons to kill you, robot."

"Very well." Doberman lowered his hand from the transmitter. "I only mention it because the same Miles Blackpit was just apprehended by the Nephyrs not two days ago."

Anna's facial muscles lost tension and her musculature tightened on her frame. "What?"

"He was found trying to kidnap a Coalition operator."

"The *Nephyrs* have him?" Anna whispered. It appeared as if, for once, Anna Landborn had completely forgotten to regulate her biorhythms. Her breathing was fast, her heart rate elevated, her eye dilation indicating total shock. "You're lying."

"He's being held in this very station, as a matter of fact," Doberman said. "If you had been paying attention to your 'background noise' like you were forcing me to do, you would have seen him."

Anna's eyes flickered toward the screens, which now showed a base football game and a Shrieker Harvest, respectively. "You're lying," she said, angrier.

Doberman sighed and replayed his recording of the operator's speech for Anna, transmitting the feed to the main screen. When he finished, he created a still frame and zoomed in on the prisoner's face. "He is the one with the decorative dermal pigmentations, no?"

"We have to help him," Anna said. Her eyes were riveted to the screen. Doberman's sensors picked up a further increase in breathing speed, the result almost classifying as hyperventilation.

*Anna Landborn seems to be having a strong emotional reaction for the first time since I made her my offer.* Doberman assessed her condition a moment, then stored the information for future retrieval and processing.

Anna's eyes narrowed. "Don't you *dare* update your profile, you stupid robot."

"Already done," Doberman said. "And, calculating the chances of getting a large, highly visible colonial out of the base without compromising our own position, I unfortunately don't think it's a wise course of action, Anna."

"Well I *do*," Anna said. "Where are they holding him?"

"Section One, H Block."

"The Nephyr compound."

"Yes, Anna."

Anna was biting her lip. "We need to get him out of there."

"I'm sorry, Anna," Doberman said. "I am not equipped to deal with Nephyrs."

"I can *make* you equipped to deal with Nephyrs," she said.

"Even though I trust your desire to free this colonial, I do not trust your intentions afterwards. In fact, it very much fits your profile for you to decide to put a time-sensitive present for me in my chest cavity while augmenting my other processes. Therefore, I am not yet willing to allow you to tinker with my internal workings."

"I swear to you I won't."

"Perhaps another day, Anna."

"Then let *me* deal with the Nephyrs," Anna cried. "I got him out of there before. I'll do it again."

"Unfortunately," Doberman said, "on this, I cannot allow our intervention. The prisoner is too high-profile to approach safely without a great amount of forethought."

Anna's body was making tiny, involuntary tremors, and Doberman saw evidence of extraneous excretions from her tear ducts. Before she could speak, he added, "It's no use faking tears, Anna. I have no latent paternal instincts to manipulate. I will not be taking you into the Nephyr compound."

Anna narrowed her tear-reddened eyes at him. "You stupid robot. I'm not faking it. Milar is my *friend.*"

Doberman carefully examined her elevated biorhythms again, then said, "You're getting very good at regulating your physiological patterns, aren't you?"

He was surprised when her capillaries expanded and she screamed, "*I'm not faking it, you stupid robot!*"

Anna's heart rate had jumped dramatically, and her chest was expanding at three times the speed of her unconscious rate. It was another aspect to her behavior that Doberman found incongruous with her profile. Further, her reaction was much more violent than he expected of a mere friend. He searched his log for instances of her using 'Milar' or 'Miles' and was stunned to find she had, indeed, shown some sort of consistent and genuine reverence for this colonist.

. . . but that was completely not within her profile.

And, while many of her comments had been compliments on the colonist's brainpower, more than thirty percent were based off of his physical attributes.

"A friend . . . ," Doberman suggested, watching her carefully, "Or an infatuation?"

Her face darkened to a shade of purple.

"We will not be mounting a rescue," Doberman said, making another adjustment to her profile. "Remember your bargain, Anna. Nothing that would seriously endanger us. A Nephyr could destroy me easily, and has the creative capacity of a human, so the likelihood of our being discovered is very high."

"What about indirect?" Anna said. "I could hack into the camp computer and deactivate the locks on the doors, give Milar an escape window."

"The Nephyrs have one of their own watching him at all times," Doberman said. "Such a window would be useless."

Anna's little fingers tightened on the magnetic disc. "Is there a Nephyr with him right now?"

Doberman checked with the camp computer. "His lifeline is within ten feet of a Nephyr lifeline. I assume they are both in the same room, so yes."

"Fry the Nephyr's lifeline," Anna said.

"No," Doberman said. "The camp computer could trace the signal back to me and determine my chip number. We are not going to get involved in this. The prisoner is high-visibility. We would risk exposing ourselves without more time to plan and prepare."

"He's *torturing* him!" Anna snapped.

"Probably," Doberman agreed.

"*Please*, Dobie," Anna said. Her eyes were leaking again.

"No," Doberman said. "It's too dangerous to approach the prisoner in any way. Finish working with your apparatus or give it to me to destroy. Then get some rest. We'll be leaving for Eiorus in the morning."

"I *hate* you," she screamed, slamming her tiny fist across the desk, scattering the parts in all directions.

"That's fine," Dobie said. "Clean up your mess or I will."

Anna's eyes flickered back to the photograph of the prisoner. Eventually, her rhythms began to settle. "Who is that girl he's looking at?"

"The United Space Coalition operator that he kidnapped from her soldier."

"What's her *name?*" Anna snarled at him.

"Captain Tatiana Eyre. An operator for the Eighth Pod, Fourteenth Squadron."

Anna's eyes narrowed. "I thought the bitch looked familiar."

# CHAPTER 28

# A Doomed Smuggler

**M**AGALI STRUGGLED IN THE SLIME, TRYING TO GET HER PRYBAR seated in the hard little tendon at the base of a purplish Shrieker nodule. A few feet away, Joel worked beside her in silence. The other eggers were spread out, hunting nodules closer to the exit. She and Joel were the only two to have ventured this deep into the mines. So deep, in fact, that at first, Magali had thought Joel was trying to escape.

Then the smuggler had sat down suddenly at a crossroads of chambers and begun prying nodules from the floor. He'd been filling his sack ever since. Almost as if that was what he'd been intending to do all along. He seemed completely oblivious to the fact that he'd briefly made Magali's heart soar with hope that he was taking her out of the mines.

*Well,* Magali thought, bitterly, *he did put the Shriekers out of business.* She had to give him some credit for that.

Joel's method, though slapdash, had been more effective than any of the various chemicals the Director made them lace into the Shrieker food supply each time Coalition scientists concocted some new wonder drug to make the aliens more docile, or, even more ambitious, render them incapable of a Shriek.

All had failed miserably, sometimes killing their victims, or even bringing on a Shriek themselves.

Yet Joel's simple cardboard trick had been so effective that within twenty minutes, ninety-five percent of the hatching chambers were completely clear. Everyone had watched in awe as the Shriekers had simply gathered around the big red cardboard displays the smuggler had set up in the far corners of the mounds, effectively giving the eggers free run of the rest of the mines. Joel hadn't even needed the two little sacks of cayenne pepper, which he had stuffed into the bottom of his harvest sack, instead.

Now Joel was kneeling beside her in the slime, filling his own sack of Shrieker nodules like a good egger, looking for all the world like he planned on dancing to the Nephyrs' tune and getting the Director as big a bonus as possible.

It didn't make sense. Joel had no reason to help them. *He should be getting as far away from here as he can,* Magali thought, casting worried looks in his direction. She would never forget what they had done to Milar. Laughing, grinning Milar, more playful than his brother when they were children, had become a dark and sinister psychopath after only three months in their hands. And Milar had been a recruit, destined for the front lines. Who knew how long they planned to entertain themselves with the smuggler.

*He needs to get out of here,* Magali thought, watching Joel work.

After Anna and her team of doctors had sewed his skin back on, Milar had stayed in his room for weeks, letting no one inside except Patrick and Anna, the former because no one could keep him out and the latter because no one was stupid enough to try. The first time Magali had seen Milar after his rescue from the Nephyr Academy, it had been in a brief moment when she had been visiting Patrick unannounced, and had accidentally caught him sitting in the kitchen, a haphazard sandwich in his hand, another of Patrick's cyborg sketches on the table in front of him. Milar had snatched up the sketch when he saw her, and the look he had given her had made Magali freeze like a startled deer, the darkness in the place of her old friend leaving her chilled. Before she'd recovered enough to say something polite, Milar had taken his sandwich to his room and slammed the door.

He never had told her what the Nephyrs had done to him. Magali hadn't asked. She'd been too afraid of what he'd say.

*Joel, you need to get out of here. Lose yourself in the caves. Fall on a Shrieker. Shoot yourself.* Anything was better than doing a round with the Nephyrs.

But as time went on, Joel showed no signs of slowing his harvest. He worked methodically, every so often glancing at the exits to the deep chamber they were in—so deep it wasn't even on the foremen's maps. The only light came from several chambers behind them, which was why she suspected Joel had stopped in the first place. To go further would have been to go blind.

"What's the difference between here and someplace closer to the exit? Nodules are gonna be the same, wherever you go."

Joel's eyes flickered toward her, but he kept working.

He couldn't understand her. Damn.

Sighing, Magali dropped her prybar and held out one hand, palm side up. With her other hand, she made little running motions with her fingers across the palm, then pointed at the tunnel deeper into the mines. "You gonna run or what?"

Joel shrugged and went back to work. Every twenty seconds, he glanced up at the tunnels deeper into the mines.

"*Look,*" Magali said, louder, now. "I know someone who had a run-in with Nephyrs. Believe me, you *don't* want to get caught. Whatever cash you think you can get from those nodules isn't worth it. If you've got a way outta here, you should *go.*" She made little fleeing gestures again, and pointed at him insistently.

The smuggler gave her an irritated look before he seated the claws of his prybar under another bright red nodule, shoved downward, and began levering his weight down against it.

"If you *can't* escape, you should shoot yourself. Really, you should. Nephyrs have this thing with skin. They like to peel it off."

Joel sighed deeply and looked at her.

*He doesn't understand what I'm saying,* Magali thought, miserable. *All he understands is I'm making noise, and Shriekers don't like noise.*

Magali picked up her own prybar with tears in her eyes. She wanted Anna back. She'd never *been* on her own before, at least not since Anna had turned five and started telling her what to do. It had been comforting, in a way. Following Anna had been easy, a habit that she had fallen into when the two of them realized that Anna's brain could do things that Magali's couldn't. Anna was special, and Magali wasn't.

That she was alone now felt . . . terrifying.

If Anna had been here, she would've had some brilliant plan for how to get every single person out of the mounds with a full harvest sack. She would have been able to flabbergast the Nephyrs and the Director with a synchronized, systematic, perfectly executed scheme that left no man, woman, or child behind. Not that Anna cared about leaving the children behind, of course. She would have done it simply to prove to the Nephyrs she was smarter than they were.

Even with Joel's cardboard traps, moving the Shriekers out of the way meant nothing if the people harvesting the nodules were too weak to work the bar effectively, like the kid in formation. Even Magali was having a hard time at it . . . she'd only gotten thirty or forty.

Hours passed, and Joel made no move to stop digging, only stopping to glance at the back of the caves every twenty to thirty seconds.

*Shriekers,* Magali realized. If there were any back here, they would have collected around his neat little cardboard traps. Yet, as she worked, she saw what looked to be flashes of light in the tunnels beyond. She frowned and pointed.

Joel had a grim look on his face. He nodded and got to his feet. In a smooth motion, Joel took the gun from her sack, then dumped his sack into hers, almost filling it. He cinched the top shut, eyed the remainder, and then got to his feet, the broken ends of his shackles jingling. Gun in hand, he wadded up his own bag and threw it against the wall.

Seeing the empty sack abandoned in the slime, Magali knew that meant Joel didn't have an escape route. No self-respecting smuggler like Joel would leave behind ripe nodules if he had a way out. He'd been helping her before he went off to die. She bit her lip against tears.

"So now you're gonna go find a Shrieker to fall on, is that it?"

Joel's gaze flickered towards her, then he moved toward the inner chambers where she had seen the flashes.

"Thank you," she cried, at his back.

The smuggler hissed and put a finger to his lips, glaring back at her. Then he disappeared beyond the edge of the mine's ceiling lights, the guard's gun clutched in his good hand.

Magali picked up her nearly-full sack, blinking back tears. She turned to head back toward the entrance to the mines. Another hour or two somewhere else and she'd have enough nodules to leave the mines.

Yet she found herself staring down at her prybar, unable to summon the interest to finish filling her collection sack.

What was the point?

Magali knew that the moment she emerged from the mounds, the Director would throw her in eggers' prison. She'd shown she had rebel training. To *coalers.* Maybe the woman wouldn't go so far as to execute her, but Magali could definitely see the Nephyr leaving her in the stocks for a few days out of sheer pettiness. She might even beat a conspiracy confession out of her and extend her enlistment, make her a lifelong egger, if the three guards didn't get to her first. Or she might just hand her over to Colonel Steele and forget she ever had an egger by the name of Magali Landborn.

So what was the point?

Somewhere deeper in the mounds, Joel was going to kill himself. Alone and in the dark, after he'd helped her fill her sack, and she was going to let him do it.

Magali jabbed her prybar at a nodule, unable to see clearly through tears. She felt a soft squish as the bar impaled the nodule and unrefined Yolk began to seep out in a red-purple ooze, the infant Shrieker inside pulsing like a bloody maggot.

Grimacing, Magali pulled her prybar out and wiped it on her glove. For a long time, she looked at the purple-red slime on her fingertips, then down at the ruined nodule that was still leaking its contents onto the transparent, bubbly slime of the cavern floor.

*It's not right.*

The smuggler wouldn't be in this situation if it weren't for her. From his first imprisonment, to his beatings and eventual outing as Runaway Joel—all of it had spawned from Magali tackling the head foreman and pounding her unconscious to save her sister. If Magali had taken the fall for that, she would have gotten a day or two in the stocks, maybe a few lashes at most.

But Anna had wheedled Joel into covering Magali's ass, and now he was wandering off to kill himself. *After* he had tried to help as many eggers as possible, herself included.

She had to do something.

Still staring at the red-purple substance on her gloved fingertips, Magali again found herself wondering what her sister would have done in that situation.

*She wouldn't care,* Magali knew. *She'd tell me to suck it up and let him go off and die alone. More nodules for us.*

Magali narrowed her eyes and got to her feet. She wasn't Anna.

◀◀ ◆ ▶▶

Joel grimaced at the lone Shrieker camped out in the middle of the chamber floor, cradling what was left of a clutch of nodules. The rest had been torn away by a black-market mowing machine, which had left more than half of the nodules broken and oozing, the tiny larvae inside writhing or dead.

Joel felt irritation at that. Only a narrow-minded fool wasted nodules.

Piled along the edge of the cave were clusters of dead Shriekers, drag marks still puncturing the slime where they had been pulled across the chamber and dumped there.

Beyond that, the beam of a flashlight bounced across the adjacent cave.

Joel frowned at the pile of dead Shriekers. It was a novice's trick, something to calm shredded nerves. He himself hadn't killed any Shriekers for almost twenty years. Anyone with any experience would have realized that it would have been just as easy—and much less dangerous—to give them a distraction.

Besides, only idiots killed the goose that laid the golden eggs. *Especially* if that goose was capable of producing a psychic scream in its death throes that would leave anyone within three hundred yards a drooling vegetable for the rest of their lives, if they survived at all. It just wasn't smart.

But then, Martin had never been smart.

Joel gingerly began to move around the lone Shrieker. He was already feeling the fuzzy beginning of a Shrieker migraine. Anger?

Loneliness, perhaps? Did Shriekers even feel these emotions? The general consensus was that they were just stupid beasts, barely above the level of a garden snail, but Joel wasn't so sure. In all his years of smuggling, he'd developed a deep-rooted respect for the creatures, one that had kept him alive more times than he cared to count.

The Shrieker tensed when Joel neared it.

Despite his qualms, Joel considered shooting it. The Shriekers were already on high alert, and having its babies and companions lying dead in the muck around it certainly wasn't going to make the creature more stable. But, when it went back to examining its ruined clutch, Joel decided if it had intended to Shriek, it would have done so already, when Geo's goon was slaughtering its companions.

Easing the rest of the way around the Shrieker, Joel found himself at the edge of the next cave, looking in at Martin.

Geo's goon was kneeling in the Shrieker mucus, plucking usable nodules from the belly of the mowing machine, tossing those that were broken or crushed into the slime behind him. He'd already filled four sacks, and was halfway through his fifth.

Joel cleared his throat.

Martin froze, and his big fingers started to reach for the gun sitting on the housing of the mower, next to the flashlight.

Joel fired at the illegal Coalition pistol, putting a hole through Martin's gun, the housing, and the mower's engine. Sparks spat and sizzled from the mower's internal workings, and the entire thing stopped humming and sputtered to a stop.

Seeing that, Martin turned red and lunged to his feet. He shoved a finger in the mower's direction and spewed an explosive series of threats and curses. Joel could tell they were threats and curses by the spit flying from Martin's lips, and the animal look in his eyes.

Now that he thought about it, Martin looked a lot like Geo. Give Geo some color, trim off a few hundred pounds of fat . . .

*A son, perhaps?*

Joel laughed, delighted. He would be able to get back at the petty old albino, after all.

Martin quieted, his piggish nostrils flaring. He spouted another long string of words, this time lower, more dangerous.

*Yes, definitely a threat.*

Joel took a deep breath, wondering how he was going to handle this. The moment he'd seen Martin, he knew he would be down here for Harvest, and he also knew that Geo's goon had a reasonable way out that wouldn't have him hiking five bags of partially crushed Shrieker nodules past the Nephyrs guarding the entrance.

Joel pointed to one of the unmarked harvest sacks—the same any hunter could use to carry starlope meat from the mountains—and then mimed throwing it over his shoulder. Then he pointed at Martin and repeated the gesture, waiting expectantly.

The albino's son gave him a flat stare that did not need to be translated. To assist in Joel's understanding, however, he gave Joel a cruel smile and, while uttering another low series of words, he drew the tip of his fat finger across his throat.

Joel shot him in the foot.

As the goon howled, Joel strode forward and kicked him over, so he was on his face in the muck. Then, foot in the middle of Martin's back, the grip of the gun secured between his teeth, Joel used his good hand to start searching Martin's pockets for some sort of map. Novices always had a map.

When he found the wadded piece of paper, he grinned. Just four caverns away, marked with a bright red X, was the word SHIP.

Joel only had a brief moment to enjoy the moment, however, before Martin's bullish body began floundering, meaty arms struggling to get some sort of purchase beneath him. Then he was spinning under Joel's grip, throwing off Joel's balance, and, with only one working hand, Joel couldn't keep him down.

Within just a few horrible seconds, Martin had flipped completely over before Joel could once more get a hold on the gun. Martin smacked it out of his hand with a meaty fist and the weapon went flying. As Joel tried to scramble for the gun, the bigger man's beefy hands were wrapped around his throat, the studded gloves biting into Joel's neck. Suddenly, it was all Joel could do to breathe.

Despite Joel's efforts to pry Martin's hands from his throat, the edges of his vision began to go black, until the smuggler's sweaty, contorted brow and his piggish brown eyes were the only things he could see.

Joel could feel himself sliding into unconsciousness.

He could feel it, because his legs were going out underneath him. He slid to his knees beside the smuggler, unable to keep his muscles taut.

A female voice came from behind him, sounding dim, like it was a good distance away. Martin's hands loosened slightly. Joel sucked in a gasping breath, his vision still narrowed to a tiny, black-rimmed field.

The voice sounded again, like it was coming from the bottom of a well.

Martin's fingers reluctantly slid from Joel's neck.

Gasping, Joel flopped away from him, crawling, sucking in breath after breath, his chest burning, his vision still dangerously narrowed to the slime between his fingers. Martin did not press his advantage, and when Joel was able, he looked up to see what had intervened.

Magali was standing near the doorway, Joel's gun in her hand. She looked confused.

Behind him, Martin started talking, his voice low and soft. As he talked, he stood. Then the evil sonofabitch took a hobbling step toward her.

Joel knew the bastard would wring her neck and screw her corpse, if Magali let him anywhere near her. He got up, even as Martin continued to speak in low, soothing sounds, and shoved him, hard, motioning at Magali to back up a pace.

She didn't move.

Martin laughed and kept talking.

Joel put his body between them, shoving Martin back a step. Martin looked at him, gave him a smile that made his insides feel sick, and continued to speak.

*Lying,* Joel realized. Martin was lying to her. Telling her some story, some fabrication, and he couldn't do a damned thing about it.

Joel glanced back at Magali. She was frowning, now. His heart began to thunder in his ears. He shook his head emphatically, denying whatever Martin was saying, but Magali's frown darkened. The barrel of the gun slowly slid from Martin, until it was hovering between the two of them, as if she couldn't decide which one she wanted to shoot first.

*What's he* saying? Joel thought, panicking as Martin's soft voice continued to fill the cavern. Martin gave him a self-satisfied look that left him cold, and the first traces of fury were beginning to tighten Magali's face. Seeing that, Joel would have given anything to know what he was *saying.*

And then, as the barrel of the gun turned to level on his chest, Joel knew.

◀◀ ◆ ▶▶

"You *are* that Landborn girl, ain't ya? The gal whose daddy disappeared a few years back? David Landborn? One hell of a legend, that guy. Everybody knew of him . . . him and his two girls."

*Killer,* Wideman giggled.

"Don't come any closer," Magali snapped, when the enormous man took another step toward her, blood squishing up from the singed hole in his boot. He had the bulk of Patrick and Milar combined, and it scared her. He was a mod—he had to be. Nobody grew that big on their own.

"Sorry, honey, sorry." The man raised big hands in supplication. "Just thought we were friends, here."

"We aren't friends," she whimpered, keeping distance between them. "Back up." She was running out of cavern to back into.

"Maybe not yet," the big man said. "But we could be." He grinned, and it looked completely genuine. He did not back up.

"Did you say he was . . . " Magali swallowed, unable to wrench the word 'tortured' from her throat. "What did he do to him?" Her gaze was focused on Joel, who had gone deathly still, looking paler and scareder than she'd ever seen him before.

The big man snorted. "Who, Joel? Nothing." Then his smile turned vicious. "Well, nothing, unless you count him letting your daddy's name slip to the nasty Yolk runners he was double-crossing. Saved his own hide by trading his life for your daddy's. The crime boss gave him the choice to give up his life or give up his Yolk source. What do you think he did? Squealed like a rabbit. Geo sent his guys out the very next day to find your daddy. Made him watch while they collapsed the mine on your poor mother—horrible accident, don't you think?—and then took him out and tied him to a tree and slit his gut open for the tree-hares to eat while he screamed his lungs bloody."

Magali closed her eyes against tears. "You're lying," she whispered.

She heard the big man take another step toward her. Her eyes snapped open and she stumbled back, her heel hitting the edge of the cavern wall. "Get back, goddamn it!" she shouted.

The big man gave her a sad grin, completely ignoring the gun. "Lying?" The man shook his head. "Just look at Joel's face and tell me I'm lying." He gestured to the gray nature of the smuggler's skin. "He would've said something before this if I weren't."

"Joel's been muted," Magali said, feeling a wave of hope. "He can't understand a word you're saying."

The big man gave Joel an unreadable look. "He can't?"

"No," Magali said. "So just back up. I know Joel a hell of a lot better than you do."

The big man laughed. "Oh, I doubt that. I'm a smuggler, girl. I don't associate with the nicest of folk, and people like Joel, you get a couple beers in 'em and they talk. Stories spread. Go to any bar and ask. Sad truth is probably everybody you talk to this side of the Snake'll know what happened to your daddy, and why. Joel, the honorless little weasel he is, broke the Golden Rule of Yolk smuggling. He gave up his source, and his source paid with his life, and the life of his wife." The man laughed. "Funny thing is, the skinny bastard named his ship *Honor,* and the guy flying it ain't got a scrap of honor to save his soul. He's a liar, a betrayer, and a cheat. I think that's ironic."

Magali didn't believe him. Despite his smile, there was something in the man's eyes that reminded her of the way Colonel Steele's gaze had felt as it oozed down her naked body. Or Anna.

She shuddered when she thought of Anna.

Still, he had known about her father. Even most of the people in Deaddrunk had thought her father had suffered a mining accident. Most of them never even suspected he was smuggling Yolk to buy weapons for Wideman's war. For the big man to have known that her father had been part of the black market Yolk trade meant he had met her father, in some way or another.

Magali looked at Joel. She knew that the black market Yolk trade was a dangerous business. Nephyrs killed suspected smugglers without even a trial. Her father had always done everything he could to keep his children and his wife as far from the actual illegal processes as possible. He had told her again and again that to breathe one whisper to the wrong person would bring men on both sides of the law to his doorstep with guns in their hands.

Was *Joel* the one her father had been selling his Yolk to? Could that have been what happened to him, could that be why her mother had gone into the silver mines alone that night? A competitor found out about him and came to collect?

She didn't think Joel had the heart to kill anybody, and if the big man had claimed he had, she would've known he was lying. Even the guards, who had tried to kill him, were still alive and breathing when most people would've yanked the gun from her hand and put a beam through their skull.

But give someone up? Betray him to save himself? When she looked, there was something in Joel's eyes that hadn't been there before. Fear . . . and guilt. Softly, she said, "Joel, did you hand over my father to the Yolk cartels?"

He emphatically shook his head and made two cutting motions with his hand, pointing at the other man. *Don't believe him. He's lying.* For a moment, Magali believed him.

Then she realized that, if Joel was innocent, he wouldn't have had any idea what she was talking about. But, seeing his anguished face, she knew that he *did* know what she was talking about. He must have known this was coming since the first day he'd met her in the foremen's chambers.

"Of course he did."

She felt the big man move closer again and Magali stumbled sideways, almost slipping against the wall. "Stay back, *please!*"

The smile grew on the man's face, crinkling the corners of his eyes. "Come on, now. You ain't going to shoot anybody." He took another limping step toward her, his hands up in supplication, a grin on his face. He reached out with one beefy hand, palm up.

Joel suddenly grabbed the collar of the man's leather jacket and yanked him off his feet, into a backwards sprawl in the slime.

The big man lunged upward in a snarl, the harmless grin vanished from his face as if a switch had been flipped. He punched Joel in the wounded leg, hard, and Joel crumpled. As Joel was falling, the big man got to his feet and kicked him in the face.

Joel's head snapped back and he went still. *Oh my God,* Magali thought, the barrel of her gun drooping slightly as she looked on in horror. *He killed him.* His face had fallen into a cluster of broken nodules, and for a moment, the reddish gore leaking from around the infant Shriekers made it look as if his face had been ripped apart. Then she noticed the shallow rise of his shoulders as his chest expanded. Once. Twice.

Joel was alive, but barely.

"Now where were we?" the big man growled. He brightened. "Oh yeah." He wiped his bloody hand on the front of his shirt. He gave her an apologetic grin and he held out his hand. "My name is Martin." He took another limping step toward her.

Magali tore her gaze from Joel's chest and once more leveled the gun on the big man. "I told you to back up!" Even to her ears, it sounded like more of a plea than a command.

The big man's brown eyes were hard. "A pretty thing like you wouldn't shoot a friendly guy like me," he said. He was still smiling, but it sounded as if it were a warning. He continued to move toward her, slowly.

"Back!" she cried, working her way along the wall.

"There's no need for the gun, little girl," Martin said. "We both know you don't know how to use it."

"I know how to use it," Magali said, still backing along the wall. "I'm an expert marksman. My daddy trained me since birth."

Martin laughed. "Birth, huh?"

"Birth," she whispered. Her knees were shaking again, and her stomach was twisting with the urge to vomit.

His eyes dropped to the gun for a moment and he seemed to consider that. "You're an awful liar, kid. Your hand is trembling like an alchie who forgot his meds." He took another step.

"Colonists know all about how to shoot," Magali blurted. "Gotta shoot starlopes to eat. Especially the town where I'm from. Everybody knows how to shoot in that town. Everybody."

His patronizing smile never left him. "Yeah, I hear you're real good at shooting paper targets," the man said. "But shooting a man isn't the same as shooting a target, is it, dearie?" He took another step toward her, and another, his hands out in a peaceful gesture. His smile widened. "Besides. The way you're holding that gun, I'd guess you'd never even shot a starlope before, have ya, kid?"

And he was right.

Though she didn't respond, his confidence grew. "So you ain't never killed nothin' before, huh? Just cardboard and straw bales, is that it? That ain't no way to start your career there, little girl. Shooting a man? I can tell you from experience it ain't fun. Changes you forever."

"Please don't," she whimpered. "I hate guns. I don't want to shoot you."

He tisked, the good-natured smile still plastered on his face. "I know you don't. I can read people, dearie. I know what they call you. I know you ain't a killer."

Magali's heart clenched. She squeezed her eyes shut against tears.

He continued to move closer, slowly. "So just put the gun down, darlin'. Okay? We both know you ain't gonna use it. Just give me the gun and let Joel and me finish up our disagreement, okay, girlie?"

*I should give him the gun,* she thought, panic a hard lump in her throat. At least if she gave him the gun, he wouldn't hurt her.

"That's right," he said softly, like he was talking to a wild animal. He held out his hand, still inching forward. "Gimme the gun, darling. That's it."

Magali felt the wall end behind her, leaving her stuck in a rocky niche with no way out. The big man continued to close, murmuring soothing sounds.

*He's not going to stop,* she thought, horror racing through her veins. More than half of her wanted to throw the gun down at his feet and collapse into a terrified ball against the wall. The other half was screaming at her to pull the trigger, pull the trigger, pull it *now*. There were too many similarities to Anna in Martin's flat, dead eyes that managed, despite the smile, to carry a cold threat within them.

Recognizing this, Magali's terror grew. If he was anything like Anna, she would pay dearly for bruising his pride. Anna did not take slights to her pride gracefully. Cruelty was second nature.

And, looking into his eyes, Magali saw that same intellect, that same utter psychopathic confidence.

"Please don't come any closer," Magali whispered. "I'll shoot you if you come any closer." Instinct was warring with dread, and it was all she could do not to drop the weapon in the slime. She squeezed her finger on the trigger just to the point of firing.

Seeing that, Martin paused. The grin faded from his face, replaced with wariness. "Okay, I'll stop," he said, holding up his big hands. "Easy."

Seeing his feet had stopped moving, Magali let out the breath she had been holding. "Thank you."

"I just want us to be friends," he said, watching her anxiously. "We know you ain't gonna shoot me, else you wouldn't look like a terrified starlope. Just put the gun down and we'll talk, okay?"

Reluctantly, she lowered the barrel.

Martin grinned at her. "There. See? Friends. That's all I wanted. Nothin' nefarious. You can keep the gun, if it'll make you feel better. I just wanted to instill some reason, that's all. You seem like a nice enough gal. I've got a ship nearby and I'd be happy to let you hitch a ride outta the Yolk camp."

Magali's relief was so great she was shaking. "You'll help me escape?"

Martin's response was a grin.

Her eyes fell to the smuggler. "What about Joel? If we leave him here, the Nephyrs are going to kill him."

Martin's face twisted in a grimace. "Frankly, that wouldn't hurt my feelings none."

"I want to take him with us," Magali said. "Is there room on your ship for two?"

Martin gave her a long, analyzing look. "Is that a request or an order, little girl?"

Under his glare, she cringed. "A request." Then she quickly babbled, "But I *am* the one with the gun."

He laughed, but his eyes were cold black diamonds. "Yeah. I see that. Kind of funny that you ain't dead yet, eh?"

. . . *that you ain't dead yet?* Then, as Magali began to frown at that, Martin lunged.

Reflex drove Magali's arm up, and instinct did the rest. Just as she'd been taught on countless paper targets, she squeezed off four beams in a tight, smoky cluster over Martin's heart. One after the other, each with a three second recharge delay. Martin's eyes were wide with confusion and, as the fourth shot hit home, his knees buckled under him, blood pumping down the front of his shirt in scarlet waves. An instant later, he was face down in the slime, motionless, the deep red of his lifeblood making ruby puddles in the transparent Shrieker mucus.

*Killer,* Wideman's voice whispered to her.

Horrified, Magali threw the gun across the room, sucking in huge, gasping breaths of disbelief. Then, as the full implications of what she had done dawned upon her, she slid to the floor and emptied her lungs in a sob.

# CHAPTER 29

# Escape from Rath

IT HAD BEEN EASIER THAN TATIANA HAD THOUGHT. MILAR HAD just tapped the Nephyr guarding the compound with the wand when he reached for him, and the Nephyr had collapsed in a blubbery mass of circuitry.

Milar had dragged the Nephyr all the way back to his cell and made Tatiana shut the door. "This way, squid," he whispered, leading them out the back, deeper into the Nephyr block.

"Where are you *going*?" Tatiana hissed back at him. "We should be going the other way!"

"I've gotten out of here before," Milar reminded her. "Just keep quiet and stay with me."

"But there's nothing but barracks rooms—" she started, confused.

"Shhh," Milar said. "I know what I'm doing."

He didn't, as it turned out.

After blundering through thirty different hallways, narrowly avoiding getting caught by Nephyrs going to and from their barracks rooms and the chow hall, Milar finally stopped, face torn in confusion. "There used to be a trash terminal here."

"Yeah," Tatiana said, fuming. "I've been trying to *tell* you that, dweeb."

He peered down at her, clearly confused. "What?"

"This section of the base got an overhaul last year. Somebody decided the trash depot wasn't secure, so they replaced it with a barracks unit."

Milar cursed. "That was the only way out. The spaceport's so tightly locked down you couldn't get a mouse in there, much less a ship. There's nowhere else to go."

"That's not true," Tatiana said.

"It *is* true," Milar growled. "Anna studied this place for two weeks before she found a way out."

"I don't know who Anna is," Tatiana said, "But there's gotta be another way."

Milar snorted.

Then, suddenly, the base alarm began to blaze around them, lighting up the walls with flashes of red, raising goosebumps along Tatiana's arms with the screeching wail. Behind them, someone raised a shout. They heard footsteps running in another hall, going the other direction.

Milar's entire body, however, had gone as stiff as if the Nephyrs had burst into the hall with them and charged. Every ounce of amusement in him was gone. His gaze flickered back and forth, and his breathing had become strained. He was beginning to act like a cornered animal.

"They're going to catch us both," he whispered.

The way Milar was looking at her, his knuckles white on the EMP wand, Tatiana realized it was time to take things into her own hands before the bastard decided they were both safer dead.

"We can still get out of this," Tatiana said.

"I've backed us into a corner," Milar said. "I should've listened to you. Now we're both going to die, if not here, then back in the cells with the Nephyrs."

*He's going to do it,* Tatiana thought, horrified. If she didn't stop him, Milar was going to EMP her and slit her throat.

Though she didn't have a plan, Tatiana forced as much calm into her voice as she could and said, "Would you stop being stupid for just one minute, collie? That colonel was on the night shift. That's the *base* alarm, not the *section* alarm. Those Nephyrs are probably off to chase some smuggler or something. Nobody knows I rescued you, else they would've fried my brain by now."

The panic in Milar's eyes cleared a bit.

"Now," Tatiana said with as much firm authority and calm derision as she could fit into her voice, "if you're done blubbering, maybe we could try out my plan?"

His eyes narrowed as he glanced down at her. "I thought you didn't have a plan."

"I didn't," Tatiana snorted. "But you sure as hell gave me enough time to *form* one, while I was spending the last twenty minutes following you around in circles. Give me the wand."

"Coaler, don't play with me," he growled. "I'm going to need it."

"To use it on me?" she demanded.

His eyes flickered away. *He's scared,* Tatiana thought.

"Come on," she said, throwing her hand out between them insistently. "Give."

She saw his fist tighten on it as he cast a look down the corridor ahead of them. For a moment, it looked like he was going to use the wand on her anyway. Then, reluctantly, Milar handed it over. "Good," Tatiana said, collapsing it and closing her fist over it. "I just stopped you from doing something really stupid. You can thank me later." She turned on her heel and started walking, having no idea what she was going to do next.

Behind her, Milar hesitated a moment, then she heard him jog to catch up. "Where we going, coaler?"

"You don't want to know." In truth, *she* didn't even know. It was the base alarm, true, but that didn't mean it wasn't for them. The fact that base security hadn't crispified her brain yet could have simply been because the Nephyrs wanted her alive when they caught her.

"You don't know, do you?" Milar growled.

"Of course I do."

"Gimme back the wand, squid."

"Screw you, crawler."

She led him to a service corridor and, lifting the lockdown code with a quick AI override, let them inside.

"I'm not gonna use it on you," Milar said.

"Bugger off," Tatiana said, closing the service door, keeping the wand tightly in a fist, out of reach.

Then, with the door to the passageway shut, she took a moment to think. "What about the Yolk drops?"

Milar snorted. "More security than the Emperor's cruise ship."

"Prisoner intake?"

"We'd stick out like a sore thumb."

Trying to think of all the places where they could get into a ship or get over the base fence, she said, "Civilian housing?"

"And you think we're somehow gonna make it two miles all the way across the base so we can boost ourselves over a razor wire fence in some engineer's backyard while Nephyrs and soldiers are boiling around us like ants?"

Soldiers.

Tatiana froze. Eyeing Milar, she said, "How much do you weigh?"

"More than you," Milar growled, stepping menacingly toward her. "Now gimme back that wand."

"What's your body displacement? A hundred and fifteen liters?"

Milar frowned. "Maybe a little less."

"Let's hope so," Tatiana said. "I'm fifty-one liters, and you add a hundred fifteen to that and you get one-sixty-six. The belly of my soldier holds two hundred and twenty, max."

Milar's eyes went wide. "You can't be serious."

"You rather die in here, collie?" she demanded, waving at the walls that were resounding with the shriek of the base alarm. "Because I can leave you here sucking your thumb, if that's what you want."

"How would I breathe?" he demanded.

"I'll put a hole in the air tube, let you suck on it." She turned and started walking.

The colonist didn't follow her. When she looked, his face was a funny shade of white.

"Oh don't worry about it," Tatiana said, "I won't let you choke too much."

She heard the colonist reluctantly follow her. "You realize," he said, coming abreast of her as she took the first flight of stairs, "that this sounds like a damned good way to get us both crushed when your soldier bounces a little too hard and there's no goop to cushion us."

"I'll be careful," she said, cresting the steps.

"Careful's got nothing to do with it," Milar growled. "You put even a bit too many Gs into a landing and we'll both be squished."

Tatiana shrugged. "So they say." She turned down the narrow south corridor and started leading them toward the soldier hangar.

"Squid," Milar warned, grabbing her by the shoulder. "There ain't an operator on Fortune who could do what you're planning without killing us both."

Tatiana gave him a beaming smile. "Guess it's a good thing I'm the best operator in the sector, then, eh?"

Milar snorted. "Sure you are." He didn't release her shoulder. "I want a different plan."

Smiling sweetly, she said, "Chicken?"

Milar's eyes narrowed.

# CHAPTER 30

# The Ferryman's Dilemma

JOEL GROANED AND ROLLED OVER, THE TINGLING, METALLIC taste of blood overwhelming even the throbbing in his face. Blood . . . or something else.

He winced when he realized his face had been mashed into a cluster of ruined nodules, the grublike larvae wriggling against the insides of his cheeks and teeth as their life fluids spilled into the slime around them, prodding their way through his lips as they sought refuge from the air.

Horrified, Joel sat up and gagged, shoving the larvae from his mouth with his tongue.

Yolk. That overpowering acrid taste of metal was raw Yolk.

Disgusted, Joel wiped the blood-red sludge off his lips and spat. His tongue and the inside of his mouth were numb with the taste of Yolk. He rubbed the top of his tongue against the roof of his mouth, trying to rid it of the overwhelming metallic burn. He was still busy spitting when Magali said, "Wideman was right."

Joel froze, turning to her.

Magali was slumped in the slime, her back against the wall, cheeks wet, eyes red and inflamed. She was dressed in clothes that were much too big for her, with a bloody cluster of burn-holes centered around her belly. Defeat was clear in her posture. "I'm a killer. All he ever said about me. 'Killer.' He was right." She gave a miserable laugh. "I'm even wearing his clothes. Like skinning a starlope."

Joel turned and saw Martin's naked corpse sprawled out in the Shrieker mucus, face down, blood puddling around him.

*She killed him,* Joel thought, stunned. He hadn't thought she had it in her. The little sister, sure, but Magali? Even after pounding in Gayle Hunter's temple and kicking Yvonne in the face and breaking Rachel's finger, it had never occurred to him that she could pull the trigger. Threaten, yes. Pull the trigger, no.

Not for the first time, he was absolutely delighted to be proven wrong. Absolutely delighted . . . and probably still breathing because of it.

Then something else occurred to him. *Why am I understanding what she's saying?* Had Martin jogged something loose when he rearranged his teeth? He opened his mouth to ask.

"Not that you understand a goddamn word I'm saying, you useless smuggler asshole," Magali said.

Joel shut his mouth with a frown.

"Not even that psychotic bastard Milar was just 'killer.' He got *odes* written about him. He got his essence put in those goddamn zucchini a thousand times. He got to see his future. *Everybody* in that damn town got more than just one word. Everyone but me and Anna." Magali paused, giving Joel a wry, pinched smile. "But I guess I shouldn't complain too much. All Anna got was screaming. Every time he saw her, the little old fart would go apeshit. Eyes would bulge out and he'd empty his lungs like they were on fire. You could always tell when Anna got too close to the little bastard. The whole village would hear it."

Joel frowned. He had heard whispers of a legendary oracle hidden somewhere north of the Snake. Geo had offered twelve mil to anyone who could capture the bastard and bring him back to the Junkyard. Was Wideman in Deaddrunk? It made sense, considering all of the rumors he had heard of the colonists and their war games. He thought they were just creeps with a death wish. But maybe they were creeps with a death wish and an oracle.

Magali laughed. "You know, when Wideman first saw me, I was just a baby in my Daddy's arms. Wideman pointed at me and said 'killer.' Most of the people there actually thought he'd said 'Kill her,' and if my Daddy weren't so good at punching people in the face, they'd've thrown me down an abandoned mineshaft, quicker than spit."

Joel nodded, frowning as he thought about David Landborn's infamous war games. The man had scared the crap out of him, talking about independence from the Coalition. Just staying in Deaddrunk had always made Joel uneasy. The whole town was armed to the teeth, funded by David's cultivation of a secret Yolk mine. The whole lot of them were dead set on starting a war.

David Landborn . . . her father.

Suddenly, everything snapped into place for him. There was a girl, born in Deaddrunk, who was rumored couldn't miss. Anything she shot at, she hit. Like, better than a robot. The colonists had kept her name to themselves, not really trusting a smuggler with that kind of information, because in their eyes, with his background in the Coalition, Joel was just one step away from being a Nephyr himself, but he was pretty sure he had heard 'Deaddrunk' somewhere along the way.

Maybe her shooting Martin wasn't as much of a long shot as Joel had imagined. In that town, anyone with the last name 'Landborn' had given him goosebumps when he'd stood next to them for too long. His eyes fell once again to the neat cluster of holes over Magali's belly. It wasn't the grouping of a terrified egger. It was the grouping of a killer.

A cold tingle worked its way down his spine as he once again met her eyes. *This* was the 'Killer'? *Magali?*

Magali hefted her gun, looking at it, seemingly lost in her own thoughts. "All that old bastard saw was 'killer' when he looked at me. Not 'mother' or 'sister' or 'artist' or a dozen other things I want to be. Just 'killer.' I spent every moment of my life waiting to get out of Deaddrunk. I hated that place. All they cared about was war. My dad had the whole town doing war games twice a week, and he'd force me to play along."

She took a deep breath, half shudder, and said, "I'd always make a mistake early and Anna would delight in killing me. Anna or Milar. They liked to work together. Team from hell. Undefeated. Once took out our entire village, just the two of them. Could read the rest of us like a book, knew what we were gonna do before we did it." Magali sniffled, and tears were once more leaking down her cheeks. "I didn't want to kill anybody," she whimpered. "I hated those stupid games. I let them find me on purpose so I didn't have to shoot people." She gave a bitter laugh. "Even when it was just paint and lasers, I couldn't shoot people. Thought I could change my future by studying art and trying to get pregnant. Would've succeeded, too, if my bitch of a sister had stayed out of things. Patrick was gonna give up the war for me. We were gonna move across the Snake, somewhere we could have kids and a normal life."

Joel nodded with commiseration.

Magali's dark look returned. "Anna was like Dad. She wanted to start a war. Was gonna see me fulfill Wideman's prophecy whether I wanted to or not. Did you know my father never let me ride in a ship while he was alive? He never let me learn to fly on my own. He paid for Patrick and Milar and Jeanne to go through flight school but he made me stay at home and learn hand-to-hand combat like a good little soldier, instead. The first time I ever rode on a ship was when Patrick and I snuck out of town. Daddy was so angry . . . grounded me for four months." Tears were streaming down her cheeks, and Joel watched, uncomfortable, as she reached up and swiped them away with her arm. "The bastard," she whimpered. "I wanted to be a pilot so badly. I wanted to go to the stars. I wanted to get *away* from here. I think that's why he wouldn't let me learn to fly. He knew I wouldn't stay. He knew I'd join up and ferry Yolk back and forth for the Coalition if it would get me off Fortune."

*Get me off Fortune . . .* Suddenly, Joel's brain snapped into focus. He drew his hand from the Shrieker slime, and still clutched in his palm was Martin's scrap of engine manual with his hasty map drawn upon it. From the corner of his eye, he watched Magali sit up to look at the map.

"Where did you get that?" she asked. "The dead guy?"

Joel gave her a bovine look, blinking with great effort. It was much too interesting to let her know he understood every word. He would have to consider that very hard in the future, when it came time to tell her the truth. *Why waste a possible lifetime of fun?* Oh, he was sure he would give up the act sooner or later, but, considering the interesting things he had already learned, it would be a lot later than sooner. He moved his tongue around the inside of his mouth, still grimacing at the metallic buzz of residual Yolk.

Then he jerked. Could it be the Yolk? Considering the way his throat was burning, he was pretty sure he'd swallowed some of it.

"Is that a *map*?" She straightened further. She looked interested, yet at the same time tired. Like she was asking if he had an extra beer.

Joel nodded again, bemused with the idea that the unrefined Yolk, rather than Martin's kick, could be responsible for jogging his memories loose. Then he winced, realizing his mistake.

Magali had gone quiet, watching him. Joel didn't like the look she was giving him. "You've been nodding a lot. You'd nod if I asked you if you were the smuggler doing business with Dad before he disappeared, wouldn't you, Joel?"

For the first time, Joel realized that the gun dangling limply from one hand was beginning to tighten in her grip. The look she was giving him was much too dark.

*Okay, Joey-baby, fun time's over.* He opened his mouth to blurt out the truth.

Magali interrupted him with a sigh. "Of course he didn't betray Dad. That bastard was lying to me. Smooth-talking me just like Anna. Hell, *he* was probably the one who betrayed Dad. How else would he have known? Joel probably just got scared because he knew the guy would just love to wring my neck." She got to her feet, steadying herself in Martin's oversized boots. "You were trying to save me, weren't you, Joel?"

Joel nodded.

Magali sighed, deeply. "She fried your ability to read, too, didn't she?"

Joel nodded.

In baby talk, complete with elaborate gestures that meant nothing to him, Magali said, "What you don't understand, *Joel*, is that that little piece of *paper* in your hand is a *map*, and that *map* is gonna lead us to Martin's *ship*. Can you fly a *ship*, Joel?" She made little bird wings with her hands.

*Can I fly a ship.* The snort of disdain was too much to hold back. He started coughing, holding his fist over his mouth to hide his amusement. Then Joel had an unnerving thought: Even the refined Yolk wore off. A few days to a week, depending on the person, and it was gone. Joel's gaze fell to the ruined nodules, then migrated to the sacks of Yolk Martin had harvested. That should keep him a while . . .

Magali marched over to him and grabbed him by the jaw, making his entire face flare up in a jolt of fire that traced through his skull and down his spine. "A *ship*, goddamn it!" she snapped. "Can you fly a *ship?*" She made like she was piloting a joystick with one hand.

Joel jerked his head away, rubbing his jaw. *What got up her undies?* he thought, glaring.

"Merciful Aanaho," Magali whispered, slumping back to the wall and pressing the back of the hand holding the gun against her head. "What are you thinking, Mag? He was dumb as a board even when he could understand you. Danced to Anna's tune like a pitiful goddamn puppet."

*Puppet?* Joel narrowed his eyes, but waited.

"Get up," Magali finally said, standing. "We're gonna go find that ship and you're gonna fly me outta here."

Joel waited for her to gesture for him to rise before he stood. Though it was against his instincts, he let her snatch the scrap of paper from his grip. He studied her as she peered at the smudged lines and tried to make sense of it, trying not to allow his resentment to show. *So I'm a puppet, eh?* After everything he'd done for her, after *everything* he'd been through, she thought he was just a stupid puppet.

"Follow," Magali eventually ordered, making a 'come' gesture.

Joel felt the resentment all the way down to his toes. It took a force of willpower to keep up the act and follow her through the cavern.

*A puppet,* he thought again as he bored holes into her back. *Does that mean they knew what they were getting me into? All that time, they knew they were sending me to get outed as Runaway?*

These tunnels, like all unaltered Shrieker tunnels, were narrow and low. Magali, being tall for a girl, had to hunch over in order to move forward. Joel, being taller than most men, really had to scrunch down not to scrape his head and back against the ceiling. After a few more minutes half-squatting, half-crawling in the maze of Shrieker tunnels, he began to frown at the odd howl he heard ahead. The Shrieker mucus, he realized, was beginning to thin under his bare feet. It had disappeared entirely when the tunnel suddenly opened up and sunlight hit him in a startling blast. Joel stood up and stared at the massive cavern that loomed before him.

Beyond the cave, the wind whipped by with such force that it howled against the rock.

Martin's point of entrance was a huge cave set into the sheer, four-thousand-foot cliff overlooking the acidic green waters of the Snake. Martin's ship—*his* ship, Joel realized, his heart giving an extra thud—was sitting like a gigantic ebony raven overlooking the titanic crevasse. He'd never seen anything so beautiful in his life. He walked up and touched a polished black leg, enraptured by its very presence. Within its titanium core, he could feel his own freedom pounding at his essence. He felt a stupid grin slide onto his face.

For the first time in three years, Joel felt the stirrings of his old self again. He felt like Runaway Joel.

"It's beautiful," Magali whispered.

Joel nodded, breathless.

"That's our way out of here, isn't it?"

*Sure is, tootz,* Joel thought, activating the ramp. *Mine, anyway. Whether you go along all depends on whether or not you happen to be in the cockpit with me in the next twenty seconds.* He started to climb the ramp before it had fully extended.

Then, from the entrance to the cave, Magali said, "Okay. Stay here. I'm going to go get the others."

That broke his reverie. Joel frowned and turned, tearing his eyes from his ship. "What?"

But Magali was already gone, the outline of her back disappearing down the tiny Shrieker tunnel.

For a moment, Joel didn't understand. *Others? What others?* Then his mind clicked back into gear. Of course she would go get the Shrieker nodules. Smart girl. Would make a good smuggler. Here Joel was all caught up with getting out of there, not thinking about anything but his own freedom, but she was already one step ahead . . . and thinking about their credit accounts when they got out. Grinning like a fool, Joel jumped down from the ramp and went to help her.

His grin began to fade when he realized that the cavern with Martin's sacks of Shrieker nodules was empty. Goosebumps began to form as he watched the Shrieker slime drip back into place where running feet had sped through it, headed toward the main entrance to the mines.

He reconsidered what 'the others' could mean, and as he did, his jaw fell open.

*Oh hell no,* Joel thought, taking an automatic step backwards. He was *not* spending the next ten hours ferrying three thousand naked eggers back and forth in a hull designed to hold no more than forty-five at a time. He grabbed a sack of nodules with his good hand and dragged it back to the ship. He tucked the sack carefully in a corner and hid it with a few crates of mechanical tools. He wasn't greedy. One sack was enough, especially when he knew that if he went back for more, he would end up ferrying a few thousand helpless eggers out of the Shrieker mounds because he was a self-acknowledged softie and if he had to look into their big, frightened eyes to tell them 'no,' it would be all over.

"Sorry, guys," he muttered. "That's a suicide run and I'm itching to get the hell outta Rath." He slapped CLOSE, then jogged past the storage bins and toward the helm, unhappily noting the mess Martin had made of the place in his absence. He actually came to a halt as he passed through the kitchen, stopping to stare at the big heart mug that now rested beside the coffee pot . . . right next to a big stuffed bear and a can of lollipops.

Apparently, Joel wasn't the only one who had been a softie.

*That,* Joel thought, staring at the bear's bright red, tinselly fur, *is weird.* He wondered for a moment if Martin could have a girl hidden somewhere on board.

Or maybe he was just secure enough in his three hundred and fifty pounds of masculinity that a glittery stuffed bear and a can of lollipops would be taken in stride.

*Of course,* Joel thought, still staring, *if anyone mentioned it, he could just wring their neck and bury them in the peat bogs.*

It reminded Joel of Geo's annoying eating habits. Like father like son? He once again thought of the big man he'd left face down in the slime. *Geo is gonna be so pissed off when I tell him,* Joel thought, delighted.

From a distance, of course. A very long, very untraceable distance. A hologram would work well. Too bad he hadn't gotten any footage of the corpse. That would've been the icing on the cake. Killing the brute, taking the Yolk, stealing back his ship . . . Life couldn't get any better than this.

He ducked through the kitchen and into the hallway that led to the bridge.

Inside the cockpit, Joel slumped into the captain's chair, expecting to find the comforting dimples his bony cheeks had left in the leather, and instead finding that Geo's thug had torn out his old antique pre-Coalition chair and replaced it with a shiny new chrome-plated Evil Warlord model, complete with lazy-man hand-pads, lumbar massage, and RoboDrink beverage service. Joel's disgust was so thick that, for a moment, he forgot about his soon-to-be ferryman status.

*Hell no, hell no,* he thought, as he remembered. He ignored the lazy-man handpads Martin had installed and shifted the chair forward to the main console, his fingers running automatically over the startup procedures. As he worked, he estimated how long it would take Magali to go back, convince the eggers she had a way out, and return. Seconds began to tick off in Joel's head like a Doomsday countdown. Joel knew he was too much of a softie. Always had been. It was one of his most expensive flaws, one that had cost him several thousand pounds of flour when a starving village kid happened to tug on his arm at just the right moment, and almost a hundred grand in antibiotics when a plague-stricken woman offered him a free cookie when he was fueling up at her station.

Joel knew that the moment he saw those three thousand wan, frightened eggers' faces, he would spend the rest of his life ferrying the poor fools to safety.

It would be the rest of his life because, gee, eventually the Nephyrs were going to start wondering why no one was emerging with their harvests and gee, a glossy black ship makes an awfully pretty target for a military-grade ship cannon.

He *had* to get out of there. He was Runaway Joel, not Ferryman Joel.

Joel warmed up the engines and was getting ready to increase thrust when a thought hit him like a Coalition freighter.

*I never wanted to be Runaway Joel.*

He'd been tricked into it by Geo, back when the two of them were still friends in the service, when Joel was a starry-eyed, fancy-flying academy grad who hadn't broken a law in his life and Geo was a thin young squadron commander whose pink eyes were only then seeing their first glints of criminal intent. Geo had spent years convincing him. He had cajoled and bullied and eventually blackmailed. Now, over twenty years later, it had gone on so long that his smuggling had become a habit, something that Joel had taken for granted right along with Geo's sadistic evil streak.

As a kid, a hotshot sixteen-year-old who had already passed his flight certs, Joel had always envisioned himself as an admiral or a justice. Someone proud, honored, respected. If Joel had had his way, he would still be flying for the Coalition and carrying a respectful rack of medals and commendations for diligent service and outstanding flying.

It was the outstanding flying that had gotten him into trouble. Joel's superiors had seen his skills and decided he would make a good flyboy for the Controlled Substances unit—Geo's unit. And Geo, seeing those same skills, had come to a much different conclusion.

With promises, nudges, and threats, Geo had slowly pulled Joel from the charmed life of a Coalition ace into the shady underground of the space station Junkyard. The change had been so slow that Joel hadn't even realized it had happened until he saw the first Wanted poster with his name on it. The shock had been so intense that Joel had set his ship to drift and he had floated in space for a week, alternating between crying in self-pity and mourning his vanished ideals.

*I never wanted to be Runaway Joel,* he thought again.

Then a small voice added, *So here's your chance to change.*

He was still sitting there, staring dumbly at the console, when Magali led the first eggers through the back of the cavern. He watched the ship's cameras as she jogged across the cave and disappeared under the belly of his ship with the eggers in tow. He saw her move for the ramp release. Saw her attempt to open the door and have the ship rebuff her. His thumb hovered over the outer seals release switch. His heart pounded. His head hurt.

He wanted to change. He wanted his old life back. His honor. More than anything, he wanted to go straight.

"Joel!" he heard Magali shout. "Open the goddamn door, Joel!" He saw her pound on the sealed door. He heard her yell in frustration, then move back, draw her gun, and fire at the ship in disgust. Joel squeezed his eyes shut.

He was home free, and yet instead of taking off, he was hunkered inside his ship, seriously contemplating heroically dying to help a few hundred eggers get lost in the woods. *For what?* he thought. *For honor?* He snorted disdainfully at the thought. Whatever honor he ever had had been thoroughly obliterated by two decades of doing Geo's bidding in order to eat.

Besides, helping a few thousand eggers escape a Harvest wasn't exactly going to get him an Emperor's Commendation. It was going to get him shot out of the sky, and once the Nephyrs dragged him out of the flaming wreckage, he'd die in the same way he was going to die before—alone and unknown, derided and sneered at, his name something to be laughed at rather than something to be remembered.

*It's the Yolk talking,* he thought, listening to the electric crackle of the gun's energy as the shots bounced off his ship. *You're always going to be Runaway Joel. That's all you are now. Just get out of here.*

The ship continued with its power-up procedure. Outside, he heard the grating sound of the legs being retracted.

"Joel!" Magali shouted, banging upon the ship's outer shell once more. "Joel, please!" Then he watched as the ship's exhaust blew her aside, to huddle in the corner with the rest of the terrified, wan-faced—

He could help them. Of anyone this side of the Outer Bounds, Joel could help these people. He had the skills. He had the ship. He knew the Nephyrs were going to kill any stragglers, any who didn't meet their quotas. He knew those quotas, at least for the Forty-Third battle squadron, were going to change depending on how pretty the girls were when they came out, or how much they decided they wanted to see someone scream.

Joel had heard horror stories of the Forty-Third. Colonel Steele had gathered a hundred and forty-four of the most despicable, most disgusting Nephyrs that could be found this side of the Outer Bounds. 'The best and brightest,' they were called. They were sent to do all sorts of missions—reconnaissance, detective work, peacekeeping—but their specialty was Harvest. His unit was one of the few that *requested* to guard the Harvest. Most Nephyrs didn't enjoy herding terrified eggers. The Forty-Third delighted in it.

He had heard the stories. He knew eggers went missing with the Forty-Third.

He could help them. He knew he could. He knew there wasn't a Coalition fighter pilot in the Sector who could catch him if he were behind the controls of *Honor*.

*Honor*. After stealing it from a government shipyard, he had named his ship *Honor,* as if some unconscious part of him had recognized what he had given up when he fell in with Geo. Joel squeezed his eyes shut. Without looking at his console, he reversed the takeoff measures. Once the ship had touched back down, he gently flipped the outer seals switch with his thumb. He heard the ramp slide down. He heard a woman storm aboard, felt the barrel of the gun touch the back of his head.

"You had to think about it, didn't you?" Magali said. "You weaselly piece of shit." He knew by the soft, quiet tone of her voice that she was very close to pulling the trigger.

Hands out where she could see them, Joel carefully got up from the console and straightened until he was towering over the Landborn woman. This close, he easily could have reached out and grabbed the gun, but he stayed well back, having no misconceptions about taking the gun from her and surviving afterward. The tight cluster of holes over Martin's heart had been proof enough of that. He just waited, afraid to move, afraid to speak for fear of saying the wrong thing, watching the indecision in her face, hoping she would give him the benefit of the doubt.

Magali's hazel eyes never left his. They both knew she couldn't fly it. There probably wasn't a single egger in the camp that could fly *a* ship, let alone *his* ship. She needed him, and they both knew it. He saw that anguish in her face, knew she recognized that fact, and hated him for it. Joel watched her over the barrel of the gun, waiting.

Magali cursed and lowered the weapon. "The only reason you're not dead right now," she said softly, "is because you can't understand a damn word I say, so I'm going to give you the benefit of the doubt and assume that you didn't realize I was coming back."

Joel nodded.

"Joel, I need you to fly these people out of here." Magali pointed to the eggers gathering in the cave, then to the cargo hold of the ship, then out past the mouth of the cavern, beyond the Snake. "I convinced them to stop the Harvest. We're gonna show the Director she can't push us around anymore. We're making a stand."

*She has got to be insane,* Joel thought.

Magali made a frustrated sound. "Nephyrs"—she jerked a thumb at his ruined hand—"are going to *kill*"—she drew her thumb across her neck—"us." She pointed to him, then to her. "If we don't fly"—she made little wings with her fingers—"away." She fluttered them toward the door.

In that, Joel wholeheartedly agreed. He nodded.

Magali made a frustrated sound. "You can't listen, you can't speak, you can't *read . . .* " She glanced at the eggers in the cavern. "Merciful Aanaho," she whispered. "We need a miracle."

"How's this for a miracle," Joel said. "You get the hell off my ship and I'll pretend you didn't just point a gun at me and together we'll start getting these people somewhere safe."

Magali jerked like a dumbstruck starlope.

"I'll save as many as I can," Joel said. "But the moment I see a Nephyr or a Coalition ship, I'm gone, and I won't be coming back."

Magali continued to stare at him.

"Either that," Joel said, "or stay, and I'll lock the ship down again and take us anywhere you wanna go and we'll let the eggers deal with Colonel Steele and the Director on their own."

When Magali finally spoke, it was an icy-cold whisper. "You were listening?"

Joel didn't need to ask when she was referring to. He nodded. "I think I got some Yolk under my tongue while I was unconscious. Fastest way to the bloodstream, baby. It'll probably wear off any minute now, then I'll be right back to that drooling idiot you know and love."

Magali looked like she was trembling, though by the hardness in her eyes, fear was the last thing from her mind. Too carefully, she said, "All that time, you could've said something. You let me think . . . " She shook as she looked up at him. Softly, she whispered, "If you're lying to me—" she stopped and hesitated, scanning his eyes, before she continued. "If you take off and don't come back, I will make what the Nephyrs did to you look like happy hour."

Joel believed her. If the console hadn't been behind him, he would have taken a step backwards. As it was, he felt pinned under her stare, his chest tight where he expected a cluster of beams to appear as she changed her mind.

Still too softly, Magali turned back toward the cargo hold and said, "I'll go see what I can do to get the eggers organized."

Glad for the reprieve, Joel said, "The hold'll take forty, forty-five if they're small." Magali looked over her shoulder at him a moment, then strode off of his ship. Joel let out the breath he had been holding.

*You might not think you're a killer, love,* he thought, watching her go. *But you just gave Geo a run for his money.*

Outside, Joel heard Magali shout orders to the amassed eggers. A moment later, a group of naked men and women stumbled onto his ship, pushing and shoving like frightened cattle. Flipping on the intercom, Joel said, "Be nice, people. You don't act civil and you're gonna find out how unhappy I can make people who ride in my cargo bay." Then Joel was sealing the gates, his career as a ferryman beginning in earnest.

# CHAPTER 31

## One, Two, Three

**M**AGALI HAD JUST USHERED THE FOURTEENTH GROUP ONTO THE ship and was standing well away from the cliff's edge, watching them go, when the little boy from the formation—a shy, grinning kid affectionately called Baby Benny by the male side of the camp—ran through the back of the cavern toward her, weaving between anxious clusters of eggers to reach her.

*He's panting,* Magali thought, anxiety filling her gut as the little boy stumbled to a halt beside her. "What is it?" she whispered.

"They're coming," Benny said, too loudly. "I heard someone in the caverns. They're *coming,* Magali."

*We're not even half done yet,* Magali thought, fighting panic. "Nephyrs or guards?" she asked.

"I don't know," Benny whimpered. His eyes were rolling wildly at the entrance, his little body tense with terror.

*Trapped,* she thought, feeling the empty void of the cliff behind her. The wind howled across the stone lip, tugging at the sweaty strands of hair against her face. She took an involuntary step backwards, imagining the endless fall to the rocky riverbed thousands of feet below.

"Did they see you?" Magali asked, her throat tight with fear. She had instructed her eggers to remove all the Shrieker carcasses from the other caverns and throw them over the cliff, along with Martin and the broken mower machine. Aside from the crushed nodules left by the mower, there wasn't anything to suggest they were back here.

"I don't know," Benny said, glancing over his shoulder and inching toward her. "I think maybe."

*Shit,* Magali thought, catching the panic growing in the eggers' eyes. She had to do something. She looked down at the gun in her hand. She remembered using a similar gun, back when Wideman's prophecy hadn't come true and she'd been shooting at straw bales and bull's-eyes, not people. She remembered how easily she had been able to hit the center ring, how naturally it always fell into place for her.

*Just think of them as targets.* She got down to one knee, readying her gun.

She heard Wideman's high-pitched giggle. *Killer.* He jabbed a crooked, arthritic finger at her, his hand still covered with green and yellow vegetable shreds. His eyes showing whites all around, he cackled, *Killer. Magali the killer. Killer, killer, killer.*

Magali hit the side of her head with her palm, forcing the image away. She wasn't a killer. She was just doing what she had to do. Saving people.

"Everyone else get away from the entrance," she said, peering down the sights. Seeing where she was aiming, the eggers quickly obeyed.

"I'm a starlope hunter," a man whispered, sidling up behind her. "I'm a decent shot."

"I'm from Deaddrunk," Magali replied, not taking her attention off the entrance. Her gun's sights never wavered.

The man's eyes widened. "Oh." She felt him back away and whisper to one of his friends. Then Magali's focus was elsewhere, back on the entrance of the cavern.

*Please be human,* Magali thought. She was a good shot, but energy weapons could only damage Nephyrs in the eyes or mouth—if the mouth was even open. And Nephyrs were *fast.* If it were Nephyrs, she'd only have seconds before they were on top of her. She prayed it wasn't Nephyrs. The three-second charge delay would cripple her with Nephyrs.

She heard a noise in the tunnel.

A whimper built in her throat. *It's just like target practice,* she told herself, fighting the urge to drop the gun and stumble to the side to huddle with the other eggers. She forced her fingers tighter around the pistol and waited.

The first human guard entered the cavern with a confused look, stumbling to a halt when faced with the vast emptiness of the Snake beyond. Magali recognized him as one of the guards who had been most likely to offer his canteen to eggers who emerged from the mines after shift. He had offered water to Magali more than once, to her gratitude.

*He's human,* she thought, and for the first time truly wished he had been a Nephyr, instead.

Then the guard's eyes found the amassed eggers huddling against the far wall and he frowned, slowly lifting his rifle.

*Pull it,* her mind screamed. *Pull the trigger* now! Magali's chest felt like it was on fire. She could feel her finger on the trigger, but she couldn't create the pressure she needed to fire. Her whole arm felt numb and unresponsive, disconnected from her screaming brain.

Breaking into a smile, the guard shouted over his shoulder at some-one behind him. He still hadn't noticed Magali kneeling silently to one side, gun shivering in her grip.

*Killer,* Wideman giggled at her.

The man turned to take in the rest of the cave. Their eyes made contact. His eyelids tightened with surprise. His mouth constricted into a tiny O. He stumbled back one step. His rifle swung toward her. His finger tightened on the trigger.

Magali shot him in the head.

Instantly, her brain began counting, just as it had with her father's targets. *One, two, three.* The READY light flashed green. Instinct took over again. Magali shot his partner, who had come jogging up to stoop beside his fallen companion. *One, two, three.* She fired at the dim shapes moving in the darkness, at the place where she approximated a chest to be. One of them slid to the ground with a gurgle. Magali was already rushing forward, toward the two dead men in the cavern entrance. *One, two, three.* She fired her pistol again, then grabbed the rifle on the dead man, fired it, dropped it, and grabbed that of his com-panion. Then she was spinning away to avoid the arc of fire emanating from the darkness.

*How many are there?* she thought, counting down in her head. She saw movement and fired again, and she heard a thud in the corridor as another guard collapsed.

Then silence.

For several moments, the silence pounded at her ears like liquid hammers. Slowly, Magali lowered her gun. She had fired six shots. Had they all hit their mark?

The starlope hunter rushed forward and grabbed the closest guard's rifle, then tentatively disappeared into the corridor beyond.

"They're all dead!" he cried. "Six guards."

Instantly, Magali felt dirty. She had intended to wound them, had hoped to put them in a corner, guarded, until Joel had finished ferrying the eggers to safety. She hadn't counted on her instincts to go for the kill.

As she stood, staring at the bodies, murmurs of fear arose from the other eggers. She understood. By killing the guards, they had crossed a line that they could never take back.

"Anyone else here any good at shooting?" Magali asked.

"Shooting *what?*" an old man asked, his voice coming from directly to her left.

"Nephyrs," Magali said, turning to look at him. Joel hadn't even gotten half of them off the cliff yet, and the Director already knew that something was wrong with the Harvest. "Sooner or later, they'll send the Nephyrs."

The old man grumbled, but stooped to pick up a rifle. There was something about the way he checked the gun's cartridge that made her think he knew how to use it. "S'pose I couldn't expect to live much longer as an egger anyway."

They found four more volunteers, and Magali stationed them at various angles around the mouth of the cave. Nothing was getting through that corridor without being shot at seven ways first. They waited as another group of eggers tossed the guards' dead bodies over the cliff.

One of the eggers stood at the very edge of the cliff as he levered the bodies one after another over the edge. Watching him, only inches from the endless drop, Magali shuddered at her sudden wave of vertigo and took another involuntary step toward the back of the cave. She reached back for the rock behind her and tightened her fingers against it as she watched the bodies fall soundlessly into the void.

*Killer,* Magali heard, as she watched the bodies go soundlessly over the edge. This time, it was her own voice speaking.

# CHAPTER 32

## A Tight Fit

Milar scooped a palmful of cushioning gel out of the belly of the soldier and made a disgusted face at it. "I'm not getting in that stuff." He turned his palm over and let the goop drip in a long, thin, slimy line down onto the body of the guard he had incapacitated on his way into the hangar. "No way in hell, squid."

"Suit yourself, knucker," Tatiana said. She began to strip.

Milar's eyes widened. "What are you doing?"

Milar visibly shuddered. "I don't think so."

Tatiana shrugged and unzipped her uniform. Sliding it aside, she stepped forth. Milar was carefully averting his eyes, pretending to wipe his hand on the unconscious man's shirt.

"I'm going to need you to connect a lot of the lines for me," Tatiana said, climbing past him and dipping her foot into the lukewarm goo. "It'll go a lot faster that way."

"I thought you were afraid of soldiers, squid," Milar growled, just above her ear.

Tatiana winced. "Don't remind me. Just do what I tell you when I tell you and we'll be okay. Starting with that line right there. Hook it into the third node down my spine."

Reluctantly, Milar picked up the line and stepped behind her. As she started cinching up belly nodes, she felt his fingers press into her back, then the bone-deep click as the node mated with the soldier. Instantly, she felt the frame of the soldier like it was her own skeleton.

She had him connect the other three spine nodes, in order, verifying systems in between giving orders.

"Okay," she said. "That one to the back of my head." She was already fitting the palm nodes in place. "We're going to have to skip a few of the waste nodes. We don't have time, and we don't plan on being in there that long, anyway. My kidneys can handle it."

"I don't think I want to know what that means," Milar said. He snapped the second line into place, and Tatiana immediately felt the data from every primary sensor in the soldier.

"Get the left leg sensors, starting with the hookup above the ankle and going up the leg," she said. "I'll get the right leg."

"How do I know which one is which?" Milar demanded, motioning at the jumble of lines laid out before him.

Tatiana had already inserted the first ankle node and was working on the one behind her knee. "There's a number code on each one that matches the number scribed on the node," she said, impatient. "Just connect the dots."

Reluctantly, Milar did as she asked, and had actually gotten two nodes seated and locked before Tatiana finished her six and started helping him.

"Arm nodes next," she said. "Same deal. I'll do the left because it's easier for me." She started pressing the lines in, biting down the urge to vomit when she felt the tug of electrodes sliding into place under her skin. She shuddered at the click as the coupling made its lock.

"That really bothers you, doesn't it?" Milar commented softly.

"A little," she admitted. She wouldn't look at him, though, refusing to let him see just how *much* it bothered her, lest he lose confidence in her plan. Then, once she had waited for him to finish her right arm, she said, "Okay, that's good. Now hook up the temple node."

At this, Milar balked. "Are you sure? I'm not trained . . . "

"You want *me* to do it?!" Tatiana demanded.

At her flat stare, Milar swallowed. "Uh . . . "

"Either I fumble around with it and try not to jam it in there sideways or you grow some balls and do it for me," Tatiana said. "Just be careful and try not to kill me."

Milar, who had already picked up the thickest line, flinched, then glared at her. "Squid." He was utterly gentle, however, when he took her head in one hand and began pushing the long, thin electrode down its receptacle column, into the center of her brain. Tatiana remained utterly still as he finished and locked it in place.

*"Welcome, Captain Tatiana Eyre,"* her soldier said, once the seal had been made.

When Milar stepped back, he looked pale and his hands were shaking. "Don't ever make me do that again."

"No promises." She grabbed a spare clip from the tray and handed it to him. "Here. Put that on. It'll keep the goo outta your nose."

"My *nose?*" Milar managed, swallowing. He grimaced down at the thing in his hand like a man gazing upon a wriggling flatworm.

Tatiana grunted an affirmative. Carefully, she pushed one leg, then the other, down into the stabilizing gel. Then she forced herself to sink into a fetal position inside. She dug around in the slime until she felt the stomach hose. She uncapped it and, taking a deep breath, began feeding the slimy thing through her nostril.

"What are you *doing?*" Milar cried.

"My body's metabolism is ramped up in here," Tatiana said. "This provides a special chemical solution that both boosts concentration and makes sure my body is paralyzed while I'm flying."

Milar's eyes went white all around. "Paralyzed?"

Tatiana rolled her eyes. "You do it every night when you sleep. Same concept. And necessary, too. Otherwise I might be tempted to run with my feet instead of run with my soldier. This is going to keep me alive. Now, any other stupid questions? Once I've got it connected, I won't be able to talk."

"Why not?" Milar whispered. In less than twenty minutes, he'd gone from a big badass colonist who knocked out Coalition guards with a single flat-knuckled fist to looking like a bug-eyed little kid who had found himself on the wrong playground.

Tatiana had to laugh. "Because after this, I'm going to hook up the mask." She motioned to the black apparatus bristling with tubes and sensors. At Milar's horrified look, she said, "I'll be fine. I do it all the time. Just strip down and join me when I motion for you, 'kay?"

Milar eyed the cockpit warily. "I don't think I'm gonna fit."

"The volume calculator put you at a hundred and nine liters. Volumetrically speaking, you'll fit."

He didn't look convinced.

"You rather stay here?" Tatiana demanded.

Reluctantly, Milar unbuttoned his pants and pulled them off, then stuffed them into the storage compartment. "Can I keep my underwear this time, squid?"

She had to grin. "Sure. Now as soon as I've got the tube in, crawl in after me and get your knees up on either side of me. It's the only way you'll make it in here. Once you're in, I want you to grab the air hose leading off the mask and take that knife and cut yourself a little air hole. A *little* one, mind you. You sever it and it's game over."

"I don't think this is gonna work," Milar muttered, leaning in to eye the roof of the inner shell. "That thing's tiny."

Tatiana was beginning to feed the hose again, then stopped. "Oh, and we're leaving the EMP wand behind. No way in hell is that thing coming on board with me."

"What about the knife?" Milar asked.

"Throw it in the cargo compartment, if you can. If you can't, we leave it."

Tatiana fed the hose up her nose, gagging as it slipped down through her sinuses and into her stomach. She wasn't as proficient at it as her technicians, and it left tears in her eyes as she prodded and scratched it into place.

"You all right?" Milar asked, leaning forward into the cockpit, looking concerned.

"No, dammit," she muttered. "Now stop asking questions." Then Tatiana positioned the clip over her nostrils and clamped it down, making sure she couldn't inhale stabilization fluid through her nose if her mask became displaced. Then she took the operator mask from its hook.

The operator mask, unlike that of freestyle pilots, had no window for her to see what lay beyond the mask. It wasn't necessary. She was supposed to be seeing with her soldier, not with her eyes.

Looking at the black faceplate, Tatiana's stomach started to churn as she remembered what was to come.

"No wonder you don't like this," Milar muttered. He was eyeing the mask like it was some strange toxic weapon.

Tatiana tapped the air line. "Cut it," she said.

Reluctantly, Milar leaned in and grabbed the line approximately thirty centimeters from where it entered her mask. Then he hesitated.

"If I cut this, and I can't fit in with you, then you're not going to be able to get out of here, are you?"

"*Hurry.*"

Muttering, Milar cut a notch into the hose, then threw the knife into the cargo hatch and locked it shut.

"Here goes," Tatiana said. "Any other questions before I seal up?"

"Couldn't we find a better way to do this?"

Tatiana slid the faceplate and its accompanying air tube in place, bit down on the air regulator in her mouth and, making a seal along the outer edges of her face, began touching the AI mechanisms that tightened the mask into place. She motioned Milar when she was ready.

Still, Milar made no move to enter the pilot chamber.

Tatiana slapped the stabilizing gel near her neck in aggravation.

"All right," Milar said, sounding very unhappy. "Fine, squid. Fine." She felt him stick his legs in first and, placing his shins on either side of her shoulders, eased himself in with her. *Careful of the lines,* she thought, itching to rip the mask off and see if he was going to tangle anything. She felt him slide forward and down.

She heard displaced cushioning gel begin to ooze out of the pilot chamber, dripping with wet plops on the floor of the hangar, and suddenly Tatiana found her knees mashed up against the colonist's chest. By the way she could feel something touching the side of her mask, Milar had had to duck his head down and to the left as he finally got his body crammed into the cockpit with her.

"I'm gonna have one hell of a neck-ache in the morning," he muttered, right next to her ear. "And hell, I can't move my arms. Can you pass me the air line?"

Tatiana wiggled until she had a grip on the air hose and, tracing it backwards until she found the notch, stuck it into his mouth.

"Thanks," he said. Then, around the tube, "You better know what you're doing."

In reply, Tatiana gave her soldier the command to shut the hatch.

Instantly, Milar went stiff as the hydraulics began to whine and the light from the hangar began to cut off.

*Hold on,* she prayed, as the lid sealed and left them in darkness. Milar's chest was heaving against her knees, and he was sucking more air from the line than it would provide.

"I'm beginning to have second thoughts, squid," Milar said.

*The worst is yet to come,* Tatiana thought. She reached out and put a hand on his shoulder. *Just calm down and trust me.*

*"Hatch locked,"* her soldier told her. *"Pumping stabilizing gel."*

Milar's body jerked when the stabilizing gel began to ooze into the chamber. "Oh, fuck this. Let me out, squid. Let me out right—" His last was lost as the gel inched past her ears.

It was obvious Milar was not happy. He made this evident by the way he squeezed her hand until she thought something would break. He was jerking it back and forth as best he could in the close quarters, basically the same as, *I want out. Right now.*

By the way he was sucking down on the hose, though, Tatiana knew he wasn't starved for air. He could deal with it.

# CHAPTER 33

# Magali's Choice

THE FIRST THING JOEL SAID WHEN MAGALI CAME ABOARD HIS ship was, "There was a Coalition ship snooping around a few miles up the Snake. This is gonna be my last haul."

He had brought Magali aboard and locked the doors behind them to talk. Now, alone with her, he waited for the response he expected.

*Okay, Joel, get me out of here.*

Instead, like a true Landborn, she said, "There's still three hundred and seventy-one people out there." Her hair was clumped with sweat and she oozed an aura of stress and frayed nerves. She kept twitching to look over his shoulder at the viewfinder, which showed the empty cavern entrance. "We need to get them to safety."

"Three hundred and seventy-one?" Joel asked, amused. "You've been counting, huh?"

"Yes," she said, with no hint of humor. "You need to keep going." Her words held the taste of a threat.

*She reminds me of her father.* Joel gave her a bitter snort. "What are you gonna do, Magali? Force me to fly with a gun to my head?

You think that'll improve my concentration somehow? They pinpoint where I'm coming and going—which I'm pretty sure they're trying to do right now—and every single person we've ferried out of here will be lined up and shot. It's time to cut our losses and go, before they figure out they've been had."

Magali swallowed, hard.

"So," Joel said, leaning back into Martin's huge leather chair. It had actually kind of grown on him, especially the lumbar support. His old chair had been as flat-backed as a board. "What do you say, Magali? You launched this little project. You wanna come with me or you wanna go down with your ship?"

"You can't leave," Magali babbled, the determination that had reminded him of David Landborn falling away, leaving in its place a scared little girl. "The Nephyrs will find us. Please."

Joel laughed. "So? The eggers got a bit unruly. Happens all the time in the Yolk mines. They *expect* things like this to happen. All part of the game. You can't keep people in those kinds of conditions and expect things to be just gumdrops and lollipops. Besides, you ain't killed anybody they care about, and they still got plenty of time to grab a few nodules outta there before end of Harvest, so they'll just whack everyone we leave behind on the ass and send them back into the mines. Hell, maybe those Nephyrs will even go in and start picking nodules themselves, to save face. Couldn't admit to their overseers they let a couple thousand eggers slip out from under their noses, could they?" He grinned, imagining the glittering circus clowns on their hands and knees in the slime, plucking nodules. The image delighted him.

Magali had flinched and grown increasingly pale as he talked. "What's wrong?" Joel asked, his smile fading.

"I killed fifteen of them," Magali said.

Joel went utterly still. "Fifteen of who?"

His world collapsed when she said, "Guards."

*Oh Aanaho, Joel. What the hell have you gotten yourself into?* His gaze fell to the gun in her hand, then out at the entrance to the cavern, expecting Nephyrs to boil out of the darkness at any moment. "Please tell me you're joking," he said.

Swallowing hard, the Landborn girl said, "They sent guards in to check on us. I killed them. Then I killed the Nephyrs that came to check on the guards."

*She killed* Nephyrs? Joel could barely think. Was she joking? No one killed Nephyrs. "How long ago?"

"An hour for the Nephyrs. Almost two for the guards."

More than a dozen trips ago. "And you let me keep *shuttling* and didn't *tell* me?" Joel screamed.

"I'm sorry," Magali cried. "I didn't think you'd keep flying."

"You're *damn right* I wouldn't have kept flying!" For the first time in his life, Joel wanted to hit a woman. He even balled his fist, rage coursing through him so hotly that his jaw ached. Instead, he whispered, "What did you do with the bodies?"

"Over the cliff," Magali said, staring at her feet. "I thought we could get all of us out of here before they sent in a second batch."

Joel closed his eyes and took several deep breaths. "Mag, all Coalition troops are fitted with these nifty little things called lifelines. All they've gotta do is get the camp computer to review their last movement patterns and they're gonna have a map right to your hideout."

Her face went wan. "I'm sorry," she whispered. And she looked sorry, too. Joel didn't know whether to laugh or cry. He was looking at a dead woman.

"Listen, Mag," Joel said, "Nobody kills Nephyrs. That's like kicking a hornet's nest. Shit, no wonder I was getting pinged out there.

A computer registers a four-thousand-foot drop on a lifeline and it's gonna know something's up. Shit. I'm getting out of here. Right now. Before the camp computer can fry my line. You can either come or stay, but either way, you're as good as dead. Everyone in that cave is as good as dead."

Magali glanced at the groups of eggers huddled against the walls through the viewscreen. He watched the guilt work its way through her, the misery. "Dead?" she said.

"They'll kill everyone in that cave, then they'll hunt down everyone who was involved. They'll sic the entire Coalition Army on you, if they have to. Nobody kills Nephyrs and gets away with it."

She took a deep breath and held it, tears glistening on her cheeks as she looked out at the eggers she had killed. Softly, she said, "Take the kids."

"What about you, Mag?"

"Just the kids," Magali said. "I'm going to stay here."

*She's insane,* Joel thought. *Just like her father.*

But he didn't have time to dwell on it. "Fine," he said, powering up the ship again. "Get the kids in here. Just don't tell anyone it's the last trip or you'll have a riot on your hands."

If she heard or understood him, she made no sign. She simply turned and left.

Joel felt sorry for her. He knew that, whatever the Director and her glittering friends had planned to do to him for his lifetime of thwarting the law, it was going to look pale in comparison to what they did to Magali for slaying their brothers.

*Poor girl,* he thought, as the first passengers began filtering into his cargo hold. He hoped she had the good sense to shoot herself before the Nephyrs found her.

◀◀ ◆ ▶▶

"He's just taking the kids this trip," Magali said, trying to avoid the eggers' gazes, feeling her shame right down to her very core. "Everyone else can wait for the next trip." She gave Benny a gentle shove toward the ship's ramp.

"Now wait a minute," the starlope hunter said, hefting the rifle he had taken from one of the guards. "You're telling me that, all of a sudden, the smuggler just wants to take the kids? Why?"

Magali felt her face heat. She'd never been good at lying. That was Anna's forte, not hers. "He just does."

"'He just does.'" The starlope hunter glared at her, then at the ship, where Benny and the other kids were climbing up the ramp. "Bullshit."

Other men and women had started to gather around him, watching her with curious expressions. Several carried rifles or knives from the fallen Coalition forces they'd killed.

*Think, Magali,* she thought, panicking. *Think!* What would Anna say? She didn't know. Some lie, no doubt. But as she stood there, watching the man's expression grow darker, no lie would come to her lips.

"He ain't coming back, is he?" the starlope hunter asked, after she'd been silent for too long.

Magali felt the lump of dread in her gut tightening into something worse. "Please," she whispered, before she could stop herself.

"Oh fuck this," the starlope hunter snarled. He turned and wrenched Benny off the ramp. Holding the terrified child out between them by a shoulder, the starlope hunter shook the boy and said "Who you think the Nephyrs are gonna kill when they get here, little Deaddrunk hotshot? The *kids?* Or the guys and gals who shot their pals?" He gestured to the men and women holding the guns they had stolen from the guards.

Magali's face reddened and she couldn't speak.

The starlope hunter shoved Ben at her. To the cavern, he said, "I'm getting the fuck outta here, and I'd suggest everyone who touched a gun today does the same. When they figure out what we did, those Nephyrs are gonna—"

The man's words broke off before Magali realized she had her gun aimed at his head.

"Just the kids," Magali said.

She heard the sound of rifles jingling against their slings around her. Absolute silence filled the cavern.

The starlope hunter broke into a bitter smile. "There's over a dozen rifles trained on you right now," he said. "I don't care how good a shot you are. You shoot me, little Deaddrunk slut, and you're gonna have twenty holes in your head before you can scream."

To Magali's horror, she realized it was true. The other men and women who had helped her kill the Nephyrs were now standing around her, their weapons aimed at her face.

The starlope hunter's voice was lifting in a sneer. "You were just gonna let us all die here, weren't you?"

*No,* Magali thought, her heart skipping as she glanced at the other eggers. He was going to scare them. "Please don't do this," she whispered. "Keep your voice down."

The starlope hunter laughed. "Keep my *voice* down? You were gonna leave us for the Nephyrs, and you want me to keep my *voice* down?" He gestured grandly to the three hundred seventy other eggers left in the cavern. "Why? So nobody panics? So they all wait for their slaughter like brain-dead cattle?"

"No," Magali whispered.

"Yeah, well, to hell with that," the starlope hunter said. "I'm getting on that ship, and those kids can just fend for themselves." And, at that, he climbed aboard the ship. Inside, he heard yelling, and the kids who had already boarded came running down the ramp in terror. A moment later, Magali heard the starlope hunter get into an argument with Joel. She heard the starlope hunter yell back. Something heavy slammed against a wall. Then nothing.

The ship continued to wait for passengers.

The starlope hunter stuck his head out the open hatch. "*Now*, people! We ain't waiting much longer."

Magali stumbled backwards as panic ensued. Where before, she had managed to instill order with logical weight calculations and calm commands, now the cavern became an echoing clamor of screaming voices and pushing bodies, all begging to be taken to safety. The ones with the guns got in first, then the strongest shoved their way in after them. Before the hull was completely full, one of the men inside pounded on the gate release and the hatch started to drift shut. Those stuck outside began to scream and plead with those inside. One woman even thrust her hand in the lock to stop the gate from shutting. A moment later, she withdrew a stump. Her thrashing body was crushed underfoot as hundreds of eggers lunged away from the ship as its engines began to increase exhaust.

Magali looked away, dread at what she had done weighing on her shoulders, suffocating her soul in despair. She swallowed and felt the burning sting of bile.

The ship retracted its legs and desperate pleas became broken sobs as the eggers realized they were going to be left behind. A moment later, the glossy obsidian ship darted through the cavern entrance and was gone.

Beside her, an old man said, "What a selfish prick."

Magali looked up at him, shame collecting deep in her core.

But the old man was watching the ship disappear along the ragged edge of the Snake, not Magali. "I mean, sure, sucks to be us, but you were trying to do the right thing and he screwed it all to hell. His mother obviously potty-trained the dumbshit too early."

Magali realized it was the old man who had picked up a rifle and grumbled about killing Nephyrs. Lars. He had dressed himself in a dead guard's outfit. He still carried his rifle, and he lifted it to his shoulder to watch the ship disappear through the scope.

"Prick," Lars said again, lowering the gun. For the first time, he turned to look at Magali. "You're David's kid, right? The deadeye shot?"

Magali's shame increased a thousandfold. She looked away.

"Thought so. Not many people I know can put a Nephyr down like that." He gave her a sideways look. "Sure, never met you before, but I heard of you. The resistance was real proud of David's kid."

"That's Anna," Magali whispered, lowering her eyes. *Anna wouldn't have done something this stupid.*

"Oh?" the man raised a unruly white brow. "Then David raised *two* kids that could kill a starlope at two thousand yards with an antique projectile?"

Anna had never made an accurate shot with anything, let alone a projectile weapon. Her child's body just wasn't ready to hold an adult-sized gun. Magali looked up.

The old man read her reaction accurately. He grinned and slapped her on the back. Then he said the most earth-shattering words Magali had ever known.

"Looks like Wideman was right. You *are* a killer. A damn good one, at that."

Magali swallowed hard. Somewhere, in the background, she heard Wideman laughing.

"You know, though," the old man said, leaning distractedly on his gun, "we aren't gonna survive this."

Magali nodded.

"So you want me to do it or you?"

She blinked up at him through tears. "Do what?"

The old man gestured at the eggers. "Kill them. Which of us is gonna kill them?"

Her mouth fell open and she couldn't speak.

"Listen," the old man said, his eyes still filled with kindness, "I fought the Coalition on Redrock as a kid. I saw the things they did to prisoners. Back then, it was bad. Now . . . " He shook his head and his eyes flickered toward the entrance. "Last forty years, Nephyrs have got a lot nastier. A *lot* nastier. A lot of guys my age have seen it. They were cruel sons of bitches when I was a kid. Now, it's like they made torture a culture of their own. Almost like they stopped being human. Started with the Yolk. They just went . . . bad."

"You want me to *kill* them?" Magali whispered.

"One of us should," the old man said. He crouched beside her, his eyes on the eggers. "You don't wanna do it, I will. We certainly won't be doing them any favors leaving them alive. Not after what we did today."

"I did most of it," Magali said, squeezing her eyes shut against tears.

"True," the old man said, "But the rest of us didn't stop you. That'll be just as damning, in their eyes."

Magali's desperation grew as she looked out over the huddled mass of crying eggers. Whimpers and broken sobs were penetrating the constant howl of the wind outside. "How?" she whispered.

"Drive 'em off the cliff," the old guy said.

*Killer,* Wideman giggled.

*Oh God.* Magali imagined them teetering on the edge, imagined the long, horrible drop to the bottom of the Snake, imagined them emptying their lungs in a scream again and again before they hit the jagged rocks below . . . Magali squeezed her eyes shut, her terror of heights becoming a raw and burning ball in her throat. "I can't." She listened to the wind howling at the entrance of the cliff and took a shuddering breath. "That's too horrible. I can't."

The old man lifted his rifle from the cavern floor and stood. "I'll do it, then." He turned toward the eggers.

"No," Magali said, getting to her feet. "We're not killing them. No."

The old man's face darkened in a frown. "Believe me, girl, if that starlope-skinning prick was right and your smuggler buddy isn't coming back, then the only humane thing for us to do is going to be give these folk a merciful end before the Nephyrs get to them. Really. We leave them alive and they're going to suffer."

*What have I done?* "I can't kill them," Magali whispered.

He put a gentle, arthritic hand on her shoulder. "This ain't a time to let your heart rule, girl. I speak from experience. These people are better off dead."

"*Stop talking about them like they're cattle!*" Magali screamed, throwing off his grip. She was shaking all over, now. She was finding it hard to think. Then, taking a deep breath, she said, "No. We'll strike a deal with the Nephyrs. I'll give myself up if they promise they won't hurt anyone else."

The old man threw back his head and laughed. "I can tell you ain't never been in a war before, Landborn. 'Cause that was one of the stupidest things I ever heard." There was an underlying anger in his expression, now. "That's like punching a Shrieker in the face and asking it not to Shriek. It's gonna Shriek whether you want it to or not—just like Nephyrs are gonna kill these folks whether you want them to or not." When he saw she wasn't in agreement, he lowered his voice and said, "You should at least give them a choice, girl. Let them make their own decision, if you're too soft-hearted to do it for them."

"No," Magali gritted. She turned away from him in disgust.

With a sadness in his words, the old man said, "Suit yourself, girl." She heard him raise his gun.

Magali pivoted and slammed her heel into the old man's gut. His gun, which had been pointed at her chest, fell away as he tried to catch himself. As he was falling, she brought the pistol up, her finger hovering on the trigger. Every ounce of her wanted to pull the trigger.

*I'm not a killer,* part of her whimpered. Yet she had killed fifteen men and women in the last ten hours. She had wounded two others, only to have her companions make the killing blows. It had been so easy, so natural . . .

Anger and humiliation boiled in the man's face as he looked up at her gun. "I was just gonna do you a favor, love. You wanna deal with this mess yourself? Fine. Then deal with it. I am not hanging around for the Nephyrs." He brought the barrel of his gun to his chin.

"Drop it!" Magali screamed.

Completely oblivious to the pistol shuddering between them, the man said, "If you know what's good for you, Landborn, you will do the right thing for these people."

She saw his fingers tighten on his weapon, saw him close his eyes. Magali shot him.

As the man's eyes were widening, the gun fell to the side, his fingers with it. His wide blue eyes moved from her face, slowly, to his hand. The first three fingers on his hand ended in bloody stumps.

"You shot my *hand!*" he screamed at her.

Magali kicked the rifle aside. "You can get someone to fix it later, after I make a deal and turn myself in."

His voice thick with disdain, he said, "You're a fool." He got up and started walking toward the cliff.

"I can shoot off ankles just as easily," Magali warned. When the old man just turned and stared at her, she said, "It'll turn out okay. You'll see." It was more a plea than a promise.

"It's my *choice,*" the man snarled. "And I choose to die."

"I'm not a killer," Magali said.

"The hell you ain't!" the man snapped. "You're as sadistic as your goddamn sister."

That hit her like a fist to the gut. *As sadistic as Anna?* Then, staring down the barrel of the gun at the man whose hand she had just maimed, a small voice asked, . . . *am I?*

What if it was genetic? What if she really was like Anna, and had been all along? They were sisters, after all . . .

*You're just a killer, Magali,* Wideman cackled at her shoulder. *Face it.*

*No!* Magali pounded his words from her skull. *No I'm not.*

The old man's eyes darkened horribly as he watched her. "And just as crazy, too."

Magali lowered her fist from her forehead and her eyes narrowed. She pointed at the group of eggers with her gun. "Get over there with the others."

"You're gonna rot in hell for this," the old man snarled. He slumped to the ground near the eggers. He made no move to bind his wounded hand.

"Magali?" Benny whispered, sidling up behind her. "Why did you just shoot Lars in the hand?"

"It's nothing," Magali said. She lowered her gun, feeling suddenly ancient. She looked at the young boy and, seeing the confusion in his blue eyes, found herself saying, "Benny, if you had the choice between falling and hitting your head really hard or having Nephyrs kill you, what would you choose?"

Benny got wide-eyed. He whispered, "The Nephyrs are going to kill me?"

"No," Magali said. "But what would you choose?"

"I'm scared of Nephyrs," Benny said.

From the darkness in the tunnel, someone laughed. "As you should be, little one."

Colonel Steele casually strode from the darkness, flanked by a dozen of his fellows. He stopped at the entrance to the cavern and his Nephyrs spread out in both directions. They glittered gold in the dawn light filtering across the Snake.

Benny screamed.

"Sounds like he'd choose the cliff," Colonel Steele said, still smiling. Then the Nephyr cocked his head at Magali. "That *was* the choice you were giving him, wasn't it? The cliff or the Nephyrs?"

Magali swallowed, careful to keep the gun at her side. She could kill one, maybe even two, but she couldn't kill them all.

Colonel Steele seemed to read her mind, because he smiled.

"So," Colonel Steele said, stepping forward. "I couldn't help but overhear you wanted to make us a deal." He cocked his head as he moved around her. "You're quite the shot, if the lifelines piled at the bottom of this cliff are any judge. Are you the one that killed my men?" He spoke almost as if they were old friends chatting over steaming cups of *fora* juice.

Shaking, Magali nodded. Her whole body was cramping with terror, but she fought her instincts and said, "I did it. I want to trade myself for their safety." She nodded with her chin at the eggers.

The tall Nephyr continued to walk around her, forcing her to turn to keep him in sight. Colonel Steele seemed to be considering that as he looked at her body. "Any caveats?"

"You do whatever you want to me, but you don't hurt them," Magali said. "They didn't do anything."

Behind her, the old man lunged to his feet and sprinted for the cliff edge, but a Nephyr caught him and dragged him back before he even made it halfway. The woman casually threw him into the huddled group of eggers, then went to stand between them and the exit. Magali's chest clamped in terror at the cyborg's speed. Standing as close as he was, Magali realized she wouldn't even have a chance to twitch her arm before Colonel Steele had her by the throat. Shaking, she looked down at her gun.

"And we can do *anything* we want to you?" the Nephyr asked. "You're sure?" Magali didn't like his smile. He seemed to be enjoying himself.

"Yes," Magali whispered.

Colonel Steele stopped circling and watched her. For a long moment, Colonel Steele said nothing as he considered. Then he said, "Give me your gun."

"I want you to promise you're not going to—"

"We aren't going to kill any more eggers," Colonel Steel snorted. "Nalle can't report she lost all her eggers . . . it would make the bumbling moron lose face. We'll satisfy ourselves with you as long as you don't bore us." He winked at her. "So better make it interesting, eh?"

Magali felt the cold, psychotic nature of the man's being all the way down her spine.

Panic almost made her turn and sprint toward the exit. Instead, trembling, she handed over the gun. Huddled in the group of eggers, Lars began to cry. When she looked, she saw that one of the Nephyrs was forcibly bandaging his wounds.

"Now those clothes that obviously don't belong to you." Colonel Steele was still smiling, but it was wrong, lifeless.

Magali swallowed, but slowly started to peel off Martin's blood-stained pants.

The Nephyr's eyes were fixed on the cluster of holes over her stomach. "That was the man's heart, wasn't it." It wasn't a question.

Magali nodded.

"Interesting. Where did you learn to shoot like that?"

"It was close range," Magali whispered, carefully setting the pants aside. The cold air from outside now hit the exposed flesh of her legs and she suddenly felt a hundred times more vulnerable than before. She squeezed her eyes shut. "Anyone can make that shot at close range."

"With this pistol?" The Nephyr snorted. "I don't think so." He gestured at her torso with it. "Now the top, please." He sounded almost friendly, like a doctor who had just asked her to flex her knee. It was his leer of anticipation, however, that spoke the truth.

*Just like Anna,* she realized, in horror. Magali suddenly found her fingers unable to grab the hem of Martin's shirt, her arms unable to pull it over her head.

"I would be happy to assist you, if you need the help." The Nephyr was still smiling, though he wasn't looking at her. He was inspecting the gun, wiping dirt and Shrieker slime from the crevices with the cuff-edge of his uniform.

Trembling, Magali pulled the shirt over her head and dropped it to the ground.

Colonel Steele finished his inspection of the pistol, then cocked his head at her. Seeing her cross her arms over her breasts, he smiled. Then he bent and retrieved the shirt on the ground. Holding it up, he said, "Whose shirt is this?"

"He said his name was Martin," Magali whispered.

Colonel Steele's hairless eyebrows went up. "You had a chance to talk to him before you killed him? My, aren't you the happy little murderess."

Shame ate wormy holes in her stomach.

Colonel Steele stuck his fingers through the singed holes of the shirt, examining it as the other Nephyrs stood back, waiting. The silence seemed ominous.

"What are you going to do to me?" Magali whispered.

Colonel Steele flipped Martin's shirt inside out and read the tag. He whistled. Then he held it up again. "Martin was a big boy.

I don't believe Nalle has any guards of that size on her rolls. He was a smuggler?"

Magali nodded.

Colonel Steele glanced over at her, curiosity in his sky-blue eyes. "And where is his ship?"

"Runaway Joel took it," Magali said.

Colonel Steele laughed. "I see." He neatly folded Martin's shirt and stuffed it under one arm. Amicably, he said, "You're afraid of heights, aren't you, Magali?"

*Oh no,* she thought.

Colonel Steele's gaze flickered to her face and he examined her expression before he casually went on, "Because I've been monitoring your heart rate for a while, now, and every time you glance at the cliff edge, it spikes. Would it scare you to go over the cliff, Magali?"

A shot of terror hit her core before Magali was able to suppress it. "No," she forced herself to say.

Colonel Steele grinned at her. "Your heart rate just doubled. Is it a phobia?"

"No," she said. It came out as a whimper.

"Oh, this is *delightful*," Colonel Steele said, beginning to pace around her again. "Here you are, a murderess who just single-handedly slaughtered nine of my companions before shoving them over the edge, and you're probably more afraid of that big bad cliff than you are of me, aren't you?"

Magali swallowed and said nothing. She couldn't, because the fear of tumbling over the edge, alive, was so horrifying to her that she was finding it hard to breathe.

Colonel Steele stopped pacing. She saw him come to a decision.

Magali squeezed her eyes shut, already feeling his hands shoving her over the ledge, the wind against her skin, sucking the scream from her lungs. *Oh God, oh God . . .*

Instead, Colonel Steele said, "We'll definitely get to that." His voice held cold promise. "Before we do anything else, I believe you gave that boy a choice. Bring him over here, please."

Magali jerked when she heard Benny's terrified whimper. At first, Magali didn't understand. Then, looking down into Benny's terrified eyes as the Nephyr shoved him at her, Magali's gut suddenly cramped. "You promised you wouldn't kill them," she whispered.

"I did," Colonel Steele said. "Which is why you're going to do it." He cocked his head at the child, his paternal smile beaming down at the boy. "I believe he chose the cliff." Then he returned his gaze to Magali, waiting, amusement glittering in his glacial eyes.

Magali felt such a sudden rush of vertigo that she fell to one knee, shaking. "No," she whimpered.

"Unless, of course, you'd like for me to do something special to him, instead." The Nephyr reached out, grabbed Benny by the shoulder, and pinched a spot on the boy's arm. Ben began to scream, and as the boy flailed in the Nephyr's grip, a strip of skin broke away and began to peel up his arm.

"No!" Magali screamed. She lunged forward and grabbed Benny. "No, please. He's just a boy."

Colonel Steele flicked the little strip of flesh aside, his perfect smile still in place. "That's just a taste of what's in store for him if you don't do as you're told, little one."

"I can't," Magali whispered, hugging the sobbing boy to her chest. "I can't."

"You *can*," Colonel Steele said. His eyes hardened as he continued, "Or you will watch him scream his lungs bloody as we peel him like an orange."

Magali shook her head and buried her face in the boy's shoulder.

Colonel Steele sighed and reached for the boy again.

"No!" Magali screamed, dragging Benny back a step. "No." Shaking, she kept backing away, until she was halfway to the cliff edge. Once he saw the direction she was headed, Colonel Steele stopped following and watched, like an interested parent. The other Nephyrs stood positioned around the edge of the cave, witnessing the proceedings with sick little grins of curiosity.

Magali got down on one knee and held Benny out. The child was still screaming hysterically, one hand clamped to the bloody spot on the skin that the Nephyr had torn away.

"You're gonna be fine," Magali whispered, looking over the boy's shoulder at the cyborgs lining the cavern. *Please, God, some sort of miracle.*

"I'll give you, say, nine minutes to get him over the edge," the tall Nephyr said, still smiling. "One minute for every one of my men you killed." He paused, watching her. "If you *don't* get him over the edge in nine minutes, our deal is forfeit and I'll start entertaining myself in other ways. If a little pinch on his arm makes him howl like that, just imagine what we could do with some . . . more sensitive areas." The Nephyr smiled at the boy and stepped forward to pat a cheek affectionately.

Benny screamed a long, terrified howl and lunged back into her arms. His thin form was shaking and Magali held him.

Nine minutes. Benny had nine minutes to live.

"Oh, and just the boy," Colonel Steele said. "If you decide to go with the little brat, you can be sure that our deal is off and every one of these maggots will die writhing for what you've done." The Nephyr was still beaming at her. "One way or another, we're gonna have some fun tonight."

*No,* Magali's heart screamed. She hugged the boy to her chest, feeling his sobs of relief against her breast as she held him, praying to God for mercy. She told herself that the Nephyrs were just testing her, just trying to find her breaking point. They couldn't possibly expect her to push a little boy over the cliff.

And yet, she knew they could.

"Shhhh," she murmured, stroking Benny's hair. "Shhhh. I've got you. It's okay." She'd always been good with kids. They loved her, for reasons inexplicable to Magali, and Benny was no different. His breathing calmed and his fingers stopped digging into her back. He let out a relieved breath, half sob, half sigh.

"That's adorable," Colonel Steele interrupted. Looking over his shoulder, he said, "Wouldn't you agree, Captain Xui?"

The female cyborg who had dragged Lars back from the edge grunted. "Picture-fucking-perfect. Just like a good little Mommy. Too bad the bitch is down to forty seconds. She almost got the kid asleep. Easier to throw 'em over the edge when they're asleep."

Magali's heart lurched. *Forty seconds?* She thought she'd had several more minutes, at least.

*Oh God,* she thought. *God, don't make me do this.*

"Make that thirty seconds," the female Nephyr said, watching Magali with cruel intent.

"Come on, Benny," Magali whispered. "We need to go."

In her arms, Benny tightened his little fingers on her back and whimpered. Did he understand what was happening? Did he know Magali was going to betray him? Would he understand why?

Magali reluctantly stood, still hugging Benny to her body. "This way," she said. She began carrying him toward the edge. Benny's eyes were on the Nephyrs over her shoulder, not even looking where they were going.

Magali was only a couple feet away, now, and her whole world seemed to lurch and teeter. Her legs trembled and it was all she could do not to drop to the ground and crawl away on her belly.

*I have to do it,* Magali thought, her heart slamming in her chest as she stared down into the empty void. Benny was still docile in her arms, watching the Nephyrs. *Aanaho, don't let him realize what I'm doing.*

"Hey kid," the female Nephyr called, "She's gonna throw you over the cliff."

Ben stiffened in Magali's arms. His little face turned from the Nephyrs to fix on Magali, fear widening his blue eyes. Then he twisted in her arms, squirming to look behind him. When he saw the cliff only a few feet away, he began to thrash.

"No, stop!" Magali cried, gripping him more tightly. "Please, Ben, you don't understand."

"Ten seconds!" one of the Nephyrs shouted behind her.

"No!" Benny shrieked, as she lowered him toward the edge. "No! *Mommy!*"

Mommy. Magali gripped his wrists as he bit and kicked her, her heart ripping arcs of agony through her chest. She wanted to be a mommy. And here she was about to throw a child to his death.

Behind her, she heard Colonel Steele laugh and start toward her.

"I'm so sorry," Magali whispered, through tears. She moved them both closer to the edge. Benny shrieked and tried to claw around her, to get back at the cave. The wind whipped at her hair as she tried to peel his fingers away from her body. Magali barely registered the drop below, so horrified at what she was doing that her fear of falling paled in comparison.

Then, hearing Colonel Steele's footsteps pause behind her, everything came into horrible focus. "Then I suppose he gets the Nephyrs, after all," Colonel Steele laughed. The Nephyr reached for Benny's wrist. She saw the glittering skin, felt the inhuman cold pulsing from his alien muscles.

Magali shoved Ben.

The child tumbled over the edge, his eyes widening as he threw his foot backwards and it found only air. His shriek was swallowed by the wind.

Magali watched him fall. Even though she wanted nothing more than to curl up and die, she watched Benny fall. She owed him that much.

Beside her, the Nephyr had stopped, his hand outstretched. He, too, watched Benny fall. When the body came to a rest at the bottom of the Snake, he turned to her and said, "You pushed him." He sounded confused.

"I had to," Magali said, trembling with rage and self-loathing. "I couldn't let you hurt him."

The Nephyr laughed at her. "I wasn't going to kill him."

Cold, unutterable shock doused away her body's nerves, leaving it utterly still. "But," Magali whispered, "you said . . . "

"I just wanted to see if you'd do it." Colonel Steele gave her an amused look. "What kind of monster kills a child?"

*What kind of monster . . .* Magali slumped to the ground, staring over the edge. The Nephyr moved back into the cave and began to bark orders. She heard eggers being escorted from the room with orders to continue the Harvest. She was still there when Colonel Steele came back to her. "Now, about the rest of our bargain."

Magali looked up. She was alone with the Nephyr.

Colonel Steele was unzipping his pants.

"Make it good," Colonel Steele said, "and I'll leave the pistol when I seal the tunnel behind me."

# CHAPTER 34

# The Red or the Black

**T**ATIANA FLEW AS LONG AS SHE COULD, SKIMMING THE TREETOPS and keeping a low profile, but every warm breath she shared with Milar reminded her of the condition of her body, of how she was trapped in an egg of goo, plugged into a hundred different lines like some sort of medical experiment, locked away in the darkness forever, should just one hydraulic arm stop working around her.

Much too soon, Tatiana began to recognize the signs of panic. She flew for another half hour, inching them closer to Deaddrunk, but her panic grew until it was an overwhelming desperation.

Finally, she had to stop.

*Let me out,* she gasped. *Let me out right now.*

*"Captain, we are in colonial territory. It is much advised that you—"*

*Now!* Tatiana mentally screamed at it.

*"Very well, Captain,"* the soldier said. It set down and began to fold open. One by one, Tatiana felt her senses return to her. She was sucking down too much air, now, and she could feel Milar crammed up against

her in the darkness, pressing her knees against her chest, making it even harder to breathe.

*Oh shit,* she thought. *I'm not going to make it.* She scrabbled wildly, trying to get out, but the soldier's cooldown process refused to open the hatch until the superheated outer shell had no chance of roasting her alive when she scrambled out onto it.

Tatiana panted, sucking down air, feeling tears under her gooey eyelids. *Let me out,* she pled with her AI. *Just open the hatch. I don't care how hot it is.*

*"We are waiting for the outer shell to cool down first, Captain,"* the soldier calmly told her. *"I can't allow you to injure yourself on exit."*

Tatiana began to struggle, and, in struggling, realized she was completely trapped. She hyperventilated, but the bot refused to give her enough air. Combined with the wet, stale stuff Milar was expelling into the tube with her, Tatiana began to see bright specks of light along the edges of her vision. Her chest heaved, but the tube refused to accommodate, and the darkness continued to press on her.

Milar, for his part, hadn't moved a muscle.

*He's dead,* she thought wildly. *His air line slipped from his mouth and I'm trapped in a cockpit with a corpse.*

It was taking too long, and she wasn't getting enough air.

Though everything that had been pounded into her in operator school told her not to, her instincts made her reach up and tear off her mask to see. The air tube left her mouth and immediately she sucked in a mouthful of the gel.

Gagging, struggling, painfully bumping nodes, her eyes flashed open and suddenly all she could see or feel was the greasy burn of the cushioning gel squeezing through her lids, seeping in against the surface of her eyes and into her mouth.

*I'm going to die,* she thought, choking, struggling, aware of nothing but her terror.

Then she felt Milar's hand on her shoulder, squeezing it gently.

At approximately the same time, the hatch slid open and blurry sunlight assailed her goop-filled eyes.

Tatiana surged forward, but Milar was in the way.

*Get out, get out, get* out, her mind screamed. She yanked the nose clip off, leaving a painful gash in the skin, and dragged the feeding line out of her throat, aware only that the goop hadn't receded fully yet and she had no other source of air. She *had* to get outside. She would crawl over Milar's bloody corpse if she had to.

*I can't breathe,* she thought, feeling the gel still surrounding her face. Her lungs began to burn. *God, I can't breathe—*

The stabilization gel fell just in time to keep her from choking on it.

"Hey, calm down," Milar said, as soon as it dripped out of her ears. "Calm down, sweetie."

"*Get out of my way!*" Tatiana screamed, trying to lunge past him.

"Hey, dammit," Milar snapped, "Hold still, all right? My neck's caught on your chest hookup."

"I don't *care,*" she gasped. Fresh air was right *there,* all she had to do was crawl past him.

"Listen, squid," Milar growled. He shoved himself closer, pressing her against the back of the pilot chamber, his forehead pressed against hers. "The chest hookup got tangled. You're not going anywhere fast, so cool it."

Tatiana panted, and slowly managed to drag her eyes away from outside the chamber and meet Milar's gaze.

Still dripping with stabilization liquid, his face was laced with concern. "There ya go. You going to be all right?"

Reluctantly, she nodded.

He held her gaze for a moment longer, then released her shoulders. "Well, at least you're not blubbering anymore," Milar grunted. "That's a start. Now. Help me figure out how to get the hell out of here before

I start having hysterics of my own. The chest line got wrapped around my neck."

The magnitude of the problem suddenly dawned on her. "Why did you let it do that?" Tatiana cried. "You yank on it and it could sever my aorta."

Milar gave her a flat look. "Do you *want* to see me hysterical?"

"No," she said.

"Well, you're about to." He sounded dead serious.

"Okay," Tatiana said. "Okay. Umm." She could see a little better now that her eyelids had cleared some of the goop out of her eyes. "Okay. Can you reach my chest hookup?"

"Are you nuts?"

Tatiana followed the chest line with her eyes. "I might be able to unwrap it, if you duck your head down."

"I *am* ducking my head down, sweetie. I've been doing it for about two hours, now, and I think my spine has realigned itself accordingly."

"Don't argue with me and do it," she snapped.

Muttering, Milar leaned forward further, giving her access to the chest tube that had, indeed, encircled his neck in transit. She yanked on it, found it secure. She grabbed it where it hooked against his ear and, because she didn't have the leverage to do anything else, started hitting it with the meat of her palm.

"You know," Milar said, his cheek hitting her shoulder with every smack, "this should be some sort of criminal punishment."

"The line's too tight," Tatiana gritted. "It only has a few feet of leeway in any direction."

"Well what kind of idiot designed the damn thing?" Milar asked from her shoulder.

"Apparently an engineer who never anticipated a two-meter meat-brained bastard to get between it and the wall of the pod." Grunting, she pushed his head down further and pried it over his ear. "How the *hell* did you do this?" she cried, frustrated.

"Somewhere between getting my nuts crushed with your foot as you hit the Gs and struggling to breathe when you started panicking like a drowned rat, I'm not sure."

"Gah!" she cried, slapping it aside. "There. It's off. Now get the hell out of here."

"Yes, your Majesty," Milar said, straightening as much as he could. To her relief, he began to ease himself out of the pilot chamber. As soon as his legs were clear, Tatiana clambered after him and out onto the deck, unhooking nodes as she went.

"Well," Milar said, cranking his neck back and forth, "I think, aside from getting skinned alive, that was probably one of the most unpleasant experiences of my life."

"Ungrateful crawler," Tatiana muttered, as she unlocked nodes and began easing the electrodes out of her body. She felt Milar step behind her, helping her with the harder-to-reach spinal nodes.

"Thanks," she said.

Milar grunted. They finished unhooking her, then Tatiana jerked open the cargo box. She thrust Milar's pants at him and began to crawl into the spare uniform she found tucked inside the pilot survival kit. It was not her size, built for someone thirty or forty pounds heavier, but she put it on anyway.

"You call Patrick," she said, shoving Milar the emergency radio. Then, needing air, she jumped off the soldier and walked a few paces off into the brush, trying to get her shaking under control.

After a few moments, Milar touched her shoulder. "I called Pat. He'll be an hour, at the soonest. You doing okay?"

"I'm fine," she growled, though her stomach was still doing hula-hoops.

"Good." He unfurled the emergency blanket and spread it out on the ground between them. Gesturing to it with the blade of his knife, he said, "On the ground, squid. Hands at your sides."

Tatiana froze. "What?"

"I'm cutting out your lifeline."

"Just wait a minute," Tatiana said. "I'm not feeling too good right now."

"Tough," Milar replied, a big hand pressing against her back. "The coalers are gonna realize something very wrong has happened sooner or later. Lie down on the blanket. Don't want to infect a node."

"I'm not lying down," Tatiana said. "I'll sit still, like you did."

"Bullshit," Milar growled. "We both know an energetic little Shrieker like you couldn't sit still if your life depended on it. Lie down or I'll lie you down."

"You can't *do* that!" Tatiana shrieked.

Milar gave her a flat look. "Do it. Now."

Narrowing her eyes, Tatiana got down on her stomach.

Milar sat down on top of her, pinning her arms to her sides with his knees. She felt his big hand against the back of her skull, pressing her forehead into the metallic material of the emergency blanket.

"Ow," Tatiana complained into the ground. "Why are you sitting on my arms, you collie bastard?"

"Making sure you don't get another cheap shot at the family jewels while I cut out your lifeline. Now stop shouting and try to hold still. These newer ones are more sensitive to jerking."

She felt the cold touch of metal on the back of her neck and winced as she felt the knife bite into her neck. Blood began to seep over the base of her skull and drip onto the metallic heat-reflective blanket beneath her chin. She heard the wet click, then began counting down in her mind as she felt pressure in her neck as he twisted the battery cap away.

Eventually she felt the tug as the electrodes began to slide beneath her skin. She stiffened.

"Careful," Milar whispered, "Don't move."

"As if I *can*, with you pressing my face into the—"

"Quiet, goddammit!" Milar growled. "This thing is rigged to pop your pretty little head off if it senses tampering. Just shut up a second. I don't want to lose some fingers, all right?"

"—ground," Tatiana muttered. Then, without missing a beat, she added, "Now *there's* an idea, collie. Maybe I should just start wiggl—"

A minor explosion less than fifteen centimeters from her spinal column cut her off with a blink. The big hand gripping the back of her skull jerked.

"Uh . . . Milar?"

"You," Milar said, "are lucky I am level-headed."

She winced. "You lost some fingers?"

"Yes."

"Uh . . . Sorry?"

Milar jerked the rest of the electrodes out of her neck and, with an unceremonious grunt, threw the lifeline into the weeds. She heard it clang against a tree with a tinny sound.

Milar released her head. "I've got to thank you, Captain. You have once again illustrated in gruesome, smoking detail, why I hate coalers."

"Does it, uh, hurt?" Tatiana asked. Then, straining to see him, she said, "You can let me up now."

Milar didn't move. "You are a pain in the ass, you know that?"

"Uh, yes?"

"From day one, you have been nothing but a gigantic pain in the ass."

"I didn't mean to," Tatiana said, squirming, trying to get a look at him. He sounded calm. Which probably meant he was madder than hell.

"A week ago, if I'd had even the slightest *clue* as to the magnitude of the ass-pain I was about to receive, I would have turned and run screaming in the opposite direction."

"Why are you still sitting on me?"

"Because I'm not sure I can stand without falling over."

"It's that bad?" Tatiana asked, trying to twist around to see. "Let me *up*."

"It's bad enough I'll probably only remain conscious another minute or two."

Tatiana's eyes widened. "Then what are you going to do?"

"Die, probably."

"Get a tourniquet on it!" she cried. "Grab that nanostrip on your chest and slap it on the wound. And get *off* of me."

"Don't think I have the strength," Milar said.

"You *bastard*, if you pass out on me, I'll kill you."

"Sorry, sweetie." Milar slumped over onto her and suddenly Tatiana was straining for breath.

"Milar," she panted. "Move. Your. Ass. Can't. Breathe."

"Too . . . weak . . . ," Milar moaned near her ear, his upper body crushing her into the earth. "Damn . . . hard to . . . see . . . "

"No!" she screamed. "I'll die under here!"

"Were they," Milar gasped, "right?" Then he went silent and still above her, the added limpness forcing the last bit of air out of her lungs.

Were they . . . *right*? Tatiana stopped struggling and narrowed her eyes. "You're faking."

After a moment, a whisper against her ear said, "What makes you think that, squid?"

"Let me up," she snapped.

"I don't know . . . you kidnapped me and tried to blow off my fingers. Maybe I like it here."

"I," Tatiana gritted, "am so gonna kill you."

"Apologize," Milar said.

"*No!*"

"Are you ticklish?" Milar said. He moved one of his hands to her ribs.

Tatiana shrieked and started to struggle.

"Careful," Milar said, easily stroking his fingers down her ribs as she panicked and clawed underneath him. "You're going to bump some nodes out of place. Just apologize, sweetie. Say, 'Milar, I'm sorry I locked you in a bubble of goo and wouldn't open the hatch when you wanted out. I'm sorry I stomped on your nuts and made you think I was going to spurt arterial blood all over if you twitched too hard even though the damn line was strangling you and the air tube wasn't giving you enough air. Milar, I'm sorry I made you strip down to your boxers and forced you to spend two hours with your head crammed down against your chest and get goo down your asscrack. Milar, I'm sorry I never listen to instructions and that I probably would've gotten you killed if your lifeline hadn't been a dud. Oh, and Milar, I'm sorry I just tried to blow off your hand.'"

"Stop," she gasped. "I'm sorry!"

"Only if you answer me one question first," he said, still stroking her ribs.

"*Anything,*" Tatiana screamed.

"Which dragon," he said. "Red or black?"

"I like them both!" she shrieked.

"Really," he said, and she could tell he was grinning. "Why?"

"They're pretty," she wailed.

"You got a thing for dragons, coaler?" He was *still* tickling her.

"Yes," she managed, gasping. "I do, I do."

Milar flipped her over, grinning as his golden brown eyes scanned hers. Softly, he said, "What about the guy wearing them?"

Tatiana's breath caught in her chest. For a long time, all she could hear was the sound of her heart pounding against her eardrums. Then she nodded.

"Better speak up," he warned, reaching for her ribs again.

She narrowed her eyes. "I think you're the biggest knucker I've ever—"

Milar closed the distance between them with a kiss. Instantly, Tatiana froze, feeling every objection flee in a rush of surprise. After a moment, she began to melt under him, and her hands reached up of their own accord to bury themselves in his hair.

When Milar finally broke the kiss, they were both breathless. "Thank you for rescuing me, Princess," Milar said. He leaned forward and touched his lips to her forehead. "I appreciate it."

Tatiana bit her lip and said, "Even if you got goo in your asscrack?"

Milar grimaced and pushed himself into a seated position, straddling her. He eyed her a minute, his golden-brown eyes alive with amusement. Finally, he chuckled and shook his head. "Don't remind me." Standing, he offered a hand and helped pull her to her feet. "Come on. I hear Patrick coming."

# CHAPTER 35

# Cliffhanger

MAGALI SAT IN THE CAVERN, SHIVERING AS THE WIND TUGGED the heat from her bruised and naked skin. Behind her, the tunnel was sealed with piles of energy-fused rock. She hadn't moved for over a day. The Nephyrs had used her body, as promised. Instead of leaving the pistol for her to finish herself off when they were done, however, Colonel Steele had dropped it over the edge.

"Oops," he had said, watching it fall. Then he'd smiled. "Oh well. Anyone willing to kill a child to save herself doesn't deserve an easy death." He'd walked back to the cave entrance, then paused. "Oh, and that cute little pact we made don't mean jack shit to me. The moment those eggers finish cleaning up after Harvest, they're all going to be executed as traitors to the Coalition." And then he'd left her there. Bruised, battered, and bleeding.

Throughout it all, Magali hadn't cried. After what she had done, she didn't deserve to cry.

But now, trapped, thinking of the hundreds of lives that were going to be lost because of her actions, she cried.

*You're not trapped,* Wideman said. He had talked her through the hours with the Nephyrs, distracted her during the worst moments with songs and little lullabies that her mother had used to sing to her as a child.

Magali looked back at the stones blocking the exit, fused together with superheated energy charges, then back at the cliff. She supposed he was right. She could jump.

She even got to her feet before her instinctual terror of falling rammed her knees back into the stone beneath her.

*Coward,* she told herself.

*You're not trapped,* Wideman said again. Then he giggled. *Killer.*

"Shut up!" Magali screamed, grabbing at her head. "Shut up, you asshole!"

Then, realizing she was screaming at a figment of her imagination, Magali got up and strode to the edge of the cliff before her mind could register what she was doing. As soon as it did, her feet froze on the stone and it was all she could do not to fall into a crouch, gripping the red-orange rock beneath her in terror.

Staring at the wind-whipped cliff, remembering Benny's hands clutching at air as he fell, she said, "I'm a monster and I deserve to die." And she knew, deep down, that they were the truest words she had ever spoken. Still, she couldn't make herself take those last two steps.

Looking over the edge, trying to work up the courage to jump, she could see Benny's body far below. It was a tiny pale dot against a red-orange background. She had given Benny one of the guards' shirts to wear, but the Nephyrs had stripped him of it at the same time they removed the Coalition bodies from the base of the cliff.

Now Ben's body was a lone, naked dot upon the rocks below.

*They didn't even bother to bury him,* Magali thought, anguished. Sooner or later, the Fortune fauna would find the boy's thin body and tear it apart. They'd had the chance to take him back with the dead guards, give him a decent burial, but they'd left him for the animals. Like he wasn't even human.

And Magali couldn't do anything about it. She was responsible, yet she couldn't do anything about it. She could either die of dehydration or jump, and neither of those ends would allow her to pile rocks over the body in a funeral cairn.

*He was just a kid. He didn't do anything to you. You could have at least buried him.*

Though she hadn't cried the entire day she spent with the Nephyrs, Magali felt tears once more heat her cheeks as she stared helplessly down at the body.

Wideman was right. In that moment, given the chance, she would kill every man, woman, and cyborg wearing Coalition colors. She would shoot them until she ran out of charges, and then would go after them with a knife. If only she had a *gun*. She could kill them with a gun.

*Then go get it,* Wideman told her.

Magali froze, staring down at the twisting green band that was the bottom of the Snake. It was so far away it looked like she was gazing down upon a child's model canyon. Slowly, her eyes moved to the rock-face beneath her.

It wasn't particularly flat. There were jagged cracks, wind-eaten hollows, even places where she could walk on narrow, slanting ledges.

Immediately, she squeezed her eyes shut, her heart thundering in her ears. *That's a four-thousand-foot drop. No one climbs down a four-thousand-foot drop and lives. It's suicide.*

Then everything seemed to fall into focus.

*Then I fall,* she thought. *So what? I am dead anyway.*

She sat there, feeling the wind tug at her skin, trying to think.

*It's four thousand feet,* her mind kept babbling at her. *The gun wouldn't survive a four-thousand-foot drop. Its lenses and chambers would shatter.*

On a fancy gun, yes. But the same irritating three-second delay that had kept Magali from putting holes in every single Nephyr who had stepped through the tunnels two days before belonged to the same safeguarding system that kept the gun cushioned from every hazard that could befall it in the dirt and grime of normal combat. The designers of the A1550-Y had been more interested in utility and durability than maximum firepower. It had been the backup weapon for standard infantry troops for over a hundred years.

*The grunts've spent a century trying to break this thing*, her father would always say when he brought it out. *Anything you can imagine, those guys have done it. Best they ever do is break the sights off.* He then showed her the welded line on his gun where the sights had been snapped off long ago, then welded back into place. *This one got run over by a tank.*

As Magali stared down at the bottom of the Snake, she thought, *Yeah, but did they drop it from four thousand feet?* She considered climbing all the way down, her body straining and trembling, only to find the gun a shattered husk.

*Don't you want to kill them?* Wideman's voice asked her.

Feeling that ocean of acidic rage eating at her stomach, Magali's fingers tightened into fists. She took the last two steps and put her hands on the lip of stone. She sought out a crevice, then put her leg over the edge. The howling wind grabbed her and tugged. Her instinctual terror struck, then, trying to unfurl in her gut and spread outward into her limbs.

*Fuck off,* she told it. And started to climb.

# CHAPTER 36

# Tatiana Flies Cargo

PATRICK GRIMACED AT THE CYBORG STANDING BESIDE HIS brother. "You can't be serious, Miles."

Milar gave him a look that could have detonated concrete. "Serious about what, Patty?"

Patrick blushed, knowing that now would be a good time to change the subject, but he couldn't help himself. He jabbed a finger at the cyborg. "She put you back in Nephyr hands. Our face is plastered on every single government wanted list there is because of her. She got the whole town of Deaddrunk strip-searched. They confiscated Veera's *ship* because of her."

"She's done with all that," Milar said. He winked—*winked*—at the cyborg. "Ain't ya, squid?"

"What can the little runt do that you or I can't?" Patrick demanded.

"Have babies, for one," the cyborg said.

Patrick narrowed his eyes at her. She peered back, completely unaffected. With a growl, Patrick said, "Really? I didn't think the Coalition wanted baby cyborgs running around."

"I signed the waiver," the cyborg said, her blue-violet eyes challenging. "Took a few drugs. It's all there. Baby."

"Maybe," Patrick said. "But how does a jumbled hunk of metal drop a kid without hurting itself?"

Milar stepped between them. "She's coming, Patty. Stop being a dickhead."

"We never hurt her!" Patrick snapped. "We fixed her broken bones, and didn't murder her twenty different times when we should have. And she turned you over to the Nephyrs and sang to the Coalition investigators like you were Satan himself. They put the interviews on the news feed, Milar. She said you *raped* her."

Milar lifted a brow. "So?"

Patrick sputtered. "She lied."

"I told her to lie," Milar said. "She did exactly what she needed to do."

Patrick frowned. "You *told* her to say that you'd made her eat her own feces?"

Milar looked a bit shocked, then turned to the cyborg. "You *said* that?"

She blushed scarlet. "Maybe."

"That's disgusting," Milar said.

"You told me to make it bad," Tatiana said.

Milar continued to stare at her.

"We can't go back to Deaddrunk," Patrick said. "They've had a group of Nephyrs in the hills, watching that place ever since they discovered the antique guns Landborn cached in the mines. Thank God they didn't find the energy weapons."

Milar winced. "What about Dad?"

Patrick froze, his eyes flickering back to Tatiana. She was watching them much too closely.

"Oh, come off it," Milar said. "Sooner or later, she's gonna know Wideman's our Pop, if she hasn't already guessed." He glanced over at her and raised a questioning eyebrow.

The cyborg flushed and nodded.

"Just great!" Patrick cried. "Anything *else* you want to tell the coalers while you're at it, Milar? You *know* she'll just go right back and start singing the moment we take our eyes off her."

"Not gonna happen," Milar said.

"Why?" Patrick demanded. "Because you rescued her?"

"*I* rescued *him*," the cyborg corrected. She jabbed the tip of her finger into his brother's chest. "*He* was running around like a headless chicken."

"Yeah," Milar said. He grinned at her. Something passed between them, and the girl blushed.

Patrick was still staring. *She* rescued *him*? How could a four-foot-nine cyborg rescue his brother? With her particular brand of cyborg, the metal actually hindered the muscles' normal movement, so she was a *weak* four-foot-nine cyborg. Not only that, but why? Why would she bother? She had been home free . . .

Patrick scowled at the cyborg. "How do you know it wasn't a setup, Miles? They could have let you escape together so she could infiltrate the rebel cause."

"She made her choice," Milar said. "Just like Wideman said she would."

*Of course he would play the Wideman card.* Patrick felt his mouth tighten. "Fine." He glared at the cyborg. "Goddamn it. Fine." He stuck out his hand. "Patrick."

The cyborg gave it a puzzled look.

"Since we never got a chance to introduce ourselves properly," he growled. "My name is Patrick Whitecliff. The oaf you just dragged out of the Nephyr compound is my brother, Milar Whitecliff. He's the one with the dragons."

She looked up at him and blushed. Then, gingerly, like she expected him to rip her arm off, she reached forward and put her hand in his. "Tatiana Eyre," she said. He felt the metal node digging into his palm as her small, smooth fingers tightened on his. Her hand was sticky, just as it had been the day they'd caught her outside her soldier.

"Call me Pat," Patrick said.

Milar snorted. "Call him Patty. Everyone else does."

"And I hate it," Patrick growled, squeezing the woman's hand in warning. "Call me Pat."

"I had a sister named Patty." She grinned up at him evilly, her odd, purplish eyes dancing.

Patrick had to smile, despite himself. "So how'd she save you, Miles?"

"Flew me out in the belly of her goddamn soldier," Milar said, shaking his head. "Disgusting stuff dried already. I think my ass cheeks are going to be stuck together for the next ten years."

"It comes off in the shower," Tatiana said quickly. "Just soap it up good."

His brother gave the cyborg an evil look. "Maybe you could help me with that later."

She turned red as a beet. "Um."

Watching the exchange, Patrick's mouth fell open. His brother was . . . flirting?

"Oh, shut your trap, Pat," Milar said, giving him a meaningful look. "It ain't like I never had a naked girl in the shower before. The cyborg and me came to an understanding, that's all."

Patrick frowned, then glanced from Milar to Tatiana. Suddenly, it struck him. *He doesn't want her to know he's a virgin.*

Patrick threw back his head and laughed.

This time, it was Milar who turned red as a beet.

Cackling, Patrick cried, "You just don't want her to know you're—"

Milar stepped forward and punched him in the shoulder, hard. Patrick doubled over, unable to stop laughing.

"He's what?" the cyborg asked. She frowned up at Milar. "You're what?" Patrick could see what she was thinking . . . *Diseased?*

That made him laugh harder, until he was choking and gasping.

Milar shoved him over. "You say one more word, Patty," Milar growled, squatting over him, "and next time people see you, they won't be able to tell you're my brother."

"Sorry," Patrick choked from the ground. "Sorry." Then, seeing the baffled look the girl was giving his brother, he started cackling again.

"Screw you," Milar growled, stepping around him and stomping up the ramp of the ship.

The cyborg stayed behind, eyeing Patrick like he was a strange new type of Shrieker. "He's what?" she asked, once Milar's heavy footsteps had disappeared inside the ship.

"He's gonna be paying me a lot of money," Patrick said. "Starting today."

She frowned down at him. "He owes you money?"

"He will," Patrick said. "If he wants me to keep my mouth shut."

"Fuck you!" Milar shouted from inside the ship. Then Patrick heard the sounds of feet charging up the metal stairs.

"Then he's"—Tatiana lowered her voice to a whisper— ". . . married?"

*Married.* Oh, that was just too perfect. Patrick threw back his head again and roared.

A few feet away, the ship's engines began to warm up. The cyborg gave the ship a nervous look, then glanced back at Patrick.

"Better . . . go," Patrick said, gasping, gesturing toward the ship. "I'll be there in a minute." He rolled onto his belly, chuckling into the dirt.

Tatiana gave him one last, wary look, then jogged to the boarding ramp and disappeared inside. Somehow, Patrick found the strength to climb aboard the ship before Milar took off. He collapsed onto the deck, still laughing. Tatiana and Milar had retreated to the cockpit, leaving him alone to get his glee under control.

He was getting to his feet to climb up to the cockpit when Milar flipped on the intercom and said, "Patrick, you need to see this."

The tone of his brother's voice put Patrick into an instinctive sprint. He slapped open the hatch and stepped inside. Tatiana looked up at him from the pilot's chair. Milar was in the copilot seat, watching a news feed. He gave Patrick a look that stopped his heart.

"What?" Patrick said.

"Yolk Factory 14," Milar said, gesturing to the screen.

It took Patrick a moment to tear his eyes from his brother's face and refocus them on the news feed. A camp-wide Shriek had decimated the population of Yolk Factory 14. Only three hundred and thirty-two survivors.

*Oh no.* Patrick stepped closer, his heart beginning to pound.

"Anna and Magali were in Factory 14, weren't they?" Milar asked.

Patrick scanned the images of the tired, wan-faced survivors as they filed out of the mounds. He didn't see the tall brunette and her creepy little sister.

*Magali.* His chest hurt. He was finding it hard to breathe. "They have a survivor list?" Patrick whispered.

Milar glanced at Tatiana, then reluctantly nodded. He accessed the data, then leaned back for Patrick to scan the lists.

Patrick read it three times. "No Landborns," he whispered.

"Maybe they changed their names," Tatiana offered.

"We've been keeping track of them every day since they were taken," Milar said. He lowered his voice and his eyes caught Patrick with apology. "They were always there."

*We didn't rescue them in time,* Patrick thought. His eyes flickered to Tatiana. *We didn't rescue them in time because we were busy with the cyborg.*

"Now, hey," Milar said, starting to stand. "It ain't her fault, Pat."

"The hell it isn't," Patrick whispered. "We left Mag and Anna to die because we were busy playing her stupid games." Then, because he couldn't stay there any longer without putting his fist through someone's eye socket, he turned and left the cockpit.

Milar found him later, sitting in a corner on the lower deck. "I'm sorry, Pat."

Patrick didn't look at his brother. "You said she'd be fine another two weeks." Patrick wiped tears from his eyes. He hadn't realized he'd been crying.

"We don't know they're dead," Milar said.

"I haven't heard from Anna in four days," Patrick said. "Ever since the day you were captured."

"Think she knew?" Milar asked.

"She would have tried to set up a rescue, if she had," Patrick said. He took a deep breath and let it out, squeezing his fingers into a white-knuckled fist. "Oh my God, I want to kill them."

Milar watched his hand, his face contorted in understanding. He nodded. "I do too."

"Then why do we keep waiting?" Patrick snapped. "I'm tired of waiting for Wideman's damn Sign. All we've done is wait. David's gone. Now Magali and Anna are gone. Who's next? You? Jeanne? We lose anyone else and there's not gonna be a war."

"Wideman never said they'd be part of the resistance," Milar reminded him.

Patrick almost hit his brother. Almost. Softly, he said, "Magali and I were gonna run off together. Build a house. Raise a family."

Milar dropped his eyes to his hands and started fidgeting with his knife. For a long time, his brother said nothing. Patrick imagined he was dealing with the shock. Then Milar said, "I know."

Patrick flinched. "You *knew?*" He had thought he had managed to keep it a secret.

"*Please,*" Milar snorted. "You're my brother, Pat. I can read you like a book. I knew you were gonna run off. Saw it coming a mile away. That's why I told Anna."

Patrick froze. The calm child's face, the utter sincerity as she told him Magali wanted nothing to do with him. The letter, in Magali's handwriting, confirming it.

"Pat?" Milar said, after a minute had passed.

"You split us up," Patrick whispered.

Milar reddened. "You were gonna give up *everything* we've worked for to chase a *girl.* Hell yes, we split you up. And I'm glad we did. The resistance wouldn't be the same without you, Pat. Like you just said, we lose anybody else and we lose the war."

Patrick lunged at his brother, knocking the knife aside and going for his throat. "You asshole!" he snapped. "It was *my life!*"

Milar kicked him off and crawled forward before he had a chance to stand. He pinned his shoulders, glaring. "You're gonna help me fight the coalers, Pat. We made a pact. You can chase tail when the fighting's over with."

"What, just like you and your little cyborg?" Patrick snarled and threw him to the side.

"That cyborg happens to be a leader of the resistance!" Milar snapped, shoving him away and getting to his feet. "We need her help."

"Oh bullshit!" Patrick snapped back, standing. "You didn't stare at her picture all those years because she was gonna put down a few coalers. You did it because you wanted to get her metal ass into bed."

This time, Milar's eyes narrowed and he lunged. Patrick stopped him with a roundhouse, but instead of going down, Milar caught his leg and jerked him off his feet. Patrick hit the floor hard with his back and head, making the metal grating clang as if it had been hit by a two-by-four. He blinked, seeing stars.

But Milar had already rammed his knee into his chest, reaching back to throw a punch.

Adrenaline was surging through him in burning waves, now. Patrick screamed an animal cry and rolled over onto his brother, once more going for the throat.

"*Boys,*" Tatiana said over the intercom, "*as interesting as all that is, you might want to know we've got Coalition on our ass.*"

Both Patrick and Milar froze.

"They give you a lifeline?" Patrick asked.

"Took it out," Milar said. "I'm lucky the damn thing was a dud or I'd be—" His eyes widened. "Oh shit."

"They put you under?" Pat cried, pushing himself to his feet.

"I was in surgery for almost two days, and drugged up for the next one."

"Shit, Milar," Patrick cursed, scanning his brother's body for extra lumps. "Shit, shit."

"*Boys?*" Tatiana said. "*You want me to bring 'em down or what?*" She sounded utterly calm.

*She doesn't know the ship has no guns.* "This ain't a warship!" Milar cried, heading for the stairs. "You can't take down Coalition fighters."

"*Watch me.*" And then the ship lurched and went into a sudden dive, leaving Milar and Patrick struggling to stay upright. "*Might wanna strap in, though.*"

"Hell no!" Milar cried, stumbling up the stairs. Patrick followed on his heels, ready to take up copilot. Instead, they were thwarted by a locked door. Milar pounded on the hatch. "Damn it, coaler, let us in there! My brother and I need to fly this thing!"

*"No you don't, knucker,"* Tatiana said. *"Just sit down, relax, and try not to vomit. Oh, and figure out where they tagged you. I'd guess the armpit or between the shoulder blades. If you can get Patrick to cut it out without cutting off an arm during the maneuvers, that would be nice, too."*

Milar stared at the locked cockpit door, then raised his arm and pounded at it again. Tatiana ignored him.

Milar narrowed his eyes and went to the locking console affixed to the outside of the hatch. He flipped open the housing and started typing in a manual override.

Remembering the scenes Wideman had shown him, Patrick caught Milar's arm. "We should let her do this."

Milar blinked at him. "Are you nuts?" Then, a bit deflated, he said, "She needs a copilot."

"No," Patrick said, remembering. "She doesn't."

*"That's right,"* Tatiana said, *"So if you could please strap yourselves in before the walls of the ship turn you both into hamburger, I would very much like to start showing these three yokels who they're dealing with. Twenty seconds until I start barrel-rolling."*

"This ship can't barrel-roll," Milar said.

*"You can gape at me in awe later. I promise I'll give you all the proper opportunities."*

"Coaler," Milar growled.

*"Ten seconds, collie,"* she replied.

"Fine," Milar snapped. He slid down the stairs and settled into a crash harness. Patrick followed. Tatiana waited until he had clicked the primary straps into place, then the world started to spin.

◀◀ ◆ ▶▶

*This is it,* Tatiana thought, watching the three Bouncer ships come in close, trying to cut her off. *No going back now.* She jammed the joystick forward and to one side, sending the ship into a spinning forward roll that should have ended in splattered Coalition operator smeared across a four-kilometer-wide stretch of Fortune flora.

Instead, she used her momentum to finish the arc and, like the toy ball on the end of the timeless cup-and-ball game, she came whipping around the other side, at the Bouncers' backs. At the same time, she flipped off her main engines, going cold.

*"Where the hell did it go?"* one of the Bouncers said, over the secure Coalition band. Already knowing the couple of dozen channels the Bouncers used, it had only taken Tatiana a few seconds to narrow it down.

*"I don't know. Shit, did it crash?"*

The three Coalition pilots were still trying to figure out where she had gone when she pulled out of their backdraft and extended her landing gear.

"What the hell are you doing up there?!" one of the brothers screamed from the belly of the ship. Tatiana still hadn't been around them long enough to tell the difference between their voices. Flipping on the com, she said, "Did you figure out where they tagged you yet?"

"One in the armpit, another behind his ear," Patrick said. "We think he might have a couple in his chest cavity."

"Aanaho," Tatiana said. "No wonder they weren't too worried about you running off. How you gonna get them out?"

"We're gonna EMP him," Patrick said. "Pulse him in a few dozen places from head to toe and it should fry anything he's carrying."

"It's above you, above you!"

Tatiana frowned, listening to the Bouncers scream at each other. Distractedly, she said, "You're not setting off EMP charges on my ship."

"*Your* ship?" This time, she could tell it was Milar. "Guess again, tart."

In response, Tatiana switched power to her main engines and dove, ripping off the closest Bouncer's left stabilizer with the screech of tearing metal. She watched as a chunk of landing gear spiraled toward the ground along with a goodly portion of the Bouncer's left wing.

"*I'm hit, I'm hit!*"

"*You going down?*"

"*I gotta turn back before I fall outta the sky. Lost maneuverability. Think it blew off a wing.*"

"*Aanaho, that thing's got guns?*"

"*What the hell do we do? It's not letting us get a lock on it!*"

Tatiana took a deep breath, then spun the vessel up and to the side, her ship's engines roaring as she rolled back and fought her own momentum. She grabbed the console hard, then went cold again as she hit the apex of her arc. Immediately, the ship began an upside-down freefall dive. The smallish wings on the colonists' ship were more for stability than carrying weight, but with the speed Tatiana had gained from her downward plunge, she used the wings to guide her fall into a wide arc, then slammed on the engines just before hitting the ground, making her feel the Gs in her brain.

"*Goddamn it, you two, that's just a collie ship. Ain't got any guns on it. Just shut the hell up and bring it down.*"

"*Easy for you to say, jackass. He didn't just turn your ship into Swiss cheese.*"

To the Whitecliff brothers, she said, "*Hold on. I'm about to put us in another spin.*"

"Sweetie," Milar replied, "You've already put Patrick out of commission. Another spin and I think I might join him."

Tatiana glanced at the camera feed. Still strapped securely to the wall, Patrick's head was lolling against his forehead harness. Beside him, Milar looked a funny shade of green.

*"Got a lock on it!"*

*"Fire, damn it!"*

She couldn't help herself. She laughed as she pulled another spin over the top of a Bouncer, forcing his companion to either break the lock or risk taking down his partner, as well. "Can't take the heat, Milar?"

"Squid," Milar said, sounding weak, "As soon as you put this thing down, I'm gonna bust in there and drag you somewhere to show you what heat is all about."

Tatiana blushed and she forgot about the Bouncers. "Um."

Milar grinned, perking up despite his pallid complexion. "I'll take that as a yes."

*"Locked again! Firing!"*

Tatiana shut off the engines, twisted the ship down, then didn't haul up on the controls until she had collided with the treetops. All around her, the sounds of snapping trees thudded against the hull with dull metal bangs as she plowed through the alien canopy. She felt the echo of an explosion somewhere behind her, as the missile slammed into flying debris and detonated.

*"Shit. It dodged the missiles. Do I have a go on the LAZ?"*

Crap. Lasers. Tatiana was hoping it wouldn't come to that.

*"Roger, take it down."*

*"Captain, I'm registering colonial structures within the regulated twenty-five kilometer no-fire limit. A miss might result in civilian casualties."*

*"I don't give a dead shit! They're all rebels and pirates anyway. Bring that junk heap down."*

Tatiana once again flipped on the com speaker. "Milar, I need you to release some stuff from the cargo nets. Everything heavy you can get your hands on. I need to drop some ballast."

"What happened to the hamburger?" Milar mumbled. He looked well and truly miserable. She was actually a bit surprised he was still conscious.

"I'll hold off on the fancy stuff until you get back in harness," Tatiana promised.

"That before or after you wreck these Coalition guys' days?" Milar asked, unbuckling himself. "Because I'm itching to drag you off somewhere and show you some fancy stuff of my own."

Tatiana blushed again. "Me too." Then, *Oh my God, did you actually just say that?*

Milar paused and looked up at her through the camera. He grinned. "Got any requests?"

"The *ballast*, you horny bastard! Get the *ballast*!"

Chuckling, Milar jogged across the cargo bay and started dragging stuff out of the nets and tossing it on the floor.

"Hurry!" Tatiana cried, as the Bouncers got into position behind her. She had put on as much speed as the ship could handle, but the Bouncers were closing. Any minute, they would start firing, and LAZ, once locked, wasn't the type of weapon to miss.

"I am hurrying," Milar cried, throwing more gear and tools onto the floor.

*"I've got the target locked. He's flying straight and level as a rookie now. Looks like the guy made himself sick."*

The other pilots laughed.

*"Roger. As soon as you can, bring him down."*

"*That's enough!*" Tatiana shouted at Milar, eyeing the pile of debris on the floor of the ship. "Get back in harness. Now!"

Milar, thankfully, didn't argue. He struggled back across the deck and fell back into the body-shaped pad. He had just secured his forehead band when Tatiana veered up and shut off power, flattening the ship against the air in front of it. She heard the two Bouncers boom past beneath her. In the cargo bay, she heard Milar yell as all the loose debris tumbled past him and hit the cargo bay door.

*"Damn, missed."*

*"You missed? How the hell could you miss?"*

Tatiana was climbing, now, putting every ounce of her ship's power into upward speed. She hit forty thousand feet, then opened the hatch and allowed all the debris to hurtle out the back with a roar of wind. Then she slammed the door shut, turned sharply toward the ground, and used gravity to boost the ship's natural speed, much like a cart coasting down a hill. Hitting one thousand feet, she saw the Bouncers ahead of her, circling back.

She flew straight at the first one.

*"The asshole's playing chicken!"*

*"LAZ the bastard!"*

Tatiana rolled out of the way at the last moment, veered to the left, then retreated back the way she had come. She pressed her ship into speed, pushing the engines for all they would go. Tatiana felt even the little bots carrying extra oxygen to her brain struggle against the Gs. The two remaining Bouncers fell in behind her, their superior ships and cockpits able to handle the sudden force of acceleration. In moments, they were zipping along the treetops at three times the speed of sound, their velocity increasing steadily with every heartbeat.

*"Three seconds for a lock,"* one of the two remaining Bouncer captains said. *"Two, one . . . "*

Tatiana kept an even course, concentrating on navigating the terrain ahead of her.

Twenty seconds later, a new voice said, *"Well? Did you take him down?"*

Neither of the two Bouncer captains replied.

*"Bravo-Four-Four-Eight-Papa-Seven-Charlie, did you get the lock?"*

Tatiana checked her viewfinder, then turned due east and headed deeper into colonial territory.

*"Bravo-Four-Four-Eight-Papa-Seven-Charlie, do you read?"*

The controller received no reply. In an increasingly aggravated voice, the woman said, *"Bouncer captains of the ships Bravo-Four-Four-Eight-Papa-Seven-Charlie and Bravo-Four-Four-One-Adam-Zero-Victor, do you copy?"*

Tatiana flipped the com off and concentrated on staying low and off of radar. To her passengers, she said, "That did it. You can come in here and stare at me in awe now."

Neither Milar nor Patrick responded. She glanced at the camera feed. Both of their heads were lolling against the forehead harnesses. Tatiana grinned and let them sleep.

Two hours later, she heard someone open the cockpit hatch.

"Enjoy your snooze?" she asked.

"Well," Milar said, stepping through, "We're not dead or entertaining Nephyrs, so I've got to assume you and your buddies had a little coaler powwow and struck a deal and that's why my ship isn't a steaming wreck in the jungle somewhere."

"I want guns on this ship," Tatiana said. "Forward and rear." Then she turned and scrunched her nose up at him. "You smell like vomit."

Milar flushed. "The only people who have those kinds of guns are coalers, and they sure as hell ain't gonna sell them to colonists."

"Then we'll steal them," Tatiana said. "Not having guns pissed me off."

Milar peered at her. "My ship can't outrun Coalition Bouncers."

She raised a brow. "You knew they were Bouncers?"

"I heard them when they flew under us at the same time you tried to flatten me to the wall." He was watching her too closely. "I also recently had an unpleasant experience with them . . . or had you forgotten?"

"Oh yeah," Tatiana said, flushing. "Right."

His eyes narrowed. "Coaler, why are we all still breathing?"

Tatiana looked up from the viewfinder. "You know that stuff you pulled off the racks?"

"My tools?" Milar said.

"Yeah. That's the thing about Bouncers—they're fast, but light-duty. At their top speeds, they don't have the impact resistance to survive a collision with anything harder than a bird."

Milar just frowned at her, his golden-hazel eyes confused.

"Your tools went through their windshields," Tatiana said. "At about Mach 3."

Milar continued to scowl at her. "Any tools you released from the hatch would have been traveling at the same velocity as the ship when they were released."

"I dropped them from forty thousand feet, then ran the Bouncers into them at ground level."

Milar's eyes widened. "No wonder I passed out." Then he frowned at her. "Come to think of it, why didn't *you* pass out?"

Tatiana shrugged. "One of the great things about my little buddies is they keep the proper amount of oxygen flowing to my brain, whatever the Gs." She glanced up at him. "Bouncer pilots have similar tricks, but they do it mostly with drugs and augmented organs."

"So," Milar said, sounding unhappy, "what you're trying to tell me is you just saved my ass again."

"Yep," Tatiana said.

"Get out of my chair," Milar said.

Tatiana gave the controls a nervous look. "But what if the Coalition—"

"Now, coaler." Milar grabbed her by the top of her jumpsuit and bodily hauled her out of the captain's chair. Then he put the ship into a landing sequence. In less than a minute, he had lowered them into a tiny swamplike clearing and powered down the ship. With the landing gear mangled, the ship rested at an angle on its belly.

"What are you *doing?*" Tatiana cried.

"Thanking you properly," Milar said, getting out of the chair.

Tatiana's heart lurched and she stumbled back, swallowing hard.

Milar saw her reaction and grinned. He went to the door and opened the hatch. The dragons bunched on his thick shoulders as he gestured. "You gonna come with me or do I need to drag you?"

Heart hammering in her ears, Tatiana found she couldn't move.

Milar sighed and grabbed her by the hand, then tugged her out the cockpit hatch and down the stairs. On the wall nearby, Patrick was slumped against the harness, snoring.

"Um," Tatiana said, as Milar dragged her across the cargo bay, toward the crew quarters located on the other side of the ship. Every nerve was on fire in the hand where he was touching her. "This really isn't a good idea. They could still be after us. What if you didn't fry all the tags?"

"We got them all," Milar said, "And waking up sleeping people is rude." He glanced at Patrick, then gave her a demonic grin.

Tatiana swallowed hard, and her feet suddenly stopped working.

As promised, Milar dragged her to a closed door, then opened it and dragged her inside.

It was a bedroom. Milar's bedroom. Tatiana's heart gave a little flutter. "This really isn't smart," she blurted.

"Uh-huh," he said, shutting the door behind them. It closed with a solid mechanical *thump*.

She swallowed again as he moved closer, his massive body pressing her into the wall behind her. "Someone should be out in the cockpit," she babbled. "What if they find another way to trace us?"

"They won't," Milar said. He leaned forward. She felt the heat emanating off his naked chest, could feel his body move closer, could feel his breath against her skin.

Surrendering, Tatiana closed her eyes and waited for his lips to find her.

Something rustled on the shelf above her head.

Blinking, she opened her eyes and looked up.

Milar was pulling a locked wooden box from the overhead compartment. He latched the shelf again, then went to the bed, completely oblivious to the fact that her heart had just been hammering a million beats a second. He opened the box and spilled little wooden pieces onto the bed, whose pillows and covers were in a tumbled disarray against the far wall, due to Tatiana's maneuvers with the Bouncers.

"White or black?" he asked, quirking an eyebrow at her.

Her back still pressed to the wall, Tatiana's mouth fell open. "You . . . you . . . " She jabbed a finger at him. "I was . . . " *You were what, Tatiana? Waiting for him to have his way with you? Make you beg for mercy? Ravish you like a true pirate?* She flushed so hot her head felt like it was going to pop like a blood blister. Frantically directing her attention to the board beside his knee, she managed, " . . . I was thinking black."

"White it is." He started setting pieces onto the board, placing the white pieces opposite him.

Desperate not to look as mortified as she felt, she sat down beside him. She watched him place the pieces, taking extra time to get them aligned just right. As casually as she could, she said, "So you're gonna thank me by playing me a game of chess?"

"You're the only one awake, so it's either play with you or play alone." He paused in placing the pieces on the board. His golden-hazel eyes found her, and they were dancing with wicked amusement. He knew damn well what he'd just done. The *bastard!* "Why?" he asked. "You want me to thank you some other way?"

*Yes!* her mind screamed. She'd never found it so hard to breathe in her life. Yet, the way Milar was watching her, his big hand poised over the board, a smug grin plastered on his face, Tatiana couldn't let him win. "No," she said, feigning boredom. "Chess is fine." She gave him what she hoped was a disinterested look. "Why, did *you* have something else in mind?" She said it as if maybe he had wanted to watch a movie, instead.

Milar's blindsided blink would have thrown Tatiana off the bed in convulsive fits of laughter had she not been trying so hard to keep a straight face. Milar's brow twitched in a slight frown, and when she continued to focus her attention on the game, she felt his shock and dismay tumble against each other in his mind.

*Ha,* she thought, triumphant, *two can play at this game, collie.*

Almost reluctantly, Milar started placing pieces once more. Tatiana watched his callused hands, swallowing. Despite herself, she became mesmerized as she imagined what those hands could do, if only she would swallow her pride for two seconds . . .

"On second thought, I've been up all night." Tatiana forced herself to yawn and then innocently stretched out on the bed beside the board. "Don't play too long, and be sure to be quiet when you go out, okay? I'm a light sleeper."

Milar's face formed into a barely controlled thunderhead. "You're *tired?*"

Yawning again, she shrugged. "Saving collie ass takes a lot out of a girl."

For a long moment, he just watched her. She closed her eyes and listened to the minutes pass to the thundering of her heart. She let her breathing slow, her chest rising and falling in the rhythm of sleep.

She had actually started to feel sleepy when Milar growled, "You're faking."

Without opening her eyes, she allowed herself an evil grin and said, "How's it feel, collie?"

The words had no more than left her lips when she heard a roar and the chess board skittered off the bed to crash on the floor with the wooden tinkle of pieces scattering. Tatiana squealed and tried to roll away as she felt Milar's weight crush the blankets beside her. He caught her by the shoulder and dragged her back to the bed.

"Careful of the nodes!" she cried, instinctively panicking under the grip. It was why she hadn't gotten frisky with a non-operator in over six years—outsiders just didn't understand how sensitive they were. She squirmed, straining to see if his fingers were brushing one of her shoulder hookups under the jumpsuit. Then she realized Milar was only centimeters away, watching her.

Milar leaned forward, until she could feel the warmth of his cheek beside hers. Into her ear, he whispered, "I know where all the nodes are." Tatiana froze, the words making a tingling rush down her spine. Every molecule of her body was aware that he had closed the distance between them to mere centimeters, and that she was pinned to the bed, with nearly two meters of brawny muscle between her and the door. She'd never been this close to anyone of his size, and it left her acutely aware of why she had never been drafted for the Nephyrs. She met his eyes and forgot to breathe.

"You do?" she whispered.

Milar nipped her earlobe. "Oh yeah."

The words sent tingles of pleasure straight down to her belly. "Um . . . "

He stifled her next thought with a gentle teasing of his lips upon hers. He drew his fingers along her scalp and she felt his thumb gently brush the node in the base of her skull. Instead of quickly moving his fingers somewhere else, like everyone else she had ever bedded, he caressed it tenderly, sending waves of sensation up and down her spine as he kissed her.

In that one gesture, she was his. Never before had she felt so accepted as with that gentle touch at the base of her skull. Tatiana felt her body respond under him, felt her entire being aching for more.

After a few more breathless moments, Milar pulled back and touched his lips to her neck, just under the jaw. So softly she almost didn't hear him, he whispered, "You wanna do this now or later?" He nipped her other ear. She felt his husky breath against her neck as her heart slammed against her ribs.

He leaned back and met her eyes. "Because, frankly, coaler, I've been waiting for this a really, really long time, and I don't wanna screw it up." She saw such honesty there, such trust and longing . . . It melted her very core.

He continued to wait for her answer.

She was flushed, panting, and moving under his caresses like a schoolgirl. Tatiana was so stunned that she could only gape at him. *Is he stupid?* she thought. He was so beautiful, so perfect above her . . . Every nerve was calling for him to rip her clothes off.

When she didn't respond, his confidence visibly shattered. "Sorry, that was too fast." He started to pull away.

"That's *it*," Tatiana screamed, throwing him off of her. Milar fell with a stricken look. As he fell, she crawled into his lap and met his startled mouth with a kiss. "You," she said, nibbling his lip, " . . . are done teasing me."

Milar's eyes widened, but she was already pushing him further into the bed, spreading her body out atop his warm length, her hands tracing the dragons on his chest as her lips found his again. This time, Milar's big arm wrapped around her, pulling her close, and his fingers settled gently around the node in the base of her spine. Tatiana's whole body trembled with excitement as his fingers paused to caress it through the cloth. Then his other hand was moving up, finding the zipper to her jumpsuit.

*Oh yes,* Tatiana thought. She shivered as his big hands found the catch and tentatively tugged down. She sat up and shrugged her shoulders forward, allowing the material to slide from her shoulders until she could feel the cool air against her back.

Looking up at her, Milar's breath visibly caught.

Tatiana froze. *Here's where he realizes he's getting it on with a cyborg.* Dismay dragged painful claws through her gut and she looked away. Then, *Maybe he'll still do it anyway.* She found herself disgusted at her own desperation.

Milar startled her by reaching up to trace a finger between her breasts. When she looked, he seemed enraptured, taking her all in. His eyes meeting hers once more, he grinned a goofy, innocent grin.

*That is not the look of a guy who is having second thoughts.*

"You're beautiful," he whispered.

*Oh God,* Tatiana thought, dropping back into the kiss. She felt his warm fingers again find the node at the base of her spine and settle there, holding her to his naked chest. She let her own fingers roam his body, following the slight bumps of the scars, tracing the dragons as they wound over his shoulder and onto his back. The fingers of her right hand buried themselves in his hair as the fingers of her left impatiently slid the jumpsuit further down her back. Then she sat up and traced her fingers down his taut stomach. She let out a little gasp as his fingers tentatively found her breast. The rock-hard bulge in his pants was almost painful where it pressed against her thigh. Giggling, her hands found his belt and she began working the clasp loose.

Under her, Milar suddenly stiffened. She caught him staring at her like a dumbstruck starlope, his eyes wide, swallowing hard.

For a horrible moment, Tatiana thought she had pinched something in releasing the clasp, and he was trying not to let it show. She carefully tugged the belt away, cursing her clumsiness, hoping it didn't break the mood.

When he kept staring at her, stock-still, as she started unbuttoning his pants, however, she realized it wasn't pain that was going through his head.

In that moment, Patrick's episode came back to her in full force, and she flinched. *Aanaho, he's probably got some incurable collie disease.*

She thought about that for all of approximately two seconds, then continued unbuttoning him anyway. She was done waiting. She'd just hope whatever he had wasn't communicable.

And then, as her fingers reached down into his pants to push the flaps aside, she heard him gasp. It wasn't a gasp of pleasure . . . It was a gasp of surprise.

*. . . surprise?*

He was biting his lip, watching her hands, looking unsure.

Tatiana lifted her eyes back to his face, it suddenly dawning on her. "No way."

That jerked his attention back to her. "No way what?"

"You're a virgin, aren't you?"

Milar reddened like his face had been dipped in acid. "No."

"You *are!*" she cried, gleeful. She smacked him playfully on the chest. "After all that crap about girls telling you you're heavy . . . You're a *virgin.*"

He swore softly, averting his eyes as he turned his head to the side, his body trembling under her with what had to be fear and anticipation. "Is it that obvious?"

She gave him an evil grin and kissed his navel. "Yes," she said. Then, when his head came around and their eyes locked, she gave him an impish smile. "But that doesn't bother me a bit. I happen to like virgins."

His eyes widened. "You do?"

"Taste like chicken." She nibbled his stomach, then gently began to ease his pants down.

He raised a big hand to stroke her temple. "Coaler," he whispered, "I'm all yours."

Those four words settled in Tatiana's chest and set it afire. Before she could stop herself, Tatiana had crawled back over him and they were kissing again. Their bodies began to move in rhythm, melting into each other, responding to the other's pulse. His fingers found the heavy metal port over her heart and began slowly tracing the sensitive edge, making her gasp.

Immediately, Milar froze.

"It's okay," she whispered against his cheek.

Gingerly, he again started tracing the outer edges with his thumb. It was so intimate, something she had never let another human being do. It left her shivering above him, eyes closed as she felt his fingers move.

"Coaler," Milar whispered.

"Mmm?" She stroked the muscles of his shoulders, down his chest.

"Why am I the only one undressed?"

Then she squealed as Milar tossed her over onto her back and tugged the rest of her jumpsuit off. Then he was kissing her from above, gently lowering his weight, pinning her once more to the mattress. Tatiana moaned, pressing her body to his impatiently.

The intercom of the ship suddenly made them both jolt. *"Milar, if you're on the ship, you asshole, get up here and tell me what the hell happened."*

"*Shit!*" Milar cried, dodging for his pants like a teenager caught necking in his mother's basement. Tatiana had to laugh.

Milar, holding his clothes to his groin, blushed a deep scarlet. "He'll come looking for us," he blurted.

Still giggling, Tatiana gestured at the door. "I'll catch up with you later."

Milar threw on his pants and bolted from the room.

Taking a peek at the clock, Tatiana flopped back on the bed and stared at the ceiling. She took a deep breath, then let it out in a sigh. It had been the best thirty minutes of her life. She still felt the electricity pulsing where he had touched her, leaving tingles of warmth in its wake.

*Next time,* Tatiana thought, *I don't care if the ship's about to explode. He's finishing what he started.*

# Chapter 37

# Hijacked

THE MAN TAPPED THE BASE OF JOEL'S BRAIN STEM WITH THE cold barrel of his rifle. "What do you think you're doing?"

Prickling, Joel gestured at the ground through the viewfinder. "I'm putting you down with the others so I can go back for those kids." Scattered amongst the trees, he could see huddled groups of eggers he had dropped off from earlier runs, watching them hover.

"Bullshit," the man—Corey, he had called himself—said. He pressed the icy metal barrel against Joel's shorn scalp once more. "You're taking us to Silver City."

Joel tensed in his shoulder harness, thinking of Magali. "That's almost three hours from here."

"The smuggler can add," Corey laughed. "Good for you." The two rifle-bearing women who had taken up positions leaning against the wall of the cockpit behind him snickered.

"Listen," Joel said, thinking of Magali, "this is a fast ship. You have no idea how fast. I can get you to a nearby town, someplace like South

Fork or Thirtymile, in under ten minutes. When they go looking, the Nephyrs are gonna check places like Sand Hills and Bridgetown. I'll put you down an extra four hundred miles out from that. You'd be safe there."

"Yeah, to hell with that," Corey said. "South Fork and Thirtymile have three hundred people, tops. A couple dozen guys with guns show up . . . word'll spread. Silver City's on the other side of the planet, and big enough to get lost in. You're taking us there."

*Magali's not gonna survive that long,* Joel thought. "What about them?" he asked, gesturing to the eggers on the ground. "Nephyrs are gonna find them if we don't get them some help."

Corey laughed. "Good. It'll give the Nephyrs a distraction."

A distraction. Joel remembered saying similar things, in his youth. *He would make a great smuggler,* Joel thought, disgusted.

Joel stared at the console in front of him. Magali was still back there, and the Coalition was closing in. If he took them all the way to Silver City, none of the eggers of Yolk Factory 14 would be there when he got back. They would be back in the camp, to be lined up, condemned, and murdered as traitors to the Coalition.

"I'm the pilot," Joel said, "and I'm taking you to South Fork." He reached for the console.

The egger behind him grabbed him by his chin and hauled upward until Joel's neck felt like it was about to break. The man's rifle was suddenly pressed against his cheek. "We ain't givin' you that option, Runaway," the wan-faced egger said softly. "You take us where we wanna go or your brains are gonna start bubbling."

Joel focused on the cold metal barrel digging into his cheek, then he looked back up at the grinning man behind it. Softly, he said, "*Honor* is one of the fastest, most customized atmo-jumping ships ever brought this far into the Outer Bounds."

The man jammed the rifle deeper into his cheekbone. "So?"

"So," Joel said, "it's a standard 450-TAG fitted with enough boosters and frame support to hit Mach 5 in ten seconds. There's maybe three people on the whole planet who can fly it, and one of them is sitting in this chair. You kill me and you're gonna have a hell of a time going *anywhere,* much less out of Nephyr search range."

The idiot grinned at him. "Guess we'll see, won't we?"

Joel narrowed his eyes. "Guess we will."

The man released him. Gesturing with his rifle, he said, "Get us to Silver City without any more lip and maybe we won't sell this fancy scrap heap to the highest bidder when we get there."

Joel leaned forward in his restraints, pressed unnaturally toward the console by the gun that was once again jammed against his brain stem. When he didn't move, the egger behind him said, "Now, Runaway."

"Silver City, huh?" Joel said. Silver City was a good choice. The Coalition would never look there. It was where Joel would go, if he were looking to disappear.

Which he was, wasn't he? He'd done everything he said he would do. He'd spent hours ferrying eggers away from that place. He had to think about himself, now.

. . . Didn't he?

"You gonna get this thing movin' or I need to jump-start your brain?" The gun tapped him again. *Tap. Tap.*

"I'm thinking," Joel muttered.

"Ain't much to think about," the egger said. "You take us where we want to go and you get to live."

Joel looked at the controls and saw Magali's face, agonized and tear-stricken, huddled against the wall of a cave, her hands still shaking from using the gun that had saved his life. He saw her spill her life's story, confident he couldn't understand a word.

Then he saw the Nephyrs get her. Joel squeezed his eyes shut, forcing that image from his mind.

*Tap, tap, tap.*

The barrel of the gun brought him back to the present.

*You are a smuggler,* Joel thought. *A smuggler can't care about the sheep.*

Joel put both hands on the accelerator. *Honor* started picking up speed, and the eggers on the ground quickly passed out of visible range.

Then, *Magali isn't a sheep.*

And, right then, Joel knew he had to save her. He started gaining altitude, putting more distance between themselves and the abandoned eggers on the ground. He casually switched off the inertial dampeners.

"Now, ain't that better? Everybody wins." Behind him, the man had relaxed, lowering the gun from Joel's head. "See? We might even let you keep your—"

The man's words were cut off when Joel jammed the forward power as far forward as it would go. The ship's engines screamed joyously, and suddenly Joel was being slammed into the back of his chair with all the weight of a thousand-pound man. The eggers fell to the back, howling in surprise.

"Drop your weapons," Joel snapped over his shoulder. "Right now."

"Stop it!" Corey cried. "Now, smuggler!" Joel heard the sizzling crackle of an energy beam hitting the wall near the floor. Joel's heart skipped and a spike of adrenaline sizzled in painful arcs through his chest as he imagined what had been damaged.

"Drop it!" Joel screamed.

"Now!" the man screamed. The gun fired again. A bolt tore through along the floor beside Joel's foot. Joel flinched. He could think of at least twelve places in the cockpit where an energy beam, if triggered in the right spot, could kill them all. His hands tightened on the controls.

Joel hadn't wanted to do it this way, but the moron wasn't giving him a choice.

Before the man could fire off another shot, Joel threw the ship into a downward plunge, making his gut roil as his body started to float, then abruptly pulled an arc, hitting positive Gs, crushing the eggers back to the floor under their own weight, then started to spin. Behind him, he heard people scream as they tumbled against the walls like bingo balls inside a mixing basket.

*Sorry,* he thought, straining to stay conscious through the added weight of his body against the chair. He hadn't flown in three years, so he wasn't sure how much he could take anymore. For the average untrained, unaugmented pilot, it was seven to eight Gs. Joel was praying he could handle more than that.

Ideally, Joel would have put his passengers to sleep, but he wasn't sure he could withstand what they could not. Joel had the training, but his ships had always been advanced enough to compensate for at least some of the added pressure, giving him no real advantage over the eggers. Even twenty years ago, when he had been flying for the Coalition, his body had been cushioned in the most advanced inertial-dampening fields available.

Which meant he was in for a hell of a ride.

Joel cut his spin, then immediately pulled up and shot skyward, nose vertical, then threw the ship into a second, more violent spin. In the back, men were screaming, now. He winced, knowing they were breaking bones, knowing he didn't have time to do it gently if he wanted to help Magali and the other eggers.

*The first thing I need to do once I get Magali,* Joel thought, as he pulled them out of the upward climb at the dark, purplish edge of the stratosphere, flipped the ship in an arc, and dove straight down, superheated atmospheric plasma blotting out his view of the ground through his viewfinder. *Is get someone to take out my lifeline.*

Joel's ship had built-in signal scramblers, in case his merchandise ever got fitted with a government tracking device. That meant that as long as he stayed within twenty feet of his ship and his ship stayed powered, the Coalition wouldn't be able to pin his location to anything closer than a two-thousand-kilometer-wide radius.

Which, if what Magali had said was true and there were dead Nephyrs at the base of that cliff, was probably the only reason he wasn't a drooling vegetable.

Even in the ship, the moment he went back into range of the camp computer, he was taking a big risk. He had been out of the loop for three years . . . Who knew what kinds of new tracking technology the Coalition had developed in those years? And who knew whether or not Martin had kept his own technology up to date. So much in the smuggling world depended on up-to-date tech . . .

Joel dragged the ship through the nadir of its latest arc at about a quarter its normal atmospheric power, knowing that full power without inertial dampeners would kill them all. As it was, he was feeling dangerously light-headed, with all the blood of his body rushing to his brain. Much more pressure and one of those teeny blood vessels would develop an embolism—which Joel knew from experience was all too often the death of a good smuggler, much more common than the firing squad.

Then he was through the nadir and building upward speed, the Gs once again tugging the blood from his brain, leaving his vision narrow and his head light.

*Just hold on, Joey-baby,* he thought, clamping down his chest and abdomen as hard as it could go, emptying his lungs in a scream as he tried to keep the blood where it belonged. *Just hold on . . .*

He brought the ship out of the arc and leveled it out. Behind him, the ship echoed with every beat of his heart. He tentatively glanced over his shoulder.

The three eggers in the cockpit with him were lying in various bloody angles of disarray.

Joel brought the ship to the ground and got out of his harness. He was advancing on the eggers, reaching for the closest discarded weapon, when Corey opened his eyes.

There was a moment where their eyes met, then Joel realized Corey had the gun aimed at his chest.

"Fucking . . . smuggler."

The man pulled the trigger.

A sudden burning in the right side of his chest made Joel blink. A microsecond later, the burning went numb. Then the flesh around it began to heat and heat, until it was an unbearable searing agony and he could feel the sickening feeling of his own flesh bubbling in his chest. He looked down, saw the air escaping from his lung, hissing through the charred flesh between his ribs, felt the awful pressure in his rib cage as the fleshy bag collapsed.

On the floor, the egger was chuckling, picking himself off the floor. "Thought you got us didn't you, smuggler? Thought you—"

Joel kicked him in the nuts. Then he kicked him again and again, until he stayed down. He was gasping, now, his body struggling for air. The edges of his vision were waffling between red and black.

Picking up the egger's gun, he collapsed with his back propped up against the console, struggling just to stay conscious. He watched the eggers sleep, his mind drifting at the edge of the warm envelope of the void.

*Aanaho, Joel,* he thought. *What did you get yourself into?*

When the first eggers woke, Joel had to strain to produce enough air to talk and stay conscious at the same time. "Grab your friends," he said, making sure they saw his gun, "and get off my ship."

The eggers eyed him warily, like a housecat that had suddenly gone feral.

"*Now,*" Joel said.

They obeyed. Joel watched them, dragging men and guns off the deck, into the swamp beyond. Joel let them take the guns. He couldn't have found the breath to stop them, anyway. It was all he could do just to keep his eyes open.

*I need help,* Joel thought. *Aanaho, I need a doctor.*

But where could he go? The doctors who weren't under Geo's thumb were gonna be earning their paycheck from Coalition coffers.

Then he had a more disturbing thought: *I can't outfly Coalition like this.* His fingers, ears, even his bones were tingling. Every breath left a sucking sound in his chest, as blood began to fill the cavity. His mind, already feverish from the festering leg wound, began to drift in and out of consciousness.

*Shit,* Joel thought. *Shit, shit.*

Nanostrip wasn't going to be enough. Not for this. He needed a surgeon, and fast. One that wouldn't rat him out to Geo or hand him over to the Coalition.

As the last eggers were dragging the last of their friends off his deck, Joel climbed into the pilot's seat and locked the doors behind him. He latched himself into place, then leaned against the restraints, panting, feeling dizzy.

*Deaddrunk,* he thought. *Landborn's place.*

# CHAPTER 38

# Playing TAG

*P*ATRICK, ON THE LIBERTY, YOU COPY? BASE JUST CALLED ME. THEY *just had an unidentified ship land at the port,"* Tatiana heard the woman on the radio say. *"Something snazzy. Not responding to hails."*

Tatiana flipped open the com. "Pat and Miles are sleeping. Who are you and what's the problem?"

The radio was dead silent for a good minute and a half. Then, *"You're that cyborg bitch, ain't ya?"*

Tatiana frowned, recognizing the voice from somewhere. "Jeanne?"

*"I ever see you again, coaler, and I'm gonna add your teeth to my necklace."*

Tatiana remembered the ring of molars the woman had worn around her neck. She had thought it looked silly. "That's nice," she said. "But like I said, Pat and Miles are sleeping. You want to talk to them, you're gonna have to convince me it's important."

*"You let me talk to them, bitch, or I'm going to strip you down for parts. My composter could use an overhaul."*

"My coordinates are 39.04771 south, 68.99057 west. Bring it on." Tatiana flipped the com off and went back to her romance novel.

In her idle inspection of the ship earlier that morning, Tatiana had found the brick of brain-candy under the greasy footspace where someone had left it as an impact buffer between the radar unit and its oversized housing, and had been boredly skimming through the grime-stained pages ever since. The plot totally wasn't doing it for her. The man, a beefy deep-space captain who had rescued the feisty-yet-fragile maiden from a horrid life of entertaining pirates, was a dweeb. He kept writing poems and buying her roses at every port. *Roses?!?!*

Not only that, but Tatiana was already three-quarters of the way through the book and no sex scene. What the hell?

Bored, Tatiana began to skim. She found the sex and slowed. The setup was picture-perfect. Candlelight. Champagne. Oils. More poems. The damaged heroine tentatively opening up, allowing the diligent captain into her heart, finally professing her own undying love as they listened to classical music on the ship's audio system . . .

No sex.

She could not believe it. She stared at the final page for a full minute. After all that, she totally could not believe it.

Tatiana gave a disgusted scream, ripped the book in half, and hurled it across the room. "I wasted *two hours* on you!" she shouted. "Two hours! Damned piece of shit."

From the door, Milar chuckled. "That's why I was using it to cushion my radar unit."

"Find another," Tatiana growled. "I'm using that one to wipe my ass." Then she jerked. "You read *romance* novels?"

Milar froze with a hunted look. "No."

"And what the hell is up with your buddy over there?" Tatiana demanded, jerking her thumb at the com system. "She threatened to add my teeth to her necklace."

Milar frowned. "Jeanne called you?"

"Yeah, Jeanne. Her. She's a bitch."

"She's a *dangerous* bitch," Milar said, slipping past her to sit in the copilot seat. Reaching for the com, he said, "When did she call?"

Tatiana yawned. "I don't know. Half an hour ago? Twenty minutes?"

Milar had no sooner flipped the com open than a sleek, gleaming warship dropped into the weeds ahead of them. A moment later, the hatch opened and a woman stormed out, a gun in one fist.

"Oh shit," Milar said. He gave Tatiana a worried look. "You gave her our coordinates?"

"Yeah," she said. "Why, wasn't I supposed to?"

Milar winced and headed for the door. "Not yet," he said. "Every soul in Deaddrunk still wants to see you strung up by your nodes."

"That's impossible," Tatiana snorted.

Milar gave her a long look that told her it was, indeed, possible. She swallowed. "Oh."

"Just stay here while I go talk to her," Milar said. "She lost sixty thousand creds' worth of goods when the coalers swept the place after they picked you up outside Deaddrunk. I imagine she's still a little sore about it."

Tatiana swallowed hard. "Are you gonna bring your gun?"

"Jeanne won't shoot anybody," Milar said. Then, he looked at her and amended, "Well. She wouldn't shoot me or Pat." He gestured at the pilot's seat. "Just stay here. Wake Pat up for me, if you can. I may need some backup." Then he turned and left.

Instead of using the intercom to wake Patrick, Tatiana yawned and activated the audio/visual receptors on the personnel hatch immediately outside the ship. Then she snagged her half-eaten bowl of popcorn off the airspeed indicator and kicked her legs up over the engine monitor, leaning back in the captain's chair to watch the 2-D scene unfold. Milar was leaning against the open hatch, casually blocking the entrance to the ship with his big body. Jeanne was standing a pace down the boarding ramp, her face contorted in obvious fury.

"*. . . of my way, Miles. She's gonna get what's coming to her.*"

"*She got me out of Rath in the belly of her soldier,*" Milar said. "*I owe her a big one.*"

Grinning, Tatiana threw a handful of popcorn into her mouth and chewed. "That's right, collie," she told Milar through the console. "A few more hours in your room and we'll call it even."

"*She called the coalers in on us,*" Jeanne snarled. "*And now the whole goddamn town is being watched by Nephyrs.*"

"*Not her fault,*" Milar said. "*She was scared.*"

Tatiana's grin caught. Scared?

"*Scared?*" Jeanne demanded. "*You're letting her get away with it because she was* scared?"

"*It ain't her fault,*" Milar continued. "*Poor girl was in fight or flight. So she flew. Happens to the best of us.*"

Tatiana pulled her legs from the console and sat up. "Fight or flight?" she demanded of the console. "What kind of horseshit is that? I called them with your gun to my head." She scoffed. "Fight or flight. Pffft."

"*That cyborg runt almost got you killed, Miles. Or are you too goddamn infatuated you can't see the land mine you're stepping on?*"

"I'll show you a land mine, lady," Tatiana said, around more popcorn. "I'll stuff it in your ear, how about that?"

"*What do you want, Jeanne?*" Milar asked.

The woman narrowed her eyes. For a long moment, it looked like she would simply turn and walk away. Then, softly, Jeanne said, "*I know you ain't got the best com, so I'm guessing you ain't been getting the message. Runaway Joel just showed up in Deaddrunk. Shot through the chest. Unconscious. Drivin' that pretty black ship of his.*"

Milar eased himself off the edge of the door. *"The TAG?"*

*"Yeah,"* Jeanne said. *"And the Coalition's gonna get their hands on it, if we don't go in there and take it before the Nephyrs come sniffing down from the mountains."*

*"Shit,"* Milar said. *"Where's he been all this time?"*

*"No idea,"* Jeanne said, *"Though he's got a lifeline, from what they tell me. Didn't realize it until they pulled the fucker off his ship, though."*

Milar's eyes widened. *"The town's been tagged."*

*"Yeah, and after the stunt your little friend pulled, I'm thinking this time they're not gonna let us off with just a contraband sweep."*

*"It's gonna be another Cold Knife."* Milar cursed again.

Tatiana wiped grease off her fingers and flipped on her microphone. "Who's Runaway Joel? And what's a cold knife?"

Jeanne's head jerked toward the intercom, then her eyes narrowed at Milar. *"Can she fly a TAG? Because Joel sure as hell ain't going nowhere fast."*

Milar grimaced. *"No, I don't think—"*

"Fly a *TAG?*" Tatiana snorted. "Please. What, you *can't?*"

Jeanne looked directly into the camera with a cold, flat green stare, giving Tatiana goosebumps. Then she shoved past Milar and into the ship. Tatiana heard her footsteps thunder on the grating at a run.

Floundering, Tatiana dropped her popcorn bowl and scrambled to hit the button to seal the cockpit. After a polite beep, the doors hissed shut with a comforting metal click. Tatiana breathed a sigh of relief and dropped her face to the console. *That was too close.*

Someone kicked the swivel lock on the pilot's chair and spun her around. Tatiana screamed.

Jeanne leaned over her chair, her toothy necklace dangling in Tatiana's face as she put her cold emerald eyes only centimeters from Tatiana's. Swallowing, Tatiana shrank into the cushioning as far as she could go.

For a long moment, the woman's eerie green gaze only searched hers. Then she said, "Whose side are you on?"

Outside, Milar was pounding on the door and shouting. Tatiana was so terrified she didn't hear the words. All she could see was the promise of death in the woman's face.

"Yours," she whispered.

For the longest time, the pirate just watched her in silence.

"And you can fly a TAG?" Jeanne finally said.

Tatiana swallowed hard and nodded.

"How about a custom 450 with boosters and fully manual control?"

She nodded again, afraid to speak.

"That's not standard training for an operator." The woman's voice was utterly flat, emotionless. Deadly.

"I was bored," Tatiana squeaked.

The pirate continued to stare at her. Finally, she reached up and grabbed a chink between the molars of her necklace, holding the gruesome thing out so Tatiana could see it. "You know what this represents, girl?"

Tatiana swallowed at the empty hole. The teeth around it were big, nasty things, with black lines of plaque in the crevices. It was downright Stone Age. "You're getting in touch with your hunter-gatherer side?"

The pirate was utterly still, utterly calm. She said absolutely nothing, just stared, and Tatiana watched her own death tumble around in the woman's head. She cringed into the leather, suddenly wishing she had taken those Personal Confidence courses the base had offered in its continuing education programs.

Then, thinking about it, she realized that the better course would have been another Operator Behavioral Reconditioning Course, OBRC, lovingly referred to as the How Not To Be A Smartass course. Most operators had to take it at least once in their tours, since all of them got cocky at some point or another. Tatiana had taken it seven times already, and had been queued for her eighth when she was kidnapped.

. . . Or was it the ninth?

"This," the woman said, dropping the necklace back so it dangled between them, the empty chink clearly visible, "is the place I reserved for you the day you handed Milar to the Nephyrs. Got rid of a tooth from one of Geo's goons so I could fit you in."

*Oh shit.* Looking at the gap, Tatiana swallowed.

"You cross the line one more time, coaler," the pirate said, "you do *anything* to piss me off, and you're going right here." She tapped the gap in the necklace again. "Understand?"

Tatiana gave a weak grin and nodded. Rule One of the OBRC— Smile And Nod.

Behind them, the door opened and Milar rushed inside. "Hey, now," he said, when he saw the pirate leaning over her. He slowed and held out a wary hand. "Jeanne, just calm down."

"I'm taking the girl to Deaddrunk," Jeanne said, straightening until she towered over Tatiana. "She's gonna get that TAG the hell outta there before those Nephyrs get curious. Then she's gonna distract them while we evacuate the town."

"She can stay here with me," Milar said. "I'll take her."

"*Liberty's* a brick with wings," Jeanne said, grabbing Tatiana by the shirt. "I can get the girl there in half the time with *Belle*."

"It's Captain Tatiana Eyre," Tatiana said. "Not 'girl.'" Then she winced. Rule Two of the OBRC—Keep Your Mouth Shut Unless You're Eating.

"I'm taking the girl with me," Jeanne said. "You got a problem with that, Miles, you can take it up with my gun." She hauled Tatiana out of the chair by her jumpsuit.

Seeing Milar wasn't going to take it up with her gun, Tatiana swallowed, hard. "Maybe I can't fly a TAG, after all. My memory's a bit fuzzy." In fact, now that she thought about it, she couldn't decide if she had been trained on a TAG or a GAT. What the hell *was* a TAG, anyway? She kept thinking something yellow with foilers, but she was pretty sure that was just the MMORPG she had played in her barracks room.

Without looking at Tatiana, Jeanne grabbed her necklace by the missing tooth and showed it to Tatiana. To Milar, she said, "She's coming with me. Wake up your brother and fly this thing back to Deaddrunk. We're gonna need every ship for the evacuation." As if the matter was settled, the pirate dropped the necklace back to her chest. "Let's go, coaler." She turned and strode from the room, leaving Milar and Tatiana looking at each other.

"I think she wants to kill me," Tatiana whispered.

Milar looked slightly pale. "You should do what she says."

They glanced at the door together.

"*Now*, coaler!" Jeanne snapped, from the steps to the lower deck. "Every second we waste, that's a second we won't have to get you situated on that TAG before the Nephyrs decide to get curious."

"What's a TAG?" Tatiana whispered to Milar.

Milar's eyes widened and he paled further.

"Don't make me come back there and get you, runt!" Jeanne shouted.

"Your teeth are dirty," Tatiana shouted back. To Milar, she said, "What's it look like? Big, little?"

"Just go," Milar said, wincing, "Before she *does* kill you."

"I don't *want* to go," Tatiana snapped. "What's a TAG? Is it yellow?"

Milar just looked at her as if she were some strange space barnacle that had affixed itself to his ship.

"With foilers?" she suggested.

"Look, squid," Milar said, his face clearing, "stop screwing around. This is the real thing. Cold Knife is the name of a town the Nephyrs slaughtered looking for you, after we blew up your soldier. Runaway was running from something. They hunt him back to Deaddrunk and they'll murder everyone there."

"Then come with me," Tatiana said. "I don't like her."

"I'm sure the feeling is mutual, sweetie," Milar said. "But of Pat and I, I'm the one best equipped to fly this baby out of a firefight."

"No," Tatiana said, "*I'm* the best one to fly this out of a firefight. What the hell does a TAG have to do with anything?"

"You wanted a ship with guns," Milar reminded her. "A TAG's got guns."

"But it's not even your *ship!*" Tatiana cried. "You want me to steal a *ship?*"

"It's not stealing it if the owner can't use it no more," Milar said.

"Then that Runaway Joel guy is dead?" Tatiana demanded.

Milar's face darkened. "No, but he will be. We'll be leaving his ass in Deaddrunk for the coalers."

Tatiana frowned. "That's not nice."

Milar gave her a flat look. "It's what he deserves."

◀◀ ◆ ▶▶

Tatiana sat in a passenger seat—not the copilot seat, despite her protestations—and picked at her nails as the pirate flew them back to the town of the crazy egger.

"So," Tatiana said, "how's my little egghead friend?"

Jeanne ignored her. In fact, for the last twenty minutes, the pirate hadn't said anything to her other than, "Get back in the seat or I'll start cutting off fingers."

"This Runaway Joel a friend of yours?" Tatiana asked.

"Was," Jeanne said. "Not anymore."

"Oh yeah?" Tatiana probed, curious how a frigid icicle like Jeanne could have a friend. "What broke you up?"

"Differences," Jeanne said.

"Like what? He stole your toothpaste?" Then she slapped her forehead. "No, it was the *fingers,* wasn't it?"

She actually saw a muscle in the woman's jaw twitch. "He betrayed a friend of mine."

"So?"

Jeanne looked over her shoulder. "So, that friend is dead now, and I've got three more teeth on my necklace."

"Oh yeah?" Tatiana asked, looking at the string of molars. "What happened to the owners?"

"I hunted them down, scalped them, took their scalps back to the thugs' employer, dropped them on the desk in front of the fat fuck, and then blew the shit out of his living room on the way out."

Tatiana peered at the woman, trying to determine whether or not she was lying. Like any good fashion model, she had *curves.* Finally, she said, "You're like, what, one-eighty? One eighty-two? Seventy-three, seventy-four kilos?"

Jeanne gave her a blank frown.

Tatiana realized that the backward colonist knucker probably didn't have the first clue about what a kilo or a meter was. She cursed the barbaric nature of the colonies and started doing the mental math. "So, like, five-eleven? A hundred sixty pounds? Hundred *seventy?*"

Jeanne said nothing.

"How does someone like you scalp someone?"

Jeanne's green eyes found her again. "How does someone like you look in the mirror without wanting to blow your metal brains out?"

Tatiana flushed and fell into a brooding silence. Rule Eight of the OBRC—Sticks And Stones Can Break Your Bones, But Commanding Officers Can Ground You. Unfortunately, Tatiana had always failed this part of the brain scan. Under her breath, Tatiana muttered, "You forget to chew your mastodon this morning? 'Cause you're acting awfully backed up."

"What was that?"

"Nothing. I'm sure flint chips take excellent scalps."

Jeanne gave her a long look of utter bafflement, then returned to the controls.

"Neanderthal," Tatiana muttered.

"I heard that," Jeanne said.

"Must be those keen hunter senses," Tatiana said.

Jeanne looked over her shoulder . . .

. . . and grinned. Tatiana's mouth dropped open.

"You know," Jeanne said, returning her gaze to the viewfinder, "I was rooting for you."

"What?"

"Back when you took *Liberty* and left us all staring at your exhaust vortexes. I was hopin' you'd talk your way out of Milar gutting you. Half the prophecies say he gutted you." She gave Tatiana another measuring look. "Wideman gave us more prophecies on you than everyone else combined. Why is that?"

"Uh," Tatiana said, flushing. "He's got a thing for cyborgs?"

"You gonna be the Face of the Revolution, there, girl?"

"Wasn't particularly planning on it," Tatiana said.

Jeanne held her gaze a moment, then returned to the viewfinder. "We're coming up on Deaddrunk. I'm gonna drop you beside the TAG and see if I can find those Nephyrs. As soon as you get airborne, I'm gonna need you to slow down the coalers while everyone evacuates. If they've at all got their shit together, they're gonna be coming from Yolk Factory 9, about a hundred and forty miles southwest of Deaddrunk. It's got its own Pods assigned to it."

"How many?" Tatiana asked, suddenly distracted by the crystal butterfly hanging from above the ship's viewfinder. It seemed oddly out of place, like the Abominable Snowman had suddenly decided to wear a gigantic yellow smiley face hat while it ripped the heads off of high-altitude enthusiasts.

"You hear me?" Jeanne demanded.

Tatiana jerked her eyes away from the butterfly. "Eh?"

"However many show up, take care of them," Jeanne said. "You can do that, right? If you can't, and you need help, let me know. We can't afford to have any of those bastards get through to Deaddrunk."

Tatiana peered at Jeanne, her mind's eye unable to rid herself of the crystal butterfly. "Deaddrunk?" A butterfly just seemed so unbelievable. Maybe Jeanne had a girly little lover who happened to like crystals. Yeah, that was it. She was a lesbian. Made total sense, now that she thought about it.

Vaguely, Tatiana heard the ship slow, felt the metallic thud of the landing gear fall into place.

She looked at Jeanne. *Could* she be a lesbian? Butch was in, sure, but would any woman really want to share bed space with *Homo erectus? All she's missing is the spear,* Tatiana thought, her eyes once again falling on the ridiculous necklace. Now that she was looking, she was pretty sure a few of them were *bloody.* Ew.

A moment later, the ship was sitting on the tarmac, and Tatiana realized she had just spaced the last half of Jeanne's instructions.

Jeanne apparently realized this, too, because her fists whitened on the stick. "Girl," she said.

"Captain Tatiana Eyre," Tatiana said.

"Girl," Jeanne said again. "You—"

"Captain," Tatiana said.

"—get in—"

"Tatiana."

"—that ship—"

"Eyre."

"—fire it up—"

"To you."

"—and blow up—"

"Collie."

"—anything that moves." Jeanne twisted around in the captain's chair. Her face was a thunderhead, daring Tatiana to interrupt her again. Silence fell between them, pounding and tense.

"Except you," Tatiana said.

The pirate narrowed her eyes. "Obviously."

"One condition," Tatiana said.

"What, girl?" she asked in a frustrated growl.

Tatiana jerked her thumb at the butterfly. "Whose crystal is that?"

Jeanne's green eyes never left her face. "Mine."

"It's pretty."

"I took it off a dead woman," Jeanne said. "After I carved out her double-agent tongue." Still deadly calm, the pirate said, "When I'm bored, I like to look at it and remind myself what it was like to hear her scream."

Tatiana scrunched up her nose. "You're worse than Milar."

"You have no idea," Jeanne said softly. "Are you going to get off my ship now?"

Tatiana grimaced and glanced out the viewfinder at the ship she was supposed to fly. Unfortunately, it didn't look all that familiar. She only had the vaguest tingling of memory, but she wasn't about to tell Jeanne that, not when she'd been threatening her with a necklace. "Yeah, sure." She stood up and moved toward the exit.

"And girl?"

Tatiana grimaced and glanced over her shoulder.

"Fuck it up . . . " Jeanne touched the notch in the necklace again. " . . . And you'll be right here."

Tatiana realized that this was an ideal time to utilize the Nine Rules of the OBRC. She took a deep breath, hesitated, then said, "Is that before or after you read your mammoth entrails to determine which day is most portentous to bathe this month?"

"After," Jeanne said. Then she smiled.

It was the single scariest thing Tatiana had ever experienced in her life. She ducked out of the cockpit and *ran* for the exit.

She was panting in the pilot's seat of the TAG, powering it up, before she realized that she had, indeed, seen the inside of this ship before.

Not *a* TAG. *This* TAG.

Remembering *where*, Tatiana suddenly didn't feel very good.

*"Girl, you gonna take off or what?"* Jeanne demanded over the com.

Tatiana stared at the windshield, remembering watching the ground rush up to meet her through it. Slowly, she got out of her chair. Every hair on her body was standing on end, and her pulse was zinging through her fingers, making them tingle.

*"Girl, what the hell are you doing?"* Jeanne snapped. *"Those Nephyrs are gonna be here any minute."*

"Stop calling me girl!" Tatiana shrieked, trying to think. The last time she had seen this console, it had been melting under intense heat. Along with it, her skin had crackled open like a suckling pig. "This is a bad idea," she finally said. "I'm coming back to your ship."

*"What are you talking about?"* Jeanne demanded. *"No you're not."*

"I'm getting off this ship," Tatiana said. "I'm not flying this thing."

*"You can't be serious."* It was Milar, this time. *"Squid, we need you to fly that thing."*

"I'm serious," Tatiana said, remembering her own blood spilling across the ship's aluminum floor. She remembered ruby puddles expanding around her as the fires spread, working their way toward her lifeless fingers and face. She watched her eyes close, watched herself die. The déjà vu was so thick that she could almost feel her own ghost tracing its icy fingers down her neck. "Serious as a goddamn heart attack."

For the longest time, Jeanne said nothing. Then, softly, *"The next time I see you, you're dead."*

"Yeah, whatever!" Tatiana screamed into the microphone. "You want to fly it, you get in here and do it. Count me *out.*" Then she slammed the switch down and unlocked the outer hatch, leaving the ship still running.

She was halfway down the ramp when she saw the Nephyr.

He was walking across the tarmac, a gun slung across his chest, a curious look on his face as he examined the ship.

As soon as their eyes met, they both froze.

*Oh shit,* Tatiana thought. Several more seconds passed, her heart thundering in her chest. A little frown built on the Nephyr's glittering face and he took a step toward her. Tatiana spun, ran up the ramp, and slapped the door lock. Then she ran to the cockpit and sat down in the chair.

She almost powered it up. Almost.

*It's gonna be this ship,* she thought, looking at the familiar console, the same outrageously huge leather chair. *This is the one that kills me.*

She heard the Nephyr hit the ship's outer lock, hard. It wasn't enough to get him inside—brute strength would never be enough to crack this particular nut—but the muffled thud made Tatiana jump.

*I'm trapped in my own coffin,* she thought, verging on hysteria.

Outside, she heard the whipping roar of Bouncers as they slowed overhead. Along with them came the sonic booms of soldiers, then the sound of the ground thundering as they dropped beside her on the tarmac. While the Nephyr couldn't force his way in, they could, and gladly.

*"Calling all colonist ships within a seventy-five kilometer radius of the civilian town of Deaddrunk. This is the Coalition Air Force. Power down your engines and exit your ships or you will be fired upon."*

Tatiana closed her eyes, remembering the fires, the horrible pain, her own charred flesh. Above her, she heard a ship blown apart. She heard the percussive sounds of the soldiers firing back. Reluctantly, she put her hands to the joystick that she had watched break her ribs.

She took a deep breath, hesitating there. *No guts, no glory.*

Then she jerked back on the nose and rammed forward the accelerator, praying she could make it over the treeline before the Bouncers realized she wasn't going to hold still. She expected a normal, gentle, computer-regulated liftoff. Instead, she shot off the tarmac at a thirty-degree angle, creating a sonic boom before she was over the treeline, sending a hurricane of broken asphalt into the group of Nephyrs and soldiers gathered on landing pad behind her.

Despite herself, Tatiana had to grin in reluctant admiration. *Nice ship.*

She spun it in an arc, hitting twenty thousand feet in seconds, barely feeling a single G as the ship's inertial dampeners kicked into gear.

*Really* nice.

She leveled out and hit the power, outdistancing the Bouncers that followed her as if they were standing still.

*I could get used to this,* she thought, spinning and going high, then backtracking and dropping down on them from above. She put holes in their engines before they'd even completed a half turn.

*Really* used to it.

Tatiana screamed her delight as she weaved between the fiery debris of the Bouncer ships, clipping the trees with no more than a meter to spare. "This is *great!*" she shrieked. She'd never been in anything so intense. It had engines built for a ship three times the size, and was utterly responsive to her every twitch.

Experimenting, Tatiana weaved over the treeline, following the contours of the ground, unhindered by the ship computer's normal calculations and trajectory corrections. The ship moved with the grace of a soldier, yet without the sensory deprivation. She saw the land rushing under the windshield, could almost feel the wind whipping across its hull.

*It's so much better than a soldier,* she thought, spinning out over the other Bouncers, taunting them. She was so thrilled it was a pressure rising up in her chest, expanding until she was laughing uncontrollably.

"Like flying a magic carpet," she giggled. She brought down four more Bouncers, dancing around them and filling them with holes as easily as if the four larger ships had been sitting still. She flipped on her microphone and said, "Milar, this thing is *awesome!*"

Instead of responding, Jeanne said, "Aanaho, Miles, we can't find Wideman. He wasn't on any of the ships!"

"Then where is he?" Milar cried. "Tell me where he is, Jeanne!"

"You think I'm fucking God?"

"I'm going in after him!"

"With *that* ship?!" Jeanne cried. "That'll get you *killed*, Miles!"

Milar did not respond.

Tatiana frowned, imagining the *Liberty* taking on a Pod of soldiers. It would not be pretty. "Miles," she told the microphone, "Stay where you are. Let me clear a path first."

Milar ignored her.

Tatiana moved her attention to the three operators that were only now leaping off the tarmac in pursuit. The remaining six were moving into the town.

She winced at the idea of the soldiers reaching the town, but gave priority to the three coming at her head-on. Out of anything in the

Coalition fleet, soldiers had the best weaponry, and one mistake would leave her a bleeding corpse in the midst of a fiery wreck.

That was a sobering thought.

*Can't let them get a bead on me,* she thought, flipping low and wide, then twisting to do a hard ninety-degree climb. The ship responded perfectly. She could almost sense its frustration, its willingness to do more.

*Good ship,* she thought again. "Milar, you're not doing anything stupid, are you?" She twisted around, found the operators beginning to take the turn upwards after her—unlike the Bouncers, they were capable of the more excruciating Gs—and quickly hurtled past them with enough sonic force to make her teeth chatter. As they were trying to work their way back, she put on speed, arced back up, and came up above and behind them, right on their tails. She turned all three into little balls of flame before they realized they were no longer following her.

Tatiana whispered an apology as they went down in pieces. It had been her deepest fear as an operator—going down with her ship. The Coalition Air Force did everything in its power to preserve the high-tech hardware of a coalition operator. That meant the entire pilot's chamber was essentially an indestructible black box.

And, if the rest of the ship was destroyed, that meant it was an indestructible black box without power. Thus, for most of her career, Tatiana had been plagued with nightmares of being trapped in her safe little bubble of goo as the machinery died around her.

From the few other operators who would talk about it, it was a common sentiment.

Realizing Milar hadn't responded, Tatiana frowned and scanned her viewfinder for *Liberty.*

Nothing but Bouncers, the smaller dots of operators, and the erratic blip of Jeanne's ultra-fast *Belle.*

"Milar?" she asked, her voice catching. "You there?"

No response. As she passed overhead, Tatiana's eyes fell on the wreckage in the jungle, the ship that had exploded above her as she sat on the tarmac. A sick welling of dread began to form in her chest. "Jeanne, what happened to Milar?"

Jeanne didn't respond.

The operators were wrecking the town, obliterating everything. Right behind them, the Nephyrs were combing through the wreckage, dragging survivors out of the rubble and lining them up on their knees, hands behind their heads.

"Jeanne!" Tatiana snapped, flying low and firing on the closest operators before pulling out of their weapons' range. She felt the five remaining launch behind her. Just skimming the treeline, Tatiana spun a wide arc and caught the operators from behind. She blindsided one with a rapid pulse, then curved low and wide as the remaining four went after her. They were faster and more agile than the Bouncers, so she had to struggle to stay behind them. Not wanting to make them nervous, she didn't bother with trying to make a lock. She just held back and waited until three of the four were clustered together in a tight curve before peppering them with energy rounds.

The fourth operator was harder, obviously more experienced. Even with his smaller engines, he was doing a good job of staying out of her sights.

*Hold still, you slippery bastard.*

The operator refused to let her get a lock. He kept going straight, darting in and out of the trees, keeping low enough that even Tatiana was having trouble keeping him in view. After several frustrated attempts, all she succeeded in doing was setting vast swaths of the forest afire. The operator, meanwhile, was setting a direct course for Rath.

*He's leading me away,* she realized suddenly. Her blood went cold. She immediately spun up, turned, and raced back to the town with every ounce of speed her engines could muster.

*Oh my God,* she thought, staring at the destruction. *Oh my God.*

A single Nephyr remained in the village. He was walking down the line of prisoners, a gun in his hand. She saw the Nephyr come up behind a woman, put a gun to her head. Through the magnified image of the viewfinder, Tatiana vaguely recognized her as one of the faces that had worked on her node and collarbone when she had drifted in and out of consciousness after her crash. A doctor.

She saw the doctor jerk and flop forward into the dirt. The Nephyr moved down the line. Put his gun to another head.

*No,* Tatiana thought.

A second colonist collapsed. A man.

*No!* Tatiana passed overhead. She couldn't shoot at him. Not unless she wanted to risk hitting the colonists if the shots bounced off the energy field of his skin.

But she had to stop him. She had to.

The Nephyr, pausing only long enough to recognize the sonic boom of her passing, moved on to the next person.

Tatiana swept over and back, then dropped for another swoop at the town. Tatiana twisted her ship at an angle and flew through the center of town, preceding her own sound waves by three times their speed as her left wing all but scraped the village's central road.

She hit the Nephyr dead-on with her wingtip, ripping him off the ground. Immediately, she dragged her nose up and put on speed. She could feel the drag his body created against the wing as she soared into the atmosphere and compensated with more power, praying the ship had enough structural integrity to hold together.

"You the cleanly sort?" she growled, flipping on her wing cam. "Because you're about to learn how to vacuum." She broke through the stratosphere, then passed the mesosphere, picking up speed. She was halfway through the thermosphere when the Nephyr caught fire and broke apart.

*Damn,* she thought. Her eyes were filling with tears, but she wiped them away. She dropped the ship back to the tattered tarmac and sat there, listening.

The skies were empty. The Coalition was dead or gone. Gingerly, Tatiana flipped open her com. "Milar?"

Silence.

She remembered the obliterated ship, smoking in the forest. Had it been *Liberty?* A growing dread was screaming at her that it had been.

Then, a gruff, *"Get back in the sky, girl. More might be on the way."*

Sucking in a breath, Tatiana flipped on the microphone. Thinking of the pieces of devastated wreckage she had seen in the jungle, she said, "Jeanne, what happened to Milar?"

There was a long pause. Then, reluctantly, *"He went down."*

*Oh no.*

Unable to stop herself, Tatiana powered down the ship and ran out the back. Behind her, she heard Jeanne shout, *"What the hell are you doing?! Get back in the air, girl!"* Then Tatiana had opened the hatch and jogged into the sunlight, all of her senses on alert, adrenaline kicking fiery arcs through her chest. In the town below the landing strip, she heard the shrieking scream of a raid siren. She ran for the woods, her nose scrunching at the smell of burning metal and polymers.

*It wasn't* Liberty, Tatiana told herself. *It wasn't Milar. Please God let it not be Milar.* She reached the edge of the tarmac aiming for the crash site she could see billowing smoke in the forest beyond. She pushed her way through the alien brush, desperate to know, now. Five minutes of grunting and panting later, she found it.

Coughing at the smoke, she stopped on the ridge carved by the nose of the ship and stared down at the wreckage, trying to compare it to the colonial utility that the twins had been flying.

Nose, engines, and size were all wrong.

It was a Bouncer ship. She felt her relief as a living thing, rushing through her core.

Tatiana spun and jogged back toward her own ship. She'd have a better chance of spotting him from the air.

When she reached the edge of the forest, she came to a stumbling halt.

The TAG was gone.

An instant later, she felt something cold and hard touch the middle of her spine.

From over her left shoulder, she heard, "You move, traitor, and I won't wait for after your trial to start ripping off skin."

# CHAPTER 39

## The Last Fifty Feet

THE LAST FIFTY FEET WERE THE WORST.

Magali had spent her first night huddled in a hollow, hugging her knees as the wind blew hot air through the Snake. Even with the scattered rests she had taken on the way down, Magali's arms ached and trembled. It was all her blistered fingers could do just to stay in the shape of hooks. Her legs were slowly giving way under her.

Her bloody toes slipped on the stone, taking off more skin, leaving her once more dangling by her hands.

Magali looked down tiredly. In a tired pang of desperation, she considered letting go.

*It's just fifty feet,* she thought. *I can drop fifty feet.*

Then a darker part of her said, *You can't kill anyone with a broken leg, Magali.*

Somehow, she dragged her feet back to the rock and slowly lowered herself another foot. She hadn't found a place to rest since the sun had hit the top of its arc. It was almost nightfall, now. Two days of climbing. The night in the hollow had sapped her body's warmth and left a runny nose and a fever in its place. Her limbs were almost unresponsive, now. She would often find herself clinging to the rock, daydreaming, with no idea how long she had been in the same position. During those daydreams, Wideman would appear clinging to the rock nearby and talk to her.

Was it a daydream, or something worse?

Then she thought, *How could it be a daydream? I* hate *Wideman.* People daydreamed about stuff they loved. They fantasized about brawny men under secluded waterfalls, not some creepy old dude with greasy white hair and bug-eyes.

Her exhausted, feverish brain was doing circles in the sky above her, feeling completely detached from the limbs that struggled against the cliff face.

Forty feet.

*I'm not gonna make it.* She felt her sweaty fingers loosening, despite her every attempt to control them. She was so warm . . . Her eyes kept wanting to shut.

"You've gotta kill them, Mag." Wideman was back, hugging the rock a foot from her face, his eyes fixed on her with his creepy, psychotic stare. "You've gotta kill them all for what they did."

Magali squeezed her eyes shut and slammed her forehead into the reddish stone to get rid of the image. When she looked back, Wideman was gone.

Gingerly, she lowered herself another foot. Her hand slid down the crevice she had put it into, skinning the already-too-sensitive flesh of her fingerpads. Some part of her was recognizing that she was going to fall, but it felt like she was watching her thoughts from a distance.

She closed her eyes, feeling the trembling in every muscle, unable to get them to work. It seemed so ironic. After a four-thousand-foot descent, she was going to fall to her death at the last forty feet. She already felt her fingers losing their hold on the rock face.

"Magali." This time, Wideman's schizophrenic eyes were half an inch from her own. "Remember Benny? Remember what they did to Benny, Magali?"

Magali squeezed her eyes shut and hit the side of her skull against the cliff.

When she looked again, she was startled to realize Wideman was exactly where she'd left him, his skinny form clinging to the rock, vegetable particles stuck to his fingers and hair. Trembling, she whispered, "I hate you."

Wideman grinned, his psychotic eyes unmoving. "I know."

And then he was gone.

"I hate you," Magali said again, louder this time. She dropped her forehead to the stone. "I hate you so much. You ruined my *life*!" Everything, from her first moments in Deaddrunk, to her sister's intervention with Patrick, to pulling the trigger on Martin, all of it was due to Wideman. Her whole life had revolved around him and his stupid little vegetables.

"I hate you," she said again. Her limbs were shaking with anger, now. "You're just a stupid, crazy old man."

She heard Wideman laughing at her.

Magali tightened her fingers against the rock and wept. For thirty years, he had commanded every part of her life. The entire village of Deaddrunk had formed every daily activity around him, dancing to his every whim, writing down even his most incomprehensible gibberish. Even now, even after she had thought she had finally gotten free of Deaddrunk, even after she had traded her freedom for the life of a doomed egger, he was still there, still directing her life, still nudging her the way he wanted her to go, still controlling her future.

Yet Magali recognized the irony. After years of avoiding guns, avoiding Milar's rebellion, avoiding anything that could possibly make her deserve Wideman's hated title of 'Killer,' now she *wanted* to kill those men. She wanted to do it more than she wanted to breathe. It wasn't just some passing feeling, something that she could put out of her mind. It was a driving, ever-present passion to see them die.

Even as she thought about putting them in her sights and pulling the trigger, she felt no regret. She wanted to see the bullets enter their brains, wanted to see the startled little look on their glittering faces before they fell, the thrashing of their confused bodies afterwards. She wanted to see them die.

She forced her blistered fingers into another crevice. She lowered herself another foot, powered by the thought of finding Colonel Steele in her crosshairs. The others, she just wanted to kill. Steele, she wanted to hurt.

Her toes found a tiny lip and she lowered herself a few more feet down the wall of rock.

She would kill him last.

The other Nephyrs would die, but she would save Steele for last. She would hunt him like the animal that he was.

She was standing on the crunchy stone dirt at the bottom of the Snake for several minutes before she recognized the fact. Magali blinked, then reluctantly let go of the stone in front of her. She fell back onto her heels, the first time she'd used them all day. The crumbly red-orange dirt dug into the soles of her feet, sticking to the blood and weeping blisters of her toes. She stared down at it, uncomprehending.

*I made it.*

She wondered if she was hallucinating again. Magali looked up.

The top of the cliff seemed to swim above her, swirling with the deep blue sky, blotting out the sun. Magali quickly returned her attention to her feet, fighting vertigo. Having had nothing to eat for almost four days, it was all she could do to keep standing. All she'd had to drink was a few handfuls of the brackish water dribbling from a crack in the stone that afternoon. She glanced at the Snake, wondered if she could stomach its venom.

Magali stood there, unable to make her feet move, feeling light-headed. She listened to the rush of liquid in the channel behind her, the watercourse that had carved its long, ribbony path across the globe. The highly acidic water had a greenish hue, its surface almost placid as it continued to eat its way through the face of Fortune.

*I made it,* she thought again, this time registering shock. She looked up again, startled. When she had first put her foot over the edge, she had hoped, but she had never once thought she'd actually make it. It all seemed dreamlike, now, something that had happened to somebody else.

*Did I really do that?* Even with her throbbing toes, her scabbed and bleeding fingers, she had trouble believing.

A humming in the distance brought her attention back to the task at hand. Somewhere down the Snake, she heard the increasing roar of an engine echoing against the canyon walls, approaching fast. Magali stumbled backwards automatically, pressing her shoulder blades into the cliff. *No,* she panicked. *Oh no.*

The *gun.*

It had to be near Benny. But where was Benny? In her grueling climb, she had sought handholds and footholds wherever she could find them, paying little attention to her position in relation to the ground. In fact, she had tried her best to *avoid* looking down. Now Magali found herself in strange surroundings, with no points of reference to match up where she was with where she had been. Had she gone north or south in her climb, and how far?

The approaching ship spurring her into motion, she hurriedly moved from the wall and started searching the rocky red earth, climbing boulders to get a better view. She found Ben a few dozen yards away, his tiny body twisted, limbs askew, his head facing the ground. Saying a mental prayer for him, Magali began searching for the gun. She looked into crevices and frantically pushed aside Fortune pin-scrub, barely feeling the biting sting the leaves left on her skin. Nothing.

*What if they took it?* she suddenly thought, freezing in place. What if, after Steele had dropped it, the Nephyrs had retrieved the gun when they had gone down to grab his companions? What if it bounced against the canyon wall and fell into the Snake? What if the canyon's gusting wind had blown it a hundred feet off course?

The engine was getting closer, coming from the direction of the Yolk camp.

*No!* a part of her screamed. She would *not* be caught helpless again. Never again. It came in a powerful inner surge, one that left her limbs tingling with the strength of her rage.

Almost as if her own stubborn will had conjured it, she saw a flash amidst the boulders to the north. She jogged up the Snake, eyes pinned to the spot, terrified she would lose track of it.

She found the gun lodged between two boulders, intact. Seeing it, beaten but not broken, Magali let out a sob of relief.

The engine was almost upon her when she ran back to Ben's body and sprawled out between the boulders beside it, her hand and the gun hidden under a pin-scrub bush. Moments later, the ship rounded the last bend in the river and the engines were an overpowering roar bearing down on her. Magali heard the vessel slow directly overhead and clenched the gun tighter. *Stay still,* she told herself. *Don't move. They'll pass.*

But they didn't pass. She heard the metal clang and the whirring grind as the landing gear extended, then the shift in tone as the engines prepared for landing. Magali lay still, though her heart was hammering, now. It was all she could do not to sit up to make sure one of the metal legs wasn't about to crush her.

Magali heard the metal pads crunch in the stony pebbles a dozen feet away, then the whine as a ship door opened and a ramp extended. *Just stay calm,* she thought. *They probably just want to make sure you're dead. Just wait it out, Mag. Don't shoot unless you have to. You can't kill them all. Not yet.* Still, her fingers were numb from gripping the gun too tightly.

She heard light cyborg footsteps travel down the ramp, so quiet they were almost imperceptible. Then the crunch of gravel as they approached, slow and wary.

They stopped a few feet off. Magali imagined the Nephyr dragging a gun from his cargo belt and shooting her between the eyes. Her heart rate began to increase its tempo the longer the newcomer stood there, watching her. Was it Colonel Steele? Would he want to take her body in to be identified and condemned?

Magali concentrated on her breathing. She focused on keeping her chest movements as shallow as possible, despite the way her blood was thrumming through her veins. A Nephyr could read her heartbeat.

If it was a Nephyr there, he would know she was still alive.

# CHAPTER 40

## The Head Doctor

**W**ALK FASTER, TRAITOR, OR I'LL START PLUCKING HARDWARE right now and save the doctors the time."

"Yeah, whatever, loser," Tatiana muttered, but she stepped up the pace, anyway. She was wearing cuffs and ankle shackles that made it incredibly difficult to do anything more than a slow shuffle, and the bigger, taller Nephyrs weren't slowing down for her.

Up ahead, surgery patients and doctors stepped aside to watch the procession of eighteen Nephyrs, two Internal Investigations officers, twelve Base Security personnel, and six specially assigned, assault-capable Gryphon units. Tatiana lifted her chin and tried to ignore the wide eyes from the side corridors and open room doors.

Screw 'em.

*Guilty.* It still rankled her. They hadn't even given her a *trial.* Sure, they'd got the whole thing on camera, right down to her getting down on her hands and knees so Milar could stand on her back and retrieve his shackles, but jeez. Not even a *trial.* What was this, the Stone Age? Surely she deserved a few minutes to explain her innocence, maybe have a few pity-parties in front of the cameras. But no, they'd kept her locked in almost complete solitary ever since they'd dragged her back to Rath. Her conviction had been delivered to her via the smug sneer of a Nephyr lieutenant general. They'd fed her gruel. *Gruel.*

Now they were going to remove her hardware before the Nephyrs got her. Full correction. To the death, spare the potty breaks. Damn, this sucked.

The Nephyr on point turned down a side corridor marked SURGERY and Tatiana slowed again, looking up at the big white letters on the sign with trepidation. "Taking a *right!*" the next Nephyr in line shouted. Several Nephyrs down the procession repeated the call. As she turned the corner, she saw the big teal double doors up ahead and Tatiana felt her feet slow further.

"Move it, tiny," the Nephyr behind her snapped, slamming a heavy hand into her back, tumbling her into the Nephyr in front of her. Nobody bothered to help right her when she fell. In fact, one of them grabbed her by the arm shackles and started hauling her forward, giving her the option of stumbling to her feet or getting dragged.

"I bet you stole a lot of lunch money as a kid," Tatiana muttered, struggling back into a standing position. "Lot of good it did you, eh?"

The Nephyr holding her wrist chains gave her a grin that left her with goosebumps. "Oh," she said, "I'm not too displeased with the results. I get to skin me a little operator bitch. Always wanted to do that."

"Such lofty goals," Tatiana muttered. "Remind me to nominate you for the school board."

The Nephyr woman holding her chain looked up to one of her companions. "I want her tongue."

Tatiana swallowed down bile and muttered, "Tastes like chicken."

"Actually," the Nephyr woman said, smiling at her, "it tastes like pork."

*She is not bullshitting me,* Tatiana realized, looking up into the woman's icy-calm face. *Fuck me, I am so screwed.*

"See," the woman continued, plucking at Tatiana's orange prisoner's jumpsuit as they walked, "sometimes we'll carve a chunk off and eat it in front of 'em. Bit of thigh or backstrap or, if they're boring, the tongue. Fry it right on the spot in a little salt and butter and garlic, slice it up nice, throw in a few onions for flavor. Hell, we'll even offer 'em a piece, if they're hungry."

*Definitely don't be boring,* Tatiana thought immediately. Then, with a sudden wave of hysteria, she realized that she was planning on doing her damndest to entertain Nephyrs as they flayed her alive. She swallowed hard.

"Taking a *left!*" the lead Nephyr shouted from up ahead. Two Nephyrs had stopped to hold open the double doors as the procession passed through, revealing row after row of dreary blue surgery rooms.

*Oh man,* Tatiana thought, seeing the first surgeon in blue scrubs and a facial mask, standing off to one side, watching. She felt her heart start to thunder in her ears. *Oh man . . .*

Then the Nephyrs were parting, leaving her a black-clad corridor of glittering bodies leading into an open surgery room. Inside, she could see an operating table and a nice, big array of tools and electronics.

They were gonna tear out her hardware. She was *never* flying another soldier. Never flying another *anything.* She was grounded, man, and she hadn't even gotten laid out of the deal. Seeing the guy with the syringe standing beside the bed, it finally started to sink in. His assistant, a *much* smaller woman who appeared to be some sort of dwarf, had everything but her eyes hidden by a facial mask. She was seated on a short stool, playing with a scalpel, shaving her fingernails.

Shaving her . . . fingernails? Wasn't that, like, against some sort of health code?

The doors slammed shut behind her and two Nephyrs set the deadbolts, top and bottom, leaving Tatiana alone with four escorts and two surgeons. Tatiana slowed again as they drew closer to the spotlit center of the room, and the female Nephyr in front of her laughed. "Aww, I think she's starting to hyperventilate." She shoved Tatiana hard, and Tatiana went careening into the operating table, upending the carefully laid out trays and spilling medical instruments in a metallic clatter upon the floor. "Get on with it, docs," the glittering broad said. "I want this bitch back in time for dinner." She gave Tatiana a wink.

The dwarf stopped shaving her fingernails and narrowed her eyes at the instruments on the floor. In a high-pitched, childlike voice, she said, "I'm sorry, did someone ask the lawn ornament to talk, Dobie?"

The man beside the bed said, "I don't believe they did, Anna."

"I see." She paused and held her tiny hand out to inspect the back of her nails. "Execute them, please."

"As you wish, Anna." As the Nephyrs were frowning, the man raised a hand and pointed a finger at the Nephyr closest to her, then raised a finger at each of the three others, and Tatiana had just enough time to see the tips of four of his fingers fold back, exposing small black tubes, before she heard a collective *pop* and jumped. In that instant, all four Nephyrs suddenly collapsed, their bodies shuddering. It had taken only a second. The man lowered his arm, blew smoke from the four steaming barrels jutting from his hand, then the tips of his fingers folded back into place and he dropped his arm back to his side. When

Tatiana looked down, the Nephyrs' brains were oozing gray-pink slime out an empty eye socket.

"Niiice, Dobie. Your aim is improving."

"I continue to modify myself as time allows, Anna," the man said.

Listening to the perfectly calculated pitch of his voice, Tatiana frowned. "Wait. Is that a . . . *robot?*"

"Wow, she's a bright one."

"Her statistical record indicates she is, Anna."

The girl—it *had* to be a girl, Tatiana realized, maybe only five or six—snorted in disdain. Giving Tatiana a considering look, she blew on her fingernails, then rubbed them on her shirt. "Dobie, help her onto the table." She pulled off her mask and flung it aside. "We're gonna have some fun."

Tatiana froze. "The . . . table? What? Why?"

The girl's smile was icy. "So I can experiment on you, of course."

Tatiana's face fell as the robot moved to grab her by an arm and pull her toward the table. "What?"

"Oh, you actually thought you were getting rescued, didn't you?" The kid laughed at her. "Oh no, sweetie. Oh no. This will be much, much better." Smiling, the girl got off her stool and started walking towards her. "You see, you killed my friend, and I didn't want the Nephyrs getting first whack at you."

As the robot bodily hefted Tatiana onto the table and cinched down the wrist and ankle restraints, Tatiana frowned down at the little girl, struggling against hyperventilation. "I don't know what you're talking about—who *are* you?"

"They skinned him, you know," the little girl said, twisting the scalpel in the light, looking at the blade. "All those pretty dragons— one of the Nephyrs decided to tan it and use it as a coat." She looked up at Tatiana with a smile that left Tatiana cold. "She's dead now."

Dragons . . . It took her a moment to make the connection. *Milar.* "I didn't kill him!" Tatiana cried, as the robot buckled her head to the table. She frantically strained against the straps holding her down. "I helped him escape!"

"I see." The girl smiled and lowered the scalpel to the metal tray. Idly, she picked up what looked like a circular bone saw. Pressing the button, the blade shrieked in a high-pitched whine as she watched it thoughtfully. "Dobie, perhaps you could replay the scene in question for our new friend?" She turned to smile at Tatiana. "Since her memory seems to be so . . . fragile."

"As you wish, Anna." The scene immediately came up on the operating screen, which the girl twisted so that Tatiana could see.

A man, hanging from his wrists in a tiny concrete cell, his skin hanging on a hook beside him. Tatiana recognized the sinuous red and black serpents and felt sick. "Oh my God," she whispered. "I thought he escaped."

*Jeanne said he went down,* she remembered. *He went down and they skinned him alive.*

"Took him four days to die," the little girl said. "The Nephyrs running the show were quite disappointed. Seems one of their techs arrived with a highly virulent form of bacteria on their sterile medical equipment. What a shame."

Four days . . . Tatiana frowned, remembering the charges that the lieutenant general had read to her the day she returned. He'd left her the paper to examine after he'd left. The date had been in the upper left-hand corner. Blinking at the kid, she said, "But I've only been back two days." They had *escaped* four days ago.

She saw a flicker of confusion in the girl's face before she shook herself and continued, "So here's the deal. I need guinea pigs, and I don't like you, so I'm going to run a few experiments before I hand you back to the Nephyrs. Sound like fun?"

But Tatiana was frowning at the skin. The dragons looked wrong, somehow. She'd gotten a really good look, earlier, back when the bastard had been teasing her, and the nose of the red one was tucked over the black one's back, instead of behind it. "Kid," she said. "I don't know who that is, but that's not Milar. The red dragon is wrong."

The girl frowned at Tatiana a long moment, then reluctantly glanced at the screen. She cocked her head at it a moment, then turned back to Tatiana. "Explain." She still had not turned off the bone saw.

"I went back and rescued him from the Nephyr compound," Tatiana babbled in relief. "Four days ago. He had a little EMP wand in his knife and he used it to disable some Nephyrs. I took out his lifeline and stuffed him in my soldier and flew him back to his brother. I took out a couple of Bouncers with his ship, then we spent a couple days laying low, staying under radar. Then there was a big firefight over Deaddrunk. I flew a TAG and took out a pod of operators and about a dozen Nephyrs."

The girl wrinkled her nose. "Dobie?"

"An unarmed cargo ship wiped out three Bouncers on patrol over the western jungle," the robot said. "Two days later, there was a fight over Deaddrunk, but the information is classified, pending a Director's code."

Narrowing her eyes at Tatiana, the girl shut off the bone saw and swiveled the console back around and began typing something into the screen. A few moments later, she cocked her head, looking genuinely surprised. "Huh. She's telling the truth."

"It appears that way, Anna."

The girl tapped her fingers against her cheek a moment, glancing at the screen, then to Tatiana, then back. "Says Miles and Patty went down in the north end of the Tear. There's a huge search out for them right now. Most operators north of the equator have been deployed.

Big firefight. They found the ship, but colonial resistance isn't allowing them to land and do a thorough search."

Tatiana let out a huge breath of relief. "Oh thank God. See? I'm on your side. You can let me go, now."

The girl spun the console away from her and gave Tatiana an easy smile. "You're right. I could."

The girl made no move to disengage the shackles holding Tatiana to the stainless-steel table. Instead, she smiled, and Tatiana felt the coldness of it in her soul.

The girl switched on the bone saw again. "But, like I said, I need a guinea pig, and I don't like you."

"Listen, you crazy little bitch, let me *go!*" Tatiana jerked at the restraints, but didn't even succeed in rocking the table.

"You see, you got a bunch of pretty pictures, where all I ever got was screams."

Tatiana blinked at her. "Pictures?" Was the girl psychotic? "What the hell are you talking about? Let me *go.* Somebody *help!*"

The little girl laughed. "Screaming is good. That's what they're expecting. The surgeons were ordered not to use anesthetics, so I figured, why not? Makes for more interesting dinner conversation later. You know . . . horror stories to tell your kids?" The girl chuckled and stepped forward with the saw.

Tatiana shrieked and tried to thrash her head aside, but the robot had strapped it brutally—and effectively—to the table.

"Now, before we start," the kid said, bringing the spinning blade within centimeters of Tatiana's left eye, "I want to be very clear about something."

Tatiana whimpered and fisted her hands, her heart shooting streams of acid through her veins. "Please don't do this."

The girl smiled at her. "If you pass out, I'm going to stop everything to revive you, then I'm going to administer a powerful stimulant.

Unfortunately, that will also make it hurt much, much worse, so please try and stay conscious, okay? I want you to experience *everything*." She gave Tatiana another icy smile, then the blade was descending, and Tatiana emptied her lungs in a scream.

# CHAPTER 41

## Jersey

STEELE? YEAH. I GOT MY EYES ON HER RIGHT NOW. NAH, TOTALLY dead."

*Killer,* Wideman giggled.

*No,* Magali screamed inwardly. *No! Go away, just go away!* Whether she was talking to the Nephyr or Wideman, she wasn't sure.

"Like what, a broken leg?" the man went on. "Nah, none that I can see. Looks like she fell on her back."

*Please go away,* Magali whimpered inside.

"I dunno, a couple days? She's cold as an ice cube."

. . . *Cold as an ice cube?* Magali's startled mind asked. He hadn't even touched her. Nephyrs had heat sensors built into their skin. There was no way he couldn't see she wasn't alive.

"Yeah, sure. Will do." She heard the footsteps move closer.

*Can't let him get too close,* Magali realized, suddenly launching into another panic. If he got close enough to take her gun from her, it was all over. *Pleaaase,* her ragged mind whispered. *Please just go . . .*

She heard the Nephyr slow and start to kneel. "Hey there," he said softly. "How are you doing?"

Magali snapped her eyes open and whipped the gun around, holding it up between them. It was a Nephyr, clad in the same jet-black gear as the others, the same gold-filigreed skin, though she didn't recognize him as one from the cave. "Back off and keep your hand from your ear," she ordered. Nephyrs had a special transmitter built into the skin under their ear that allowed them to make calls to camp computer systems, ships, or other Nephyrs.

The Nephyr hesitated, looking down at her gun warily. Very slowly, he held up both his hands, palms facing her, and ducked his head in a gesture of peace. "I heard what you did for those eggers." He gave her a timid smile.

*Lying,* she thought, trembling as she watched him down the barrel of the gun.

After a long pause, he gently offered, "My name's Jersey."

"I have to kill you," Magali whispered.

He made a nervous laugh. "Uh, Miss, you could always lower the gun and we could talk."

Magali shuddered inside. She could, too, couldn't she? But if she did, he would take her gun away, and she was *never* letting that happen again. Never. Her entire body shaking, she said, "It isn't happening again. I'm sorry."

"Hey," the guy said softly, "I know this is gonna be hard to believe, considering I look just like that psycho Steele, but I'm not gonna hurt you."

"That's right," Magali whispered hoarsely. "You're not." *Never again.* Her finger tightened on the trigger.

The Nephyr's blue-green eyes widened and flickered to something above and behind her. Her mind stumbling from exhaustion, Magali hesitated, and in that horrified moment, she realized she had never ascertained he didn't have a partner. She turned to look over her shoulder.

Inhumanly fast, the Nephyr lunged forward, catching her arm with his glittering fingers and pushing it sideways. Magali, her body bruised and exhausted, was too slow in pulling the trigger. The round glanced off the side of his cheek, hitting the cliff behind them. Magali screamed and tried to wrestle it free, to get off another shot, but the arm that held her had all the hydraulic strength of a crane, keeping the gun inexorably pointed at the sky.

Then the Nephyr swallowed and glanced over his shoulder, saw the singed mark in the rock where the round had penetrated, then looked back at her, his aquamarine eyes searching hers. He reached up with his other hand and, with something akin to gentleness, pulled the gun from her fingers and set it behind him. "You want something to eat?"

Magali shuddered and went limp under his brutally strong grip. His unnaturally smooth fingers felt like warm glass against her forearm. She remembered the last time she'd felt that unnatural smoothness, the crystalline hardness against her skin, and she swallowed back bile. She ducked her head to her chest in despair, her entire body shaking around her. "Just kill me. Please."

"Erm. How about hot chocolate, instead?"

Magali frowned at the sand between their knees. Then, slowly, she lifted her head so she could see his face.

Under the glittering circuitry, he offered her a shy smile. "You know how to remove a lifeline, right?"

Magali's exhausted mind stuttered. *A trick,* she finally thought. It had to be some sort of trick. She glanced over her shoulder, looking for the other Nephyrs.

"I'm alone," the Nephyr said softly. Very slowly, he released her forearm and lowered his hand, watching her reaction closely. When

Magali didn't scramble away from him, he offered, "If you get on the ship with me, I'll take you to Silver City."

*A trick!* her ragged mind screamed. *Another trick!* She couldn't trust him. Couldn't trust *them.* They lied with smiles on their faces, gentleness in their touch. Just like Anna. Magali felt like she was swimming. She could hear Wideman chanting in the background, could see the edges of her mind fraying, the corruption eating inward. She felt herself teetering, very close to falling—somewhere. Close to letting go. Close to—

The Nephyr lowered his head so he could peer up into her face. "My name's Jersey Brackett, of the original Brackett clan that helped colonize the South Tear. I was born in Six Bears, thirty-five years ago zoomtime. They drafted me when I was fourteen. Spent five years in cryo, each way."

Magali felt part of her snap back into place. The Bracketts were a legend—before they were all killed in the Yolk mines. Six Bears was a ghost town south of the Tear. Between the Yolk drafts and the Nephyrs, there was nothing left. Her world came back into focus as she frowned at him. "What?"

Very slowly, still holding his hands up in peace, the Nephyr got to his feet and retrieved the gun. Then, tilting his head sideways at the ship, he said, "Come on? I'll tell you the rest onboard, once we've got some food in you, okay? You don't look too hot." He eased his way sideways, to the base of the ramp, gesturing into the ship's bowels.

*Another trick,* Magali thought, the remaining strands of her mind straining to the edge of breaking. *It has to be another trick.* Half of her wanted to just follow him up the ramp, and half of her wanted to hurtle into the Snake and suck as much of its acidic water into her lungs as she could before he could pull her out.

"Please," the Nephyr said. His voice actually sounded anguished. "Trust me. I'm not gonna hurt you. I've been looking for you for a really long time."

*They want me alive,* Magali's mind babbled. *Alive for more of their games.*

The Nephyr seemed to droop, watching her. He glanced up at the sun, then back at her. Then, gingerly, he set the gun inside the ship and started walking back towards her, pulling off his shirt.

. . . pulling off his shirt?

Then he was kneeling beside her again, poking her head through the hole in the jet-black cloth, then easing her hands through the arm holes, the unnatural hard-smooth of his hands brushing her skin as he dragged the hem downward to cover her chest and back.

Magali could offer no resistance as the Nephyr then took her by the palm and gently pulled her to her feet. "Come on. I've got food and water on the ship. Nice little bunk, too, so you can lie down."

*He wants to put me in his bed.* Magali froze, coming to a halt, her heart starting to pound like a jackhammer.

The Nephyr hesitated, giving her a pained look. "It only fits one person. It's a scout ship. Only built for a crew of two, and somebody's supposed to be at the controls at all times."

Magali didn't believe him. She *couldn't* believe him. But when he gently put an arm around the small of her back and guided her into the tiny belly of the ship, she let him ease her into the shadows beyond.

"Okay, stay here a second," the Nephyr said. He hit the button for the ramp and triggered the airlock, then, with a last glance at her, turned and ducked through the entrance to the forward compartment and she heard tinny rustlings inside.

Magali's eyes found the gun, still sitting on the carpet where he'd set it. In a daze, she squatted and retrieved it. Then, seeing the tiny

bunk the Nephyr had mentioned, she sat on it and stared at the clothing and gear racks on the other side of the narrow hallway, considering
what it would be like to finally put the muzzle to her brain and pull
the trigger.

A few minutes later, the Nephyr returned with a steaming cup in
one hand, a bowl in the other, his glittering chest covered with another
ebony shirt. He had already ducked through the aft compartment door
when he saw the gun in her lap. He hesitated. His blue-green eyes
shifted to her face and she saw anxiousness there. Clearing his throat,
he completed the last few steps to ease himself down onto the bunk
beside her.

"Hot chocolate," he said, offering her a plain steel cup filled
with steaming liquid. Magali glanced down at it, saw the glittering fingers clutching the handle of the cup, then looked back up at
him, feeling like she were watching a puppet in a traveling peddler's
show.

The Nephyr cleared his throat nervously, then set the cup aside
and offered her the bowl. "Chicken soup," he said, moving the spoon
along the rim so that it was facing her. "With extra helpings of chicken,
'cause the Nephs would bitch if Supply skimped out on the meat." He
laughed uncomfortably. When Magali didn't even look at it, he lowered his voice and said, "Please?"

Magali dropped her head. For a long moment, Magali just stared
down at the carrots and noodles floating amidst the yellowish broth,
unable to comprehend it. Then, almost as if her limbs were powered by
someone else, she reached up and took the bowl.

The Nephyr seemed to relax slightly as her numb fingers found the
spoon and she began to eat. He watched closely, but made no move
to take the gun from her lap. Instead, after a moment, he reached up
and dragged a fuzzy green blanket out of the overhead bin and gingerly wrapped it around her shoulders as she spooned the soup into her

mouth. When she was finished, he again offered her the hot chocolate, handle first.

Magali took it mechanically, still waiting for the trick. Her eyes found the mark of captain on the Nephyr's bare arm, embedded in the glittering skin just above the elbow. A golden profile of a wolf, head low, one leg lifted. It rested in the same little black-and-gold patch as Steele's arrow-clenching fist of colonel. In bold golden numbers above the wolf stood a proudly emblazoned 43.

Seeing her stare, the Nephyr cleared his throat uncomfortably and crossed his arms, dropping his hand nonchalantly over the patch. He got up and, one hand still covering the skin of his arm, dragged a black, unmarked long-sleeved shirt from one of the clothes bins, then tugged it over his head. Magali watched the wolf disappear under another layer of black before he sat down beside her again. "Would you like water, instead?"

Magali's eyes remained on the spot above his elbow, where she knew the golden 43 rested just under the thin layer of cotton . . .

"Hey." The Nephyr touched her chin and dragged her face up to meet his. "I'm not like them. I swear." He looked so genuine, so honest . . .

Magali had to look away. She glanced down into the swirling brown liquid, instead. If it had been Anna, it would've been laced with some sort of chemical . . .

"It's not drugged," the Nephyr said softly.

Magali's eyes lifted back to his face. For several long minutes, she just studied his face, trying to determine the catch. "How do I know," she managed, through dry, cracked lips, "this isn't a trick?"

The Nephyr's blue-green eyes darkened for the first time. "I went through enough mind games in Nephyr Academy. Was hard enough to keep myself on the straight-and-level." His eyes grew distant and his mouth twisted in distaste. "I don't need to spread it around."

*Like he's talking about a disease,* Magali realized, watching him.

The Nephyr seemingly shook himself, then took her hand and gave it a gentle squeeze. "Okay then. I'm gonna go head up the controls and get us the hell out of range of the camp computer. You should probably get some sleep. If you don't want the chocolate, drop the whole thing in the waste bin and I'll take care of it later." He started to stand and turned, his back to her.

"Aren't you going to take the gun from me?" Magali blurted.

The Nephyr hesitated and looked back at her. "You gonna use it on yourself?"

Magali thought about it. "No."

"Then no." He ducked through the door and disappeared. A few minutes later, she felt the ship's engines power on and the entire vessel jiggled as the landing gear began to retract.

Magali looked down at her hot chocolate, thinking about the sorts of things that Anna would have put into it. Her eyes flickered to the gun, then to the blanket around her shoulders and the empty soup bowl resting on the bed beside her. After a long moment, she brought the cup to her mouth and drank.

# CHAPTER 42

# That Night in the Desert . . .

JOEL WOKE TO THE COLD MUZZLE OF A SHOTGUN IN HIS MOUTH. He knew it was the muzzle of a shotgun by the distinctive *sha-shunk* as someone pumped the action. When he opened his eyes, a voluptuous, green-eyed beauty scowled down at him over the barrel.

God, he had horrible luck with women.

"What did I do?" Joel asked around the barrel of the gun. It came out like, "Waa thid aa thoo?"

The woman leaned close, jiggling the ring of teeth hanging from her neck. "Why did you do it, Joel?"

Then he placed the necklace and Joel froze. Jeanne Ivory. The pirate who collected debts in the form of molars. Oh shit. *Horrible* luck with women. Last time he'd seen Jeanne, it had been stranded in an equatorial desert just west of the Tear, watching him take off with about two hundred mil in raw Yolk that she'd carefully laid out and prepped the night before—right before he'd given her the night of her life. He swallowed, deciding not to bring it up, just in case she had forgotten.

"Uhm. Dhoo wath?" He knew better than to ask a pirate like Jeanne to jog his memory.

Jeanne did not remove the gun and continued to give him a flat green stare. "Why'd you save those people, Joel?"

*Save those people* . . . Joel frowned, wondering what the hell she could be talking about. Last people he remembered saving had been a starving village by 'forgetting' a few thousand pounds of flour in their main square.

"Thley were uungry?"

"Not only the folks in Deaddrunk, but the eggers in Yolk Factory 14, too. That's not in your nature, Joel. Who are you double-crossing this time?"

Joel frowned and shoved the gun out of his face, sitting up. "Eggers? What egg—" Then he felt his face go slack as he remembered. "I saved *eggers.*"

Jeanne took a step back, the shotgun still aimed at his face. "They say you were spouting some horseshit about changing your name to Ferryman Joel. Why would you do that, Runaway? Or should I just blow your lying tongue through your lizard brain and call it good?"

Joel sighed and gave her an irritated look. "So I took your virginity and fibbed a little bit. I didn't leave you without resources, and only disconnected the power supply to your ship's command console. Easy fix. And you *told* me it was the best damn night of your life, so don't give me your crap, Jeanne."

Jeanne's pretty green eyes narrowed.

He shoved himself to the side of the rickety, rough-hewn bed and put his bare feet on the dirt floor. He was actually surprised he was alive. He had dropped into Deaddrunk as a last resort, on the off-chance that maybe they wouldn't remember who he was long enough to patch him up. And it had been sheer, blind luck that the joyriding idiot who had stolen his TAG had gone off lollygagging into the woods like a rookie, giving Joel just enough time to load the rest of the survivors on board and ferry them to safety. He barely remembered that. Mostly, he remembered someone yelling at him to stay conscious, slapping him when he tried to run the ship into a mountainside. That had been annoying. He'd been so tired . . . He had almost done it just to make them leave him alone.

Joel groaned and pushed his palm to the side of his head. He guessed he had always been lucky, in a weird sort of way. Twice in one day, he should've wandered off to meet his Maker, but it looked as if not only had the surgeon patched him up, but he'd also stayed awake long enough to land the ship, which he didn't even remember. Hell, somebody had even put some work in on his hand. He bent the fingers the Nephyr had crushed, grimacing. They ached, but were mostly whole, so either someone had spent some time and money patching him up or he'd been unconscious for several weeks. He hated to consider the latter.

"You'd live longer by not bringing up ancient history, Joel."

Rubbing his head, Joel peered up at Jeanne and said, "Why? I'm sure you've had tons of other guys since me that made that 'best night of your life' pale in comparison."

Her flat scowl was all he needed.

"Oh." Joel laughed. "Okay. So I guess I'm just that good."

Jeanne's face remained utterly impassive behind the half-yard tubes of black steel.

"Geo had me pinned between a rock and a hard place," he sighed. "I *needed* that money, Jeanne. He was gonna take a finger." He held up his left hand and wiggled them for her. The shotgun shifted from his face to his hand. Seeing that, Joel quickly made a fist and dropped his hand back to the bed, clearing his throat nervously. "Uh. How long have I been under? And where's my ship?"

"How about you answer my questions first, considerin' I'm the one with the gun, and I'm going to blow your head off if I don't like what you've got ta say, just like I *should* have done back when you were plugging my ears with bullshit."

Joel snorted. "Please. You do that, you'll miss out on all these pretty teeth." He smiled for her, showing dimples. "No cavities, baby."

He saw Jeanne's trigger finger twitch and his heart skipped. He swallowed hard. "Uh, Magali Landborn wouldn't let me leave without them." It wasn't *exactly* true, but it was probably an answer that Jeanne would believe.

"You want me to believe that, Joel?"

He grimaced, peering down the dark double barrels of the gun. "Uh . . . yes?"

Jeanne rushed him and made a commendable attempt to shove the gun up his left nostril. "Magali wasn't *with* the eggers, Joel," she snarled. "And she sure as hell didn't arrive with you in Deaddrunk, and she wasn't in the pile of corpses the Nephyrs threw out in the bogs after they finished with the three hundred you left behind. Where is she?"

"Uh," Joel said, his head tilted back by the pressure of the gun. "I got hijacked. I had to leave her on the cliff. They probably killed her and left her in the mines." It wasn't going to be what Jeanne wanted to hear, but it was a fact of life, and Magali had known the chances.

"Or maybe she shot you, eh, Joel?" Jeanne snarled down the gun. "That how you got that nice hole in your chest?"

"Jeanne," Joel said carefully, "I'm sure your killer instincts are in overdrive, looking at these beautiful chompers, but if you want to ever see Magali Landborn alive again, this is really important. How long have I been under?"

For a long time, the pirate simply studied him, and he watched the gears churn in her mind as she considered killing him anyway. Then she lowered the gun and said, "Four days since you crawled back to the controls and shuttled the Deaddrunk survivors to safety."

Joel felt his heart start to hammer. "Shit." A lot could happen in four days, and if they'd killed three hundred eggers . . .

Jeanne was watching him with the acuity of a cat. "The Nephyrs got her, didn't they?"

Joel grimaced. Magali Landborn was a sort of legend to those who followed the babblings of the weird little 'oracle.' "Like I said, we had a hitch in the plans. A bunch of assholes with guns decided to hijack my ship when I was working on one of the last runs. I left her halfway up a cliff."

"Any way she climbed down?

"No," Joel said, shaking his head. "No way."

Jeanne gave him a long look, then said, "Miles and Patrick went down in the Tear four days ago. Nephyrs went in looking for them and vanished and the Coalition sent a few Pods and a dozen ground teams. Whole place is like a beehive. I need you to fly me in after them."

Rubbing the kinks out of his nose, Joel hesitated at the last. "You've got a funny way of asking for my help."

The pirate gave him a cool smile. "Who says I'm asking?"

"They've got *Nephyrs* on the ground and you think *we* should go waltz in and check it out?" Joel demanded. "Are you *nuts*?" The Tear gave him the creeps. Sure, there were plenty of Shrieker mounds in it, if you knew where to look, but entire colonies had disappeared on its metal-rich banks. Followed by the investigation teams that went looking for them. Followed by the military teams that went in after *them*. There was a good reason why it was a no-fly zone, and Joel would rather leave it that way.

"You misunderstand," Jeanne said, giving him a cruel smile. "You're taking me to the Tear, Joel." Leaning forward, still grinning, she said,

"And you're going to shoot down as many of the bastards as you can. We've never had so many in one place before."

Joel's lips formed a little round O. "Uh. I don't shoot people, Jeanne. I kinda left that behind when I left the service. This ship didn't even have *guns* on it until that rat-bastard Geo stole it from me."

Jeanne's smile was sinister as she plucked at his shirt. "Tell ya what. You're going to take a hint from that fancy ship and you're going to start doing something *honorable* with your damn life, or *I'm* going to take you out back, shoot you in the head, and bury you in a bog like those three hundred eggers you abandoned before I go give your ship to someone who can use it properly."

Joel laughed. "What, no necklace for me?"

"You don't deserve the necklace." Her emerald eyes were flat. "You deserve a bullet."

Seeing the sincerity on her face, Joel cleared his throat. "What about the Whitecliff boys? We snap off a bunch of wings and drop a bunch of ground-pounders in their lap, they're gonna be a might bit irritated with us, don'tcha think?"

"It'll give Milar more to shoot at," Jeanne said.

"Oh." Joel cleared his throat. "What if I want to go check on Magali, instead?"

"Magali can take care of herself."

Joel narrowed his eyes at the pirate. "I think we'll check on Magali, *then* go do whatever the hell it is you want me to do."

Jeanne smiled at him. "You know what the difference between a pirate and a smuggler is, Joel?"

Joel immediately winced. He did, indeed, know the difference, and much of it had to do with the massive gun she carried in her hands and her willingness to use it. "One of them likes to pretend she's the tooth fairy?"

"One of them kills people." Jeanne patted the gun. "So," she said. "Last chance, Joel. You gonna die Ferryman Joel or you gonna go out in a ball of flame as Fireman Joel?"

Joel laughed. "Lady," he said, standing. Then he caught himself, looking Jeanne up and down, eyes catching on the leather clothing, the hunting knife, the shotgun, and the string of molars. "Well . . . *woman,* at least . . . " He cleared his throat, returning his eyes to her face. "If I take us into the air to do battle with *Honor,* I'll be landing again in time for dinner and a hot bath. No ball of fire for me, babe."

Jeanne gave him a grin that unsettled him. "We'll see."

# CHAPTER 43

# Science Is Fun

TATIANA GROANED AND OPENED HER EYES. IMMEDIATELY, SHE found she could move her arms and legs, and she screamed and threw herself off of the operating table, yanking IV lines free of her body and tumbling to the floor in a metallic clatter of nodes and operating instruments.

*. . . taking too long. We should go in there.*

A knock thundered on the double doors, making the deadbolts rattle. Stumbling, Tatiana noticed that the door to the surgeon's prep room was open. In a panic, she dragged herself across the cold, antiseptic-smelling tiles, trailing an IV bag. The shackles, along with a good portion of her forehead, were haphazardly cast into a pile near the door. Seeing the circular chunk of skull—and the floppy piece of eyebrow muscle and skin that the girl had cut away, Tatiana's stomach heaved and she retched a thin stream of bile onto the floor.

*They shouldn't be taking this long. She stopped screaming an hour ago.*

The double door pounded again. "Hey, guys! You in there? What the hell, man? What's taking so long?"

Tatiana crawled across the cold tiles, her fingers trembling as they scrabbled for purchase against the indentations in the grout. Whimpering, she yanked the IV loose and pulled herself into the darkened prep room and, her arm shaking, pushed the door shut behind her.

The prep room was about twenty feet wide, with two armless chairs, a sink, several cubbies, and, above the sink, a mirror. Tatiana let out a moan and dropped away from the sheet of glass, clutching at the floor. She had seen it all. The girl had adjusted the operating screen and made her watch.

Tatiana retched again, then just huddled under the sink, shivering. A few feet away, she saw another door, a single one leading to the doctors' entrance. Tatiana just stared at it, unable to make her arms and legs move.

*"See that, Captain? That's your frontal lobe. Now we're just going to slide the scalpel in right there and make a small incision . . . "*

Tatiana moaned and curled in on herself, shuddering.

*Something is wrong. I should break down the door.*

"Hey, man, last chance! What the hell is going on in there?"

Tatiana started to whine. It sounded odd, coming from her throat, but she could no more stop it than she could stop breathing.

*"See that? Those twisted little gray lumps are generally accepted to be the driving force behind your memory, your motor function, and your ability to problem-solve. They're also your emotional control center, your language center, and the seat of your individual personality. If I were to carve out a little chunk here, for instance, you'd no longer be a cocky, know-it-all pilot. If you could still talk afterwards, you'd probably have trouble finding joy in, for instance, sex with smart, muscular men you don't deserve. Science is fun, isn't it?"*

In the other room, the double door exploded from its hinges.

*Oh fuck. We are so screwed.*

"She got away! The bitch got away! Alert the base! Four men down and we've got a fugitive in the medical wing! Female operator, hundred and fifty centimeters, blue eyes." *I am so gonna kill someone.* Tatiana heard thunderous footsteps hurtle to the center of the room, then something heavy and metal went careening across the room, to crash into the far wall. She huddled further into herself, muffling the whine against her forearm.

*"There are some people, however, who believe the frontal lobe is also the slowly evolving center for crude psychic activity in humans. That's why you're my guinea pig today. I'm going to see if we can stimulate your primitive little brain into producing its own form of Yolk. Wouldn't that be neat?"*

*How the hell did she get these off? I had the only key . . .* She heard chains jingle, then drop back to the floor. Then she heard leather creak as someone squatted. *What the hell* is *that? Somebody's* forehead? *That little shit is so gonna die.* The heavy footsteps thundered the rest of the way across the operating room and the operating room door slammed inward on its hinges, hitting the sink above her hard enough to crack the basin. Tatiana shuddered and pulled her knees closer to her body.

The Nephyr stepped through the prep room door and slammed it behind him, making the wall rattle against Tatiana's back. Looking up at his tall, glittering form, Tatiana felt her heart shoot streaks of acid into her arms and legs.

The Nephyr hesitated, reaching up and touching his skull. *Damn, my head hurts. Need another migraine pill from the doc.* Then he took three strides forward, yanked the far door off its hinges, and threw it aside as he disappeared into the corridor beyond. *So dead . . .*

*"Not that I expect you to understand this, my wide-eyed little lab rat, but basically, the native fauna of Fortune—that's the animals, for those of us who are too stupid to know what that means—exhibit innate*

*psychic development that far surpasses anything in the human body. Thus, because you have such pitiful material to work with, I'm going to be inserting a device into your brain that will affect the cells during mitosis. What that means, my little guinea pig, is that it will randomly stimulate your pathetic little brain cells to replicate, and when they do, it will begin to make small changes to your DNA during each division. And, just so your head doesn't explode, I programmed in something special, just for you. One half of each dividing cell will basically receive a self-destruct mechanism after final division and will be absorbed back into the brain. You better be grateful—it took me an extra ten minutes. I just hope I got the frequency right, otherwise they'll die too fast, and you'll become a vegetable."*

Tatiana couldn't stop shaking. Her forehead was an aching, pounding throb, but she couldn't bring herself to touch it. She turned slightly and vomited again, though nothing came out.

In the other room, she heard more footsteps, softer this time.

*Dumbass is gonna get what's coming to him. This is his baby, he said. Let him do his job, he said. Director is gonna string him up by his pretty, glittering balls.*

A woman stepped through the door that the first Nephyr had cracked off of its hinges, then switched on the light and shut the door behind her. She slowed when she saw the second door utterly pulverized and lying to one side. She sighed deeply, then lifted her glittering face to the cubbies. *Doctors must've been in on it. No one was scheduled for this room . . .*

The Nephyr walked over to the cubbies and started rifling through the scrubs and clean white shoes contained therein. Huddled on the floor behind her, Tatiana heard herself start to whine again.

*Damn, my head. Must be my period again. Hell. Just what I need.*

Tatiana shivered on the floor, watching the woman lift her hand to her head and bend forward, groaning.

*"Now here's the really cool part—the longer it's in there, the more alien you'll become. Fun, huh? Oh, and I took a hint from Dobie. Try to take it out and you die. Disconnect it and you die. Disable it and you die. Hell, you should be* very *careful with it, because if it gets tapped just a bit too hard, you die. But then, you should be used to that, right? Nothing new for an operator with a temple receptor. Just think of it as another node, sweetie. But, in case you're not convinced, let me show you something . . . "*

Tatiana whimpered, remembering the little blades the girl had shown her, protruding from the end of the device. They had extended and started whipping back and forth the moment the girl pushed a tiny pink button on a keychain-sized transmitter. The girl smiled at her over the churning blades.

*"Basically, my little pet, do anything except be a good lab rat for me, and this thing is going to scramble that inadequate little brain of yours with these nice little blades right here. See them? Look kind of like a food processor, right? You fiddle with this thing and it'll eat its way through your brain in a matter of, oh, a second. Isn't that right, Dobie? Now hold* really *still while I slip it in there . . . "*

The Nephyr frowned and lifted her head, turning.

*"Now I want you to remember something when this is all over. I own you, now. See this little pink button? I push it, I get to watch you die. Doesn't matter where you are, or how much interference it's got— you piss me off, you die. Now. I know you're listening, 'cause you're bleeding like hell. So here's your first command from your new owner. You stay the hell away from Milar. Keep your hands off him, got it? He's mine."*

The Nephyr's dark-brown eyes found Tatiana huddled under the sink and she frowned. "What the—" *What the hell is that in her head?*

Tatiana's throat started to burn as her scream came out as another high-pitched whine.

The Nephyr winced, then stumbled slightly, her hands clutching her skull. "Shit," she mumbled. Raising her voice, she called, "Guys! I found her! She's in here on the floor under the sin—"

Tatiana cried out in animal terror and started sliding sideways along the wall, panting.

The Nephyr grunted and felt to one knee. "What the hell?" she muttered. "My *head*."

Four more Nephyrs piled into the room, and immediately their glittering faces turned to find Tatiana whimpering against the wall. One of them sneered and started toward her. "Looks like the docs had a bit of fun with her," he laughed, bending down to reach for her. *Man, this is going to be so much fun.*

"P-please," Tatiana whimpered. She cringed away from him, the whine coming in quick pants, now.

The Nephyr woman on her knees frowned. *It's her. It's the little shit doing it.* "Don't touch her!" the woman shouted, reaching for something on her belt.

Ignoring his comrade, the Nephyr man wrapped his glass-hard fingers around her throat and smiled at her. "Why? I'm just gonna have a little fun of my own." Tatiana felt something flip inside of her, like an explosion of terror, shoved outward. Instantly, the Nephyr's eyes went wide and he crumpled. The others, too, dropped. The woman on the floor, who was further away, had just enough time to pull her gun from its holster before she, too, slumped forward, the pistol still clutched in a fist.

Seeing the bodies, feeling the man's rock-hard fingers slide slowly from her throat and down her chest as his body slumped to the floor in front of her, Tatiana felt another burst of terror slide out of her, bigger this time, along with a puddle of urine. Out in the adjoining room, she heard other bodies drop.

Cringing, Tatiana tugged her knees back to her chest and stayed there, staring at the corpses. None of them moved. The woman's crotch grew wet with urine. The room started to stink of feces.

Several minutes passed before one of the Gryphons stepped into the room, his footsteps absolutely silent as his big, dark body entered the blindingly lit space. He was carrying a gun out and ready. He surveyed the corpses, then looked down at Tatiana. Tatiana glanced up at him and cringed, her blood thundering like bile in her ears.

"Detainee Eyre, you are hereby placed under arrest for the deaths of nine Nephyrs, pending further investigation." The robot started toward her, and Tatiana let out another low moan and tried blindly to slip back down the wall, away from him. The Gryphon's movements started to grow jerky as he approached, then came to a complete standstill beside her, half-crouched, frozen in place like a wax statue.

Tatiana let out another babble of terror and crawled across the room, away from him.

*"Now remember. Be a good girl. Kill enough coalers for me and maybe I'll let you live after it's over."* Her tiny face had twisted into a violent smile. *"Then again, if you touch him again, maybe I'll just have to re-visit my little lab rat and make some adjustments. It's got a tracking device in it. I will know exactly where you are, so don't think you can hide from me, you retarded little monkey."*

Tatiana's whine built into a chest-deep moan as she crawled on her hands and knees through the doctor's entry and into the sterile white service hallway. A nurse was collapsed on the floor a few meters down the hall, a clipboard in her hand.

Seeing the body, Tatiana whimpered and struggled to her feet. She had to hold herself on the wall, her knees going weak, her vision blurry.

*"Now, you'll probably be dizzy from blood loss for a couple days, so drink plenty of orange juice and take your vitamins. Oh, and there's a*

*soldier prepped in Hangar 3, if you can make it that far. Don't worry about getting gel in the wound. I sealed it up nice and good. Reinforced it with titanium bands and screws, but then again, you already saw all that, after I peeled away your face. Why bring up bad memories?"*

Tatiana stumbled forward, the whine once again building in her throat. Two blue-coated lab technicians stepped from around a corridor and hesitated. *Dear Lord, what is that?*

"Are you looking for someone?" the closest asked gently.

"Please help me," Tatiana whispered. "Please."

They glanced at each other. *She's wearing a prisoner jumpsuit.* "Are you here for surgery?" one of them demanded, his tone becoming more aggressive.

*Surgery* . . . Tatiana felt her heartbeat skip in a sudden, uncontrollable surge of panic. Both of the technicians groaned and crumpled forward, clutching their heads. One of them, the taller one, whimpered on her knees. *Hurts, oh God it hurts so—* The technician folded forward and her body started to convulse on the floor.

Tatiana let out a terrified cry and bolted down the corridor, teetering as she stumbled, trying to keep her balance.

*"Now the neat part about this thing is that it runs on solar energy. I could've made it nuclear, but that would've taken away half the fun. So every few days, you've gotta go outside and let it recharge. If you look close, there's ten little green lights around the edge. Each light represents ten percent battery. If a light turns red, you've got ninety percent. If two go red, you've got eighty, and so on. If you don't recharge it, at ten percent charge it'll trigger the* nuclear-powered motor and we'll have scrambled operator brain, won't we, Dobie?"

Tatiana stumbled onward, ignoring the startled cries of doctors and technicians as she bolted past them.

*That's her. The escaped operator.*

"Stop!"

Tatiana let out an animal wail and bolted faster.

*"Now, I could've just put something simple in there, like an explosive, but that shows a distinct lack of creativity. Hell, a* robot *could think of something like that. This, now, this is a thing of beauty. A work of art. You hear that, cupcake? You're my latest work of art."*

"I said *stop!*" Booted feet ran up behind her and something grabbed her by the back of the jumpsuit. Someone strong yanked her around, and suddenly, Tatiana was looking up into the masked face of a surgeon.

Tatiana screamed and flailed and kicked, shoving him away from her even as his eyes went wide and his grip weakened. He slid to his knees, groaning. Tatiana kicked him in the mask and ran.

Babbling incoherently, Tatiana ducked through another door and drew it shut behind her, gasping in the darkness, trying to think. She had to get away. She had to escape.

All she could think, however, was that she had motorized blades lodged in her brain, waiting on the press of a button. Whimpering, she slid back down the wall and dragged her knees back to her chest. "Please," Tatiana whispered. "God, please . . . "

*"Oh, and don't try to EMP it. Just . . . don't. I will spare you the details of exactly what will happen because my time is precious and I'm starting to get bored, but let it suffice to say if you do, it involves your brain on the wall."*

With a moan, Tatiana scrunched further in on herself, her chest shuddering in a sob.

*"Now, you'll have to be fast. Gotta get back to your soldier before they figure out what happened. If you're too slow, they'll just catch you and put you back on this nice table, here, and do it all over again. You wouldn't want that, would you, cupcake?"*

Shaking, Tatiana stared into the darkness, rocking back and forth, trying to ignore the pounding in her head. *God help me,* she whimpered to herself. *Please . . .*

She had only the warning of the slow click of the surgery doorknob turning before someone opened the door and stepped into the darkened room with her. Her breath caught and she choked on a scream. Tatiana heard the door close, but the light never came on.

For long moments, there was a deep, profound silence in which she was afraid to breathe. Tears burned her cheeks, and her heart tore ragged streaks through her chest. Then, with the calm, precise voice she had come to dread, the kid's robot said, "I did not fully understand what she was planning to do until after she'd already begun, and I realize what happened to you was partially inspired by my own actions. I feel the need to apologize and make amends."

From across the room, the robot flipped the light on, and Tatiana whimpered and cringed away from him. He lifted a small, oval device that Tatiana had last seen in the little girl's hand. "This is the only control to the device in your head."

Tatiana let out a wail of terror, seeing it.

The robot then pinched it between his fingers, crushing the circuitry, pulverizing the plastic into tiny pieces. He dropped the pieces on the floor between them. "You'll still need to keep it charged to stay alive," he added, his face twisting in a grimace, "but she does not 'own' you." Then, without another word, the robot turned and disappeared into the surgery, flipping the light off behind him.

# CHAPTER 44

# Incentive

Really, Jeanne," Joel said, as his ship sped towards the Tear, "you can put the shotgun away now. I'm finding it hard to concentrate with a gun aimed at my spine."

Jeanne kept the weapon slung across her lap at him, glaring at him from the tiny, fold-in passenger seat that she'd pulled out of the wall. She had also buckled in. Damn.

"I'm thinking you need the reminder, Joel," Jeanne said.

"C'mon, Jeanne," Joel protested, for the eightieth time. "I just wanted to see if she was still alive. That's all."

Jeanne gave him a long, flat look. "I don't care *who* you're trying to save," she said. "You do something like that again and you're a dead man."

Joel believed her. Despite Jeanne's wishes—and her screaming at him and shoving her gun in his face, once she'd figured out what he was doing—Joel had taken them to the Snake looking for Magali. All they'd found was the tiny, twisted corpse of a child before Jeanne had put a round through the tinselly red teddy bear to get his attention.

So he'd switched off the inertial dampeners and done a little fancy flying. So what? It wasn't like he'd tried to *kill* her or anything. He'd just wanted a few more minutes to look for Magali before he had to scurry off to the Tear like a good errand boy. "We're at eighty thousand feet and you don't know how to fly this thing. Really, Jeanne. What are you gonna do?" Joel demanded. "Shoot me?"

She gave him that unnervingly wicked smile she was so good at.

Joel groaned. *Horrible* luck with women . . .

"You know," he said, adjusting the fuel supply, "this is not really the right way to get a guy like me to cooperate." He checked his gauges, then, satisfied he'd found the right mixture, set the ship into cruise.

"Oh?" she asked, sounding only half interested.

"Yeah," Joel said. "I mean, a guy like me, I don't got much to fight for, right? I got a ship, but that's it. No family, no kiddos, no pets . . . I got girls fawning over me, but they don't want anything more than one-night stands. Maybe a weekend, if we're both feeling frisky. Nobody likes a smuggler. Not really. They're cheesy. Lame."

"Sounds about right," Jeanne said.

"I had lots of goals in life," Joel said, "before Geo got his hooks in me. Wanted to find a girl, start a family . . . All of it kinda dissolved in the grind. I just became another cog in the system. Just one of the links in the chain of black-market Yolk."

"Sounds to me," Jeanne said, "that you don't have much to live for, Runaway. Would ending your miserable existence for you now spare you the need to commiserate?"

"*Pirates*, on the other hand," Joel went on, "now *they* got flair. Flash. Finesse." He glanced behind him at her necklace and made a face. "Well, flash."

"Do you *want* me to kill you, Joel?"

"Not especially," Joel said. He checked a regulator, then sighed. "I mean, imagine it. Forty-five years old, probably had upwards of six, seven hundred women, and I still don't have a kid. And I've *checked.*"

"Sounds like divine mercy," Jeanne said.

"I mean, you had fun, right?" Joel continued. "Hell, sounded to me like you had a blast."

"Fly the ship, Joel."

"I do this thing," Joel said, "I want a date."

Utter silence descended in the back of the cockpit. Joel adjusted throttle, then turned to look.

Jeanne was glaring at him with a deadly scowl. "Not in your lonely, pathetic dreams."

"C'mon, Jeanne, it would be fun," Joel said. "When was the last time someone romanced you properly? You know, wine and roses? A good massage? Dancing? I'd wager it was a helluva long time, considering the pretty little mementos you've got warning off everyone with half a brain."

"What does that make you?" Jeanne growled. "Brain*less?* I said no date."

"Babe," Joel laughed, "I've sampled the wares. I know what they're missing." He could *feel* her scowling at him as he continued, "So that's my proposition. I win your little dogfight for you, I get a date."

"I've got a shotgun aimed at your kidneys. You *don't* win the dogfight, I pull the trigger. That is your date."

"*Incentive,* Jeanne," Joel reminded her. "You gotta give a guy like me *incentive.*"

"Blow it out your ass, Joel."

"Fine, dinner," Joel compromised. "Someplace fancy, with a dance floor. An entire night with you."

"Do you *want* to get shot? Oh my God, I think you want to get shot."

"You'll have to ditch the necklace for the date," Joel added thoughtfully. "Don't want to startle the maître d'. And we'll get you in something fancy. Red. I get to pick."

"You are this close, Joel."

"A dress, I think," Joel said. He glanced over his shoulder. "You ever worn a dress, Jeanne? You know, strut your stuff? You'd blow people away."

"I'll tell you who I'm about to blow away, Joel. And it isn't the Easter Bunny."

"Why Jeanne," Joel said, grinning, "I do believe you're blushing. You *like* that idea, don't you?"

Jeanne's face purpled and she found something to inspect on the wall beside her.

"So," Joel said. "Dinner, dancing, a dress."

For several minutes, the cockpit was silent. "I have a condition," Jeanne said. It was a gruff mutter.

"Oh?" Joel said, glancing at her.

"We go in my ride," she said. "And you pay."

Joel felt himself grin. "I think we can manage that. Should I schedule you for six? Six-thirty?"

"You still gotta win the dogfight," she muttered.

"*Babe*," Joel laughed, patting the console. "*Please.* This is *me* we're talking about, here. Runaway Joel. The guy who spent two decades running the entire Coalition Space Force in circles. I'm gonna make whoever that ham-fisted idiot was that stole my baby back in Deaddrunk look like the incompetent moron he was."

"I'll believe it when I see it." But she set the shotgun aside.

Joel grinned, feeling a flutter of excitement. Jeanne had always been . . . interesting. He hadn't actually thought he'd get a dress out of the deal. Hell, it was a little shocking she'd given in on the dinner and dancing. He'd expected more of an argument, or at least a counterproposal involving a twelve-gauge catheter.

"We're coming up on the Tear," Jeanne growled. "Here's your chance to earn that dress."

Feeling quite happy that he hadn't lost his charm, Joel turned just in time to see the hornet's nest popping up on radar. He blinked and leaned into the screen, counting the little black dots. "Holy *shit*, Jeanne!" he cried, pointing. "There's *hundreds* of them."

She gave him a sly little grin and shrugged.

No wonder she had capitulated so easily. She didn't intend for the two of them to make it out of this alive.

"What the *hell*, Jeanne?" Joel cried, as a dozen Bouncers veered upwards from their patrol, headed right at them. "What's going on down there?!"

"Miles and Patty've got Wideman," Jeanne said. "Somehow, the Coalition found out about him. They're throwing everything they've got at finding him. We've been throwing all *we've* got at keeping them off the ground."

Joel swept to the side, avoiding the Bouncers and coming in a wide, sweeping turn to give himself more time to assess the situation. "Jeanne," he said carefully, "that's not a dogfight. That's a *war zone*."

"You *did* say a dress," she said, giving him a smug look.

Joel glared at the pirate over his shoulder a long moment, then heaved a huge sigh and glanced back at the screen. He studied the scene a moment, watching the hundreds of ships in their explosive merry-go-round, then shook his head. "Well," he said, taking a deep breath, "God hates a coward." He nudged the joystick downward and ducked *Honor* into the fray.

"You mind running the com for me, Jeanne?" Joel said, sweeping into the mess. He caught a soldier from behind, setting it ablaze as he passed. He hit the full-screen, giving him a bug's-eye view of the surrounding battle. Making a mental lock on a Bouncer in his general trajectory, he started pushing on the throttle to catch up. Verdant alien jungle slid underneath them at Mach 6. Joel hit the Bouncer going about twice the speed of his quarry, then spun upwards and out, rocking the world in a spin of glory that had them at a hundred thousand feet in the span of a couple of heartbeats. Behind him, there was nothing fast enough to keep up. Joel brought *Honor* to the apogee of its arc just as it was starting to break free of gravity, then hammered the controls forward and went spinning downward with all the grace of a stooping hawk.

He came in from above, peppering two soldiers that were chasing a colonial scout ship, then yanked back the stick with a foot or two to spare, grazing the jungle with his backblast.

"You got us patched in yet, Jeanne?" Joel called over his shoulder, flipping the ship onto its side and swinging wide, chasing after a couple of Bouncers following a colonial ship. He didn't reach them before they hit their quarry, and Joel had to twist and pull up and over the dying ship as it plummeted to the alien forest. As soon as he was clear, he dropped back into an arc to catch up with the Bouncers. The Bouncers split up, one going east, the other going up. Joel followed the latter, hitting enough Gs to make the dampeners sputter. He nailed it, then spun through the rubble as it exploded around him.

"Yee*haw!*" Joel shouted at the console, spinning back down for another go. "I forgot how much *fun* this was!" When he got no response, he glanced behind him.

Clinging to the passenger seat, Jeanne was looking pale.

Joel frowned and tapped the com unit. "Patch us *in,* Jeanne," he said. "I'd like to hear what our good friends are saying out there." He frowned at her. "You *do* know their bands, don't you?"

"You almost hit the ground," Jeanne said. "At Mach 6."

"Meh," Joel said, waving disinterestedly. "It would've been quick."

Jeanne slid a shaking hand over to the communications console and started setting the bands. Almost immediately, he heard *"—that freakin' TAG!"*

*"It's back?! Where the* hell *does this guy keep coming from?!"*

Joel grinned. "Music to my ears, Jeanne. Turn it up. Time for a pre-dinner mood piece."

"They've been at this for three days already. There's no way we're gonna be done in time for dinner."

"Watch me," Joel said.

She gave him a green grimace, but spun up the volume dial.

"Louder!" Joel shouted, over the booming of his stereo system.

"Are you *nuts*?!" Jeanne shouted back. But she twisted the dial.

Listening to the chaos around him reverberating like an old friend in his lungs, Joel once more relaxed into that trance of the sky. "All right, you pups," he said, grinning, "time to take you back to flight school . . . "

# CHAPTER 45

# Milar's Experiment

PATRICK WATCHED THE SOLDIER HURTLE UP THE TEAR, SHAKING the trees behind it as it broke the sound barrier. Behind it, four more soldiers were right on its tail, weaving in and around boulders at speeds that perplexed the human eye.

"Got five more incoming," Patrick said over his shoulder.

"I see 'em," Milar said. He grabbed the radio. "You see 'em, guys?"

A moment later, Jeanne replied. *"Got 'em. Joel's taking us in now."*

But Patrick was frowning at the way the soldiers were weaving around the debris of the Tear. It was almost as if they were *chasing* each other. "Hold up a sec," he said, lowering the scope. Sure enough, the lead soldier spun suddenly, kicked off the wall of the cliff, and used its sudden change in course to fire at the closest vessel trailing it. The second soldier exploded in a blinding white-hot ball of flame and went careening into the Tear in pieces. The remaining three began returning fire, but the first was already spinning up and away, heading skyward.

"What the hell?" Patrick said. "You see that, Miles?"

Milar was frowning at the soldiers as they danced around each other. Joel swept in from the side, and suddenly the jungle on the opposite bank of the Tear was alive with explosive rounds. The third soldier veered off, then careened into the jungle and embedded itself into the cliff.

The lead soldier ducked, swept through the jungle, following the same path its brother had just carved with its body, and, as the other two ships were trying to comprehend that, wove out of the canopy, around, and put a grouping of holes through a third soldier's engines. It sputtered and dropped out of the sky, though the operator slowed its forward momentum with enough leg hydraulics to keep it from plowing into the cliff.

Patrick turned just in time to see a huge, stupid grin on his brother's face. "It's her."

"*Her*, her?" Patrick demanded, looking back. It was hard to keep track of the soldiers, with the speed at which they were moving. "How the hell did she get a soldier?"

But Milar was on the radio again. "Tell him to hold off, Jeanne. I think that's Captain Eyre."

"*Bullshit,*" Jeanne retorted, "*I saw them take her away in handcuf—*"

Above them, the fourth soldier went up in a blinding gout of flame. It swept downward in a billowing pillar of debris and smoke, rocking the Tear as it hit the ground and exploded. The survivor immediately spun into the mess above them, hitting a Bouncer cockpit with its balled-up fist as it went by. Then Patrick lost it in the sun, and he wasn't sure which it was again until another soldier exploded. And another. Between the soldier and the TAG, within minutes, the sky above them was clear.

"*Milar?*" the croak across the radio sounded barely alive. "*Give me your coordinates.*"

Patrick frowned. "That didn't sound like—"

But Milar was already babbling their location into the radio. "Come on, sweetie. We're right he—"

The soldier dropped out of the sky and hit the ground with enough force to toss them both onto their backs.

"Milar, what the hell is wrong with you?!" Patrick screamed, getting back to his feet. "If any of them heard that—"

Then the belly of the soldier was opening and an operator rolled out onto its steaming hull, covered in transparent gel. Ripping the mask off of her face and sucking in deep, sobbing breaths as she yanked the nodes loose, the operator slipped off of the soldier and into the grasses. She immediately started to vomit into the brush.

Behind him, Wideman started screaming, "*Saw, saaaww!*" and began flailing and kicking at the blankets they had wrapped around him.

"Calm down, Paps!" Patrick cried, rushing to grab Wideman and stop him from thrashing his head into the propane campstove where they were boiling water. As Patrick ran to tackle the little old man, however, a sudden, painful buzz in his head almost threw him to his knees. "Shit, Shrieker!" he cried, glancing around them, looking for the telltale neon flesh of an alien blob. All he saw, however, was the naked, dripping body of an operator, head down, retching into the brush. He frowned. Had they made camp on a Shrieker mound? Had the operator's impact triggered a Shriek? "Shrieker, Miles," he repeated, as the pain increased. "We need to get the hell outta here. *Now.*"

"Milar," Captain Eyre whimpered, between heaves.

Milar, completely oblivious to Patrick or their father, got to his feet and ran to the operator, sliding the last bit on his knees. "Tat, sweetie, are you okay?" Beside Patrick, Wideman had devolved into full-throated screams. "*Boooones! Saw booooones!*"

"Shut *up*, Joe!" Patrick hissed, his heart hammering as he tried to figure out where the buzz was coming from. He slapped a hand over Wideman's bearded face and started searching for trails of Shrieker slime.

Still facing the ground, the operator started babbling mindless sobs about little girls and robots and surgery. As if a switch had flipped, the agony in Patrick's head increased tenfold. He groaned and backed instinctively away, dragging Wideman with him, cradling his temple.

Then the woman looked up at him and Patrick saw the circular metal bulb protruding from her forehead, the blinking little green lights ringing the side. The pain began to become a numbing roar in his head, and it was all he could do to stay upright. In his arms, Wideman started screaming himself hoarse.

*It's her,* Patrick thought, stunned. *Oh shit, it's* her.

On the ground, the girl was crawling forward, whimpering, clutching at the air between her and his brother, a weird whine forming in her throat.

"Milar," Patrick called, "you need to get away from her. Right now." He kept backing away, dragging his father, until the buzz lessened in his head.

Patrick watched his brother freeze a moment, seeing the strange new circular node in the woman's head. His whole body went stiff, and Patrick saw him grimace. For a moment, Patrick thought his brother would do the smart thing and back away.

"Please help me," the operator whimpered, curling in on herself. "Please don't leave me. Please."

It was as if his brother melted. One moment, Milar was stiffly getting back to his feet, the next he was reaching for her, softly murmuring, "Nobody's gonna leave you, sweetie. Nobody." Patrick had never seen his brother act as gently as he did when he reached down and plucked the slime-covered operator from the sticky alien grasses and pulled her into his arms.

The operator responded by shuddering and clenching her fists in his shirt as she started to sob. The wave of relief that followed knocked Patrick to his knees. . . . *relief?* What the hell? He glanced down at Wideman, who had passed out, drooling on his shirt. He dragged his father several more feet, further easing the nagging static in his head.

Hunched over the operator, Milar glanced at Patrick, then began stroking the woman's sticky scalp. "It's okay, love. Tell me what happened."

"Little girl. Robot. Table," she sobbed into Milar's chest. "Strapped down, couldn't move. Blades in *braaaiin.*"

Even at this distance, Patrick felt the nasty buzz increasing again in his head, and, holding the girl, Milar grimaced in obvious pain. "Calm down, sweetie. Calm down. You're safe now. Nobody's gonna mess with you again, got it? Pat and I got your back, and we're both carrying really big guns."

Patrick *felt* her relief as the operator shuddered and buried her face in his brother's chest. She cried for several minutes, babbling her gratitude, until she suddenly just stopped, and the mental fuzz went silent. Patrick breathed a sigh of relief, figuring she'd somehow killed herself.

"She fell asleep," Milar said over his shoulder, careful to move only his head so as not to jostle his charge. "Poor little thing's had a really rough day. Any idea what the hell that was all about, Pat?"

Patrick was still fighting the headache from being too close to her. "They put something in her head, obviously. We need to get rid of her, Miles."

The sudden snarl on his brother's face was enough to make Patrick back up a pace. "You shut your goddamn mouth and help me figure out what's wrong with her, Patty, or I swear to God you're taking the next flight to hell."

"She feels like a *Shrieker*, Miles! Look what she did to Dad! It could be a *bomb*, for all we know. Why would they *operate* on her and then let her *go* unless it was to *kill* us, Miles?"

Milar gave him an utterly dark look. "Then it's a bomb and we're all dead. I told her I wouldn't leave her. Get me a blanket."

*You stupid bastard*, Patrick thought, in shock. It was obvious to him that whatever this was, it was some sort of trap. His prodigy brother, being twice as smart as him, should have seen it as well. Yet he continued to brush the girl's bald head and coo to her in gentle baby talk. For a long moment, Patrick stood there watching in disbelief.

Milar turned to glare at him again and made an impatient gesture toward their gear. Realizing Milar was serious, he almost left his idiot brother to his own grave. Then, reluctantly, Patrick went to their supplies and pulled a blanket from the pack. Instead of walking the last ten steps into the area of emanation, however, he tossed the blanket at his brother's lap.

"Chickenshit," Milar muttered, but he grabbed the blanket and tugged it around the operator's unconscious form. She whimpered in her sleep and Milar cast him another glare. "It's all right, sweetie. Nobody can hurt you anymore."

On the radio, Jeanne said, *"You boys okay down there? We saw that operator drop onto your position . . . You need backup?"*

Patrick made a wide circle to the radio and said, "Yeah, Jeanne, we're fine. I think. It's Captain Eyre. She finally got that node we kept seeing."

There was a long silence before Jeanne said, *"They let her go?"*

"Uh," Patrick said. "Maybe? Not quite sure on the details yet, Jeanne."

*"Why would they let her go, Patrick? Good behavior?"*

"Jeanne," Patrick said uncomfortably, "I'm not sure—"

*"What's it do?"* she interrupted. *"How do you know it's not a bomb?"* Patrick gave the tiny woman huddled in his brother's arms a long look. "We don't," he said. "But I'm sure we'll figure it out."

*"I'm coming down there,"* Jeanne said. *"Tell your idiot brother that I'll deal with this."*

"And you tell her," Milar said, much too softly, "if I see Jeanne within a mile of here before I ask for her presence, I'm going to put a bolt through her brain and start a necklace of my own." He had lowered his chin to the operator's bald head, and his eyes were like cold, hard topaz as he scowled at Patrick.

"Uh," Patrick said, "you need to stay in the air, Jeanne."

*"Why's that?"* the pirate demanded. *"His precious little cyborg needs to disappear, and if he's too much of a chickenshit to do it, I'll pull the trigger for him. What are friends for?"*

"He says he's gonna kill you if he sees you," Patrick said, meeting his brother's psychotic stare, "and I believe him."

There was a long silence. Then, *"Joel says he's tired of flying and he wants to go have dinner. I'm leaving you two to your own graves. Might wanna cover up that soldier, before they come looking for it."*

Patrick swallowed, watching his brother, feeling the aftereffects of the operator's panic still throbbing like a hot fuzz in his head. Still resting his chin on the operator's head, Milar closed his eyes and started to hum a lullaby that their mother had sung to them before she died.

Patrick realized, in that moment, that Milar wasn't going to listen to reason. Nothing that he, Jeanne, or anyone else was going to say was going to keep Miles from pulling the gun off his hip and pulling the trigger if anyone tried to separate him from the time bomb in his arms. Patrick had known that the Nephyrs had changed his brother, but this was the first time he wondered if they'd actually driven him over the edge. "Hey, Jeanne?"

*"What, you retarded dumbass prick?"*

"I think it might be best for everyone if Milar and Captain Eyre stayed away from civilization for a few days. Until . . . *they* . . . get some things figured out."

*"What the hell does that mean?"*

Patrick took a deep breath, then let it out between his teeth, fighting the instinct to argue with his brother's lunacy. "Come get me and Dad. We'll be out on the ridge. Milar's got this under control." To his brother, he demanded, "Don't you, Miles?"

Without even opening his eyes, his brother made a rude gesture off in the direction of the ridge.

*"We'll be there in two minutes. Run."*

◄◄ ◆ ►►

The high buzz of a circular saw shrieked in her ears as it descended for her brow . . . Tatiana screamed and opened her eyes, panting.

*Jeez that hurts. Wonder if she's gonna give me the Wide.* "Easy," a big voice rumbled against the top of her head. "I'm here. Calm down before you turn me into a vegetable, sweetie."

*Milar.* Tatiana shuddered and clenched the colonist's big leather jacket in white-knuckled fists. For a long moment, she just huddled there, listening to him breathe, taking strength in having him around her. Then, cautiously, he moved above her, pulling away gently. Dropping his head to meet hers, he touched her chin with a big, callused finger and lifted it. "You okay?" he asked, his honey-brown eyes flickering to the thing in her forehead.

Tatiana whimpered and looked away.

Milar's face darkened. *I'll kill them all, I swear to God.* "Who did that to you? Nephyrs?"

Tatiana shook her head, feeling tears stinging her eyes. "Little girl," she whispered.

"A little . . . girl." Milar seemed confused. *She must've been drugged.* "You sure?"

She nodded.

Delicately, he offered, "You sure you weren't drugged, princess?"

"Robot. Anna."

*Anna.* Every muscle in Milar's body went stiff around her, like rigid steel. "Brown eyes? Short black hair?"

Just thinking about the little girl's face made Tatiana's next breath come out in a long, terrified whimper.

He cursed. "Don't worry, sweetie. Whatever it is, we'll get it out."

"No!" Tatiana screamed, lunging away from him and scrabbling backwards across the alien plant life.

Immediately, Milar groaned and put a hand to his temple. *Wideman was full of shit. She's gonna kill me.* Wincing, he said, "Okay! Calm down. Please calm down. We'll leave it. Okay? We'll leave it."

But Tatiana was shaking all over, dragging her knees back to her chest. "What's happening to me?" she whimpered.

Milar met her gaze under the hand on his temple and she saw him scared for the first time since she'd met him. "I don't know. But we're gonna find out, okay?"

"You know Anna?" Tatiana whimpered. "What is she? A robot? She told me to stay away from you."

Milar's face darkened to a thunderhead. "She did?" *That little bitch. I'll kill her.*

Tatiana nodded through tears. "She said you were hers. Told me not to touch you or she'd make it worse. Turn on the blades in my brain." She felt herself start to hyperventilate again, remembering.

His eyes flickered to the thing jutting from her forehead. "That's got blades—" he winced and held his head again. "Okay, sweetie, no offense, but let's talk about something nice again. Butterflies and rainbows and nonsensical bullshit, okay?"

Remembering the doctors and Nephyrs and security personnel that had collapsed around her, Tatiana squeezed her eyes shut and nodded.

Milar inched closer to her and, almost timidly, pulled her back into his warm embrace. "Okay," he said against her skull, "what do you want to talk about? Something happy, right?"

Her forehead started throbbing where his throat touched it, and Tatiana once again saw the little girl standing over her, lecturing her on the stunted brains of lab rats as she cut at her forehead with a scalpel.

"How about movies, you watch movies?"

Tatiana shook her head and once again felt the whine building in her chest.

*She's gonna fry me like a toaster.* For a long moment, Milar said nothing. Then, "The first time I saw you, I was three. We had kids. Nice house. Land. Good life. Happy. No war."

Tatiana swallowed, dragged from the memories of surgery out of sheer curiosity.

"When I was five, I saw the two of us playing chess on the floor of a ship. I remember feeling bad because you were bleeding and I hadn't offered you any bandages, so I gave you my shirt. Didn't even realize where I'd seen that one before until my shirt was halfway off and you were staring at my dragons."

Tatiana continued to listen, the sound of his voice forcing away the whine of the bone saw.

"Saw your escape before, too, except I remembered it as I was tucking your cast under the blanket. Gave me the holy willies when I did, let me tell you. Thought I'd keep you from rabbiting by leaving you naked and reading a book on the sofa beside you. Much to my surprise, you did it anyway. Tart."

Tatiana felt herself give a weak smile into the cotton folds of his shirt. "Ogre."

She felt Milar's arms tighten around her. *Oh thank God. Thank God, thank God . . .* His big body started to shudder. After a few minutes, she heard him sniffle.

"Don't you know that snot and open wounds don't mix?" Tatiana whispered, after a moment.

He sniffed and lifted an arm to wipe his face. "Nasty stuff, snot."

"All germy and gross," Tatiana agreed.

"Really gross."

"So Wideman's been having people draw me for a long time, then?"

*She's gonna find out sooner or later. Grow a spine, you coward.* "My dad didn't carve you until I was twelve."

Tatiana frowned.

"Everybody says I'm crazy and they think Patty's the only one," Milar whispered, his hot breath against her skull, "but I've been dreaming about you a really long time, Tat. The things I saw . . . " He kissed the top of her head. "Worth waiting for, you know?"

*He's telling me he's . . . psychic?*

"Runs in the family, I think," Milar said. "First Dad, then me and Pat. I didn't get the whole shebang, though. Just dreams."

Tatiana was so stunned she couldn't speak.

*She's gonna freak out. She's gonna freak out and kill us both.* "Now before you—"

"I'm not going to freak out," Tatiana said, leaning back to look up at him. "Did you just say you *dreamed* about me?"

Milar licked his lips as he met her stare. "Uh." Then, quickly, he babbled, "I don't know where they came from, or why, but I know we're supposed to have kids together."

For a long moment, Tatiana could only stare at him. After waiting for him to recant his words—which he didn't—she finally croaked, "That's the worst come-on line I've ever heard."

Milar laughed, his amber eyes nervous. "Uh . . . yeah. Sorry." *She doesn't believe me.* He looked away.

"I believe you," Tatiana said.

Milar jerked his head back with a frown. "You do?"

"I dreamed about you, too," Tatiana said.

Milar froze. "You *did?*"

"Yeah," Tatiana said, feeling a tentative grin stretching her lips. "When I was in solitary, after they read me the charges. I had to sleep a lot, and it got . . . interesting. I think I popped your virgin cherry, oh, twenty or thirty times."

He blinked at her a startled moment, then slowly grinned back. "Squid."

"Brute." Then, cocking her head up at him, she tentatively offered, "You saw us with kids?"

Immediately, his eyes flickered to the thing in her head and fiercely, he said, "Sure as hell did."

"Then this isn't going to kill me."

"Not a chance."

Tatiana cleared her throat. "Well, that's . . . comforting. You dream about anything else?"

Milar's eyes flickered back to her and he gave a nervous chuckle. *Just don't tell her about the crash.*

"What crash?" Tatiana demanded.

Milar froze. "Did you just . . . " His eyes narrowed and he glanced at the thing in her forehead, then back at her face. He stuck a finger out and poked her in the chest. "There somethin' you wanna tell me, squid?" He leaned closer, until they were eye-to-eye, his voice low and dangerous. "Like something *important?*"

"What crash?" Tatiana insisted.

He narrowed his eyes at her. "You're on a need-to-know basis."

"Did I die?"

"No."

"So I *do* crash."

"Squid," he warned.

"Tell me!" she cried, slapping his chest.

"*No*," he snarled with startling vehemence. He grabbed her wrist and held it in a vice, dragging her face to meet his. "Some things are better left unsaid."

After a minute or two of Tatiana glowering up at him, his eyes flickered nervously to the thing in her forehead. "All right. Tell me the truth, now. How much are you picking up?"

"All of it," Tatiana said immediately.

His nervous look fell away and Milar grinned. "Oh, really."

"Yeah." She stuck out her tongue. "Collie."

*She's clueless.* "So why aren't you blushing? Hmm?"

Struck by the triumph in his face, Tatiana said, "Uh. What?"

"'Cause I was just reminding myself what a naked coaler looks like under all that goo, and I'm pretty sure I'm hard as a rock."

Tatiana felt her face heat. "Oh."

His grin became predatory and he lowered his voice to a husky rumble. "So what was that you were saying about popping my cherry, coaler?"

Tatiana felt a little thrill under his intense stare. She swallowed, hard. "Uh, we are sitting in the smoking remnants of a massive aerial battle that may or may not be over—"

"I always got the idea that danger turned you on."

She gaped at him, feeling herself heat up in all the right places. "I was just molested by a five-year-old with a bone saw," Tatiana babbled. "'Not in the mood' doesn't *begin* to describe—"

Milar muffled the rest of her retort with a kiss.

When he let her back up for air, Tatiana gasped and sputtered something about malfunctioning robots. With a rumbling growl,

Milar pushed her backwards onto the blanket, pressing her into the ground and nibbling on her ear. "Scaalllllpels," Tatiana moaned, melting into him.

*Oh my God, that stuff tastes disgusting.* Above her, Milar hawked and spat into the alien grass.

Tatiana narrowed her eyes and unflexed her body, dropping her butt back to the blanket. "Did you have to do that?"

"Uh," Milar said, reddening instantly. "I got a bug in my mouth."

Immediately, Tatiana felt a wave of inner evil. "Oh? That's it? Come on, then, gogogogo!" She grabbed his head and wrenched it back to her ear. "Right there, baby. Mmmm, oh yeah."

Milar didn't nibble on her ear. In fact, he lifted his head and gave her a narrow look. "Squid."

"You know, it really turns me on to get licked. Yeah, I love that."

He narrowed his golden-brown eyes at her. "Licked, huh?"

"Yeah," Tatiana said. "Licked all over. You can start with my feet." She pointed, for his clarification.

Milar didn't look. He leaned down, very close, until their noses were touching. *So how much can you hear, coaler?* His amber eyes scanned hers with interest.

"Uuhhh," Tatiana swallowed. "Wow. That was weird."

*Heard that, then?*

"Umm. Yes?" she squeaked.

He lowered his weight on top of her and put his elbows to either side of her face, studying her. *So can you send back? Or just receive?*

"Uhhh," Tatiana giggled nervously. "I'd actually rather not experiment on the oaf who weighs like six times as much as me and is pinning me to the dirt. I killed some people, I think, and you're *heavy*."

*I can stay here all day, coaler.*

She narrowed her eyes at him. Then, thinking as hard as she could, she thought, *You knucker.*

Milar winced and said, "Point taken."

She raised a brow. "It worked, then?"

"I'd say," he grimaced. "A little harder and I think I'd be drooling." Then he slowly relaxed again and looked at her once more, his amber eyes glinting with mischief. *You know, this could get fun.*

Tatiana made a nervous laugh. "I told you I think I killed people, right?"

*We could totally screw with Patty's world.*

"Yeah, let's *not* tell anybody, okay?" Tatiana said.

*We'd be awesome at poker.*

"I don't play poker," Tatiana said. "They accuse me of cheating."

*Totally unstoppable at charades.*

"I'm already unstoppable at charades."

He gave her a long look, grinning. *Twenty or thirty times, huh?*

Tatiana felt her face heat. "Uuhhhm. Something like that."

*Care to demonstrate?*

Oh, did she *ever!* To get this kind of hunk into bed was, like, totally beyond any of her expectations. Considering the billions of little black check marks she'd lodged under Too Cocky For Her Own Good, she had always been sure she was gonna end up with a warty, buck-toothed hillbilly with bad breath, just to get laid. But *this* . . . This was like, too good to be true. But she couldn't tell him that, huh-uh. It would pop his already-pressurized ego like a ten-ton hydrogen balloon. If he didn't simply catch fire and explode right on the spot, she'd never hear the end of it.

"Sorry," Tatiana said. "Like I was saying before, I was just assaulted by a demonic child—"

Milar began to grin at her evilly. "Hunk, huh?" he said.

Tatiana felt her mouth fall open, realizing that he must have heard part of her brainless, sex-starved inner monologue. "N-no," she blurted.

But his grin only grew more devious. "You know," Milar said, as she sputtered, "I could get used to that." He bent down and kissed her again. Against her ear, he breathed, "You have any idea how long I've been waiting for this, squid?"

" . . . this?" Tatiana managed, feeling her face heat. She could actually count the days since she'd been aching to get in his pants—hell, the hours. She'd been craving it ever since he'd stepped out of the alien jungle and his sexy beetle-green sunglasses had looked so cool in the firelight.

Milar lifted his head and gave her a thoughtful look. *Now's a good time to ask.* "Tell me something, coaler," he said, meeting her gaze. "And think about it long and hard before you answer. There's no going back on this one."

"I'll pop your cherry for you," Tatiana blurted. "I'll be gentle, I swear."

Milar grinned. "You've been gaping at me like a horny starlope ever since I stepped out of the woods by your fire, so I wasn't real concerned about that, to be honest."

Tatiana's mouth fell open and she felt her face catch fire. "I *never*—"

"The question was actually about us," Milar interrupted.

"Us?" Tatiana squeaked.

"Us." One of his deliciously big hands started idly roaming down her thigh. He gave her a long, pensive look. "*Is* there an 'us,' coaler?"

Oh yes. Yes, yes, yes, *yes*! "I dunno, I kinda have to think about that one," Tatiana said. "I've had a really crummy day and—"

But Milar's infernal smile was growing with lazy confidence. "A really crummy day, huh?"

"Hellacious," Tatiana babbled, unsettled by the confidence in his golden-hazel eyes. "I was slated for execution, pushed around by Nephyrs, manhandled by a robot, experimented on by a psychopathic child, shot at by soldiers from my own Pod . . . "

She trailed off when Milar just grinned at her.

Tatiana narrowed her eyes, bristling. "You heard me, didn't you, you knucker?"

His infernal grin grew wider. "Just say it."

"My mother told me it's best to play hard to get," Tatiana muttered stubbornly. She met his gaze. "Especially when you're falling head-over-heels for the sexiest hunk you've ever seen."

He raised a brow at her. "Sweetie," he said, "you're wasting time."

"Yes, there's an 'us,' you ape," she muttered. "Why else would I have rescued you from the Nephyrs?"

He continued to peer at her from behind a single raised brow.

"Well, I mean, you might've helped," she admitted. "A little."

He let out a low rumble, almost a growl, and sank down to meet her lips with his. Tatiana let out a moan as his big fingers found the back of her head, then forgot all about her crummy day.

# CHAPTER 46

# Mind Games

MAGALI WATCHED THE NEPHYR SORT GEAR ON THE OTHER SIDE of the hotel suite, the gun still in her lap. Seeing it was a Nephyr who was checking in, the hotel manager had put them in the biggest room they had, which gave Magali a full thirty-four feet to watch him from a distance. She hadn't said anything to him in four hours.

The big Nephyr moved like a predator, same as Steele. And, Magali noted, not like a pretty predator, either. A *deadly* one. An evil one. One that played with its food.

He still wore the long-sleeved black shirt, so all she saw of his glittering skin was his hands and head. Still, she found that even that much—seeing his skin catch the light in golden flickers—set her nerves on edge. *He's one of them,* she thought, watching the inhumanly strong fingers pick through tool bins and duffel bags. *This has got to be a trick.*

The Nephyr caught her watching him and gave her a shy grin.

*Anna could fake a shy grin,* Magali thought, not smiling back.

His grin faded into a look of concern, then he quickly smothered it and glanced away again. He brought out more tools from the ship's medical kit, then found other items from within his own personal supplies. He set out everything onto a small blanket, then rolled it up and came back over to her with a drill and what looked like a surgeon's soft-tissue spreader. Then he sat on the bed across from her chair, looking at her. He cleared his throat. "You, uh, haven't said much."

Magali glanced at the drill, then back at the Nephyr. His blue-green eyes looked nervous, she noted. Anna could fake that, too.

He cleared his throat again. "Uh, okay. Pretty soon, they're gonna start wondering why I went to Silver City, instead of back to Factory 14, if they haven't already. I kinda need you to do a little surgery, all right?"

When Magali didn't respond, he cleared his throat uncomfortably and his eyes flickered to the side before they returned to her face. "Okay," he said, picking up the supplies he had laid out. "I'll go lay the stuff out and come back for you." He started to stand.

Magali lifted the gun and pointed it at his face.

Seeing that, reluctantly, the Nephyr sat back down.

"How do I know," Magali said, watching him down the barrel, "that this isn't a trick?"

He gave an uneasy laugh. "I already gave you all the reasons I could think of."

"My little sister is a sociopath," Magali said.

His eyes flickered back to her with a slight frown. "That's . . . not good?"

"She could fake all this stuff you're doing right now," Magali said. "And she would, too, if it would make it more fun for her later."

The Nephyr looked nervously at the door. "Okay, I guess we can put it off a little longer." He set the roll of tools aside and slid down to the floor, his back against the mattress. "Let's talk about your sister."

"Her name is Anna," Magali said. "She got drafted for the Nephyrs."

He winced. "Okay, yeah, I can see that."

"She's really smart," Magali said, still holding the gun aimed at his face. "Smarter than me. And she's evil."

"Well," the Nephyr said, his face giving a wry twist, "she'll fit right in."

Magali narrowed her eyes. "And you're not?"

The Nephyr laughed. "Oh, well, I'd say there's probably a little darkness in me, considering. But no. Not evil."

"Prove it," Magali said.

The man on the floor grimaced. "All right." He sighed deeply. "Well, to be truthful, all I'd have to do to take that gun from you right now is turn my head so you can't get a good shot. I mean, the eyes and mouth are really the only vulnerable part of a Nephyr's body. Even the ears are sealed, and replaced with sensors."

"I saw that, back on the ship," Magali said. She didn't lower the gun.

"Soooo," the Nephyr said, "I could be a total dick and just walk over there and take it from you, but I'm not going to."

"Or I could shoot you in the eye like I did your friends," Magali said, "then take your stuff, sell it on the black market, and hire a ship to take me home."

The Nephyr let out an explosive sigh and dropped his head. After a few moments, he looked back up at her sideways. "You realize what I'm asking you to do, right?"

"You're asking me to let you get close enough to touch me."

He winced. "Uh . . . yeah."

"I don't want you to touch me."

He gave her a pained smile. "I know. But kinda necessary to get the thing out, ya know? Otherwise they'll just make a satellite linkup and zap me . . . " When she just continued to watch him with a flat expression, he held up both hands, glittering palms facing her. "I swear I won't move unless you tell me to. Hell, I'll lie on my stomach and keep my hands behind my head the whole time."

She just watched him.

"I'm running out of time," he said quietly.

"Get me an EMP wand and I'll think about it."

The Nephyr froze. "Uh." He swallowed, hard, and lowered his hands.

Flatly, Magali said, "You're not gonna get me the wand."

He glanced up at her, then away again, his face contorting in a grimace. He took a deep breath, then let it out between his teeth. After a long moment, he said, "Stay here a moment." He unfolded and got smoothly back to his feet, and after giving her a quick, considering look, turned and strode from the room, shutting the door gently behind him. His footsteps hadn't made a sound.

*Like a predator,* Magali thought, fighting a chill.

She considered following him out and getting lost in the slums of Silver City, but she was pretty sure a Nephyr could track via scent, and she wasn't about to leave that kind of loose end to come back and bite her later. Wideman was right. Something had changed. She realized she'd rather kill this man than let him live.

About an hour later, the Nephyr returned and stepped back into the room, again without his footsteps so much as scuffing the carpet. He shut the door behind him again, then extracted a steel tube from the cargo pocket of his pants and held it up, again with a gesture of peace. "Here. They keep one passcoded on the ship, in case we have a robot that gets too close to a Shriek." He came just close enough to put the tube on the floor near her feet, then backed off several paces.

Magali glanced down at the tube, then up at him. Reluctantly, she moved forward and took it off the floor. Uncapping the tube, she was stunned to find an EMP wand inside. Then her eyes narrowed. *A trick. Has to be a trick.* She pulled it out and extended it, then switched it on.

The Nephyr's eyes widened and he took a quick step back. Then, at her lifted eyebrow, he made a nervous chuckle and scratched at the back of his neck. "Uh, sorry. Just habit."

Magali got to her feet and, still keeping the gun between them, went over to the entertainment system. She switched it on, and it immediately showed a huge dogfight over what looked like the Tear. Then she hit it with the wand.

The system went dead.

Magali stared at it for several minutes, unable to believe it. Behind her, the Nephyr waited in an uneasy silence.

*Maybe he only gave it one charge,* she thought. *Maybe he knew I'd test it . . .* Anna would do something like that, just so she could gloat about how stupid Magali was later. Still keeping a wary eye on the Nephyr, she went over to the little r-player he'd unpacked with his belongings, switched it on, and hit it with the wand. The player went dead. She turned on his personal computer, then zapped that, too. Then his massage assistant. Then his personal alarm clock. For a long moment, Magali just stared down at the lifeless pieces of metal and polymer spread out on the bed, then she looked up at the Nephyr.

He gave her a weak grin. "Satisfied?"

Magali looked down at the wand, then back up at him. *Anna never would've given me a real wand,* she thought, stunned. *She likes to hold all the cards.*

The Nephyr cleared his throat. "Still need convincing, huh?" He let out a long breath, giving her a wary look. "Okay. Don't freak out." Then, very slowly, the Nephyr began to ease forward. Immediately, Magali's hand spasmed on the wand and she shoved it between them in warning.

"Easy!" the Nephyr cried, hesitating. Then, after watching her anxiously another moment, continued to ease forward until all Magali would've had to do was reach out and tap him on the chest, and he would've collapsed in a puddle of useless mechanics. Then he went still, less than an arm's distance away, waiting, watching her face and not the wand. In the heart-pounding silence that followed, Magali heard peddlers out on the street, hawking their wares, and the constant low buzz of the refrigeration unit.

"Believe me now?" the Nephyr asked softly, looking down at her.

Magali looked down at the tip of the wand, which was only an inch from his body, then up at him. She swallowed, considering. "You were taken from Six Bears?" she managed.

"South end of the Tear," he agreed.

"And your name is Jersey?"

"Yes."

"And you want out."

His smile was tortured. "Yeah."

Magali scanned his blue-green eyes for several moments, searching. Then, swallowing, she said, "Gimme the drill."

Jersey's face melted with relief, then he turned and plucked the tools from the bed. He carried them into the bathroom with him, dropped onto his knees, and, setting the roll of items beside him, stretched out on his stomach on the tiles. "In case there's blood to clean up," he said, as he put his hands behind his head and laced his fingers against his glittering scalp.

*In case there's blood* . . . Magali heard his skin clank like stone against the tile floor as he settled himself, and she suppressed a shudder. *That's a Nephyr,* she thought. *I'm sharing a hotel room with a Nephyr.*

. . . a Nephyr that had given her an EMP device and was waiting for her to cut his ties to the Coalition. Magali swallowed and shut off the wand. Reluctantly, she set it down on the bed beside the darkened r-player and went to join him.

She eased her way gingerly into the room with him and carefully lowered herself to the tiles beside the roll of tools. With trembling fingers, she found the drill.

"You're not gonna bring the wand?" he asked the floor.

She froze.

"Never mind!" he said quickly. "I'll keep my big mouth shut, okay? Just please keep going. Please. I don't have a lot of time left."

Magali hesitated another moment, the drill shivering in her hands. Then, very carefully, she set the drill tip against the glittering back of his neck and said, "You got a good bit on this thing?"

"Diamond tip," he said.

"And you know not to move, right?"

"Yes, ma'am."

"Good." Magali took a deep breath, then sat up and put her body weight behind the drill and switched it on. Under her, the Nephyr grunted, but didn't try to move. "Okay," Magali said, under the grinding buzz of the bit as it started to react with the Nephyr's skin, "the trick is gonna be stopping once I get through the skin, before I puncture the spine."

"I hope it's not too much of a trick," he said, with a nervous laugh.

"You'll be fine," Magali said, "I've always been good at this." The drill was, as advertised, strong enough to slowly start piercing the liquid-energy plating of the Nephyr's skin.

Jersey looked thoughtful as he stared at the floor. "You've had practice, then?"

"Sure," Magali said, as she worked.

"On who?"

"People who are dead now," Magali replied.

"Ah." He seemed to consider that. "Hopefully, their deaths were not an unfortunate result of the procedure."

"Eh," Magali said, shrugging. "Milar got 'em to himself for a few days afterwards, so you could say that."

He scanned the tile a moment, then said, "Anything you'd like to talk about? This is creeping me the hell out. A distraction would be nice."

"The less you talk, the less I want to kill you."

The Nephyr went silent a moment, listening to the grinding whine of the drill piercing the back of his neck. "I would've thought that would be the other way around," he finally offered softly.

Magali snorted. "You guys can lie as easily as you can breathe."

"That much is true," Jersey said.

"Not even going to deny it?" Magali demanded.

"Miss," Jersey said, "in order to survive the Academy, you have to learn to lie. It's part of coping."

"Coping." Magali gave a bitter laugh and shoved the bit a little deeper than she needed to before she retracted it. "Sure it is." She retrieved the bit and, before the wound could close, grabbed the surgical spreaders and stuck them into the wound, then started ratcheting it wider, exposing the red muscles underneath.

"The big trick," the Nephyr said, "is keeping them from realizing you're lying about being just like them. That's where like ninety-nine percent screw up and get caught. Then it's over for 'em."

"Didn't I tell you to stop talking?" Magali demanded as she grabbed a scalpel and started peeling the tissue away from the glistening lump of steel in his spine.

The Nephyr's breath caught as she began cutting. "See, they don't let you out of the Academy until they're sure you're as screwed up as they are."

"Your lips are still moving," Magali growled, exposing the lifeline.

"That's where most of them go wrong. They *pretend* to be like their instructors, doing all that psychotic crap, thinking they can change back, once training is over. But between the lack of sleep and the terror, it sinks in."

"I don't want to talk about Nephyrs," Magali growled, wiping the blood away from the thumb-sized device. "I need to concentrate and I hate Nephyrs."

"Sorry," the Nephyr said. He went quiet.

Magali tugged the two halves of the capsule apart, exposing its innards. The Nephyr flinched at the click, his entire body going rigid.

Magali hesitated, eyeing the battery cap. "You know I could kill you, right?"

A pause.

"Just fidget with it and leave it to self-detonate. You'd never know the difference."

For a long moment, he stared at the tile. "Probably not," he agreed softly.

"Now I've got it open, it's gonna explode in thirty seconds if I don't disarm it," Magali said. Then, when he said nothing, she added with a sneer, "Just pop off your glittering head, leave it for your psychotic friends to find next time they go looking for a colonist to fuck, how would you like that?"

The Nephyr continued to stare at the tiles. "Now who's playing mind games?" he whispered.

Every muscle in Magali's body suddenly went stiff with shame. She looked away. It was true. In all the hours since he'd dragged her off the banks of the Snake, fed her, clothed her, and given her a place to sleep, he hadn't played a single mind game. In the long silence that followed, she watched blood well up around the lifeline. Then, reluctantly, she said, "Fine. But you ever lie to me or try to screw with my head, you're dead."

For a long moment, the Nephyr just looked at the grout under his nose as the seconds ticked away. Then, very quiet, he said, "Sounds fair to me."

She reached in with a screwdriver and twisted the little black ball of the battery cap until it popped free. Then she grabbed the device with pliers and began, very slowly, easing the four long wires out of the man's spine and brain stem. Once it was free, she threw it aside, where it detonated against the bathtub.

For a long time afterwards, the Nephyr continued to stare at the floor, unmoving. Then, slowly, he unclasped his hands, reached behind him, yanked the spreaders from his neck, and dropped them to the floor. Muscles bunching, he got to his feet with a smooth, eerie grace as the glittering skin sealed along his spine. When he turned to look at her, Magali was stunned to see tears. He turned to stare at the scorch mark in the porcelain bathtub for several long heartbeats as she huddled against the wall in silence. Then, without another word, he turned away from her and strode from the room. Magali jumped when she heard the outer door thump shut behind him.

Magali let the drill slide from her fingers, biting her lip. What she had just done was . . .

. . . horrible. *Evil.*

She thought about that for several minutes, watching the closed door, as tears came unbidden. What had happened to her? Had she really changed that much? That she would *taunt* a helpless man?

Never in the past would she even have *considered* herself capable of what she had just done. It was loathsome. Repulsive. Disgusting.

She had to make it right. She had to explain . . .

. . . But explain what? That she had changed? That he looked like Steele? Did that matter? In some deep part of her core, she had the odd realization that she could not stand the thought of the Nephyr hating her. And, even worse, she had the strong feeling that, unless she found him quickly, he probably wasn't coming back.

Anna wouldn't have cared if he never came back. Anna would have taken his stuff and slipped off into the slums to sell it so she could get on with her life.

Unsteadily, Magali picked up her gun and got to her feet, knowing she had to find him. His belongings were scattered across the bed and in duffels against the wall, but she had the feeling that wouldn't matter. She felt a need to find him, to tell him, to *apologize* . . .

She hesitated a few more minutes, looking down at his abandoned possessions, then nervously grabbed the EMP wand from the bed and stuffed it back into its slim metal tube before she tucked it into her pocket and followed the Nephyr out of the room. She had been wrong in what she had done, but she had promised herself she was never going to be caught off guard again. Never.

*Killer,* Wideman giggled.

*Shut the hell up, old man,* Magali thought back.

She wasn't sure how she knew where to find him, but Magali went outside, ignoring the hotel supervisor who greeted her as 'the Nephyr's missus,' and crossed the street to the little pub where she knew the Nephyr waited.

Sure enough, the Nephyr sat in a dark, abandoned corner of the bar, the rest of the patrons giving him a wide berth. Absolute silence had descended on the place, and most of the customers were watching him with outright hostility. He had a tall drink in front of him, probably on the house. He was slumped forward in silence, staring at it. His eyes flickered to her tiredly as she slid into the booth beside him, then went back to his beer.

A long moment passed in silence, neither of them speaking. Magali watched a droplet of condensation slide down the glass and puddle on the table. Then, haltingly, Magali put the unmarked EMP tube and the gun on the table in front of them, where he could see the weapons, then slowly pushed them across the table, out of her reach. Heart pounding, she reached out and touched his stony hand where it rested on his thigh. When he didn't jerk it away, just glanced down at where their skin touched, she curled her fingers around his and gave a gentle tug.

Looking up at her in confusion, Jersey allowed her to pull his arm around her in an awkward embrace. Magali levered his arm over her shoulder, then forced herself to stay there, fighting down the carnal urge to bolt at the glass-hard feel of his body against hers. It was the only apology she could think of, and it had been delivered to her, not an hour before.

After a moment of watching her face, the Nephyr's arm tightened around her, locking her in his grip, cinching her to the side of his big body with the hydraulic power of a machine. Magali felt a spasm of panic and her breath caught, her heart hammering like bullets against her ribs, but she viciously forced herself not to shiver. After a moment, Jersey turned back to look at the beer. Once she managed to convince herself he wasn't going to simply tighten his arm and crush all of her ribs, spine, and scapulas, Magali followed his gaze.

Together, they watched the condensation form on the outside of his glass, listening as the other patrons of the bar spoke in hushed tones or got up to leave. After what seemed like an eternity, Magali slowly began to relax in his grip.

"My skin's in storage in the Inner Bounds," Jersey eventually said to the glass.

. . . Which meant, now that he'd removed his lifeline, he would never get it back.

"I'm sorry," Magali whispered.

He just frowned and gave a slight shake of his head, eyes still on the water droplets. "It was my fault. I should've waited. Served out my term and just gone back and gotten discharged. I just couldn't take it anymore. I needed out. I was starting to break. I could feel it." He took a deep breath, then let it out very slowly. "The Forty-Third is . . . " his voice cracked and he trailed off.

He stared at the glass and was still for so long that Magali started to wonder if he would continue. Finally, he said, "They made me do things . . . " He trailed off in a whisper and, swallowing, he closed his eyes.

"You had to."

Jersey flinched and Magali caught a glimpse of agony before he turned his face away from her. For a moment, he just sat there in silence, not looking at her. "Things like what happened to you," he finally told the tabletop.

Magali felt her body stiffen, felt the bile at the back of her throat as she again felt the urge to scrabble out of his inhuman grip, but she forced herself to not cringe away from him. "You had to," she whispered again, stronger than she felt.

"No I didn't," he said, with vehemence. "I was a coward. I could've let them kill me."

She digested that a moment. "If you had let them kill you," Magali finally said, "we wouldn't have been able to save each other."

He glanced at her briefly before he turned back to the beer and was silent for a long moment. He took an unsteady breath, and his voice seemed to quaver. "I've been struggling for weeks and I almost lost it today. I never thought a colonist . . . " He swallowed and started scratching his artificial fingernail into the wooden tabletop. "Let my guard down. Just assumed you'd . . . "—his voice again started to crumble—" . . . want to help me."

Again, Magali fought a sickly flood of shame. "You don't have to keep your guard around me," she promised. "I won't do it again."

She heard an explosive sound escape him, almost a wail, and the Nephyr hung his head, touching his glass-hard brow to the table beside his hand. She felt his body start to shake.

After a few minutes, Jersey glanced at her, tears once again wetting his eyes. "Can I call you Mag?" There was so much yearning in that single sentence, such *need* . . .

Seeing the bare sincerity, there, knowing that there was no way to fake such genuine *anguish,* she forced out, "Sure."

"Can I . . . stay . . . with you for a while, Mag?" he said softly, raw, wretched hope straining his face. Then, quickly, he added, "Just as friends. I won't hurt you. I'll keep my distance unless you tell me. I just need some . . . time . . . with a real person."

Magali had never considered spending any more time with the Nephyr than necessary, and every ounce of her being stiffened at the thought. He *looked* genuine, but . . . *What if he changes his mind?* she thought, anxiety spilling acid into her system. Anna changed her mind. All the time. Whenever it suited her.

He judged her reaction correctly, and agony tore at his face. "*Please,*" he whispered. "I'm so tired of being . . . " He swallowed and looked up at the empty bar.

*Alone,* Magali thought, following his gaze. Everyone was gone, even the barkeep. The entire place was silent. She swallowed, imagining the solitude in being so despised. "You can stay," she said softly. It was all she *could* say.

"Thank you," he whispered. It came out as a moan. "Thank you so much." He ducked his forehead into the crux of her shoulder and started to sob, and Magali realized, for the first time, that this creature had been broken a thousand times more cruelly than she ever had been. She put her hand around his inhumanly hard fingers and squeezed.

◀◀ ◆ ▶▶

"I love all the exposure this is getting," Anna said, stuffing another potato chip into her mouth as she watched the three-day dogfight over the Tear. "I mean, it's kinda hard for them to hide there's a Rebellion now. *Look* at it. They've thrown like, what, forty soldiers at that TAG alone?"

"The tipoff to the media was a brilliant move on your part, Anna," Doberman said.

"Of course it was," Anna replied, eating another potato chip. "What's important, now, is that people *know*. It's no longer something whispered about in dark alleys and in the back corners of bars. People *know*. They're gonna be talking about it. Discussing it. Wondering. Planning."

"The seeds have been planted, it would seem," Doberman replied.

"I hope that TAG pilot survives," Anna said, thoughtfully crunching another chip. "I'd like to meet him."

"I doubt the sentiment is mutual," Doberman said.

Anna laughed. "Are you still upset about what I did to that operator brat?"

"I did find it unnecessarily brutal," Doberman replied.

Anna snorted and waved a dismissive hand. "We needed her to scream." She ate another chip, returning her attention to the screen. "I made her scream."

She was glued to the firefight for three more hours, until the last operator spun back to earth in a powerful explosion, with only Captain Eyre and the TAG pilot still in the sky.

Anna grinned. "Oh good. They won. That'll look *great* on the news."

Then Captain Eyre's ship hurtled out of the clouds to make a sudden, rough landing in the jungle at the tip of the Tear. Anna frowned and sat up, leaning forward. "I'll be damned," Anna said, as if she could not believe it. "She's stupider than I thought."

"She does have a history of mental trauma concerning enclosed spaces," Dobie replied. "And, more recently, sociopathic little girls with surgical implements, if I am to guess."

Anna snickered. "Not for long." She grabbed the little oval device from where Doberman had left it on her dresser.

"Don't you think that's a little extreme?" Doberman asked.

Anna snorted and pressed the pink button. "I *told* her to stay away from Milar." Then, yawning, she tossed the device into the trash. "Never really intended to let her live anyway. Just needed her to put up a good show for the sheeple. Get 'em thinking." Finishing off the chips and crumpling the bag into a wad, she tossed it in after the device. Then she glanced up at him, catching his stare. "Oh, I'm sorry, did that just disturb you, Dobie?" she jeered.

"I find myself less disturbed than one might expect," Doberman replied.

Anna snorted. "Little twit had it coming. She was *way* outta her league with him. And even an idiot could see he was obsessed with those pictures, but nobody was willing to do anything about it." She took a swig of bottled water and tipped it at him. "So I did something about it." Then she cocked her head in a frown. "She did good with the soldiers, though. I *thought* we might be able to get one last use out of her, before we got rid of her."

Doberman analyzed Anna's face. "I can understand why you would do that, Anna," he said.

"You see, Dobie," Anna said, yawning and opening another stolen bag of potato chips, "if one is to lead, one must know how to make full use of one's resources."

"It seems to me," Dobie said, "that killing the only operator the Rebellion had in its ranks was not the best use of our resources."

Anna scoffed. "Yeah, well, I didn't like her." She crunched a handful of potato chips. "You ever figure out what happened to my sister?"

"The registry says she died in Yolk Factory 14, Anna."

Anna's face darkened. "Good. Nobody needs her, anyway."

# CHAPTER 47

## Dance Lessons

"You know, this isn't exactly what I had in mind," Joel muttered. He hadn't eaten much of his filet mignon. Back at the reception area, the maître d' kept glancing over at them nervously. Probably had something to do with the gigantic gun that Jeanne had slung over her exquisite shoulder, then shoved in the man's face when he tried to tell her she couldn't carry it into the restaurant.

"Really?" Jeanne said, chewing on a forkful of sautéed shrimp. Her green eyes were twinkling with delight. "Why, I'm pretty sure you got everything you asked for, Joel." Indeed, the cherry-red dress showed off her ample cleavage with breathtaking results.

Joel cleared his throat and tilted his head at the egger.

Jeanne glanced down at the tiny man spreading out his lasagna on the tablecloth. "Oh, him?" She grinned at him and ate more two-hundred-credit shrimp. "*Somebody* has to babysit the little cretin, and Pat had a headache."

Joel narrowed his eyes. In one corner, a trio of musicians played a harp, accompanied by the piano and violin, beside the open dance floor. At her smug look, her luscious lips poised around another crustacean as she bit it off her fork, Joel wadded up his napkin and stood.

"What, going so soon?" she laughed. "Be sure you pay the waiter on the way out."

"Get up," Joel said.

Immediately, Jeanne's eyes darkened dangerously. "You got everything you asked for. No complaining."

"I'm not complaining, and no I didn't. You still haven't danced with me." Joel gestured at the dance floor.

Jeanne glanced over at the dance floor and paled with satisfying quickness. "Um."

"I said 'dancing,' Jeanne," Joel said, grinning at her. "And, as evidenced, we saved your crazy little egger." He gestured at the mussy-haired little man who was now poking toothpicks into his large lasagna smear.

She coughed uncomfortably, her face going purple. "I don't . . . "—she swallowed—" . . . know how," she muttered.

Joel felt his grin widen. "So I'll teach you. All those years in Officer's Corps, heh, I've had enough practice."

"In front of *them*?" Jeanne demanded, gesturing at their audience.

"Who, them?" Joel turned and looked at the other wide-eyed patrons, who were watching the two of them over their tuxedos and expensive wines. "Why not? They're *already* staring. I think the assault rifle and those massive combat boots had something to do with it."

Jeanne put down her fork, looking sick all over again. "I don't know . . . " Beside her, Wideman was now pouring warm cream onto the toothpicky mess.

"Deal's a deal," Joel said. "Besides, you're gorgeous. Nobody's gonna be watching your feet, believe me."

Immediately, the confident, badass pirate was stripped away, leaving a blushing, lip-biting beauty in her place.

"Come on," Joel urged gently, holding his hand out.

She stared at the empty dance floor for several minutes. "What about Joe?" she finally asked.

Joel glanced at the tiny egger who was now smooshing his upturned plate into his toothpick-creamer-lasagna mixture, trying to hold it up with toothpicks. "He looks rather occupied, wouldn't you say?" He wiggled his fingers. "Come on."

With a pained grimace, Jeanne reluctantly took his hand. Joel kissed it. "Milady?"

She rolled her eyes, but got to her feet. To the egger, she said, "Stay here, Joe. The smuggler and I are going to go 'dance.'" The way she said the word, complete with a disgusted twist to her crimson lips, one might have thought she were about to muck a pigsty.

The greasy little egger nodded vigorously, spinning the plate through his lasagna. Jeanne watched him a moment, then sighed. They walked to the dance floor together, and Joel knew from experience that the stares they were getting were not all due to Jeanne's assault rifle or massive combat boots. The lady, almost at eye level with him with her four-inch soles, was magnificent. He brought them to a halt at the dance floor.

"Boots off," he ordered.

Jeanne, already moving toward the open hardwood floor with obvious nerves, immediately froze and gave him a look of suspicion. "Joel, if this is an attempt to catch me off guard while you make off with my ship—"

"—you'll kill me, I know." Joel bent and tugged his own shoes off, still keeping a grip on the pirate's hand, lest she decide to bolt like the frightened rabbit she appeared. "I'd rather you not crush my feet while we do this," Joel said. "I think I've broken enough bones for a lifetime, wouldn't you agree?"

Her eyes fell to his hand, still twisted and bent from the Nephyr's attentions. Muttering, she wrenched her hand out of his grip and, almost timidly, crouched to start unlacing her footwear. When extracted, her stockinged feet looked surprisingly delicate. She shoved the boots—still dirt-covered from slogging through the mud on some pirating adventure, no doubt—against the wall, smearing brown across the cream-colored paint. Then she stood, licking her lips.

"Gun, too," Joel said.

"Why?" she growled, instantly clutching the rifle like a lifeline.

"Because assault rifles get in the way of a good tango," Joel said.

She gave him a long, hard look, then glanced at the other patrons, all of whom quickly looked away.

"You'll have to get used to it sometime," Joel said. "I have the feeling we'll be coming here a lot."

She turned back to scowl at him. "Nobody said anything about doing this again."

"You *do* want me to fly for you again, don't you?" he asked, quirking a brow.

She gave him a long, flat look.

"I mean," Joel continued rationally, "I think this is a fair trade. You get a few hours in the sky, I get a few hours on the dance floor. And to top things off, I'll even pay."

"You bastard," she muttered. But she lowered the rifle against her boots.

Seeing that, Joel smiled from his heart. "My dear?" he offered, once more giving her his hand. "Care to dance?"

"You're *never* getting me in a dress again," Jeanne growled. "I don't care what you do."

"Why not?" Joel asked. "You look stunning."

Jeanne narrowed her vibrant green eyes at him, but took his hand. Joel led her across the floor to a central area, then stopped and showed her the proper hand placement. Folding her fingers to his was like bending the fingers of a steel statue. She kept glancing over her shoulder at the rest of the dining area.

"Now," Joel said easily. "The thing about dancing is you need to trust your partner implicitly, and follow his lead."

"*His* lead."

"Yes, *his* lead."

"What if *I* want to lead?"

"You don't get to lead," Joel said. "Now there are only a few basic steps. Once you learn them, you can do anything you see those guys on the waves doing in all their fancy jumpsuits."

She was glaring at him, but she rigidly let him move her feet into place with his toes.

"Now," Joel said. "I'm going to take a few steps to the right. Move with me on three, okay?"

"This is ridiculous." But she did it.

He showed her the most basic ballroom dance he could think of, leading her patiently through the steps, keeping time to the music, and eventually, she started to relax into the rhythm. The feel of the woman's slender hand easing into his, the warmth of her waist against his fingers, was intoxicating. When she looked up at him, her beautiful green eyes laced with timid uncertainty, Joel felt himself melting, felt his heart pounding beyond anything he'd felt in the rush of the dogfight.

"Am I doing okay?" she whispered, nibbling a luscious lip.

"Like a pro," he managed, trying to hide the way he'd been staring.

At her beaming smile and girlish giggle of relief, followed by a deep blush and quick, anxious look at the restaurant goers, however, Joel could no longer help himself. He bent to meet her, intending to remind her of that one fantastic night in the desert, years ago.

The barrel of a revolver found its way into his left nostril. "Joel?" Jeanne said carefully.

"Yes, Jeanne?" he said, swallowing.

"I think that's enough dance lessons for the day, don't you?"

"My thoughts exactly," Joel said.

"Go check on the egger, Joel."

"Good idea," he said quickly. Then, backing away, he looked down at her skin-tight dress and blurted, "Where the hell did you get a revolver?"

"It's called a leg holster, Joel," she said, still aiming the gun at his nose. "Go. Now."

He did. And, walking back to the egger's ever-increasing mess, Joel had to smile. Now *that* was a woman who knew how to give a guy incentive . . .

# CHAPTER 48

# Fortune's Rising

MAGALI JUMPED AS THE DOOR TO THE BAR SLAMMED OPEN WITH enough force to embed the latch into the opposite wall. She froze, her heart falling into a shuddering march of terror when four Nephyrs stepped into the room from the brightness of the outdoors. Her gun was in her hand in an instant.

Jersey touched her arm and gave her a slight shake of his head, his eyes on the intruders.

"Well, well," the lead Nephyr said, his dark eyes coming to rest on Jersey. "Was passing through on a Draft and heard there was a pussy in here bawling his eyes out to a colonist." He paused, looking Jersey up and down with derision. "I'll be goddamned, looks like they were right." The cruel sneer of the man's filigreed face was unmistakable.

In an instant, Jersey had launched the table off to the side, leaving his path clear to stand and put his body between Magali and the four Nephyrs.

The lead Nephyr whistled. "Girls, I do believe he wants to tango." Beside him, the three women grinned.

"Let's do it," Jersey growled, cracking his knuckles as he made fists. "I was getting bored sweet-talking the whore, anyway."

Magali flinched, her breath catching in her lungs. Facing off the four Nephyrs, Jersey didn't even look at her.

The lead Nephyr's cold blue eyes flickered to Magali and he chuckled. "That ain't the way I heard things, pretty-boy." He looked Jersey up and down, stopping on Jersey's face. "You need to go back to finishin' school or somethin'? Havin' a little breakdown somebody needs to know about?"

Jersey snorted. "Get the hell outta my way." He started toward the Nephyr, aiming to move past him, when the man stepped in front of him, meeting his eyes.

"Oh my," he said, his sneer spreading. "He's been blubbering like a baby." The Nephyr motioned, and two of his companions slipped around Jersey, one on either side. A third worked her way through the billiard tables to get behind him. Jersey watched them surround him with an icy-steel complexion, then turned back to the leader, his face a mirror. He stepped up, then, into the man's face, gritted, "Get out of my way."

"Hmm," the lead Nephyr said. "No." He gestured again, and the two women on either side of Jersey lunged inward, grabbing him by the arms, holding him in place. "Get that ridiculous shirt off of him and hold up his arm."

"No!" Jersey shouted, kicking out, trying to launch the three of them backwards. The fourth Nephyr ducked in from behind and took him in a headlock, then held him still as the other two ripped the shirt off of him. Jersey screamed in fury, kicking a table in half.

"Such rage," the lead Nephyr chuckled. "It's not *winter* out there, buddy-boy, so why the long sleeves? Almost as if you're trying to hide—" The man's glittering face froze as he got a good look at Jersey's arm. Then his eyes slid back to Jersey's face and stayed there. "The

Forty-Third is guarding the Yolk harvest in Factory 14." His voice was low and deadly.

"I got some time off," Jersey snarled. "Let go of me."

But the man didn't budge. "Girls," he said, "remind me again of that last APB that hit the waves?"

"Rogue Nephyr from the Forty-Third stole a ship, went AWOL," one of the women said, grinning into Jersey's ear. She licked the side of his face and giggled. "Can we have some fun with him, Captain?"

Magali watched Jersey go stiff, watched him reach that little tipping point, recognizing it, because she, too, had been there, only days before. She raised her gun and put a bullet through the lead Nephyr's left eye.

*Killer,* Wideman giggled at her.

*One, two, three,* she automatically began to count, as her pistol recharged.

As the Nephyr was falling and the other three were turning in confusion, Magali took three steps forward, swiveled, and kicked the Nephyr holding Jersey in a stranglehold, right in her startled face. At the same time, she put the gun to her comrade's face and pulled the trigger.

"The fuck?!" one of the women cried, dropping Jersey and backing away, staring at her two convulsing comrades.

*One, two, three.*

Magali shot her, too. Then, as the last Nephyr turned on her, confusion turning into cold, deadly promise, Magali kicked Jersey away from her and slammed the EMP wand into the woman's shoulder. Her eyes went wide and she slumped to the ground in a tremor of shakes.

*There will be more outside.* Magali tucked the EMP wand into her waistband, bent, took a gun from the closest woman's belt, and stepped past Jersey, who stood in place, staring at the four dead Nephyrs at his feet. She opened the door and stepped into the sunlight.

A group of several hundred Yolk draftees were chained together in lines along the road outside. Six Nephyrs were laughing and surrounding a voluptuous, mousy-looking woman who was keeping her eyes carefully downcast. She had a shackle around her throat, chained to the next draftee ahead of her. She was shaking as they played with her hair and bent to whisper things into her ear.

Three more Nephyrs—all female—were leaning against the wall of the hotel, yawning, watching the action around the mousy woman with disinterest. Two other males were walking up and down the three prisoner lines with riding crops, reciting the Draftee Act. Another one was seated on an upturned flowerpot—the pot's occupants upended into the road a few feet away—and holding an r-player, a set of headphones over his ears, bobbing his head to music.

Magali didn't stop to think. She raised her gun and fired at the Nephyr that was holding a lock of the girl's wavy brown hair. The man's head snapped back, pushed that way by the explosive, armor-piercing bullet of the Nephyr's gun. With her other hand, she swung around and shot the closest crop-bearer.

*One, two, three,* she thought, automatically, as she started walking toward the line of prisoners and fired the Nephyr's pistol at another of the six surrounding the girl. He jerked and slid to the ground, shuddering. With her other hand, she shot the second startled crop-bearer, who had spun around to stare.

*That's right,* Magali thought. *Look at me, you assholes.* She shot two more of the ones around the girl before they snarled an alarm and started to charge her. She dropped the recharging pistol and yanked the EMP wand from her belt. The Nephyrs were inhumanly fast, but when Magali dropped into her trance, it felt like her hand was guided by Time itself. She pulled the trigger once, then spun and stepped to the side and hit the second with the EMP as they both came crashing toward her. They hurtled past her, burying themselves in the wall of the pub.

The three Nephyrs leaning against the wall were straightening, now, frowns on their faces. Two of them started jogging across the road. One of them pulled her gun.

In smooth, rapid precision, Magali killed the woman with the gun, then the furthest of the two approaching. The third she hit with the EMP. Then she was walking, striding up to the last remaining Nephyr, who had his back to her. He was still moving to the music, watching something on his r-player.

*Killer,* Wideman giggled.

Magali lowered the activated EMP rod into the Nephyr's field of vision, aiming at his face with the gun. He froze. Very slowly, he looked up.

"How many of you were there?" she asked.

The Nephyr swallowed and his eyes flickered to the glittering corpses littering the road. "Uh. Twenty, counting me."

"Where are the other four?" she asked.

"Checking into the hotel," the Nephyr said.

Magali hit him with the wand. He slid off of the pot, convulsing into the sidewalk. She picked up his gun and crossed the road, ignoring the way the colonists were whispering amongst themselves, and kicked open the door to the hotel. Inside, two Nephyrs were reading magazines on sofas. They looked up, confused. She shot them with each of her pistols, then dropped the right pistol and, snagging her EMP wand, swung to find a fourth Nephyr charging her from the desk. She hit her with the wand and let her crash through the front door of the establishment, into the dust outside.

The last Nephyr came out of the bathroom buckling his pants, chewing on a candy bar. He froze, eyes wide, staring at his dead comrades. The candy bar fell from his mouth.

"Get out here," Magali said, backing through the front door of the hotel and gesturing with the gun. "Outside."

Licking his lips, the Nephyr's hand started sliding toward his gun. "Don't," Magali said. "I won't miss."

His face contorted in a sneer. "We'll see about—"

She shot him. Then she backed through the door and glanced behind her at the Yolk draftees. "That all of them?" she demanded. "Twenty?"

Several hundred startled faces just stared at her from the dusty road, the only sound that of the tinkling chain linking them together. Further down the streets, a few hundred more city-goers had gathered to stare. Frustrated, Magali turned to the hotel supervisor. "How many Nephyrs registered to spend the night?" she demanded.

It took the manager a long, startled minute to answer. "Aside from yours?" His voice sounded like a rough whisper. "Twenty."

"Okay," Magali said, lowering her gun for the first time since she'd started shooting. "Which one was the leader?"

"He went in the bar," one of the closer colonists offered, after a moment.

Stuffing the guns into her belt, Magali crossed the road again and re-entered the bar. Jersey was still standing inside the door, looking at the four dead Nephyrs. Magali knelt beside the leader and began searching his pockets. Finding the keys she was looking for, she got back to her feet.

A warm, glass-hard hand caught her wrist and held it.

Magali froze, reality suddenly slamming back into place. She knew, without even trying, Jersey could rip the limb from her body if he so desired. Slowly, she looked up into Jersey's face. He was still staring down at the four dead Nephyrs.

"Was that all of them?" he asked softly. "Should be twenty."

Her body trembling with the sudden, cold terror of being gripped by those stony hands, Magali nodded.

He continued to hold her by the wrist, anchoring her in place with all the authority of a five-hundred-pound statue. "What you just did," he whispered, "is impossible."

She swallowed uncomfortably, but didn't try to struggle against his grip. She knew better than that.

Very slowly, Jersey lifted his head to look into her eyes. "You're the one they call Killer, aren't you?"

Magali grimaced and looked away.

He lifted a warm, stone-hard finger to her chin and forced it inexorably back to face him. "Aren't you?"

Magali felt tears stinging her eyes. "I have to go free those people."

"Not even a robot could've made those shots," he whispered. "Nobody could have."

"I know," Magali whispered. "Anna told me enough times. Made fun of me. Teased me that I really was a robot that they'd dressed up and made to think it was human. Please let go of my arm."

"You shouldn't have enough strength in your whole body to kick a Nephyr like that," he said softly. He was looking down at her in awe.

"Please let go of me," Magali whimpered. Being this close to a Nephyr, her wrist locked in his vicelike grip, it was all she could do not to raise the gun again and pull the trigger until the gun overheated.

Jersey seemed to blink and catch himself, and dropped her hand with the suddenness of someone who had touched a burning stove. "Sorry," he muttered. "God . . . sorry." He held up his hands in peace.

Magali took a quick step back, then, when it was obvious he wasn't going to reach for her again, she turned to go. She was most of the way outside when she paused at the door, feeling his eyes burning into her back. "I'm not a robot," she said, giving him an unhappy smile over her shoulder. "Believe me. I already checked." Then she turned and went outside to free the eggers from their shackles.

Absolute silence reigned as she stepped back outside into the dusty sunlight. The road outside glittered with the bodies of Nephyrs, their corpses already buzzing with the fat black bodies of tadflies. People were staring at her as she stepped over the black-clad bodies, the keys in her hands.

*They're staring at me,* Magali thought, utterly uncomfortable as she started working her way down the ranks, unlocking the shackles with the key from the dead Nephyr. No one moved or said a word. They just *stared.*

When she was three-quarters of the way through the prisoner lines, a gray-haired woman peered back at her as she worked the key in the shackle, her weather-lined face holding that same wide-eyed awe she'd seen in Jersey's face. "You're Magali Landborn, aren't you?" the woman said, much too loudly. "The one they call 'Killer.'"

Magali hesitated, flinching in on herself. Her voice wavering, she said, "You must have me confused with someone else."

"The one who could shoot a bull's-eye at a mile, with iron sights."

Very slowly, Magali released the woman's shackles and handed her the keys. "I've gotta get going. You can release the rest of them." She turned to leave, suddenly needing to get away from the silence, the *stares* . . . She crossed the road, feeling every eye following her every movement, and pulled open the door of the bar, glancing into the darkness inside.

"Jersey!" she called into the interior, hating the way her voice cracked. "Let's go."

A moment later—much too long for Magali—the Nephyr stepped out into the sun beside her and shut the door gently behind him, his body covered with weapons from those she had slain. She felt the tension in the air stiffen, felt the colonists flinch away from him.

"Come on," she said, grabbing him by the hard, glittering hand. "Let's go. Now."

But Jersey was staring at the dead Nephyrs, looking in shock. "Magali, you just killed twenty Nephyrs in less than a minute," he said softly.

"She turned a *Nephyr*," someone gasped, nearby.

"It *is* Magali Landborn!" someone in the crowd shouted. "The Killer is here!"

"She beat them at the Tear, too!" someone shouted. "She killed two dozen operators with her rifle, hanging out the door of a cargo ship!"

"And Deaddrunk, too!" someone else shrieked. "And Yolk Factory 14!"

"*Landborn!*" someone else screamed. "*Landborn! Landborn!*"

More mouths started to take up the chant, and Magali cringed backwards, intending to back into the bar to escape the stares.

Jersey's hand once more found her wrist and held her there. "They need this," he whispered. "Stay."

"*Land-born, Land-born, LAND-BORN, LAND-BORN!*" The very walls of the buildings around her began to shake, and the air in her lungs started to vibrate in her chest. More people were coming out of buildings and joining the gathering in the street, and as the sound reached an ear-splitting crescendo, it seemed the whole city started to chant her name around her.

"Please let go of my hand," Magali whimpered, trying to back behind Jersey to hide from the people screaming her name. But they had surrounded her, filling the streets, packed dozens deep. There was nowhere to hide as they chanted at her with wide, awestruck eyes and mindless smiles.

"Jersey," she whimpered. "Please."

The Nephyr, who had been scanning the faces in stunned amazement, turned to look down at her, a look of shock on his face. "I think you just did it."

"Did what?" Magali whispered. All around her, men were picking up the dead Nephyrs, dragging them off, taking their weapons, sifting through their vehicles and belongings. She saw a glittering foot raised above the crowd, then a leg, as someone hoisted a dead Nephyr up a flagpole to hang upside down, naked and limp.

"Oh my God," Jersey whispered, as the roar around them became so loud she could no longer hear herself think. "Mag . . . you just started the Revolution."

◀ End Book 1 ▶

# Outer Bounds: Book 2

## Fortune's Folly

**Editor's Note: This is an uncorrected excerpt,
and may not reflect the final product.**

**EXCERPT:**

"Greetings, fellow ex-Nephyr draftees!"

Now that the shooting was over, utter silence hung in the air as Anna paced briskly in front of the group of kids, hands clasped behind her back. Doberman stood off to the side, cannons still protruding from his forearms, watching the scene indifferently.

"As you've probably noticed," Anna continued, "you are *not* skinless ice-cubes hurtling towards the Inner Bounds, and your former escorts are now dismantled pieces of space-junk. Some of you are probably wondering why."

She saw the flicker of curiosity across their faces, but none of them asked. Good.

Anna smiled at them. "Glad you asked. For the duration of this meeting, I'm your new Evil Overlord, and this is my pet robot, Dobie. We've come to the decision that sending our best and brightest off to the Nephyr Academy is counter-productive for the future of Fortune, so we commandeered your shuttle. If you please me, *some* of you will get offered a job. If you don't . . ." Anna shrugged. "You'll go home and forget this ever happened." She waved a dismissive hand. "Make babies, spread the genetic, that sort of thing."

"Evil Overlord," one of the older boys, probably twelve or thirteen, scoffed. "Riiiight. What are you, like *six*?"

Anna stopped and gave him an irritated stare. "Dobie, how old am I?"

"You are nine, Overlord," Doberman said obediently. They had agreed not to use her real name at the outset of their mission, and Anna loved the ring it had coming in the form of a robot's matter-of-fact reply.

"But I thought that government robots couldn't be hacked," the kid said, blinking up at Dobie.

Anna sighed, deeply. "They can't. Dobie, send that kid back home to his mommy. He's obviously outta his league." With a swiftness that delighted her, Doberman stepped forward, grabbed the kid, who screamed and struggled, shocked him senseless, then administered a forgetfulness serum mixed with a bit of long-term knockout drug, and dragged him off to a corner, where the kid slumped against the wall and started to drool. One down. Twenty-five to go. Anna scanned the remainder. "Any other stupid questions?"

Most of the kids started to babble and step backwards in obvious terror, but there were a handful that stood their ground. A fat little pumpkin of a girl and a twiggy boy with long ice-blonde hair tied at the nape of his neck, for instance, just watched her as placidly as if they were all sitting around at a tea party.

"All right," Anna said, clapping her hands together. "Dobie is going to start asking you each a series of questions with increasingly more difficult answers to determine just how useful you are to us. If you fail more than six questions or if your overall score displeases me, you join that idiot over there and forget this conversation ever took place." She gestured to the drooling kid, then motioned to the closest kid. "It's all pretty basic stuff. Go ahead, Dobie."

The first kid peed himself and started stuttering so badly he couldn't answer Dobie's questions, and he got added to the corner. Two girls passed, though barely. Then a third girl failed. "Aren't you going to tell me what I got wrong?" the girl sobbed, when Anna shook her head a seventh time and gestured for Dobie.

Anna laughed. "This is a *test*, not a *learning experience*, dipshit. Dobie, get rid of her." The fourth girl likewise failed. "He said *cubed*, not *squared*, Aanaho *Ineriho!*" Anna cried. She yawned and sat down with her r-player in disgust, only half-listening to the rest.

Most missed seven of Dobie's questions, or couldn't list all of the timed examples required of them, or were too frazzled to do the mental math. Those were all added to the pile. Pumpkin-girl, however, only missed two.

"Keep her!" Anna called over the sound of her heavy metal, not even looking up from her r-player. Even a tubblet could be useful, if she didn't have to run from anything.

The whole room went silent, however, when the robot reached the twiggy blond and, instead of answering Dobie's first question, he gave Anna a really long look and said, "You're shorter than I thought you'd be."

Anna frowned and glanced up from her device. When she saw Dobie waiting for her response, she snorted dismissively. "That counts as a failed question." She cranked up the volume and waved Dobie on.

Dobie asked another, this one a chemistry question.

The blond smiled. "I always thought strawberry soda reacted unfavorably to hydrochloric acid."

Anna froze. Very slowly, she lowered her volume, then scowled at the kid. "Another fail," she told Dobie, glaring at the kid. "Ask him something else." To the blond, she said, "You better answer his questions. You only get four more fails, and he's got some *doozies*."

The blonde just gave her a placid grin.

This time, Dobie gave the kid a logic problem.

"Funny way to die, killing yourself on a nugget of silver," the boy replied.

Anna set her r-player down and got up to scowl at the kid. "Three more fails."

He just grinned at her.

Dobie asked about botany.

"A vegetable that carves on veggies. Some would call that a horrible waste of food."

Anna fisted her hands and walked up to peer at him, eye-to-eye. "Two more fails."

Doberman hesitated, watching the two of them. "He doesn't seem to be responding to my questions, Overlord. At his current rate, I would not expect him to pass. Would you like me to administer the serum?"

"Overlord, huh?" the kid said. "I would've gone with something like Maximus or Daimyo or Khan or Fuhrer. Or, hell, just Boss. Overlord is kinda corny."

"*Continue*, Dobie," Anna growled, without taking her eyes off the kid's smug face.

Doberman shrugged and offered him a pattern recognition problem.

"Hmm, let's see," the kid said, still grinning at her. "Little Anna Never Diddles Batteries Or Rusty Nails."

Anna scowled. Getting close enough that their faces almost touched, she said, "One more fail."

Doberman asked about dermatology.

"Always wondered what it'd be like to stitch someone's skin back on," the kid replied. "Hiding the scars must be difficult."

Leaning in close, Anna said, "You're all out."

The kid grinned. "Oops."

Anna narrowed her eyes. "Keep going, Dobie."

Doberman asked, "Add all the integers one through one hundred."

"Five thousand fifty," the blond replied, in less than a second, without taking his eyes from Anna.

"Give him something harder," Anna growled. "That was just trivia."

Doberman said, "A Shrieker, a starlope, and a goat shared a stable and two feed bags. Their feeding conditions were thus: One: If the Shrieker ate oats, then the starlope ate what the goat ate. Two: If the starlope ate oats, then the Shrieker ate what the goat did not eat. Three: If the goat ate hay, then the Shrieker ate what the starlope ate. Which of the animals always ate from the same feed bag, and which bag was it?"

Without missing a beat, the blonde said easily, "Aside from the fact that hay is not stored in a bag and starlopes have a chemical intolerance to the gluten in the seeds of some terragen grasses that will kill them within thirteen hours of ingestion, it would be the Shrieker always eating hay." His grin widened. "That all ya got?"

"*Harder!*" Anna snapped. She barely noticed Doberman glance between the two of them out of the corner of her eye. He was *toying* with her. She was so angry she was seeing red.

The kid then proceeded to answer every following question correctly, taking only a fraction of a second to form his response, sometimes even answering before Dobie finished his question. Anna watched him the whole time, face-to-face, watching the smooth workings of his mind as he stared back at her, unflinching.

"So," the boy said, when Dobie finished. He still had that idiotic grin plastered over his face, and he hadn't backed down from Anna's stare. Looking her up and down, appearing as if he were thoroughly enjoying himself, he said, "Did I pass, Boss?"

"Judging by his responses, Overlord, I would put his score at—" Doberman began.

"I know what he scored," Anna interrupted. "Dobie, how did this kid get in here?"

"The ship computer has no records on him, Overlord."

"What the hell is his name?"

"I'm not aware of that information, Overlord. His facial structure has no matches above eighty-five percent."

The kid continued to grin at her. "You like sweets, Anna?"

"What the hell is your name?" Anna demanded, a fraction of an inch from his face.

"How about candycorn?"

Anna felt a cold sweat rush over her and her heart stuttered a bit.

The blond kid's grin widened. "Thought so." He cocked his head at her. "How about we go kick these bastards off our planet, eh?"

Regaining some of her composure, Anna growled, "BriarRabbit."

He inclined his head minutely.

Immediately, the pumpkin waddled over and said, "*You're* BriarRabbit? And *you're* CandyCorn?"

Anna glanced at the pumpkin. "Who the hell are you?"

"SexGoddess," the fatso said.

Anna scoffed, looking her up and down. "Sure you are." She had *thought* SexGoddess had been compensating for something.

The fatso gave her a flat fatso stare. "And the two questions I missed were four million, six hundred and thirty thousand and forty-two-point-eight-nine-five and the black pony." She glanced at the blond. "Forgive me if I'm wrong, but aren't you the two instigating the rebellion?"

Anna snorted derisively. "Rebellion? How could *kids* be instigating a rebellion?"

"I want in," the pumpkin said. "Nephyrs killed my mom and sisters six nights ago when they came to get me. I've got a brother in the mountains who also had in-utero Yolk and I know how to contact Everywhere666 and BabyDoomsday. I think we could get MadMorga and FlameOn easy enough."

Anna felt a slow, predatory smile cross her lips as she looked at the tubblet with new respect. "Oh, this is gonna be fun."

### ◀ Continued in Book 2 ▶

# Author's Note

I've had countless readers write me to say they hate science fiction, but they love my books. Literally hundreds, starting with those exact words. Believe it or not, I write science fiction, so that got me wondering . . . what is it about *some* science fiction out there that they are hating?

Here's what most *readers* don't know, but most *editors* do: There are two kinds of science fiction. Like all of my novels, the book you're about to read is pure, unadulterated *character-driven* fiction. Character-driven fiction is that delicious mental ambrosia where, regardless of genre, the story revolves around the characters and their problems, wants, and general screw-ups, delving into the emotion of a situation, not the setting. (Think your favorite thriller, your favorite television crime drama, your favorite action-adventure series . . . applied to space.) *Hard science fiction*, a.k.a. technobabble, is the dry stuff that reminds you of college physics textbooks explaining cool new ideas in a very logical way. I mean, it's neat, but you can forget the main character's name in a couple days. So, while Fortune's Rising takes place in the future, instead of spending half the book detailing out the schematics of machines or expounding upon possible technology *ad nauseam*, the story gets into the gritty substance of the people themselves, immersing the reader in their hopes and fears, their joys and sorrows, their triumphs and mistakes. As with all good character-driven fiction, this book is about *people,* not their surroundings.

That said, in this story, 'people' is a term I use loosely . . .

# MEET STUEY

I have a Muse. His name is Stuey. As you may have noticed, Stuey and I are all about character. Stuey, like other temperamental, misunderstood, eccentric geniuses, can be a petulant little turd sometimes. He'll randomly decide to ditch me in the middle of a glorious scene because I somehow ignored His Majesty's subtlest of hints, flouncing off in some self-righteous snit until I cave, acknowledge his superiority, and beg his triumphant return. But in every book that Stuey and I have created together, when I do somehow manage to translate his ridiculously vague and whimsical requests, we have forged characters that people remember for years—even decades! Take Anna, for example. Probably not gonna forget a sociopathic child with a scalpel fetish anytime soon, will ya? Or Stuart (yeah, Stuey slipped himself in there), the tragic last-of-his-kind alien survivor in *Millennium Potion*. Or Joe Dobbs, the intergalactic badass in *The Legend of ZERO*. Or Jack Thornton, the curmudgeonly, violence-prone wereverine in *Alaskan Fire*. These are all Stuey's carefully-designed brainchildren, the actions of which he oh-so-magnanimously doled out to me a single word at a time, with absolutely no hints as to what he planned to do with them beforehand. Bastard.

So I'll warn you now. Stuey delights in toying with you. He likes to make you laugh, cry, and yell. If you decide to continue with my other books—and I hope you do—just keep in mind that you're in for a roller coaster ride of character-driven fiction in each and every one. It's the only way I can get the little dude to cooperate . . .

# SARA RECOMMENDS

If you enjoyed the characters in <u>Outer Bounds: Fortune's Rising</u>, I've got some other character-driven fiction recommendations for you . . .

First off, try <u>Changes</u> by Charles Colyott. Colyott is a natural character writer, and he, like me, has spent way too many years being the undiscovered diamond in the rough. His hero, Randall Lee, is a Tai-Chi master and homeopathic herbalist by day, a down-and-dirty detective by night. The entire series is a delightful mix of dark humor, mystery, and deeply human emotions, and I highly recommend it.

Obviously, if you haven't read <u>A Game of Thrones</u> by George R.R. Martin, get off your ass and do it. This man is the best character writer I can think of living today. Early in my career, I recognized this, and his gut-wrenchingly deep, delightfully faceted characters have set the standard for me ever since. I also recommend his short story, *Sandkings*. Utterly brilliant.

Lastly, if you want to see, bare bones, what makes a character novel a character novel, read <u>The Long Walk</u> by Stephen King. All that happens, the entire book, is kids walk down a road. And yet, you will find yourself glued to every page, desperate to know what happens next. This is the epitome of character fiction, and it shows, quite vividly, how characters—not setting—are what keep things interesting, because everything else has been stripped away.

# ABOUT THE AUTHOR

(a.k.a. Join My Alaskan Army)

*Patricia Lauer, 2006*

Email me.

No, seriously, email me. kingnovel@gmail .com. Go do it. Right now. I love keeping my ear to the very heart of the publishing industry— which means I have to talk to *you*. I think entertaining and inspiring others is the most important thing about writing, and if I'm doing my job right, people will actually want to tell me what they think. So, dammit, if you were entertained or inspired, I wanna hear from you.

I'm utterly freakin' serious.

In case you're still not convinced, consider this: I'm a lifelong Alaskan. We do things differently here. With the roving grizzly bears (yes, I live in the Bush, not like those pussies in town) and my closest neighbor a mile away, it gets kinda lonely when it's just me and my computer and a big, vast wilderness out my back door. I want to talk to the people who are reading my books, because who the hell else am I going to talk to?!

In case you're concerned about writing to a complete stranger, I assure you I'm totally approachable, in my random, quirky, too-much-time-without-sun kind of way. I've spent my entire life (starting at three years old!) working on writing as an art form, and I've poured my heart and soul into the twenty (ish) books I've written, so you can be damn sure I want feedback. I mean, putting together these (utterly brilliant, totally awesome) masterpieces and then getting nothing but silence is like building the Eiffel Tower and having people go . . . meh.

So shoot me an email at kingnovel@gmail.com and let me know your thoughts on the book! I respond to every email I get (though sometimes it takes longer than others). Oh, and friend me on Facebook at https://www.facebook.com/kingfiction (authors need friends, too) and check my Author Page https://www.facebook.com/sknovel for the latest writerly news and updates. Or, even better, hop on over to Amazon and check out my other character-driven series, like *The Legend of ZERO*: http://www.amazon.com/dp/B00BTKA42Y/ or *Millennium Potion*: http://www.amazon.com/dp/B007W6RBSE/ or, heck, even my Alaskan Paranormal/Fantasy series *Guardians of the First Realm*: http://www.amazon.com/dp/B0073WZ01C/ to see some of my other compelling characters in action!

# Acknowledgments

Getting a novel from rough draft to final proof is a gigantic undertaking that no one person—however awesome, talented, and generally kickass she may be—can accomplish alone. To my utterly brilliant brainstorming team for this book: Chancey, Logan, and Kyle; to my trio of amazing editors: Stephen, Sarah, and Karen; to my wonderful, enthusiastic agent David Fugate; to Robert, my rock in times of writerly crisis; to my hordes of ravenous, plastic-spoon-wielding first-readers; to my own personal cheerleader, Kim; to my very understanding family and friends; and to David Pomerico, the man who made this all possible at 47North, I give a heartfelt thank you. Through their various indispensable contributions, this book has evolved from Stuey's and my haphazard mindsplatter into something almost resembling Art. Almost.